"ONE OF THE MOST
ORIGINAL NEW VOICES
IN SUSPENSE FICTION."
—Nelson DeMille

"A MARVELOUS DEBUT."
—Bernard Cornwell

"ONE HELL OF A READ!"
—David Hagberg

PRIDE
RUNS
DEEP

R. CAMERON COOKE

JOVE BOOKS, NEW YORK

THE BERKLEY PUBLISHING GROUP
Published by the Penguin Group
Penguin Group (USA) Inc.
375 Hudson Street, New York, New York 10014, USA
Penguin Group (Canada), 10 Alcorn Avenue, Toronto, Ontario, M4V 3B2, Canada
(a division of Pearson Penguin Canada Inc.)
Penguin Books Ltd., 80 Strand, London WC2R 0RL, England
Penguin Group Ireland, 25 St. Stephen's Green, Dublin 2, Ireland (a division of Penguin Books Ltd.)
Penguin Group (Australia), 250 Camberwell Road, Camberwell, Victoria 3124, Australia
(a division of Pearson Australia Group Pty. Ltd.)
Penguin Books India Pvt. Ltd., 11 Community Centre, Panchsheel Park, New Delhi—110 017, India
Penguin Group (NZ), cnr. Airborne and Rosedale Roads, Albany, Auckland 1310, New Zealand
(a division of Pearson New Zealand Ltd.)
Penguin Books (South Africa) (Pty.) Ltd., 24 Sturdee Avenue, Rosebank, Johannesburg 2196, South
Africa

Penguin Books Ltd., Registered Offices: 80 Strand, London, WC2R 0RL, England

This is a work of fiction. Names, characters, places, and incidents either are the product of the author's imagination or are used fictitiously, and any resemblance to actual persons, living or dead, business establishments, events, or locales is entirely coincidental.

PRIDE RUNS DEEP

A Jove Book / published by arrangement with the author.

PRINTING HISTORY
Jove mass-market edition / March 2005

Copyright © 2005 by R. Cameron Cooke.
Cover illustration by Ben Perini.
Book design by Kristin del Rosario.

ISBN: 0-515-13833-9

JOVE®
Jove Books are published by The Berkley Publishing Group,
a division of Penguin Group (USA) Inc.
375 Hudson Street, New York, New York 10014.
JOVE is a registered trademark of Penguin Group (USA) Inc.
The "J" design is a trademark belonging to Penguin Group (USA) Inc.

PRINTED IN THE UNITED STATES OF AMERICA

10 9 8 7 6 5 4 3 2 1

Prologue

BLOOD stains never came out of cotton khakis, Russo thought, flicking at the dried blood on his sleeve. It was not his blood. The day was gray and the clouds were low, making the stains look almost black. Strangely, it was the only thing he could think about. The whole patrol had been a blur.

"Sir!" Chief Konhausen shouted from up by the bow, where several sailors stood on deck gaping over the starboard side of the ship. Two of them held a line for the diver whose bubbles broached the surface of the water near the hull.

"Captain!" Konhausen shouted again, this time from the deck just beneath the conning tower.

The cool North Pacific air whisked across the bridge and broke Russo's trance. He leaned over the coaming and held his hand to his ear as if he had not heard Konhausen the first time.

"How's it look?" he called.

"It's worse than I thought, Captain. The torpedo's fouled

in the shutter mechanism. We can't move her and I don't want to. The exploder could be armed, sir. Anything might set it off."

Russo nodded. There were a couple of officers on the bridge with him, but he felt very alone. Russo looked at the blood on his sleeve again. He couldn't stop looking at it. The submarine's rolling deck, the idling diesel engines, the dull hum of the rotating radar mast all disappeared from his senses and all he could see, hear, smell, or feel was the dried blood on his sleeve that was not his.

"Shit!" one officer muttered behind him.

"What do you want to do, Captain?" the officer next to him asked.

Russo gave no answer.

"Get Hunt out of the water, Chief, and get below," the officer called down to Konhausen. "We're sitting ducks up here."

"Aye aye, XO," Konhausen answered, looking puzzled at Russo's behavior.

"Bridge, radar," the bridge intercom suddenly squawked. "SD radar contact, range five thousand yards! Aircraft approaching fast, sir!"

Everyone on the bridge exchanged white-faced glances and Russo snapped out of his hypnotic gaze.

"Clear the bridge! Clear the decks!" he yelled. "Helm, bridge, all ahead flank!"

The two officers scurried down the bridge hatch, followed quickly by the lookouts who had dropped down from their high perches in the periscope shears. Within seconds Russo was the only one on the bridge, and as the resonance of the powerful diesels shifted to a higher octave, he could already feel the hull accelerating through the water.

The men on deck also scampered to get below. All of them bolted for the forward torpedo room hatch, the only open hatch on the main deck. All except for Konhausen, who remained behind to pull Hunt, the diver, up from the water.

Russo scanned the low gray clouds above the submarine, but it was no use. The Japanese plane had the jump on them.

"Bridge, radar, aircraft at three thousand yards now, sir," the nervous voice reported over the speaker.

Konhausen finally had Hunt out of the water and climbing up the submarine's side. The rest of the men were now below and Konhausen and Hunt were the only two left on deck.

Russo desperately wanted to dive the ship. He was putting the ship and crew in jeopardy for the sake of two men, but the blood on his shirt kept catching his eye, and he couldn't bear the thought of losing another man on this patrol. He decided then and there that he would not dive the ship until Konhausen and Hunt were safely below.

The submarine's screws churned the ocean behind her and she quickly surpassed fifteen knots, leaving a white wake that would make it even easier for the Japanese plane to spot her. Her bow began to crash through the waves, spraying the two men on the bow with a cold salty mist.

"Aircraft at one thousand yards, sir!" the speaker intoned.

Konhausen had pulled Hunt up to the deck now. The big chief helped the diver rip off his fins and then both began to run across the rocking deck to the open hatch only thirty feet away.

Russo saw Konhausen get to the hatch first and disappear below. As Hunt reached the hatch, Russo pulled the diving alarm lever near his right hand and shouted into the bridge call box.

"Crash dive!"

On the second blast of the diving alarm he could hear the rushing water and see the spraying mist in the air as the sub's ballast tanks vented and rapidly filled with the sea.

He also saw the wing-like surfaces on the sub's bow deploy from the vertical position to the horizontal.

He thought Hunt was home free and had almost turned to drop down the bridge hatch before he heard a rapid staccato sound that could only be one thing. In the blink of an eye, dozens of geysers shot up in the water around the bow. The 20-millimeter shells from the Japanese plane walked across the submarine's bow from port to starboard and made sickening sounds as they struck metal hull and then wooden deck, blasting splinters in all directions.

Russo started to shout to Hunt, who was leaping for the protection of the open hatch cover, but before he could say anything a 20-millimeter projectile sliced Hunt's left leg off at the thigh like it was made of putty. A shower of blood and cartilage instantly fountained up only to splatter down on the deck seconds later.

Russo instinctively ducked when the roaring engine of the low-flying Japanese fighter blared overhead. He looked up in time to see the silver-painted aircraft with the red sun on its fuselage pull up and disappear into the low clouds, obviously to prepare for another pass.

Down on the deck, Hunt was rolling around near the hatch, blood squirting from his stump and turning the wooden deck red. Several feet away his severed leg lay grotesquely twitching.

Russo stared at the grisly spectacle and froze. The horror had happened so fast, within seconds. And now he didn't even remember that the submarine was in the middle of a crash dive. As the water reached the scuppers of the main deck, he saw Konhausen emerge from the forward hatch and with lightning speed yank Hunt below. The hatch slammed shut just as the first wave swept across the deck and immersed it completely. The swirling water carried away Hunt's leg and it quickly disappeared beneath the foaming surface.

As the waves struck the conning tower and rose still further, Russo felt a hand on his arm. One of his officers pulled him toward the bridge hatch and forced him below without much care. He reached the safety inside the conning tower and heard someone slam the hatch shut above him. He clutched the cold metal rungs of the ladder and felt the deck tilt downward as the submarine rapidly descended to a safe depth where the circling plane would no longer be a danger.

Russo did not have the wherewithal to notice the blank and dejected faces of his officers and crew staring at him from every direction. They were looking to him for guidance. They were defeated and they needed their captain.

But Russo had trouble remembering their names. He simply fixed his eyes on the dried blood on his cotton sleeve and wondered if he would ever be able to get the stain out.

PART I

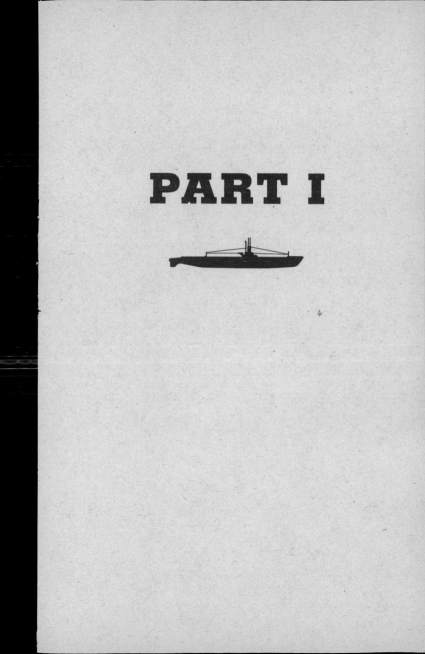

Chapter 1

THE attack had taken place over a year before but much evidence of that terrible day still remained. From his second-story window Captain Ireland could just see the ill-fated "battleship row" across Pearl Harbor. *Oklahoma* still lay rolled on her side, exactly where the Japanese bombers had left her. The shipyard engineers were making preparations to right her someday. Nearer to Ford Island, *Arizona*'s great funnel poked above the water marking her shallow grave, where over a thousand of those killed that day were still entombed. Oil from *Arizona*'s gargantuan fuel tanks still covered the water's surface. Her great fourteen-inch guns would be removed and used in a newly commissioned battleship, but the *Arizona* herself would remain where she lay as a solemn reminder of what the Japanese were capable of and what they had done.

Ireland lost some good friends that day.

He tipped the blinds with one finger and sipped at his coffee as he scanned the pier just below his window. The

waterfront below was frantic with activity. A dozen submarines sat at their moorings while water and supply trucks
drove up and down the pier providing their services like
busy ants. Sailors worked everywhere and speckled the pier
and the submarines with their blue dungarees and white
"dixie cup" hats.

Ireland focused his attention on one of the submarines,
halfway down the pier. Even from this distance, he could see
the holes in her conning tower, left there by a Japanese heavy
caliber machine gun. A sign loosely draped across the submarine's brow identified her as the USS *Mackerel* SS-244.
Ireland sighed and took another drink. This boat was his current problem and he had to fix it before things got out of
hand. He had dealt with these kinds of things before but the
solution he was about to enact made him uncharacteristically
uneasy and he could not understand why.

Captain Steven Landis Ireland came from a navy family
with a heritage as old as the navy itself. Several distant an-
cestors served on the old American frigates that the British
feared so much in the War of 1812. His grandfather sailed
with Farragut at the Battle of Mobile Bay and supposedly
heard the admiral utter his famous "Damn the torpedoes!
Full speed ahead!" His father was with Dewey when he sank
the Spanish fleet in the Philippines, which he recounted to
young Ireland not less than once a week for every week of
his childhood. And when young Steven Ireland came of
age, he dutifully followed the call from his family's naval
tradition and accepted an appointment to Annapolis in
1906. Ireland's first submarine assignment after graduation
placed him aboard the USS *Skipjack*, captained by Lieutenant Chester W. Nimitz. Nimitz had been quick to note
young Ireland's ability to solve problems and had com-
mended him on several occasions. On Ireland's successive
sea tours on other submarines, this quality was noted by all
of his commanding officers. However, as he rose in rank,

his problem-solving ability became less and less admired and more and more a nuisance to those above him. When he stepped on the toes of some of the senior navy leadership, they blackballed him, and his career quickly became somewhat less than extraordinary.

Several years later, in 1937, the review board grudgingly acknowledged him to be "a trustworthy and skilled, if somewhat eccentric and manipulative, leader of men" and they eventually gave him command of his own boat. His command tour was highly successful and his boat won several unit citations, but when his tour ended in 1939, he was far behind the rest of his academy classmates and had no chance of receiving a higher command. So the navy sent him to a quiet desk job at the War Department in Washington D.C., where Steven Ireland was expected to spend the rest of his naval career.

Those plans, along with many others, changed on December 7, 1941, when the United States entered the war. After the devastating blow to the Pacific Fleet at Pearl Harbor, the navy department quickly determined that submarines would be a major factor in holding the "front lines" in the Pacific—until replacement ships and fleets were constructed to start America's counter offensive. Commanders with submarine experience were desperately needed. Thus, Ireland was pulled from his desk job and sent to Pearl Harbor to take command of Submarine Division Seven.

Submarine Division Seven was a newly formed division. It had been created, along with several more divisions, to accommodate the arrival of newly constructed replacement submarines that were supposed to be arriving "soon." For his new division's headquarters section, Ireland had been given some of Submarine Division Three's office space until a new building could be constructed. Three offices and a small waiting room were all Division Three could afford to give up. Despite the grumblings of his headquarters staff,

Captain Ireland had gladly accepted the offices and reminded his staff that their submarine brethren at sea were serving under far worse conditions.

Now Ireland had a far more serious problem to worry about than office space. He walked over to the great chart spanning most of the adjacent wall. Sipping his coffee, he shook his head. The chart showed the current patrol zones of his deployed boats. Of the six boats in his division, three were deployed. One of those boats was missing and presumed sunk. Of the three boats in port, one was in retrofit, one was two weeks away from its next patrol, and one was . . . his current problem.

He did not like this part of the job but it was perhaps the only part of his job that mattered. He had a problem in his division. A "problem child" so to speak. A boat with an unusually high number of "hard luck" occurrences. Using his keen problem-solving ability, Ireland had done the only thing he could do. He had determined the "root cause" of the problem and eradicated it. Unfortunately, the "root cause" of any large problem on any ship was almost always the ship's commanding officer.

There was a knock at the door and an enlisted yeoman entered the room in the customary white "cracker jack" uniform of sailors assigned to shore jobs.

"Lieutenant Commander Tremain is here to see you, sir," the yeoman said.

"Very well. Send him in, will you please."

Ireland took a deep breath and sat his coffee cup on the desk. He hated being the bearer of bad news. This would be the second time today.

There was another brief knock before a smiling but worn-looking officer entered the room in service dress khakis. Jack Tremain held his hat under one arm. He looked youthful and inexperienced but Ireland knew better. If one missed the insignia of a lieutenant commander proudly displayed on his uniform, one would certainly not miss the Navy Cross above his left breast pocket. Both marked him as a seasoned veteran of naval combat. Tremain had jet-black hair swept loosely to the side. His eyes bore the crow's feet brought on by many tours of duty spent squinting into the sun. He was trim, the result of extreme physical discipline and many years of physical exertion.

Ireland smiled and met Tremain in the center of the room with a heart-felt handshake.

"Hi, Jack. How are you? How was the flight in?"

"Good, Captain. Pretty uneventful. One helluva layover in New Guinea, though."

"Two weeks, wasn't it?"

"Something like that, sir."

"And how's Judy? Been able to get through since you hit Pearl?"

"No, sir. Lines were tied up this morning. I'll try again later. She was doing well in the last letter that caught up with me."

"Good, good. Go ahead and have a seat, Jack." Ireland motioned to the chair in front of his desk while he walked to the sidebar.

"Coffee, Jack?"

"Yes, sir, thank you."

Tremain's face immediately became stone. He had been in the navy long enough to know a "butter-up" treatment when he saw it.

"You're probably wondering why I asked you to come by, Jack. I know you have a flight scheduled back to the States tonight. Leaving from Hickam, isn't it?"

Jack took the steaming cup of coffee from Ireland. He did not answer the leading question but instead changed tack.

"I just assumed you wanted to say hi to an old shipmate, Captain. I was hoping this was a social call."

"It's not. You know me better than that, Jack."

"I most certainly do, sir. So why'd you send for me? And before you begin, might I point out that I have not seen Judy for over a year now. Also, may I remind you that I've been ordered to take command of a pre-commissioned submarine fitting out in New London. That's two damn good reasons I'm determined to be on that plane tonight!"

The captain raised his hand and sat down at his desk. "Now, don't get all excited. Hear me out."

"Right, sir."

"You know Sammy Russo?"

"Yes, sir. Spent some time together in the Asiatic. Last I heard he had command of a boat out here."

"*Mackerel*. One of my boats."

Ireland paused for a moment and took several sips of coffee.

"*Mackerel* just returned from a patrol last week, Jack. She had been assigned to a position off the northeastern coast of Honshu. From the get-go the patrol was Fubar. First week on station, they sighted what they thought was a freighter coming out of Tsugara Straight. They conducted a night approach on the surface and when they got within a thousand yards, you guessed it, their 'freighter' turned out to be a *Fubuki* destroyer. What's more, before they could submerge and get the hell out of there, the *Fubuki* saw them and opened up. The bridge was peppered with twenty-five millimeter shells. One lookout, up in the shears, had his head taken clean off. Another lookout, covered with the blood of his shipmate, panicked and jumped over the side. Russo had no choice but to dive and leave the poor boy to the mercy of the sea. Of course, once they were finally down, that *Fubuki* unloaded every one of its depth charges in a four-hour attack. Close ones, too. Light bulbs blown, valves ruptured—they even had some minor flooding. Eventually, Russo was able to give the *Fubuki* the slip and the flooding was brought under control. The lost sailor was never recovered."

"Could've happened to anyone, sir. A tough break for Sammy, though."

"There's more, Jack. After this brush, Russo assessed the damage, which was relatively light, and ascertained that the patrol could continue. Two days later, they did spot a freighter, a real one this time, and conducted a textbook submerged approach. They shot four fish inside one thousand yards and got no hits. One fish must have run under the target, because they didn't see any explosion. Two fish exploded prematurely several hundred yards in front of the bastard. The last fish never left the tube and got fouled in the shutter door mechanism."

"Rotten luck." Tremain heard himself say this, realized he was being pulled into the story, and determined to himself to remain detached and emotionless.

"All efforts to dislodge it from the tube failed," Ireland continued. "So they spent the rest of the patrol wondering if the torpedo's exploder had armed itself—knowing that any heavy sea could set off the warhead and mean instant death for them all."

"Those damn Bureau of Ordnance idiots keep giving us faulty torpedoes!" Tremain said. He hated that his anger had compromised his promise to himself to remain uninvolved. He told himself to clam up and concentrate on catching his hop back Stateside tonight. Let Ireland fix his own problems without sucking him into them.

"There's more than that, Jack."

When only silence followed this remark, Ireland continued.

"Yes. After the torpedo mishap, Russo decided to break off the patrol and head for Midway Island. Before making it out of Japanese waters, they were caught on the surface and strafed by a Zero. Russo submerged the boat and got away, but another man was seriously injured before they could clear the bridge, bringing their total casualty list up to three. After this incident, Russo decided to bring the boat back to Pearl instead of Midway as his patrol orders stated. They arrived last Friday with twenty good torpedoes on board and well over fifty percent of their fuel."

"Was Sammy okay?"

"He's just fine . . . physically."

Tremain eyed him suspiciously. Then he said, "Captain, I am almost afraid to ask, but why are you telling me all this?"

Ireland rose from his desk and walked over by the window. He said nothing and clasped his hands behind his back. Finally he said, "I lost a boat this month, Jack. She's missing and presumed sunk."

"Sorry to hear that, sir."

"I've got another boat with a shell-shocked crew. Do you know what that means?"

"A load of bad luck, sir."

"Wrong!" Ireland said, suddenly agitated, turning away from the window to face Tremain. "It means that two out of the six submarines in this division are no longer in the war! It means my fighting force has been reduced by one third! It means that this area of Japanese water," he gestured to the chart on the wall, "which my squadron has been assigned to contain, now has only two submarines guarding it—instead of four!"

Tremain did not know how to respond and so he chose to remain silent.

"It means that Japanese shipping is getting through our submarine net, Jack. Japanese shipping to resupply the Japanese war machine and provide fuel, weapons, ammunition, food, and supplies to the hundreds of enemy outposts throughout the Pacific—outposts that young American soldiers and marines are going to have to land on and fight and die to take. Every ship that gets through means American lives lost.

"I'll come to the point, Jack. You and I both know that this 'bad luck' line is bullshit. To claim "bad luck" is to simply shirk responsibility. It is simply a way to hide problems—serious problems lurking in the unit. The ultimate responsibility in any command resides with the commander. I don't have to tell you that."

"No, sir."

"Well, here it is. I need *Mackerel*. I need her back in the war—fast. I need her and her twenty-four torpedoes out there sinking enemy ships." Ireland drew a deep breath. "In peacetime we have the time and convenience to nurture and aid a commander when he's not cutting it, even to give him a break. Hell, if we had enough boats to cover everywhere we could even give Sammy a break now. But this is not peacetime, Jack, and we're definitely short on boats. Russo's been in the war since the beginning. He's made six war patrols and done more than his part for the war effort, but he's all used up and his command is suffering for it."

Tremain cringed inside at what he could see coming a mile off.

"I relieved Sammy of his command earlier this morning, Jack. It was one of the hardest things I've ever had to do. I hated to do it, but it had to be done." Ireland shrugged his shoulders and shook his head. "So now I come to the reason you're here. I need someone to take Sammy's boat and crew and get them both back into the war. I've considered it long and hard. And come to the conclusion you're that man."

"Sir, there have to be plenty of qualified PCOs in the pipeline to—"

"Sure there are, Jack. I could put a green CO in Sammy's place and chances are that things would work out just fine—but I don't have the time or the resources to gamble on that green CO. I need someone who's been there. Someone who knows how to pick up a crew that's taken a beating and make them want to go out there for some more." Suddenly he clapped his hands. Then he leaned forward and wagged his index finger. "Now I know you've done your share and you're looking forward to seeing your wife and getting to that new boat of yours, but I need you here."

Tremain leaned back in the chair and breathed a long sigh. He thought of Judy's beautiful red hair waiting for him on the other end of that plane tonight. He wanted so much to see her. She wanted to see him, her husband that had abandoned her to go off and fight in this terrible war. Would she understand again? Or would this be the proverbial straw that broke the back of their strained marriage? Would this be the final blow to their war-blighted domestic bliss?

"Have my orders been changed, sir?" Tremain asked carefully.

"I haven't taken that step yet, Jack. I owe you that. I'm asking you to take *Mackerel* and turn her around. Just one patrol. After that, I promise I will personally speak to Com-SubPac about placing you on the priority list for the next pre-comm boat. Whatta you say?"

Tremain sighed as he ran his fingers once through his hair. He stared at the wall. He hated to be manipulated like this, by a call to duty, the same old trick his father had used on him all his life. He thought: This decision was not really his. His career pivoted on what he did here. Be a good sailor and his rising career was assured. Be difficult and his status was fixed as static for the duration. He would go no higher.

"By the way, Jack," Ireland said, suddenly in a somber tone. "I forgot to tell you. I'm sorry about the *Seatrout*. She was a good boat."

The remark struck a nerve in Tremain. He shot a glance at Ireland, whose eyes quickly went to the floor. Tremain knew Ireland had not really forgotten to tell him. Tremain knew how he operated. He had saved that little tidbit for just the right moment.

"What'll it be, Jack?" Ireland said, all business again.

Tremain closed his eyes and nodded. "Is there really a choice, Captain?"

"Not for good men like you, Jack. Thanks. When can you take over?"

Tremain rose. "I suppose I can get over there this afternoon, sir. After I place a call to Judy and break the bad news, that is. I'll need your support to do this. My own run of the roost."

Ireland patted him on the back.

"You've got it."

They shook hands and Tremain headed for the door.

"The yeoman outside has the official orders typed up and everything has been cleared with ComSubPac. Ask the yeoman to arrange a priority line for you to get through to Judy."

"You certainly have thought of everything, sir."

"Wouldn't think of operating otherwise. Good luck, Jack."

"Thank you, Captain."

After Tremain had left the office, Ireland returned to sipping his coffee by the window. From his office he could just see the USS *Mackerel* sitting at her moorings at the end of the jetty.

And good luck to you, he thought. I'm sending you a shining star.

Chapter 2

JACK Tremain took a long drag on his fourth cigarette while standing beneath some shady palms in the courtyard near the headquarters building. He had intentionally chosen the spot so that he could enjoy his cigarette out of the flow of pedestrian traffic. He did not feel like saluting three or four times a minute—or at all for that matter.

He tugged a little at his khaki jacket. The humid air did little to soothe his perspiring skin in the heat of the afternoon sun. The heat seemed to disturb him more than it had when he first stepped off the plane. Perhaps the meeting with Ireland had made him sweat more. Or perhaps it was the thought of going back to sea so soon. He had fully been expecting to hold Judy in his arms in a few hours. Now, who knew when he would see her again? The emotional strain was taxing, as it had always been. They had been through unexpected delays before at various times throughout his naval career and had grown accustomed to the ever-present "needs of the navy," but this time hurt worse than the others did. The other separations had not been during wartime. They had not been after he had suffered the loss of a boat. And a crew. Judy had always helped him sort out the senseless. She had always helped him to see the silver lining. He needed her now. He needed her to confirm that there was a still a reason for living. To confirm that there was still something left worth fighting for.

In his nostrils he caught the aroma. An aroma seldom missed but never forgotten. That distinct smell that accompanied his profession. The heavy muggy stink of diesel fuel oil. It came from the boats at the pier, just across the courtyard. It permeated everything it came in contact with.

The scent brought to mind different things in different people. In the far reaches of his mind it represented death. He felt a cold shiver and suddenly the sweat felt icy on his skin. He closed his eyes and he could see their faces. Was it years ago, or only weeks, when he had received word of their loss?

Lieutenant Commander Robert J. "Jack" Tremain came from a different stock than Captain Ireland. Like Ireland, he was a graduate of the Naval Academy. Unlike Ireland, he had been the first in his family to wear the naval uniform. Most of the male relatives had served in the army at some time or other but none had ever made a career out of it. Tremain's love of engineering had led him to join the navy. Then his love of the navy led him to stay and make it a career. From his earliest days at the academy, he had no doubts about which branch he would choose. Submarines were the vessels of the future. They appealed to his passion for all aspects of engineering. Strange that he would later find out that his real strength lay in leadership.

As an ensign, he served in his first sea tour out of Manila on an old S-boat built during the First World War. The little submarine displaced barely more than nine hundred tons and bobbed on the surface like a cork. She was extremely slow on the surface. So slow, in fact, that most of the shaft horse-power produced by the diesel engines was used to fight against the stiff currents around the Philippine Islands. He learned a great respect for the power of the sea during that tour. In later years he would often say "there really is nothing quite like standing on the twenty-foot bridge of an S-boat with a forty-foot wave about to hit you." All in all, it had been a good tour for him. With less than nine months on board he had qualified to wear the coveted "Gold Dolphins" of the submarine officer society. He made Lieutenant (Junior Grade) while on board as well. It was basically a run-of-the-mill submarine junior officer tour. Run-of-the-mill—except for one event that happened toward the end of his tour.

After an extended overhaul and drydock period in Pearl, the S-boat had put to sea to conduct a routine dive to test depth to test the rivets and seals, standard operating procedure for all submarines coming out of a maintenance period. This dive, however, turned out to be anything but routine. On the initial dive, the boat submerged with an uncharacteristically high rate of descent and it soon became apparent to everyone on board that the shipyard engineers had grossly miscalculated the amount of negative ballast needed to keep the ship on a level trim. They had loaded several thousand pounds too much. The captain immediately ordered the ballast tanks blown, but the ship's momentum was too great and she dove straight for the bottom. The bottom was at four hundred feet, well below an S-boat's test depth, but the little boat's hull held together. The boat hit the ocean floor nose first and quickly settled into the sand.

Tremain was in the engine room when it happened. Men were seriously injured from the shock, pipes ruptured everywhere, and the compartment began to flood with seawater. The ship was rigged for deep submergence, so Tremain and the crew in the engine room were isolated from the rest of the ship and thus had no hope of any assistance in their efforts to fight the dozen leaking pipes and valves. The flooding seemed insurmountable and the men in the engine room, believing their efforts to be in vain, gave up and prepared to meet their fates. But Tremain kept a clear head and snapped them out of their delirium, taking over the damage control coordination. It took more than six hours to finally bring the flooding under control. Eventually, the flooding stopped and the hull held out at 408 feet. Then they were able to pump enough water off the ship to give her a small positive buoyancy, just enough to get her off the bottom. This allowed the powerful electric motors to propel her to the surface.

It had been a close call but a defining moment in Tremain's career. From that moment, he was placed on the fast track for success. He was sort-of-a-celebrity at every officers' club social and a poster child for the local admiral. As a reward for his good leadership, he was sent to Prospective Executive Officers' School well before the rest of his classmates. It was while he was at the PXO School in New London that he met and fell in love with Judy. Upon graduation he was placed aboard the USS *Barracuda* as Executive Officer under an aged skipper, Commander Steve Ireland.

Ireland may have been aged and out of touch in the minds of many, but Tremain could attribute most of his submarine expertise to him. Tremain had reported on board with an understandably large head, and Ireland quickly showed him that he still had a lot to learn. He taught him how to be a good XO and, more importantly, how to be a good CO. Ireland spent years fine-tuning Tremain with the devotion that a father has for his son, but the two men had kept their relationship completely professional throughout. Ireland was not one for "boozing it up" with his officers and the junior officers feared him for his angry scowl. Tremain respected this and the two became an excellent team.

Tremain's peacetime exploits paled in comparison to the feats he had accomplished in the first months of the war. After a brief shore tour in 1939, he was selected to attend the Prospective Commanding Officer School and six months later he was appointed as Commanding Officer of the USS *Seatrout*, a P-Class submarine, once again stationed in Manila. When the Japanese invaded the Philippines, *Seatrout* had been one of the first American submarines to challenge the Imperial Navy. Before Manila was evacuated in late December, the boat had already sunk a Japanese destroyer and a troop transport. With Manila in Japanese hands, *Seatrout* transferred to the makeshift submarine base in Darwin, Australia, from whence she continued to exact punishment on the Japanese, sinking a total of 15,240 tons of enemy shipping during a span of four major war patrols.

Before the fifth patrol, Tremain was awarded the Navy Cross and received new orders to proceed to New London, Connecticut, where he was to take command of a new boat still in the yards. Sadly, Tremain bid his crew a fond farewell and waved to them from the pier as they shoved off for that fifth patrol without him. He then spent a few weeks in Darwin doing an odd assortment of administrative tasks before embarking on the long trip back to the States by hitching a ride with every mode of transportation heading in the right direction. It had taken him two weeks just to get to New Guinea, and it was there that the news had reached him. His beloved *Seatrout* had been declared missing and presumed sunk. The news had shattered Tremain. He had locked himself in his BOQ room and drunk himself to oblivion. Then he had slept for two days without stirring.

I wonder what you'd say, Old Captain Ireland, if you knew about that, he thought. The last time he had smelled that diesel aroma he was waving goodbye to his crew on the way to their doom. Thus, in his mind, the aroma now became the smell of death, and it made him cold all over.

He lit the fifth cigarette.

Why did he get this job, anyway? Why him?

Old Ireland had said that Sammy Russo was "all used up." What did Ireland think Tremain had been through over the last year, a shore desk job? Four patrols can take a lot out of a man.

And what about Judy? Poor soul, she sounded so torn today when he told her the news. As always she supported him but he could feel her resentment building. At some point the strain would get to her and she would lash out because he was putting her through the emotional roller coaster again. Had their marriage been a submarine the pressure on the hull would have been popping the bolts. Military marriages were among the hardest to hold together. They always had been, and especially so in wartime. Judy was a great gal, but what the hell? How much could she take? And for what? To quell the anxiety of a crusty old submariner who's upset because he doesn't have enough boats to cover his zone?

He took a long drag on the cigarette and exhaled with a loud sigh.

He was not fooling himself. He knew why he had taken the job, and it wasn't because he was the "good man" that Ireland had so graciously dubbed him. It wasn't because he felt it was his duty either. It was for one reason—and one reason alone. He wanted revenge. He wanted to kill the enemy that had killed his beloved crew. He wanted to kill the Japanese that had killed his friends. He wanted to kill every damn Japanese bastard who had started this bloody war.

Had Judy sensed all this in the phone call? He felt sure that she had. She knew him all too well. But what could he tell her? How could he make her understand the demons that haunted him in his sleep? The ninety lost souls that cried to him for vengeance on those who had robbed them of their youths.

He looked up from the ground. There she was, just

across the jetty. The infamous *Mackerel* sitting silently at
the pier. The would-be instrument of his vengeance. Her
gray-green camouflaged hull sharply contrasting against the
shoreline beyond. A solitary sailor stood watch at her brow,
a .45-caliber pistol hanging loosely from his hip.

The *Mackerel* sat well down the pier from the other submarines and seemed to be abandoned. No sign of life, save
the bored sentry, picking his nose.

The black sheep, Tremain thought.

Then he shook himself. This was silly. What was he doing? He should march right back up to that office, look Old
Ireland straight in the eyes, and tell him he simply would
not do it! And if Ireland put up a fight, he would threaten to
bypass the chain of command and take his case straight to
ComSubPac! He was going to be on that plane tonight, by
damn!

Just then, he noticed a khaki figure emerge from *Mackerel*'s forward hatch. The figure had a white laundry bag in
one hand and a leather attaché case tucked under his arm. He
stood slouching on deck facing the conning tower for a few
moments, then another figure emerged from the same hatch.
He was in khaki, too. The two men shook hands and exchanged warm smiles, then the first headed across the brow.
Halfway across he gave the customary salute to the colors at
the submarine's stern. The ship's bell then rang out, clearly
audible from where Tremain stood.

Ding-ding. . . ding-ding. . . ding-ding. . . ding.

That must be Sammy Russo, Tremain thought. Leaving
his command for the last time. The man headed straight for
the headquarters building. As he drew closer, he caught
sight of Tremain. He stopped momentarily, as if unsure of
what he should do. Then he smiled and waved and crossed
the courtyard to meet him.

Tremain smiled and extended his hand.

"Hello, Sammy."

"Hello, Jack."

"Smoke?"

"No . . . thanks, though."

Russo looked like a broken man. His eyes shifted from side to side. His uniform hung on him like loose rags. He had not shaved that day. Could this be the strait-laced, confident man Tremain had known years before?

"So I hear you're going to take over, Jack?"

Tremain did not respond. He did not know what to say.

"They're a good crew, Jack. They've just been pushed too hard. And I can't push them anymore."

"I heard about that last patrol, Sam . . . sorry about your lost men." Tremain tried to say it in the most consoling way he could.

Russo nodded and looked away, back toward his former boat. Tremain thought he saw a tear start to form in his eye.

"It may sound funny, Jack, but I'm glad you're taking my place. I trust you rather than some untried moron who'll just take them out and get them killed." He paused, fighting for emotional control and a steady voice. Then he said, "This crew can do the job. They're the best in the fleet, but . . . shit." He broke off talking again and Tremain said nothing.

"You will take good care of *Mackerel* for me, won't you? Go and sink a few for me, and bring her back safely, won't you, Jack?"

"Sure I will, Sammy. I'll even send you an autographed photo of our first kill." Tremain smiled and winked.

Russo smiled. He wiped the moisture from his eyes and seemed to regain his composure. "Well, I better get up to Old Ireland's office. I'm sure he already has a desk picked out for me!"

"Take care, Sammy."

"Good luck, Jack."

As Russo headed for the steps of the headquarters

building, Tremain took another drag on his smoldering cigarette and turned to look at the *Mackerel*. As the smoke left his body, his eyes grew cold and hard, as if he was sizing up an opponent in a prize fight. One more drag and he straightened his back, standing as tall as he could. He threw the cigarette to the ground and crushed it with one turn of his heel. Shouldering his sea bag he marched straight for the unsuspecting submarine at the pier.

SEAMAN MacDougal twirled the whistle in his hand as he attempted to enact the tedious motions of standing guard at the brow. He could not know what was about to happen to him. If he had known he would have run. He was about to be made an example of.

He had seen the officer coming from the headquarters building. But he thought nothing of it. Several officers unknown to him had been on board that day. And he did not recognize this one either. It did not really matter. After all, what Japanese would try to sneak on board in the middle of Pearl Harbor?

This officer, however, was approaching at a most alarming rate, swinging his free arm wide and taking strides as if he was on his way to a fire. His eyes seemed fixed on Mac-Dougal. They did not blink. They did not waver. They simply stared. The eyes were filled with hatred. For what, MacDougal could not know. But it alarmed him. These fixed eyes were fierce.

MacDougal swallowed hard. What was the rank? He had better check. But those eyes, holy shit! Still locked on him and ever so steady. What should he do?

"Seaman!"

MacDougal snapped to attention. Before he could blink, the officer stood before him.

"Permission . . . granted to go aboard . . . sir." MacDougal fumbled with his speech.

"What's your name?" the officer demanded. He had not moved an inch.

"Seaman MacDougal, si—"

"Do you know who I am?"

"N no, sir."

"I'm Lieutenant Commander Tremain, the new commanding officer of this boat." Tremain flashed his identification card in front of MacDougal's face. "And the next time I catch you or any other sentry allowing someone onboard without checking identification, failing to salute an officer, improperly standing a watch . . . you'll wish the Japanese had got you first. Is that clear?"

MacDougal shot up a salute.

"Yessir."

Tremain abruptly returned the salute, hefted the bag on his shoulder, and stormed across the brow. A lieutenant (j.g), obviously the duty officer, the same man that had bid Russo goodbye, was on deck and hurried to meet Tremain as he stepped aboard. The lieutenant had witnessed the incident on the pier and shot up a sharp salute to avoid similar treatment.

Tremain returned it. "Permission to come aboard."

"Permission granted, sir."

"And who are you?" Tremain snapped.

"Lieutenant (j.g) Salisbury, sir."

"And what is your billet?"

"I'm the sonar officer, sir."

"I see. Tell me Mr. Salisbury, do you always have such shabby standards for your duty section?"

"No, sir . . . I—" Salisbury seemed a little irritated by Tremain's remark, "I apologize for MacDougal, sir. It won't happen again."

"I'll say it won't," Tremain shot back, dropping his bag on the deck and marching aft.

Salisbury didn't know whether he should follow him, pick up the bag, or do nothing. He looked at the crumpled bag lying on the deck, then back at Tremain already conducting an inspection of *Mackerel*'s topside deck. Tremain walked all the way aft, stood and stared at something for a moment, then came back to pick up his bag.

"Mr. Salisbury, I am your new Commanding Officer. Lieutenant Commander Tremain is my name."

"Yes, si—"

"Mr. Salisbury, this topside looks like a typhoon hit it! Why?"

Salisbury had no answer.

Tremain did not wait for an answer and began to point out the deficiencies.

"Those lines need tending," he said. "They shouldn't droop into the water like that. And coil up that excess line. But before you do that, I want this deck scrubbed and washed down. What are that broom and those two buckets doing topside? They should be stowed below. That sanitary connection is leaking all over the place. Have it tightened. Why are there two food crates topside? Can't you get enough hands to stow them below? This is a warship, not a grocery store, Mr. Salisbury. Also, get those damn shore power cables out of the water! You're lucky if you haven't had a ground by now. And send some men over to clean up the pier. I'll be damned if it doesn't look as bad as topside."

Salisbury didn't know what to say. To Tremain he seemed defiant, yet embarrassed.

"Sir," Salisbury said, "I don't have that many men available. We just have a skeleton duty section on board."

"Why?" Tremain asked, slightly surprised at Salisbury's response. "Where is everyone?"

"They're all staying at the Royal Hawaiian, sir."

Tremain inwardly cursed Ireland: He expects me to turn this ship around, but, meanwhile, he lets this crew go on liberty. They're probably scattered all over the island by now.

"You the only officer on board, Mr. Salisbury?"

"Yessir."

"Then I suggest you get on the phone to the exec. Tell him from this moment on all leave and liberty has been canceled, and I expect every man to be back on board by 0700 tomorrow morning. I don't care if he has to send the shore patrol after them or even if he has to search every corner of the island himself, but I want them back on board. Is that clear?"

"Yessir."

"Then call over to Squadron and reserve the sub base theater for 0715 tomorrow morning. Understood?"

"Yessir."

Tremain glanced around the deck once more and shook his head before starting down the forward hatch.

Salisbury called after him. "Sir, shall I show you to your cabin?"

"No, that won't be necessary, Mr. Salisbury," Tremain yelled back up the open hatch. "I suggest you get your section started on that deck. If you have only a skeleton section, it might well take most of the night."

"Aye, sir."

After Tremain disappeared below, Salisbury visibly slouched and let out a large sigh. Why on earth did they send us this guy? he thought. Haven't we had enough?

TREMAIN stood at the base of the ladder for a few moments. He had come down into the forward torpedo room. He slowly took it all in. It was the first time he had been inside a boat since he had left *Seatrout.* He already felt confined.

The room bristled with valves and gauges. The six torpedo tube breech doors at the forward end of the room glimmered in the dull light. He walked aft, passing between the long ominous torpedoes and racks. They took up most of the room and created a passage barely wide enough for a man to get through. Ducking his head, he passed through the watertight door and into the next compartment. Here were the officer and chief petty officer quarters, a short passageway with rooms on either side: three for the officers, one for the chief petty officers and one for the captain. By landsman's terms they could not be characterized as rooms at all but more adequately as large closets with bunks. Instead of doors, curtains hung for privacy, but there really never was any privacy on board a submarine. At the far end of the passage was the officer wardroom, a slightly larger closet with a table that the officers could squeeze around and use for meals and meetings. The captain's cabin was just across the passage from this room.

Tremain drew the curtain to one side and entered his new home. He tossed his bag onto the bunk. It was just like he remembered on *Seatrout,* cramped and plain, with pipes of all sizes running through it. In addition to the bunk, a fold-out chair and a small desk further crowded the room. The desk was more like a writing board attached to the bulkhead. A sink hung from one bulkhead and a small safe sat beneath it. Though it all seemed like a meager existence, the captain's dwelling was far superior to that of any member of the crew. He at least had a space of his own.

Tremain sat on the bunk and relaxed for a moment. He opened his bag and took out some Dutch chocolates he had been saving for Judy. A lot of good they would do his beautiful wife now. He might as well eat them. There was no way they would survive this tour of duty intact. He only hoped he would.

This was going to be difficult. The crew was going to hate him for canceling their liberty. Tremain had not needed that. Damn Ireland! Why had he allowed Russo to let them go?

Maybe Ireland did it intentionally, Tremain thought. Maybe he wanted me to have no choice but to play the hard line, the ornery old son of a bitch. He's going to owe me for this.

There was a small knock outside his cabin.

"Excuse me, Captain." A burly sailor in dungarees, wearing the insignia of a yeoman first class, poked his head in. "Petty Officer Mills, sir. Mr. Salisbury told me to see if you needed anything."

Tremain was surprised Salisbury had thought of it. Maybe he would be useful after all.

"Yes, Mills. Bring me a cup of coffee, would you?"

"Aye, sir."

"And Mills. . . ."

"Yessir?"

"Do you know where the XO keeps the service records for all the chiefs and officers?"

"Yessir."

"Please bring those, as well."

"Aye, sir." Mills ducked out and within moments Tremain could hear him preparing to brew up a pot of coffee in the wardroom.

Tremain bit into a chocolate. It tasted bittersweet. Now it was time for him to do his homework.

Chapter 3

ENSIGN Ryan P. Wright stepped off the darkened navy bus and onto the gravel sidewalk. A low cloud hid the moonlight making the Oahu evening pitch black. Wright could not tell where the bus stop was in relation to the rest of the base, but then it would not have mattered if he could. He had never been to Pearl Harbor before.

Several drunken sailors in white cracker jack uniforms filed off the bus behind him and headed off in one direction. He could still hear their cackling voices after they had disappeared into the night. He considered following them and the realization suddenly hit him that he was already lost.

Wright leaned back into the bus.

"Is this the sub base?" he asked the enlisted bus driver, whose face was lit only by the vehicle's instrument panel and a smoldering cigarette.

The driver eyed him for a moment then removed the cigarette from his mouth and jabbed it in the direction of

an unlit sign near the side of the road. The sign read PEARL
HARBOR SUBMARINE BASE.

"That's it there, sir," the driver said. "And make sure
you keep bearing to the right, otherwise you'll end up on
the fleet base."

"Thanks," Wright said, smiling. He still did not know
how to get to his boat, but at least he knew the way to the
submarine base.

Wright had hardly removed his face from the door before the driver shut it and drove on. Standing in the middle
of the street with his bags in both hands, he watched the
bus drive away like he had watched his mother drive away
on his first day of kindergarten. As the bus lights faded
around a distant corner, it became more apparent just how
dark it was. The base was under blackout conditions so as
not to assist the Japanese aircraft if an attack was ever
again attempted. The dark shapes of several buildings became visible as his eyes adjusted. All was quiet and appeared to be devoid of human life.

His plane had landed at Hickam Field just before sunset,
so Wright had had a chance to see the layout of the base
briefly as the aircraft banked to line up with the runway.
Wright recalled the layout vividly and he had noted several
landmarks to help him find his way, but he had not considered what little good they would be in the dark. From five
hundred feet, he had seen in great detail the different military and naval complexes surrounding Pearl Harbor and he
had managed to pinpoint the location of the submarine base
in relation to the other bases. The Pearl Harbor naval complex was divided into several sections. He had seen the surface fleet base and the shipyard, which took up most of the
western side of the base. The shipyard, with its four massive
drydocks, each equipped with one-hundred-foot cranes, had
the capability of rebuilding a vessel the size of a battleship.
The waterfront there had been crowded with ships of all

sizes, some of them moored two and three outboard of each other to save pier space. Aircraft carriers, battleships, cruisers, destroyers, and auxiliaries of all types filled the harbor; so many ships and such a tempting target that he had wondered why the Japanese had not yet tried another air attack.

The submarine base had been easy to distinguish from the rest. Occupying a smaller area than the main base, it was nestled in the far eastern corner of the naval complex on a triangular jetty extending into the harbor. He had quickly identified the long slender hulls of submarines tied up next to two long piers extending from the jetty. From the air the surface ships across the water dwarfed their small sisters, but Wright felt a quiet thrill at the first sight of the small boats.

Wright squinted in the dark. He assumed that the jetty was beyond the sign so he began to walk in that direction. The jetty covered only a few acres but it contained the entire submarine base: headquarters buildings for all of the squadrons, maintenance workshops, barracks for the crews and maintenance personnel, a one-hundred-foot water tower for submarine escape training, a theater, a small exchange, an enlisted club, a chief petty officer's lounge, an officer's club, a bachelor officers' quarters. All of these buildings fit onto the oddly shaped jetty and were pleasantly arranged among a series of grassy courtyards dotted with clusters of tall palm trees.

Ensign Wright's eyes soon became accustomed to the light as he walked from building to building. He hoped he was heading toward the water where his boat would be. He could hear it and smell it, but he still could not see it yet. He began to see signs of life, too. A few sailors lounged here and there in front of their barracks, but he did not feel like asking them directions. He was green, and desperately trying not to show it. But his dress khaki uniform was fresh from the rack, and if the new gold lace on his single-striped ensign shoulderboards did not give it away, his oversized seabag would. He did not want to call any more attention to himself.

Wright followed the sidewalk as it led between the barracks and up to a large three-story building bordered on one side by a grassy lawn. He stopped in front of the building and found something that looked like a sign but it was too dark to read. The building's windows were covered with blackout curtains and it would have appeared to be abandoned but for the light coming from the arched doorway. The doors were open and there was light and the sounds of life inside. Wright heard the clink of glasses and the jovial laughter of happy people. Happy or drunk people, he could not tell which.

The moon suddenly appeared from a break in the low cloud cover, lighting the area in a soft blue hue. The blowing grass and palms were enchanting in the moonlight. This place was nothing like Massachusetts.

He thought he heard something for a moment, and then listened more carefully. Just above the sound of the breeze passing through the palm fronds and the voices inside, Wright heard the soothing rhythm of a Hawaiian ukulele playing a dreamy melody. He closed his eyes and listened. With the smell of the sea and the warm evening breeze hitting his face, the lazy music sounded simply divine.

How could war exist in a place like this? he thought.

The moonlight made the writing on the sign visible. The building was the bachelor officers' quarters.

Perfect, Wright thought. He did not have to report until tomorrow. He could get a room for tonight and get a good night's rest. He needed it after the long flight from the mainland.

He walked up the steps and entered the open foyer. It was deserted save for a solitary petty officer in a white cracker jack uniform standing behind the front desk.

"Good evening, sir. Can I help you?" the sailor asked.

"I'd like a room for the night, please."

The sailor smiled and shook his head, "Oh, I'm sorry, sir. There aren't any rooms available tonight. We're all booked up."

Wright slumped in visible dejection. The brief thought of sleeping in a real bed tonight had been enticing.

"Come a long way, huh, sir?" the sailor asked, sympathetically.

Wright nodded wearily, "From San Diego, today. Before that, New London."

"Well, sir, a piece of advice, if you don't mind my saying, but this BOQ will probably always be booked solid for ensigns."

"So what you're telling me, there are rooms available, but they're reserved for more senior officers, that it?"

"In a nutshell, sir."

"Lovely."

Wright glanced down the hallway. He noticed that the laughter and voices were coming from a set of double doors at the opposite end of the hall. The ukulele music came from there, too.

"What's going on down there?" he asked.

The sailor smiled. "That's the officers' club, sir. The officers from the *Wahoo* are kind of lively tonight. *Wahoo* got back from patrol today and I guess they got some kills."

The thought of a cold beer suddenly entered Wright's thoughts. "Do you have somewhere I can leave my bag?" he asked.

"Sure thing, sir. If you put it in that closet over there, no one'll bother it."

"Thanks."

Wright placed his bag and hat in the closet then walked down the hallway to the open double doors. He found that the doors led him back outside, and that the actual officers'

club was located in the L-shaped building's courtyard.
Round foldout tables and chairs were everywhere. A huge
awning covered the area to keep the club within blackout
regulations, and Tiki lamps ringed the area to provide dim
lighting. A large Hawaiian in a flower shirt propped on a
stool in the corner played the ukulele. Once in a while he
would sing a few high notes but he mostly played his instrument. The place was half full of mostly officers. Some
sat, others stood. All wore the customary officer working
uniform: long-sleeve cotton khaki shirt, trousers, and black
tie. Here and there an officer sat alone enjoying a beer, but
most of the officers were drinking, conversing, and cackling in groups. Some groups were louder than others.

Wright strolled over to the bar on the opposite side of
the club. He perched atop a barstool and ordered a beer. The
Hawaiian bartender placed the drink on the bar in front of
him with a kind smile. Wright tipped him and nodded his
thanks.

Wright took several swallows of the ice-cold beer. It
tasted good as it slid down his throat. He had not realized
how thirsty he was and he finished the bottle in four or five
large gulps. The alcohol instantly sent a warm soothing
sensation to his sore muscles and back. He then propped
his head in his hands and began to massage his temples,
thinking about the long day he had had. The bumpy plane
ride from San Diego had worn him out. It was two o'clock
in the morning California time, but his body was still on
Connecticut time.

The bartender appeared in front of him with another bottle and whisked the empty one away. Wright had just finished paying the man when a couple of noisy officers, both
lieutenants junior grade, bellied up to the bar and demanded
six beers from the bartender. The bartender seemed accustomed to their boisterous behavior and gave them six bottles,
accepting their tip with the same smile he had given Wright.

The larger of the two, a burly red-haired fellow with virtually no neck, noticed that Wright was watching them.

"What's your fucking problem . . . Ensign?" he asked, placing his red sweaty face in front of Wright's nose so close that Wright could feel his acrid breath. The large-shouldered man was obviously drunk and looking for trouble wherever he could find it. His intoxicated state aside, he was a clean-cut looking young man and he reminded Wright of several college football players he had known when he was at Yale.

"No, sir." Wright replied simply. He turned back to his bottle hoping that the drunken man would lose interest and go away. Unfortunately for him, the big man was not satisfied and brusquely gripped Wright by the arm to swing him back around.

"Maybe you're like all the others, huh?" The man spat his words in Wright's face. "Maybe you think you're better than us."

Wright did not know what to do. He had been on base for less than half an hour. He had no place to sleep and already he was about to get into a fight with a drunken lieutenant he didn't know from Adam.

"Easy, Tee. This ensign doesn't know any better." The less boisterous of the two officers seemed to understand Wright's plight and was suddenly much more sober than he had appeared a few moments ago. He placed a steadying hand on Tee's shoulder to pull him back a few inches. Wright did not know if the intervention was to protect him or to keep his friend out of trouble but, whatever the reason, he was thankful.

"You just get in, pal?" the officer asked.

Wright nodded his appreciation for the man's interference. "Yes, sir. Just arrived this evening."

The man smiled, extending a hand, "You can cut the 'sir' crap. We're all JOs here. My name's O'Connell,

Rudy O'Connell. This here's Tucker Turner. We call him T-squared, or Big T, or just Tee for short. Don't mind him, he's just drunk. Our boat just got back from patrol and we've got nothing to show for it. We've been catching a lot of crap from the other wardrooms here tonight."

O'Connell's interference seemed to calm Tee down a bit and he eventually extended his hand as well.

"Sorry, pal," Tee said as he took a long swig from his beer. He seemed to lose interest in Wright and began scanning the room as he choked down the beer. The apology was insincere, almost condescending—but Wright was happy enough to avoid a fight.

"No problem. My name's Ryan Wright."

"Well, well," O'Connell said with a big grin. "You the same Ryan Wright going to the *Mackerel*?"

"Right, I—"

"That's our boat, shipmate. We've been waiting for you to show up so we can get some relief on the watch bill. It's about time you got here."

Tee's red face was suddenly grinning devilishly. "So you're our new ensign, huh?"

"C'mon over and join us, Wright," O'Connell said. "The other officers are here too. We'll introduce you."

Wright nodded. He was glad to join them and relieved at having found some people that at least knew who he was, even though they were still complete strangers.

O'Connell and Tee led Wright to a table where three other officers and one woman sat. O'Connell proceeded to introduce him to each one.

"This is the engineer and diving officer, George Olande," O'Connell said.

A gray-haired lieutenant who looked like he was in his forties rose and shook Wright's hand. The gray hair suited the lines at the corners of his eyes and Wright could feel the man exuding the experience of many years at sea.

"George has been in the navy awhile. He's the saltiest of us all. He knows diesels better than the rest of us know dames."

Everyone around the table chuckled and the woman giggled a little with her hand over her mouth. The engineer gave a small smile and returned to his seat.

"Next to him is Carl Hubley, our torpedo and gunnery officer."

Hubley was a slightly chubby lieutenant and appeared to be not much older than Wright. With flushed cheeks and a warm smile he rose from his seat and shook Wright's hand.

"Welcome aboard, Wright." Hubley said, then motioned to the woman seated next to him. "This's my wife, Barbara."

The woman was rather homely. She had the signs of strain in her eyes and face that resulted from the many sleepless nights of uncertain waiting that accompanied the profession of navy wife, but her smile was pleasant and sincere as she greeted Wright. He nodded warmly to both of them.

"And this," O'Connell said, pointing Wright in the direction of the last officer, "is Lieutenant Frank Cazanavette, our XO."

"Hello, sir," Wright said, shaking Cazanavette's hand.

"Welcome aboard, Ryan."

Cazanavette had a soft-spoken, easygoing manner and kind eyes, Wright thought. He had a considerate and mild nature about him. He was certainly not what Wright would have expected in an XO. It was difficult for him to believe that this man was second in command of the submarine he would be serving on. The guy had a medium build which he carried with a slight slouch. To Wright he looked more like a church camp leader than a naval officer.

"Where you coming to us from, Ryan?" Cazanavette asked.

"From officer candidate school, sir. I went to Yale."

"Holy shit!" Tee blurted. "Not only a ninety-day wonder but an Ivy Leaguer to boot! What the hell're they sending us these days?"

"Shut up, Tee." Carl Hubley said. "Wright's not the only one here who didn't go to the Academy."

"At least you've got experience," Tee said. "I was hoping our replacement would be able to help us, but I guess we're going to have to wet-nurse his ass."

Wright said nothing. He could see that he was going to have trouble with Tee. The man had a chip on his shoulder a mile wide and now he was using Wright's inexperience to try to get a rise out of him. There had always been a rivalry between officers from the Naval Academy and officers who came in from different sources. Academy men had traditionally looked down their noses at their ROTC and OCS counterparts with the belief that only the Academy had the credentials to produce a qualified officer. This war had changed the minds of many, but not all. With the number of ships being built for the war in the Pacific, the non-traditional sources for officers had become essential to manning the fleet. Obviously Tee was one of those who still needed convincing. Either that or he was just looking for an excuse to harass the new ensign.

"Don't worry about him," O'Connell said to Wright. "He's a lot more pleasant when he's sober. Well, maybe not," he added with a grin.

Tee seemed to ignore O'Connell and shifted his concentration back to the bottle on the table before him.

"In case you were wondering, Tee is the damage control assistant *and* an Academy grad," O'Connell said. "We put up with him only because his dad is an admiral. Go figure. And I'm the electrical officer. And now you've met everyone. Everyone except for Joe Salisbury, that is. He's the sonar officer. He's got the duty tonight."

"Poor Joe," Carl Hubley said, shaking his head. "What a shitty day to get stuck with the duty."

Everyone at the table chuckled, except Wright. O'Connell saw his confusion and placed one hand on his shoulder.

"Young Wright." O'Connell said. He was no more than a year older than Wright himself. "You have come to join our little boat at a rather onerous time. We have just returned from what may quite possibly be the worst war patrol in submarine history. The only saving grace is that the boat made it back alive."

"Our boat made it back, but not Ecklund and Withers," George Olander said in his deep Georgia drawl.

All smiles vanished from their faces as if the old engineer had just reminded them of some bad deed they had done.

"They were good sailors," Hubley said, somberly. "Good men."

"Gentlemen and Mrs. Hubley," Cazanavette said and raised his bottle, "here's to our dearly departed shipmates. May they rest peacefully."

Everyone touched their bottles in the middle and took a long drink. Wright did not know who Ecklund and Withers were or how they had died, but he decided it would be best to join the toast.

They all sat in somber silence for several minutes while the large Hawaiian with the ukulele strummed out a soft rhythm. It sounded serene and sad at the same time. It matched the new mood at the table.

"We lost two sailors last time out," O'Connell finally said to Wright.

"And a captain," Hubley added.

"And a captain," O'Connell said, nodding. "Our captain was relieved of command this afternoon. Relieved because of our poor performance on the last patrol. So you see, Wright, you're coming to us at a rather awkward time. Our crew is at their wits' end. They've lost two of their ship-mates, they've had a patrol jinxed with bad luck, and now they've lost their captain, not to mention their nerves. And to top everything off, Squadron has just sent some asshole to take over the ship and whip us into shape. And this one's a real beauty. Tremain's his name. He's supposed to be some super sub ace or something like that. He came on board this afternoon and had Joe call the XO here to get the whole crew back on base by tomorrow morning."

Cazanavette appeared devoid of expression like he was only half paying attention to what O'Connell was saying.

"XO, I still can't believe it!" O'Connell said. "The man's crazy! Doesn't he realize this crew needs a rest? After all we've been through?"

"I don't know what he was thinking," Cazanavette said neutrally. "I've got the chief of the boat searching every bar on the island. I hope he can find them all. Don't overre-act though, Rudy. Maybe our new captain just wants to show us his face, tell us his policies, and then send us on our merry way. I'm sure he'll cut everyone loose after the meeting tomorrow. He's got to know the crew's been through a lot."

"I don't know, XO," Hubley interjected. "I talked to Joe on the phone a couple hours ago. He said the new captain's already given him enough housekeeping items to keep his whole duty section working until tomorrow morning. Joe also told me this new captain has somehow arranged a fuel, torpedo, and stores load for tomorrow. I don't know how he pulled that one off. He must have some connections up at squadron. He's probably related to Ireland somehow. Joe said the guy's just sitting in the wardroom going through the service records, drinking cup after cup of coffee."

"A perfectly normal thing for a new CO to do, Carl."

"I hope you're right, XO."

"I hope he's wrong, Carl," Olander said abruptly.

Everyone appeared taken aback by the southern engineer's statement.

"For God's sake why, George?" Hubley asked.

"Captain Russo was relieved for a reason, boys. And it wasn't because we lost two sailors. It's because we came back with twenty torpedoes on board and no ships sunk. The patrol before this one was a complete failure too, and you all know it."

"The captain did everything he could, George," Hubley protested. "You can't blame him for bad torp—"

"Who else is there to blame?" Olander interrupted. "How can ComSubPac keep a skipper in place when his boat has two hard luck patrols in a row? Other boats are sinking ships and they use the same torpedoes we do. They don't seem to have torpedo problems."

"I just think our patrols were bad luck," Hubley said. "Captain Russo had nothing to do with the way they turned out."

"I know how you feel, Carl," Olander said. "That's understandable. Captain Russo has had some good patrols on other boats, but not on ours. Everything he could do was not enough to make our boat succeed. And that's all that matters to ComSubPac."

Wright could tell that the other officers respected the experienced engineer's opinion. Most stared into their bottles, the memories of the last patrol obviously vivid in their minds.

Olander seemed to sense the mood he had created at the table.

"Now don't get me wrong, boys," he said. "I have as much respect for Sammy Russo as the rest of you. He's a good man. But I've been in boats longer than any of you. I've served under captains of all types, and I tell you that Sammy Russo is not the kind of captain this crew needs right now. Russo cared more for his crew than he did for the mission. Right now, this crew needs someone who doesn't know them so well. Someone who won't be afraid to tell them to stare death in the face and still get the job done."

"You're always gloomy, George," Hubley scoffed. "And I still think Russo beats any captain ComSubPac could try to replace him with."

"Well, I suppose we'll find out tomorrow in any event," O'Connell said. "Drink up, boys."

As Wright listened to the conversation among his new shipmates he began to dread this new assignment. When he was at submarine school, the instructors had always said, "Above all else, pray that you get a happy ship." They had explained that there was nothing quite so depressing or miserable as a ship with an inner turmoil. *Mackerel* certainly had internal problems, and Wright found himself now wishing that he had not been assigned to her.

"There's Margie, Tee," O'Connell said as he motioned toward the club entrance with his bottle. "You better straighten up."

A group of WAVES in their skirt uniforms entered the club and migrated to different tables throughout the place. They were obviously all nurses who had probably just gotten off shift at the base hospital and they had the instant attention of every man in the club. The fact that they were the only women in the club, besides Hubley's wife, made them beautiful by definition. They were not wearing much perfume, but the little they wore managed to waft across the room and stimulate every over-worked, sex-starved man in the place.

Wright watched with growing interest as two of the WAVES waved and came toward their table. They both looked cute and curvaceous in their uniforms and Wright thought for a moment he might change his mind about the *Mackerel*. Then one of the WAVES removed her hat to let her auburn hair fall to her shoulders. There was something oddly familiar about her and Wright knew that he had seen her before. She held her purse close against her side and a smile appeared on her face as Tee rose from his chair to greet her. The other men followed suit to greet the ladies, but she approached with her arms outstretched to embrace Tee.

"Margie," Tee said. "Don't you look gorgeous, girl. You get prettier every time I see you."

Tee's demeanor had completely changed from the violent drunk he had been only a few moments before, although his speech still slurred a little. He lifted her off the floor and swung her around a few times.

"You're such a liar, Tucker," she said, laughing giddily in his arms.

Wright suddenly remembered how he knew this woman. The uniform had thrown him off, and the fact that she was in Pearl Harbor half way around the world from where he had last seen her. The realization set in like an icicle as he looked up to see that Tee had put her down and her eyes were now coldly fixed on him.

They stared at each other in silence. Her smile had disappeared and her face grew paler with every passing second.

"Margie," O'Connell said, totally oblivious to the tension between them. "This is Ryan Wright. He's the new guy on our boat."

Margie said nothing but moved closer to Wright, never taking her eyes from his. Her eyes said it all, and Wright should have seen the blow coming before Margie slapped him across the face.

"You son of a bitch!" she shouted. "I hate you!"

She would have struck him again if Tee had not stepped in front of her to block it. That was the good news. The bad news was that he seemed more intent on continuing

Margie's onslaught himself as he stood chest to chest with Wright.

"You know this guy, Margie?" he said over his shoulder. "What did he do to you?"

"I didn't do anything to her," Wright said, rubbing his cheek. "I'm a friend of her brother."

"You mean you *were* a friend of my brother. Past tense, Ryan. And you weren't much of a friend at that."

Ryan saw that the other officers were exchanging confused glances. Cazanavette looked at him and raised his eyebrows.

This was just what he needed, Wright thought. What a first impression this must be making on the executive officer of his new ship.

"Margie, I don't think this is the time or the place for this," Wright said, looking past Tee at her.

"Some friend you turned out to be," Margie said quietly as her eyes filled with tears. Then she turned and stalked out of the room, her friend following closely behind her.

"If I find out you've done anything to hurt her, asshole," Tee said as he jabbed a finger in Wright's chest, "I'll kick your fucking ass from here to the emperor's fucking palace."

Tee then hurried off after her, leaving Wright and the others standing around the table.

The four officers regarded their new ensign with puzzled looks. The still-seated Barbara Hubley sipped her drink and tried to avoid eye contact with him. Wright himself was confused. He never thought that Margie could harbor such ill feelings towards him for so long. It had been six months and she still blamed him.

"I'll say this for you, Wright, you've got a way with the ladies," O'Connell said. "What was that all about?"

"It's a long story," Wright said. He did not feel like talking about it. He sat down with the others and O'Connell must have sensed his mood and did not press the issue. Instead, he called for another round of beers from a passing waiter.

O'Connell and the others talked and drank but Wright sat and sipped his beer in silence, his thoughts drifting to Margie Forester, and to her brother. Her brother who was now dead. His friend Troy Forester was dead and Margie still blamed him for it. Troy Forester, his college roommate, his role model, his best friend, his virtual brother, had been dead for almost six months now. He could still see Troy's smiling face when they said goodbye a year ago, when Troy had left for Marine boot camp and he had left for Navy Officer Candidate School. He could cite every feature of Troy's face, as if it had been yesterday. They had argued about which one of them would bring home more medals. Wright had joined the navy first and, not to be outdone by his best friend and chief competitor, Troy had joined the Marines the next day.

When Margie found out that her brother had joined the Marines, she called Wright immediately and demanded that he make Troy change his mind and join the navy instead. She thought her brother would have a better chance of surviving the war in the navy. Wright did not know Margie that well. He had met her only a few times during brief stays at Troy's parents' house. She was a couple years older than he was and she never really paid much attention to their college antics. The few impressions that he did get left him thinking she was a condescending snob. He had assured her that the Marines were just as safe as the navy since much of the war would be fought on the water. Troy of course had felt differently. He had joked that he would see more action than Wright and that all of the real men were in the Marines. He had been right about seeing more action. After boot camp, Troy had shipped out with the First Marine Division and within a matter of months he had landed on Guadalcanal. Wright remembered the last letter he had received from his friend. It described the brutal horrors of jungle warfare and the suicidal Japanese banzai attacks at night. Troy had even noted that he wished he had joined the navy with Wright. That was the last word he'd ever have directly from him.

The next letter arrived during his last week of OCS. It was from Margie. In it she bluntly informed him that Troy had been killed by a sniper in the Guadalcanal jungle. The letter went on to blame him for Troy's death because he had not stopped him from joining the Marines like she had asked. Wright had not thought much of Margie's comments at the time. She was being irrational and he was having a hard-enough time grappling with the fact that his best friend was dead and gone. Wright had felt sure that both he and Troy would survive the war and go into business together and grow old. Now that would never happen, and Margie still blamed him.

What did she know? he thought. She was still the little selfish snob he remembered. The fact that she was friends with Tee said it all.

Wright and the others sat there for a couple hours more listening to the music, smoking and drinking, and Wright got to know more about the *Mackerel* and her crew and her new captain. As the evening came to a close and the others finished their beers and got up to leave, Cazanavette pulled Wright aside.

"I don't know what the story is with you and Tee's girlfriend," he said. "It's none of my business just as long as it doesn't affect your performance. But if anything needs to be resolved you better get it done quickly."

Wright saw in Cazanavette's eyes that he was being very serious. He no longer looked like a church counselor.

"Never mind what I was saying to these guys before.

I think our captain is going to want to go out as soon as possible, so be ready to get underway tomorrow."

Wright nodded as he suddenly realized that the XO was much more aware of things than he had let on. He had told Wright to be ready. Wright only wished that he knew how to get ready.

Chapter 4

THE submarine base theater was used for showing movies every night to the sailors living on the base. They would file in and forget their troubles for a few hours while enjoying a good western or sometimes even a war movie. It gave the men a few moments of feeling close to home when they were all so far from it. The smell of buttered popcorn and cigarette smoke filled the air, just like the theaters they took their girlfriends to back home.

The sub base theater, however, was also used as a briefing room for the submarine crews. Space limitations on board ship precluded a space large enough for the whole crew to meet, and the pier, with its working cranes and myriad of shrilling pneumatic tools, was much too noisy for important crew announcements.

The grumbling crew of the *Mackerel* shuffled into the theater at 0700. They could scarcely believe they had been called back to the base for a simple change of command ceremony. They knew it had to be something more.

Instinctively, several of the wiser ones carried their laundry bags at their sides in the event they should have to go back to sea today. They were the wise old salts. The rest were simply in a state of denial.

Like a lazy snake in worn blue dungarees, the eighty-six-man crew slowly filed into the first few rows of seats on either side of the auditorium. The alert ones grumbled as they made their way to their chairs. The others simply sat down in silence as their bodies detoxified from the alcohol of the night before.

Wright, in his fresh khakis, came in at the tail of the blue snake. He did not know where to go. He had spent the night in a rack on board the boat and his wrinkled uniform showed it. He had at least managed to shave and comb his hair in the Officers' Club lavatory. He saw O'Connell motion to him from the front row where the other officers and chiefs sat. Wright went down to the front and occupied the seat next to O'Connell. He felt like every member of the crew's eyes were on his neglected uniform until he saw that his was one of the better-looking ones in the place. This was, after all, a submarine crew, Wright thought, and uniform regulations must be stretched to make up for their cramped quarters at sea.

"You don't look so bad," O'Connell said with a grin. "Carl had to bang on my door this morning to get me up."

"I feel like shit," Wright said. "That rack was smaller than a crib."

"Just wait until we get to sea, it'll rock you to sleep like a baby every time."

As Wright looked at O'Connell he caught Tee staring at him from several seats down the row. He had a lot of anger in his eyes.

"So, Rudy, what's the deal with Tee and Margie?" he whispered to O'Connell.

"You mean your friend?" O'Connell said sarcastically.

"Yeah, my friend. Are they together or something?"

"I guess so. They're engaged."

"It figures she'd end up with someone like him," Wright said bitterly.

"Do I detect a little jealousy, Ensign?"

"What, over that little snob? Hell no!"

O'Connell laughed out loud. "I think they met when we were in port a few months ago," he said. "Tee got invited to some flag officers' function—you know his dad, the admiral, has connections. Some of the new nurses on the island were there too. I guess she was one of them."

"Do you know her?" Wright asked.

"Not particularly. She hangs out with us whenever we're in port, but I've never really gotten to know her all that well. She seems okay." O'Connell grinned and held his hand to his mouth and spoke under his breath. "Actually, I was thinking about warning her about Tee someday. His true colors, you know, which you were lucky enough to experience last night."

So they were engaged, Wright thought. He wondered if Troy would have approved of someone like Tee for a brother-in-law. Troy always was protective of Margie, more so than Wright thought she deserved. Troy more than likely would have beat the shit out of Tee the first time he met him.

Wright looked down the row again to see Tee still eyeing him. Tee's slightly twisted mouth gave his face a disdainful quality as if he loathed everything about Wright. Wright wondered what Margie had told him last night. Maybe she wanted Tee to enact her vengeance on him. If so, she had picked a perfect instrument. Tee was higher in rank and thus Wright would be subject to his ridicule at sea. And if he meant any violence toward Wright, Tee had a good thirty pounds on him. The ensign decided that he would have to be alert and watch his back at all times.

Lieutenant Frank Cazanavette stood at the front of the theater auditorium and took the report from the slim and scraggly Chief of the Boat—or Cob—Chief Machinists' Mate Freund.

"Three unaccounted for, sir," Freund reported.

"Very well, Cob. Thank you."

Three. Not bad, Cazanavette thought, considering what Freund had to go through to get them here. And some of them even looked like they were sober. As the crew mumbled in their seats, Cazanavette looked at his watch. It was 0714. He looked up in time to see the doors at the back of the theater open, letting in the bright sunlight.

"Attention on deck!" Cazanavette shouted. The crew at once came to their feet, the sober ones standing a little straighter than the others. The room was suddenly silent.

Tremain entered through the sunlit door and walked briskly down the aisle to the front of the auditorium. He glanced at the men briefly, trying to see how they looked without pretending to be bothered by their pathetic appearance. Their mood was obvious. Even though they were all obediently at attention, an air of resentment filled the room. Tremain could sense it. He could even feel it on his skin as he passed them. He had prepared himself for this during the walk over from the boat. He knew that he was going to have to be tough. And he also knew that this was only the beginning. Yet it had to start somewhere.

Tremain approached Cazanavette, who was waiting for him at the front. This was his first look at his new XO. He had already sized up his new XO's capabilities by going through his service record the night before. Cazanavette presented himself just as he had expected him to appear. He stood at a slouched attention. His khaki shirt and trousers looked crumpled and unserviced, as did his loose black necktie. Tremain made a mental note for later. For now, he would keep silent.

"Ship's company reporting as ordered, sir," Cazanavette said. "Three unaccounted for."

"Who are they, XO?" Tremain asked, unemotionally.

"I don't . . ." Cazanavette paused, "I will find out, sir."

"Please do, XO. And let me know who you select as mast investigating officer." Tremain said it loud enough for the crew to hear.

"Aye, sir," Cazanavette said hesitantly. He seemed astonished that Tremain would actually consider sending the missing men to Captain's Mast, the navy's form of trial with no jury.

"Thank you, XO," Tremain said impassively. Then, facing the crew, he removed a folded piece of paper from his pocket and read it aloud: " 'From: Commander Submarines, Pacific Fleet. To: Lieutenant Commander Robert A. Tremain, USN. You are hereby ordered to proceed to Pearl Harbor Submarine Base and report to Commander, Submarine Division Seven for assignment as Commanding Officer, USS *Mackerel* (SS-244). These orders are effective immediately upon receipt. In keeping with the . . . so on and so forth . . . I congratulate you on receiving this command. Good hunting! Signed, Charles A. Lockwood, Rear Admiral, USN.' "

Tremain then folded the paper and placed it in his pocket. "Seats, please."

The crew immediately took their seats and Cazanavette took an empty seat in the front row.

Tremain placed his hands behind his back and began to pace on the stage, letting them all get a good look at him. They were all watching him intently, waiting for those first words from his mouth. The words that would define what kind of CO he would be.

"Good morning, gentlemen," he said finally, with a small unemotional grin. "As you must have guessed by now, I am your new commanding officer. I arrived on board yesterday afternoon. I'm sure you were all quite shocked to hear that you had to come to the base today. Well, that's understandable. You come in off patrol and are told to go on liberty, then, before you know it, that liberty is canceled. It can get kind of confusing. Now, I am going to clear up some of the confusion for you all. Leave and liberty is canceled until further notice from this moment on."

This brought a loud rumble from the crew, which was quickly silenced when Chief Freund stood and shot them all an evil scowl.

Tremain paused, allowing what he had said to sink in. He waited for the mumbling to cease, then continued: "I am going to be straight with you, men. Your last patrol left something to be desired. And looking at *Mackerel*'s records, the patrol before that was also what I would call shabby. Up at division, they told me that this boat is the ship of bad luck. They told me that the crew I was getting was down-and-out. They told me how you had all been through a lot and that how maybe all you needed was a good rest to get you back up to par. Well, you might as well know that I don't believe that. Not for a minute. The word 'luck' is simply another way for incompetents to excuse poor performance.

"Now I know that last patrol was tough. Tough by anyone's standards. Sure you had some setbacks. You had a few things that did not go your way. Hell, you even lost two men. But it's how a ship's crew deals with these setbacks that separates the professionals from the amateurs in combat, and most often the winners from the losers."

Tremain paused for a moment. Every eye was focused on him. He could not tell whether they were staring at him with hatred or curiosity, but at least he had their attention.

"I am glad to see that some of you brought your seabags today. That's good. You'll need them, because we're getting underway this afternoon."

This brought a sudden outburst of grumbles.

Tremain talked over their noise: "Stores and torpedo load will be carried out this morning and we get underway at 1530."

Once again the Cob rose out of his chair to silence the men, and Tremain waited for their rebellious noise to cease.

"I have concluded that this crew has forgotten how to be submariners, so we are going to practice it all the way to our patrol zone. We are going to go back to basic submarining, gentlemen. I do not know where your problems lie and I do not have time to locate them. So we are going to go back and relearn those fundamental skills that make submariners lethal killers of the deep."

"That's bullshit—!" shouted a petty officer in the third row.

Chief Freund rose again to silence the crew, but he did not have to. They all fell silent when they saw the cold hard face that appeared on Tremain as he stared down the petty officer. Within seconds the man's confident dissension was transformed as he slumped in his chair trying to avoid Tremain's locked eyes. The man could see that Tremain's face had no emotion in it. Not anger. Not hate. Just a simple stare that bridged the ether gap between them with an unmistakable message: "You are mine!"

Tremain continued: "Some of you probably feel like you deserve some time off, some time to yourselves to wallow in the misery of that last patrol, and, frankly, I don't care. This is war, gentlemen. You are not here to enjoy the nightlife on Oahu. You are not here to feel sorry for yourselves or to spend your days on the beaches while your brethren are out there across the ocean fighting the enemy. Just take a look across the harbor if you need reminding. You'll see the graves of the two thousand men that went before you. You are all here for one purpose. To destroy Japanese shipping! We are going back out there, and that is exactly what I intend for us to do. Any man that is not here to do that, any man that is not ready to do that, raise his hand."

No one responded. Several were staring at the floor with shameful eyes. A few still had defiance in their faces.

"Now, you thought that last patrol was tough, it's going to get a lot tougher. This boat is going to go in harm's way, gentlemen. I won't promise you anything but plenty of enemy ships to sink. Don't worry, you'll get your share of the fight. That is all. Mr. Cazanavette, torpedo load begins at 0740. Dismiss the crew."

"Aye aye, sir."

Tremaine hopped off the stage as the crew again came to attention, then he walked briskly back up the aisle and out the theater door. Stepping outside the building and into the sunlight, he stopped and took a deep breath. He wondered if the men had believed him. He wondered if he believed himself. Did his words hit home with any of them? It only took a few to get it started. It only took a few to change the command climate. A few well planted seeds could grow and germinate the rest.

He needed to have a talk with Cazanavette. They would have to work in tandem. Cazanavette would need a little work but Tremain was sure that, with a little encouragement, he would measure up to the task before him. The rest of the officers looked as they had in their service record photos, all except the young ensign. Tremain had not been aware that there was an ensign on board. He must have just arrived. Tremain had been scanning the officers' faces as he spoke, looking for their reactions. The most notable had been the ensign's. He had sat at attention the entire time, eyes wide. He had not flinched even once throughout the whole briefing. This ensign must think I'm a pretty tough guy, Tremain thought. I would, if I was in his shoes. The tougher he thinks I am the more he will pay attention, the more he will learn.

Tremain wanted to place a call to Judy to tell her once

again how sorry he was and that he loved her. He checked his watch. There was not enough time. There was never enough time. Maybe he could call her later.

I'll write a letter underway and mail it to her when I get back, he thought. He closed his eyes and banished the thought of his wife from his mind. He could not think of her. He couldn't afford it now. He could not think of her and keep a clear mind. He needed to focus on the task that lay before him. He was in command.

He gave a short sigh, then headed across the jetty to his waiting boat.

Chapter 5

MACKEREL took on new form as her monstrous diesel engines sputtered to life one at a time, and then fell into a rhythmic combustion cycle together. The exhaust manifolds near the waterline spewed first white smoke, then black, then settled into a dirty brownish semi-transparent vapor. The men working the lines near the exhaust manifolds covered their noses and mouths to avoid the nauseous fumes.

"Bridge, maneuvering," the voice box on the bridge squawked—it was George Olander's voice. "Placing a warm-up load on the diesel engines."

Carl Hubley, the officer of the deck, glanced at Tremain on the other side of the bridge before keying the microphone and acknowledging the report.

"Maneuvering, bridge, aye."

Hubley looked as though he expected Tremain to voice some kind of disapproval about something, but Tremain said nothing, so he carried on.

They were all on edge. Captain meets crew. Crew meets captain. But it was a marriage of necessity.

The morning's preparations had gone well for the most part. The six torpedoes had been loaded without event to bring *Mackerel*'s magazine back up to a full status. They had taken on a sixty-day load out of food and supplies, and the diesel fuel oil tanks had been topped off. All had been completed without incident. The only issue of note to Tremain during the morning's events had been the crew's apparent laziness with regard to procedures. Tremain responded by reprimanding each sailor he caught loading fuel or torpedoes without following an approved procedure or even having the procedure present at the work site.

From time to time Tremain had seen this type of behavior on the various boats he had served on. This crew had fallen into a rut that many crews, and even captains, often allow themselves to slip into. Their knowledge base was in people and not in procedures. Tremain needed to change that. He needed to change it before their laxity caused a serious accident or oversight, which might get one or all of them killed.

But that would have to wait. *Mackerel* was getting underway now, and Tremain would need to focus all his attention on that operation. He noticed a signalman standing idly on the cigarette deck, aft of the bridge, with the ship's colors in his hands. The sailor was standing by to hoist the wrinkled flag up the mast the minute the ship got underway.

"Seaman, where is our battle flag?" Tremain asked.

The seaman looked embarrassed at first and then shot a pleading glance at Hubley on the other side of the bridge, but Hubley pretended to be preoccupied.

"We haven't been displaying the battle flag, sir," he finally answered.

"Why not?"

"Well, sir, we don't have anything on it except for a few sampans we sank a couple patrols ago."

"Indeed?"

The sailor added reluctantly, "You see, sir, we came upon these sampans off Saipan a couple patrols ago, it was near the beginning of the patrol. We sank them with our deck gun and then we thought it would be kind of funny to sew three sampan silhouettes on our flag. You know, until we sank some real targets. We didn't think anything of it. Kind of a joke, you know, sir. Well, we were sure we would sink some real ships later on, and then we'd be able to add some warship patches to the flag, too. But then we didn't sink any more, sir, so now we have this flag with nothing on it but sampans. And that's why we don't dare run that thing up. We'd be the laughing stock of the harbor, sir."

"I see."

Tremain turned to Hubley. "Mr. Hubley, from now on when this boat enters or leaves port it flies the battle flag. Is that clear?"

"Aye aye, Captain." Hubley nodded. He also seemed embarrassed for the boat. "Ross, go below and get the battle flag."

Seaman Ross started down the ladder at a trot.

"And leave the sampans on it, Ross," Tremain called after him.

Tremain and Hubley exchanged glances before Hubley went back to his preparations to get the ship underway.

Tremain leaned over the bridge coaming on the starboard side, watching the sailors on deck prepare for departure. Each man had his job and they all seemed to be engaged in what they were doing. Russo had trained them well in this aspect and they did at least appear to be efficient seamen, though they were not yet adept at following procedures.

Tremain watched as the chief of the boat, Chief Freund, strode up and down the deck, barking orders. He was inspecting the quality of stowage, looking for anything on the sleek hull that might come loose when it felt the force of twenty knots of water. When he reached the conning tower, he checked each of the equipment access hatches and pounded on them with a large rubber hammer to make sure they were properly secured for the open sea. He kept one eye on the men handling the large hemp lines. Whenever he saw a sailor doing something wrong or dangerous, he would threaten to use the rubber hammer on him as well.

"Do you want to lose your fingers?" Freund shouted to one of them. "Because you will if you hold that line like that!"

"Don't stand there!" he yelled to another. "Not unless you want to lose your leg at the knee when that line parts!"

Tremain smiled. He knew that he would be able to count on Freund. One look at the wiry Freund and anyone could tell that he had been in "boats" for a long time. He was a grizzled old sea dog from the early days of submarining, from the days when the enemy was the least of the fears. When the number of dives and the number of surfaces did not always match.

Cazanavette emerged from the conning tower hatch. He was followed by two lookouts that shuffled past the officers and continued climbing to their station up in the periscope shears.

Cazanavette nodded to Hubley and then cleared his throat to get Tremain's attention. "All departments are ready to get underway, Captain." He paused before adding, "The unaccounted for men, Mitchell, Stallworth, and Sykes, are now on board, sir."

"Very well, XO," Tremain acknowledged as he continued to watch the activities on deck.

"Sir, do you still wish me to carry out mast proceedings for these men?" Cazanavette added in a low voice.

"Yes, Mr. Cazanavette," Tremain said, turning his attention to the XO, "can you think of any reason I shouldn't?"

Cazanavette glanced over to Hubley, who was again

pretending to be deeply involved with the preparations for sea. "Captain, I do not think it would be a good idea to go through with it, considering the circumstances of the short notice recall. I mean they did get here in time for underway, that's the important thing after all. No need to further complicate their lives, sir. These three are good sailors, and good submariners. This is very unusual for them." Then he added, under his breath, "Besides, the crew might not correctly interpret a mast proceeding at this time. I just think it would be an error in judgment, sir."

"XO, it was an error in judgment to release this crew on liberty in the first place," Tremain said in an equally low tone. "That would not have been my call, had I been in your place."

Tremain could tell that the comment had dug deep. Cazanavette visibly took it to heart. So much so that Tremain almost wished he had not said it.

"But, sir . . . surely nothing can be served now by punishing these men unfairly?"

"Punishment on a navy ship never is fair, XO. You've been around long enough to know that. It's there to serve as an example to the rest of the crew and to set standards. It is a tool for the captain to use at his discretion. By punishing Mitchell, Stallworth, and Sykes I'll show the crew what I expect of them—and what the price of disobedience will be."

"Sir, you can't expect them to know that they are being recalled when they are on the other side of the island." Cazanavette had said it with slight sarcasm, and it struck a small nerve in Tremain.

"I expect them to get their heads in the war, Mr. Cazanavette," he snapped. "I expect them to be mindful of what's going on with this submarine at all times, whether they're standing watch in the control room or sunning on the north shore. I expect them to anticipate going on patrol, and being ready to do so at a moment's notice with seabags packed and ready to go. I expect them to be constantly thinking of ways they can contribute to helping this boat sink enemy ships. In short, I expect them to live, eat, and breathe this boat at all times, XO. This boat needs to be their only reason for existence," he stated flatly, then paused before adding, "and yours too."

Cazanavette started to say something, but was cut off by the bridge voice box.

"Bridge, maneuvering." It was the engineer's voice again. "A full load has been placed on the diesels. The ship is divorced from shore power." The sound of the diesel engines confirmed this as the vibrations surged through the hull. The pitch lowered and steadied as they picked up the ship's electrical loads.

"We'll discuss this later, XO." Tremain did not want to have a scene on the bridge. Cazanavette looked as though he was going to say something, but he held his tongue. He nodded then headed down the hatch to take his station in the conning tower.

Tremain knew he would have to finish the talk with Cazanavette later. He could understand Cazanavette's thinking. He himself might have even voiced the same opinion a few years ago. But he knew what had to be done to make the crew come around quickly. Cazanavette would learn it too someday. Hopefully, he would learn it before he got a command of his own. Had it been peacetime, things would have been different. Perhaps Tremain would have used other methods. But this was war and they simply did not have time for any other way.

"Captain, shore power and phone cables have been removed. Both shafts have been tested ahead and astern," Hubley said. "The ship is ready to get underway."

Seaman Ross had reemerged with the battle flag and was once again standing on the cigarette deck.

"Very well, Mr. Hubley," Tremain said. "Take us out of harbor."

"Aye aye, sir," Hubley answered. He cupped his hands to his face and yelled down to the deck. "Cast off one, three, and four!"

Chief Freund acknowledged the command then ordered the linesmen to cast off their lines. The *Mackerel* was moored starboard side to the pier with the bow pointing toward land and the stern pointing out into the harbor. Within moments several sailors from other boats had removed the lines from the cleats on the pier and then dropped them into the water to be hauled in by *Mackerel*'s sailors on the deck.

"One, three, and four cast off, Officer of the Deck," called the Cob with a wave of one hand.

Tremain observed closely but pretended not to. Casting off all lines except for number two would aid in angling *Mackerel*'s stern out away from the pier. She would have to back out away from the submarine base jetty in order to get into the harbor. It would be a good test of Hubley's skills as a conning officer.

"Helm, bridge," Hubley spoke into the voice box. "Port engine ahead one third, starboard engine back one third."

Tremain envisioned the helmsman, standing at his wheel in the conning tower beneath them as he heard the man repeat the order over the voice box. The helmsman could not see what was going on outside the submarine. He had nothing more than a wheel, an engine order telegraph, and a ship's heading indicator at his station. Landmen would find it strange that the sailor with his hands on the wheel, the man who was physically steering the ship, was essentially driving blind. In the navy it made perfect sense since the helmsman's duty was to steer exactly the course ordered by the officer of the deck and nothing more.

Tremain looked aft to see frothing water churn up near *Mackerel*'s screws, confirming that the maneuvering room had carried out the order. Slowly the stern began to drift away from the pier.

Hubley waited until the ship made a thirty-degree angle with the pier and then ordered, "Helm, bridge, all stop. Cast off two!"

The men manning line number two removed the line from the cleat and let it slip into the water. At the same time the seaman standing next to Hubley activated the ship's whistle by holding down an air valve lever on the port side of the bridge. The deafening prolonged blast sounded more like a horn than a whistle as it signaled to the other ships in harbor that *Mackerel* was now underway. The whistle then followed with three more short blasts to indicate that *Mackerel* was operating astern propulsion.

Instinctively, sailors working on the jetty and the cluttered decks of nearby ships stopped what they were doing and glanced up to see which boat was getting underway. At a nod from Hubley, Seaman Ross pulled on his lanyards and hauled up the flag of the United States over *Mackerel's* sparse battle flag. Several sailors on the pier broke out in laughter at the sight of it. Several of the men on *Mackerel's* deck muttered curses under their breath at the sight of their pathetic flag. Tremain noticed several of them glance up at him with indignation as they stowed the lines.

So they do have some pride, he thought. I hope they never forget that feeling. If a sailor was not proud of his ship then he was not proud of himself. If he was proud of his ship then he would go to hell and back for the sake of his ship's honor. He might curse it ten times a day but he would fight every drunken headscrubber or lollygagger who insulted it to his face. Tremain knew this and he hoped that it would work to his advantage.

Mackerel in all her glory drifted away from the pier stern first. She floated through the residual disturbance that had been created by her churning screws and when line number two was finally clear, Hubley ordered, "Helm, bridge, all back one third."

Mackerel slowly backed away from the pier and into the channel. When she was well clear and there was enough room to maneuver, Hubley ordered, "Helm, bridge, right fifteen degrees rudder."

The submarine pivoted around gently, leaning slightly to the left. The astern propulsion and right rudder combination caused the ship's head to turn to the left. Hubley kept the right rudder on until *Mackerel* was lined up in the center of the channel.

"Helm, bridge. All ahead one third," he said, once the ship was nearly aligned with the channel. "Come left, steer course three five four."

The helm responded and *Mackerel* slowed her backward motion, came to a complete stop, then slowly picked up speed in the ahead direction. Slowly, her bow inched over to steady on the base course that would drive her just to the right of the channel's center.

Tremain watched as the figures on the pier resumed their work and the submarine base's one hundred-foot tower used for escape training slowly fell astern. He took a deep breath and let it out again slowly. He was on patrol once again. Just yesterday, he had been looking forward to seeing his wife. If he had refused to accept this command, he could be waking up with her in his arms at this very moment. Now, instead, he was on patrol again, and his body was fast accepting all of the familiar sensations it had tried so hard to forget. How long had it been since he had left *Seatrout*? Two or three months? It seemed like years. He felt the wind on his face, the poignant exhaust fumes of the diesels, the low putter of his ship's engines vibrate and surge through his body. It gave him an indescribable energy that he could never explain it. He had tried to explain it to Judy many times but for all her good intentions he knew that she did not understand. It had to be felt, it had to be experienced to understand its pull. The call of the sea—one had to hear it personally to really know about it, to really get it.

Drifting by on the left, the two dozen or so cruisers and destroyers at the naval base swayed gently at their moorings as *Mackerel*'s wake rolled out to reach them. Then came the shipyard, with its immense three-story cranes working away like giant ants.

On the right, Ford Island drifted by. *Mackerel* passed the spot where the *Arizona* lay and the boatswain's mate sounded his whistle to bring the men on deck to attention. They faced the battleship's final resting place and in unison saluted the watery grave of their fallen comrades. It was a tradition carried out on every United States Navy vessel as it passed the hallowed spot where so many were lost. It gave every man a strong sense of the job that had to be done—and why it had to be done.

They were doing well so far, Tremain thought, as the *Arizona* fell behind them. Hubley and the crew had shown him that they were at least skilled in seamanship and that was a great comfort. He had something to work with.

Mackerel continued on its journey and wound around the bends in the channel. Hubley expertly conned the ship through the harbor, around to the southerly channel and then out into the open ocean. Hickam Field passed by on the port side, just as *Mackerel* started to feel the first large swells of the Pacific, and through his binoculars Tremain could see several Army Air Corps officers eating brunch on the green lawn in front of the base officers' club. A few of them waved to the submarine as it left the shelter of the land. A few of *Mackerel*'s sailors on deck waved back.

Tremain was generally satisfied with the crew's performance. They had successfully brought the ship out of port and Hubley had done a fair job at the conn. He then ordered Hubley to set the normal watch.

"Secure the sea and anchor detail," Hubley announced on the 1MC circuit, a shipwide announcing circuit that could be heard by all hands. "Set the normal underway watch, section one."

Tremain rested his hands on the bridge coaming and inhaled a full breath of the fresh ocean air. The deck was now cleared of personnel and rigged for surface running. *Mackerel* was making a good fifteen knots through the white-capped waves, fast leaving lush Oahu astern. She was traveling against the direction of the seas and every few minutes a wave would crash against the deck below, sending cold spray over the men on the bridge. Soon Tremain's and Hubley's shirts were soaking wet.

Tremain thought about what was transpiring below as the ship's crew adjusted to being at sea once more. The watch stations were being relieved below. A third of the hands would be coming on watch. Another third would be eating and performing routine maintenance. And the last third would be going to their racks for some attempted sleep. The crew would follow this routine everyday for the next two months.

"Contact!" one of the lookouts up in the periscope sheers called out, above the crashing seas. "Ship, sir. Hull down and fifteen degrees off the port bow!"

Tremain scanned the horizon off the port bow. He spotted the small object on the horizon where the lookout had indicated. He fixed his binoculars on it and saw that it was the pilothouse of a small patrol craft. It was battling the waves several miles away from them and appeared to be headed in their direction.

"That would be the escort, sir. PC-128." Hubley had sighted it too.

"Very well, Mister Hubley," Tremain said. "Close her and signal her to follow us."

"Aye, aye, sir."

Tremain held his binoculars up to look once more at the distant patrol craft. It was standard operating procedure for a submarine leaving on patrol to rendezvous with an escorting patrol craft. As long as the patrol craft was nearby any American aircraft flying overhead would identify *Mackerel* as a friendly submarine and not attack. The patrol craft would stay with them until they were outside the aircraft's search radius or "kill zone." After that, *Mackerel* would be on her own and fair game to all attackers, friendly or enemy.

"I'm going below, Mr. Hubley," Tremain said, starting down the ladder. "Notify me when the patrol craft has taken station."

Tremain passed down the ladder through the conning tower and into the control room. He stopped at the chart table where Cazanavette was hovering with a quartermaster, reviewing the ship's projected track.

"How does it look, XO?" Tremain asked.

"Good, sir," Cazanavette answered impassively. "We have rendezvoused with the escort on schedule and are making a good fourteen and a half knots on two engines."

"Good," Tremain said. He nodded and then headed forward through the watertight door and on to his stateroom. He knew that every eye in the control room had been on him, and that every ear had been listening to his every word. He knew that all conversations would cease in every room he entered for weeks to come. Sailors had a peculiar way of letting a person know he was not welcome. They had a habit of shifting to an almost defiantly businesslike attitude and would not speak unless spoken to.

Tremain smiled as he drew his curtain and sat down at the tiny desk. It was all for the better, he thought. The crew would be united in their defiance of him and that would help them to merge together as a team—or so he hoped.

His body ached. The day had been a long one and he

almost could not believe that *Mackerel* had actually made it to sea. He could smell the dinner being prepared in the galley, two compartments aft. He could also hear the off-watch officers talking in the wardroom, just across the passageway from his stateroom. He could make out bits and pieces of the conversation. From what he could tell, the others were harassing the new ensign about some woman he had run into the night before. The ensign was emphatically denying every accusation they threw at him.

Tremain chuckled to himself. *What was the ensign's name . . . ah yes, Wright. Let's see if I can help you out, Mr. Wright.*

Taking the key from his pocket, Tremain unlocked and opened his safe from which he removed a manila envelope marked "Top Secret." It contained the patrol order. He set the envelope on the desk in front of him and stared at it for a few minutes. *The moment of truth*, he thought. *Where will they be sending us this time?*

He tore the envelope open, removed the papers and began to read them. Even in his exhausted state, he could not help but flip through the new order with a surge of excitement.

It contained nothing unusual. It was just a standard patrol order assigning the *Mackerel* to a zone with light shipping activity. Ireland was giving him a run-of-the-mill patrol to get the ship up to speed. That much was obvious to him.

After a cursory glance Tremain keyed the call box on the bulkhead activating the 1MC throughout the ship. "May I have your attention," he said. He could hear his own voice emanating from the passageway and spaces beyond. "This is the captain. I have just read our patrol order and now I will read it to you." Tremain paused long enough to notice that the noise coming from the wardroom had ceased. "'Item one, sink enemy shipping. Item two, proceed to 150 degrees East, 7 degrees, 20 minutes North and patrol in the designated patrol zone. Item three, conduct coastal reconnaissance whenever possible.' The rest of the order is just the standard verbiage that you've all heard before."

He paused for a second before continuing, choosing his words carefully. "Now, today has been a long day for all of us. I want to congratulate you all for an expert job in getting the ship underway on time. Tonight we have an escort by our side, but tomorrow we will leave our escort behind and from then on we will be all alone against the world. So stay sharp. Lookouts should use a good relief rotation. Any more than two hours of looking through a pair of binoculars and a man's eyes become worthless up there. Remember your basic submarining, gentlemen. You've shown me a fine bit of it today. Let's keep it up. That is all."

Tremain released the call box switch and sat back in his chair. He wondered if he had done the right thing by letting up on them a little. The hardest part was done now. They were at sea. He had pried them away from their moorings and their desire to wallow in drunken misery on dry land. The ship was now at sea and he could train them out here.

Yes, he thought to himself. He had done the right thing. Now he had to see how they worked together at sea. He had to see how they handled the day-to-day routine of a war patrol. That would be the test.

A knock came at the bulkhead and Petty Officer Mills poked his head through the curtain.

"Can I get you anything, Captain?"

Mills was right on cue, Tremain thought.

"Ask the steward to bring me a cup of coffee, will you, Mills." Tremain considered for a moment. "Oh, and Mills . . ."

"Yes, sir?"

"Ask the XO and Chief Freund and the torpedo chief to meet me in the wardroom at 2100, please."

"Aye, aye, sir," Mills said and then disappeared again behind the drawn curtain.

Tremain considered what he was about to do. No matter how good this crew was at submarining, nothing could help them if their torpedoes did not hit the targets. Tremain was going to get to the bottom of the *Mackerel*'s torpedo problems, once and for all.

Chapter 6

CHIEF Torpedoman Ike Konhausen did not know what to make of the new captain. He had seen many captains come and go during his fifteen years in the navy. Most of them he had been able to size up after the first meeting, but this captain was different. He was harsh one minute and complimentary the next. Stoic and cold, and then suddenly warm and personable. He was indeed a hard one to figure out.

As Konhausen walked down the passageway to the wardroom, he pondered why the captain had summoned him. The burly chief had been busted many times in the past. He did not have a spotless record by any sense of the word. In fact, he knew that he was lucky to be wearing the anchors of a chief petty officer. His mouth had always gotten him into trouble in the past. He had a knack for speaking his mind to senior officers, and most of them did not like to hear what was on Konhausen's mind.

Ever since he got promoted to chief petty officer back in '42, Konhausen recognized that his habit of speaking out at every opportunity would hurt his chances for further promotion, and now he made every effort to hold his tongue. He had been on good behavior—an entire year without any disciplinary action against him. It seemed almost like a miracle. The salty chief took it as a sign of getting older, or becoming more responsible, or both. Three months ago he became the Chief Torpedoman of the *Mackerel,* and he was determined not to ruin this new opportunity. But after hearing the captain's speech this morning, he could not help but simmer. He could not muster up enough self-control to contain his anger, and his ugly temper had flared again.

Earlier that morning as Konhausen led his division through the unexpected torpedo load, he had cursed the captain's name many times under his breath, sometimes audibly. The stress made him do it even though he knew better. The unreasonable expectations of the new captain made him do it. Now he was sure that somehow the captain had overheard him. Or maybe another officer had overheard his tirade and reported it to the captain. Or maybe it had been the Cob. Maybe even one of the sailors in his division had turned him in. Every scenario ran through the chief's mind as he approached the officer passage. This was it, he thought. This time he would lose his anchor, his billet, and maybe even his career.

Reluctantly, Konhausen knocked on the wardroom bulkhead then pushed the curtain aside to enter. He found Tremain, Cazanavette and Chief Freund all sitting around the small table.

"Chief Konhausen reporting, sir."

"Chief, come in," Tremain said cordially and motioned to a chair. "Have a seat."

Konhausen seated himself at the table, waiting for the worst. He felt their eyes locked on him like vultures.

"Chief," Tremain said. "I've called you here to talk about our torpedo problems."

Konhausen visibly breathed a sigh of relief. He couldn't believe it. This was a professional meeting and not a disciplinary one. His anchors were spared once again.

"Now, Chief," Tremain said, "we both know that Captain Russo wasn't a bad shot. He was an experienced skipper who knew submarines and knew how to fight with them. I checked out the squadron records from *Mackerel*'s last run on the torpedo range just a few months ago. Among other things, I noticed that *Mackerel* scored a ninety-eight percent overall in torpedo firings. I find that very impressive."

Konhausen nodded.

"That's a good score, Chief. With that kind of shooting on the exercise range, Sammy Russo should have been sinking ships right and left on patrol. Agreed?"

"Yessir."

"So, it had to be something else." Tremain fingered the notebook in front of him. "The ship's logs indicate that the last eight torpedoes fired from this ship failed to hit their mark for one reason or another. Right?"

"They were all Mark 14s. They're supposed to be good fish, so they should've hit." Konhausen felt like Tremain was about to turn the tables on him, and he suddenly feared the loss of his anchors again. He decided he would not volunteer any more information unless Tremain specifically asked for it.

Tremain paused for a moment. "If you have any theories, Chief, I'm ready to entertain them."

Konhausen hesitated for a moment. He certainly did have a theory. But he had to keep himself in check. He didn't want to risk ruining his career by speaking too quickly, the way he used to. He needed to be careful.

Tremain eyed him suspiciously, setting the logbook down on the table and leaning back in his chair.

"Look, Chief," he said. "I'm not going to fry you. I want

to get to the bottom of this. Anything you say will not leave this room. Understood?"

"Yes . . . sir," Konhausen replied. He still was not sure he trusted Tremain.

"Well?" Tremain said.

"Well what, sir?"

"You have any theories or don't you?" Tremain snapped.

Konhausen could see that the captain was losing his patience and it suddenly occurred to him that this time he might be putting his career in jeopardy by being tight-lipped.

"I have theories, sir," he said finally. "But, I've been told that's not my department, sir."

"By who?"

Konhausen shot an accusatory glance across the table at Cazanavette.

Cazanavette appeared flustered for a brief second, then spoke up. "Chief Konhausen approached Captain Russo and me during the last patrol, Captain, suggesting that we modify the Mark 6 magnetic detonator on our Mark 14 torpedoes. He believes that the exploder and arming mechanisms are suspect."

"And what became of your investigation into the matter?"

"Investigation?"

"Surely you looked into that possibility if you were failing to sink ships."

"No, sir," Cazanavette said. "We didn't."

Tremain's expression indicated that he was not satisfied. It was obvious that he wanted more of an explanation than that.

"Sir, Bureau of Ordnance regulations specifically prohibit unapproved modifications to any weapon by ship's force personnel," Cazanavette said quickly. "The modifications suggested by Chief Konhausen were exactly that, unapproved. Captain Russo and I felt that—"

"Chief," Tremain interrupted Cazanavette and turned to

face Konhausen. "Why d'you believe the detonator is causing the problems?"

The interruption visibly irritated Cazanavette, and
Tremain's tone made it clear that he did not want to hear
any more quotes from the BuOrd regulations.

"Well, sir," Konhausen answered a little reluctantly, "I
started thinking about what exactly happened on those
eight shots that didn't hit. Four exploded before they made
it even halfway to their targets. First, I thought it had to
be wave slap. I thought maybe our fish were running too
shallow and the surface waves were setting them off. So, I
checked the depth settings we were using and bounced that
against the sea state on those days. But, all the fish were set
to run deep enough to make it all the way to their targets.
So I ruled out wave slap as the problem."

"What about the other four?" Tremain asked.

"Well, sir, one of those never left the tube. We know that
one was due to a mechanical failure in the tube itself. As for
the other three, we assumed that they ran under the targets
because we never saw or heard any detonations. But, even if
the depth setting on those fish had been wrong, the magnetic
detonator should have gone off when they ran under the enemy ships. And that leads me to think that there must be a
problem with the detonator. Sometimes it goes off prematurely and sometimes it does not go off at all."

Tremain considered for a moment, exchanging glances
with Cazanavette and Freund. Cazanavette was fidgeting in
his chair, obviously not happy with Konhausen's assertion.

"All right, Chief," Tremain said. "Suppose I buy it. What
do you propose?"

Konhausen looked once more at Cazanavette before
continuing. He had already thought all of this out, but he
could hardly believe the captain was asking his opinion on
the matter. "Sir, I think it's the magnetic component. I want
to disable the magnetic component on the detonators in our

torpedoes. Just on the ones in tubes one through four. I want to make them strictly contact torpedoes. If we shoot them and they screw up like all the others, then we really haven't lost much. But if they run hot, straight, and normal, and we get hits, then we may have solved our problems."

"That won't solve our problems, Chief," Cazanavette blurted out. "It will only give us more problems."

Tremain silenced him with a glance.

"Very well, Chief," Tremain said, folding his hands in front of his face. "Draw up your work order and bring it to me for approval."

Konhausen's face broke into a big grin only equaled by the one on Freund's face. Cazanavette sat red-faced and silent.

"Aye, sir. I already have it prepared from the last time I wanted to do this. If you'll excuse me, sir, I'll go and get it."

Tremain nodded. "Let's cut the torpedo officer in on this too, Chief. Pass the work order through him first. How long'll it take you to do the work?"

"With the back hauling of each weapon, it should take roughly ten hours, Captain."

"Very well. Thank you, gentlemen."

Freund and Konhausen both rose to leave, but Cazanavette stayed. Tremain knew that he would. Cazanavette ushered both of the chiefs out of the wardroom and then abruptly closed the curtain behind them. "Captain, I must protest this. Bureau of Ordnance regulations are not negotiable. They exist for a reason. They're there for our safety. Chief Konhausen did not design the Mark 14 torpedo nor did he design the Mark 6 detonator, and he's certainly not qualified to open one up and work on it at sea. It simply is not authorized, sir!"

"What about sinking ships, XO. Is that authorized?" Tremain paused and Cazanavette started to respond but the captain stopped him with a raise of his hand. "Look,

I know what BuOrd regs say. But the simple fact remains that this ship's torpedoes are not hitting the targets while other boats' fish *are*. For some reason our torpedoes don't work. Now, either we have the great misfortune to get all of the bad torpedoes in the lot, or the other boats are getting the same bad fish we do and they are finding ways around it."

"So you're saying the other boats are getting hits because they tamper with their weapons, sir?"

"Very likely. I'll admit to you, XO, Chief Konhausen is not the first one to come up with the faulty detonator theory."

Cazanavette eyed him skeptically. "You mean to say this is how you conducted business on the *Seatrout,* sir? Breaking regulations to test theories floating around the fleet?"

Cazanavette's scornful tone struck deep. Just the name of his beloved lost ship sent an uncontrollable surge of grief through Tremain. He had to fight back the urge to let loose on the inexperienced Cazanavette. He could not let him know how close to the mark he had hit.

Tremain had to wait until he had internally collected himself before he responded. "No, XO. But I have shot my share of torpedoes that mysteriously went awry. Perfectly lined up shots would miss clean. I discussed it with several other boat captains in Darwin, and found that they were having problems too. We all agreed that there had to be something wrong with the torpedoes themselves. Chief Konhausen has a good theory, and I believe it's a sound one."

"Fine, sir, I agree. Let's write down his whole theory with all the modifications as he suggests, then we can submit it through the proper channels when we return. But, for crying out loud, let's not do anything to our weapons without proper approval while we're at sea and without the expertise of the shipyard technicians."

Tremain shook his head. "I don't have time for all that,

XO. It'll take months for that paperwork to get processed through BuOrd—and you know it. This crew needs a good patrol, and they need it now. I can't afford to risk their lives taking them inside an enemy convoy, only to have our weapons malfunction. I'm using commanding officer's prerogative here."

"With all due respect, sir, commanding officer's prerogative will not save us at a general court martial. What you've ordered Konhausen to do is illegal, in my opinion, and I intend to place my objection in the deck log." He paused, then added, "And I intend to report this to ComSubPac when we return."

Tremain nodded. He thought about how he would have responded if he were in Cazanavette's shoes. Several years ago, he would have said the same thing. Back when he was too focused to see the big picture. Back when his career meant more to him than anything else.

"Fair enough, XO. I respect you for voicing your opinion. But consider this. Item number one in our patrol order tells us to 'sink enemy shipping.' It's a general order. Why is it general? Because ComSubPac knows that he can't be out here on patrol, telling us how to do our jobs. He can't place contingencies for every situation in our patrol order. He would be wrong to do that. He simply gives us tools and expects us to bring back results. Our tools are eighty-five men, a *Balao* class submarine, ninety thousand gallons of fuel, a five-inch gun, and twenty-four torpedoes. ComSubPac expects us to use our own judgment. My judgment says that we can't accomplish the mission unless we modify those detonators." He paused. "Now, make whatever entries you like in the log, but we are going through with the modifications. Is that clear?"

"Aye, aye, sir." Cazanavette's response was reluctant and overly professional. His expression showed that his opinion had not changed. "Will that be all, sir?"

"Yes, XO." Tremain smiled politely.

Cazanavette rose and left the wardroom.

Sipping his coffee, Tremain considered the path he had chosen. He was sure that the detonators were the problem. Either way, there would be no covering up his decision. As soon as Cazanavette made his report to ComSubPac his career would be over, whether this turned out to be a good patrol or not. But at least he would have this one last patrol to pay back the bastards that killed his ship and crew. He would make them pay come hell or high water or BuOrd regulations.

And, besides, a general court martial would also mean that he would be with Judy sooner—and the sooner the better. She would be able to cure him of the burning hatred he felt inside. Her soft voice would cleanse him of the intolerable madness he felt coming over him of late during the nights, when all his thoughts were of the *Seatrout,* and of visions of the faces of her dead crew, and of revenge.

"YOU'RE doing it wrong, Mr. Wright," the petty officer electrician said as he yanked the tool from Wright's hands. They were both lying on their sides in a crawl space not quite three feet high. The wooden grating upon which they crawled covered the ship's massive forward battery. The battery itself was the size of a two-car garage. It and its twin in the aft compartment could provide *Mackerel* with enough power to run submerged for nearly one hundred miles at five knots, or enough power to blow the submarine a hundred feet in the air, according to the electrician. The batteries were the oxygenless power source that made *Mackerel* a true submarine. They were also one of her greatest weaknesses because they did not last long and it took several hours on the surface for the diesel engines to recharge them. Several hours during which *Mackerel* was exposed and vulnerable.

Wright was being instructed in the fine art of lining up for one such battery charge. O'Connell had informed him earlier that since he was the junior officer on board, it would be his task to check the battery charging line up. O'Connell had suggested that he should get some practice so that he could do it quickly when they reached hostile waters. Wright had just climbed into his rack for a few hours of desperately needed sleep when the lieutenant knocked on the bulkhead outside and informed him that it was time to do the line up.

Now Wright tried to keep his eyes open as the scrawny petty officer showed him how to check the electrolyte level in each of the battery cells. He felt slightly sick, and the irregular rocking of the ship did little to help, especially in the confined space of the battery well.

What time was it? Wright wondered. He could not tell. He just knew that it was late and that he had never felt so tired in his whole life, and this was still the first night of the patrol.

It had been a long day for him.

During the weapons load that morning, he had learned how to load a torpedo into the torpedo room using the weapon-shipping hatch. During the fuel load, he had learned the intricacies involved with the transfer and storage of diesel fuel. During the stores load he had discovered most of the nooks and crannies on the cramped submarine used to stuff the thousands of tin cans and boxes of dry goods that would be consumed over the course of two months.

When the ship got underway, O'Connell had placed him on the main deck in charge of a section of linehandlers. Actually, he had gotten in the way more than he had assisted, but the seamen seemed to understand the incompetence of the young new ensign and they had worked around it. No sooner had he come down from the deck than O'Connell had whisked him away to the control room and shoved

him in front of the chart table to plot periscope bearings
for Cazanavette as the ship navigated away from Oahu.
Cazanavette had swung around on the periscope, marking
bearings to different landmarks in the blink of an eye, while
Wright scrambled to write them down and plot them as fast
as he could. Whenever he fell behind, the XO harshly repri-
manded him, prompting the enlisted quartermaster at his
side to step in and help him to catch up. He had begun to
sweat profusely when the realization overcame him that
the safety of the ship depended on the accuracy of his plotting. If he was off even a tenth of a degree the XO might
make the wrong course recommendations to the officer of
the deck and run the ship aground on any one of the many
sandbars in the channel. It was all stuff he had learned at
submarine school. But now, it was real. When the ship had
opened the distance to land considerably, the piloting party
was finally secured. Only then had Wright noticed that his
shirt was soaking wet from perspiration. He felt physically
and mentally drained. The XO suddenly became informal
again and complimented him on his plotting

As if he had not suffered enough for one day, dinner
came as no relief. The whole meal, the other officers chided
him about his interlude with Margie the night before, and
they did not let up. He knew it was all in good humor—all
except for the harassment from Tee, who made it clear that
he wanted Wright to stay away from Margie when they got
back to port. Wright assured him that he wanted nothing
more than to stay away from her, but he could tell that Tee
would probably bring the issue up again many more times
in the next two months. Then O'Connell had tried to
change the subject and mentioned something about how he
should get started learning how to rig the ship for dive.
Next thing he knew, he was following a petty officer around,
checking dozens of valves in each compartment, making
sure they were in the proper position for safely submerging

the ship. After two hours of checking valves shut and open, he had secretly retired to the small stateroom he would be sharing with O'Connell and George Olander. He just wanted to get a few hours sleep, just a few. But that had been wishful thinking. His eyes were shut for no more than a minute when O'Connell walked in and told him he should watch the electrician do the line up for the evening's battery charge. Reluctantly, Wright had obeyed.

Wright knew he was getting the "firehose" method of teaching. It was the navy way. The other officers wanted him to be a contributing member of the wardroom as soon as possible, and deep down so did he. He only hoped that he could retain all that he was learning and that he would not let them all down.

"We're all done here, sir," the electrician said, rousing the drowsy Wright. "Electrolyte levels are good. Cell voltages are good. Specific gravity is good, too."

Wright nodded. He would believe anything the electrician told him at this point.

They both crawled up through the access hatch, which opened into the officers' quarters' passage. Wright then followed the electrician aft through a hatch into the darkened control room, then through another hatch into the galley and crews' mess, then through another hatch into the crews' quarters, then into the forward engine room with its two noisy diesels banging away. Another hatch led into the aft engine room with two more diesels. Finally they reached the manuevering room. Here they found three sailors standing watch at the panels that controlled the ship's diesel generator loading and the ship's electrical distribution system. George Olander, the gray-haired southern engineer, leaned against the bulkhead behind them with his arms crossed, his eyes conducting a cursory review of the gauges on the multiple control panels in the room. He nodded to Wright briefly, then continued scanning the panel readings.

The electrician checked off the last blocks on his check-list and went to confer with the electrical control panel operator. As the two sailors discussed how they would conduct the battery charge, Wright struggled to find the energy to pay attention. It was hard to hear what they were saying over the loud diesels. He felt as though his brain had been drained enough for one day.

Olander noticed that he was having trouble staying awake and reached over to jostle him.

"Oh, sorry," Wright said, feigning alertness.

The engineer shrugged and yelled above the engines, "It happens, Wright." Looking him up and down, he added, "Why don't you go to the rack? You look like you've had enough for one day. You don't need to be back here around all this machinery dead on your feet. Just about everything back here can kill you or seriously mangle you in one way or another. Go get some rest."

Wright nodded. He didn't say anything. He was too tired to find the words. He just headed forward, thankful for the kindness of the emotionless engineer. He made his way back to the forward compartments and headed directly for his stateroom. As he was passing through the darkened control room, one of the sailors on watch stopped him.

"Mr. Wright? That you, sir?"

The room was rigged red for night so it was difficult to distinguish faces.

"Yes."

"Mr. O'Connell wants you to come up to the bridge, sir."

"What?" Wright could not believe it. What was O'Connell doing to him? He was now convinced that O'Connell was either trying to kill him or deliberately prevent him from getting any sleep whatsoever.

"Mr. O'Connell wants you to come up to the bridge. You're his JOOD."

Wright looked at his watch and sighed. It would have

been nice if O'Connell had let him know he was going to have to stand watch tonight. Maybe he could have gotten some sleep somewhere between the stores and weapons load, the line handling, the piloting, the rig for dive, or the battery charging line up.

Somebody handed him a pair of binoculars as he headed up the ladder to the bridge. Emerging from the bridge hatch and into the cool ocean air, he waited a moment for his eyes to adjust to the darkness. The red light was supposed to reduce the adjustment time, but he hadn't been in the control room long enough for his eyes to get conditioned.

He felt a wisp of cool spray touch the back of his neck. It somewhat revived him, as did the fresh air. Then it suddenly occurred to him that he had not been outside the hull since he had come down from the line handling that afternoon.

"Ryan!" O'Connell's voice came out of the darkness. "Good to see you. How'd the battery charge line up go?"

Wright's eyes adjusted and he could make out O'Connell's form leaning against the bridge coaming, his grinning teeth glimmering in the moonlight.

He must think this is really funny, Wright thought.

"Lieutenant Olander told me to head to the rack. Said it was dangerous for me to be this tired. Frankly, I agree with him."

Wright immediately wished he had not said it. He did not want to look like he was some kind of whiner. He glanced up at the lookouts in the periscope shears, fearing that they too might have heard him. He didn't want them to think he was not willing to do his fair share. He didn't want them to start passing around the crew's mess that Ensign Wright was a slug.

O'Connell's grin did not disappear. If he had heard Wright's comment, he gave no indication of it.

"Come here," he said. "I want to show you something."

Wright walked over to the bridge coaming.

"Look out there." He was pointing away from the ship.

Wright looked out at the sea. It was a crystal clear night with a cool moist breeze in the air. An occasional cloud dotted the star-filled sky. The ocean was calm and the moonlit water stretched unimpeded all the way to the horizon. *Mackerel*'s white wake glowed fluorescent green with the microorganisms it stirred up, leaving a phosphorescent trail to mark the submarine's path. The only sounds to be heard were the purring of the diesels and the crashing of *Mackerel*'s knife-like bow as it cut a path through the ocean waves. It was all beautiful. In fact, it was the most beautiful and breathtaking thing Wright had ever seen. He had imagined how it would be, but to see it and feel it was something different altogether. It felt like their little ship was all alone in the world, traveling through an infinite space to a destination unknown.

Wright suddenly felt very small and he forgot about his fatigue. He forgot about the war. He forgot about everything.

" 'If I take the wings of the morning, and dwell in the uttermost parts of the sea, even there shall thy hand lead me, and thy right hand shall hold me,' " O'Connell quoted, quietly. "I always think of that psalm on the first night out. It's kind of fitting, don't you think?"

Wright nodded, still overcome by the view.

"Why don't you go below and get some sleep, Ryan." O'Connell smiled at him. "You did good today. Don't worry, you're going to fit in just fine. You've been assigned to my watch section as junior officer of the deck. I can take care of it tonight, but be ready to stand watch with me tomorrow." He pointed to the darkened shape following astern of the *Mackerel*. "Tomorrow, we lose our escort and then we're officially on war patrol. Okay?"

It was the first time O'Connell had spoken to him without the joker tone in his voice.

"Thanks, Rudy." Wright smiled back at him then headed down the ladder and straight to his stateroom. He didn't even remove his uniform. He simply collapsed on his bunk and fell sound asleep.

Chapter 7

"**CAPTAIN** to the bridge! Captain to the bridge!"

The 1MC speaker blaring near his head stirred Tremain out of a REM sleep. He had just been enjoying a dream in which he and Judy sat chatting in a coffee house in some cold New England town like they had done so many times before. He could not remember what she was telling him in the dream, but the absurdity of her last statement, "Captain to the bridge," woke him.

It was the first time he had been called to the bridge using 1MC since *Mackerel* arrived in the Caroline Islands a week ago. He glanced at the clock on the bulkhead. It was nearing noontime in this part of the Pacific Ocean. Rolling out of his rack, he sat for a second and slurped down a lingering half cup of cold coffee that was sitting on the desk. Pulling on his shirt, he wiped the sleep from his eyes and headed to the conning tower where he met Cazanavette peering over the radar operator's shoulder.

Earlier that morning they had sighted a convoy of two

ships. Tracking the ships from a distance on the SJ radar, they had obtained a fairly good solution on the potential targets. Then, just as they had been preparing to go to battle stations, the convoy had changed course and left *Mackerel* in a disadvantageous approach position. After a short discussion with Cazanavette, Tremain had opted for an end around run in which the submarine would sprint ahead and out of sight of the unsuspecting convoy to lay in ambush somewhere further along its path.

It was normal for the XO to come to the conn whenever the captain was called for, but Tremain sensed something other than duty in Cazanavette's eagerness. It was as if Cazanavette did not fully trust in him, even now. The episode with the torpedo detonators certainly did not help that any. In the three weeks since Chief Konhausen had made the modifications, Cazanavette had voiced his disapproval more than once. He had treated Tremain with a kind of sadistic professionalism.

"Looks like we've regained that convoy, sir," Cazanavette said. "It bears two eight zero. Range is eleven thousand yards."

Tremain checked the compass on the bulkhead. *Mackerel* was heading north. When they had last sighted the convoy it had been heading east, straight for Piannu Pass in the Truk Atoll, still over a hundred miles away. If the convoy maintained its present course, they would soon intercept it, long before it reached Truk where the Japanese had their mighty Central Pacific fortress on Tol Island.

Checking the chart and the radar screen once more, Tremain headed up the hatch to the bridge. There, Carl Hubley and Tee, along with the lookouts, held binoculars to their eyes as they scanned the western horizon for any sign of the convoy.

The sky was hazy, just enough to keep the sun from glinting off the water. The sea rolled in gentle swells, yielding an adequate surface disturbance to hide a periscope well. Tremain guessed that visibility could be no more than ten thousand yards. Conditions were ideal for a submerged attack.

"Ship off the port beam!" The call came from one of the lookouts in the periscope shears.

Tremain looked through his binoculars. Far off to the west, a ship emerged from the haze.

"Get me a bearing, Mr. Hubley, and pass it along to the conning tower."

Hubley swung the target bearing transmitter around and pointed it toward the ship. He clicked a side button to transmit the bearing to the tracking party in the conning tower.

"Two eight five," Hubley read off the bearing.

Tremain could hear the SJ radar mast squeaking in its well behind him, as it rotated to point down the same bearing. A few seconds later, the radar operator's voice squawked on the call box, "Bridge, radar. SJ contact, bearing two eight eight. Range nine thousand five hundred yards."

"Bridge, conning tower," it was Cazanavette's voice this time. "The contact is just visible, now. Two-masted freighter."

Cazanavette had been watching the ship through the periscope. His height of eye would allow him to see farther over the horizon than anyone standing on the bridge. A few feet of height meant miles of visibility on the ocean.

"Bridge, conning tower." It was Cazanavette's voice again. "The second ship in the convoy bears two eight zero by radar, just to the left of the first ship, range ten thousand yards. This one has a smaller return. Possible escort."

Tremain winced invisibly. He had expected the convoy to have an escort, but the reality of it touched a post-traumatic nerve inside him.

"Battle stations torpedo, officer of the deck," he said to Hubley.

. Hubley immediately keyed the 1MC. "General quarters! General quarters! All hands, man battle stations torpedo!"

The general alarm, a monotone successive fourteen bell gong, bellowed throughout the ship as the crew scrambled to their stations. As was customary during battle stations, Tremain took the conn from Hubley, and Hubley dropped down inside the conning tower to man the torpedo data computer. Tee took charge of the TBT and continued passing bearings on the convoy down to the tracking party. The bearings would be entered into the torpedo data computer, along with the range data from the radar, to refine a firing solution that could be passed on to the torpedoes sitting in the tubes.

Tremain allowed just enough time for the men to reach their stations before keying the 1MC. "This is the captain. Lady Luck has shined her face on us today, gentlemen. We have a large freighter with an escort steaming nine thousand yards off our beam. Remember your training. We're going in!"

Tremain noticed several of the men on the bridge grin at each other. This was the moment of truth they had been waiting for for three agonizing weeks. The trip to the Caroline Islands had been uneventful as far as the enemy was concerned, but not as far as *Mackerel*'s crew was concerned. Tremain had made them conduct drills during the entire voyage. They had averaged six drills per day, which was twice the number normally prescribed by their former captain. Tremain made them drill from one longitude to another. He made them drill as they crossed the international dateline. He made them drill at all times of the day. With every drill he harped on good practices of basic submarining and banged it into their heads the only way he knew how. Days had turned to weeks, and as the patrol dragged on without sighting any enemy vessels, the crew's morale began to sag even further. Cazanavette had been growing less cooperative with each passing day, and Tremain was sure that his executive officer was starting to doubt his abilities to find and engage the enemy.

Tremain knew that what they all needed was a target. They needed something to prove that all of their efforts and all of his theories were not a waste of time. Tremain had resolved that he had to find a target no matter how small and sink it for the sake of his crew's morale. All he needed was a contact. Unfortunately, *Mackerel*'s sector of the Carolines had been starkly quiet. The sector was so quiet, in fact, Tremin had considered breaking radio silence to ask ComSubPac if there was still a war on. But instead he had chosen to exercise discretion and this morning it had been rewarded. The small convoy that they now tracked had appeared.

"Bridge, conning tower." It was Carl Hubley's voice this time, the TDC operator. "We have a good solution on the freighter now, sir, and we're in a good position to intercept its track."

"Conning tower, bridge, aye. Stand by to dive," Tremain replied as he lifted his binoculars to look at the freighter once more. The target's structure was clearly visible now. He could even see its bow plowing up white water. He did not yet see the escort, but it was out there somewhere.

It must have slipped behind the freighter, Tremain thought. It was time. Any closer and *Mackerel*'s low silhouette would not be able to hide her any longer. She would be sighted by the freighter's lookouts.

"Clear the bridge!" he shouted.

Anticipating the order, the lookouts slid down from their perches and dropped down the hatch. Within seconds, the last lookout was below, and Tremain keyed the 1MC.

"Dive! Dive!"

Tremain depressed the diving klaxon with his thumb.

"AAOOOGAAAHH! . . . AAOOOGAAAHH!" It blared in all compartments, and he repeated the order.

"Dive! Dive!"

Tee headed down and was practically knocked off the ladder as Tremain came down behind him, shutting and dogging the hatch with one hand. Then all became abruptly silent as the diesels shut down and propulsion shifted to battery power. The only sound was a faint hissing as the last of the air escaped from the main ballast tanks. The deck lurched backward slightly as the bow planes dug into the water at nearly fifteen knots and *Mackerel* started her rapid descent beneath the surface.

Steadying himself on the ladder rungs, Tremain yelled down the hatch to the control room, "Take her down to sixty-five feet!"

"Sixty-five feet, aye sir," came the reply from Olander, now standing at his battle station as the diving officer. He stood behind the two planesmen in the control room and directed them as they pulled and turned on their controls to reach the ordered depth.

Tremain watched the depth and speed gauges in the conning tower as *Mackerel* slowed and leveled off at her new depth.

"At sixty-five feet, Captain," Olander called back up the control room hatch.

"Very well, Dive," Tremain replied. "Helm, all ahead one third."

Tremain knew they were well ahead of the freighter now. If the freighter held course and speed it would pass directly in front of them, lining up perfectly for the coveted beam shot desired by all submarine captains. He only hoped that *Mackerel* was still undetected. The next periscope observation would tell.

Tremain noticed Cazanavette hovering over a ship identification book laid out on the small chart desk.

"Did you get a good look at her, XO?"

Cazanavette nodded without taking his eyes from the book, then slapped his finger on the opened page.

"That's it," he said. "The *Mirishima Maru*. Fifty-three hundred tons."

Tremain looked at the black silhouette on the page. The two masts, the short smoke stack, the raised superstructure. It was almost certainly the same ship he had seen plowing the seas above them. The book gave several dimensions on the freighter. Tremain noted the mast height and pointed it out to Petty Officer Smithers, the periscope assistant, who quickly wrote it on the back of his hand. Smithers would need the mast height to read ranges off the stadimeter mounted on the back of the periscope.

Tremain looked at the clock. It had taken several minutes to submerge and to stabilize. The freighter would have closed the distance considerably in that time.

"What's the generated range and bearing to target now?" he asked.

"Four thousand five hundred yards, bearing three zero zero," Hubley said, reading the information off the TDC.

Tremain closed his eyes to get a mental image of what he should see through the periscope.

"Up scope," he ordered.

Smithers raised the number one periscope and Tremain met it at the floor, slapping down the handles as it rose out of the well. As the ocean spray cleared off the lens, Tremain conducted a quick sweep of the horizon. Satisfied that there were no other contacts, he focused the scope down the expected target bearing. Between wave slaps he saw the freighter's starboard bow move slowly across the field of view. It was harder to see it now over the waves because, at *Mackerel*'s current depth, the scope lens just barely poked above the surface of the water. Most of the hull was beyond Tremain's visible horizon. He turned the handle to increase the magnification and lined up the reticle on the freighter's smokestack.

"Bearing . . . mark," he called.

"Three zero five." Smithers read the bearing from the compass on the scope well.

It was only five degrees off from the bearing Hubley had taken from the torpedo data computer, so the solution had to be very close to the freighter's actual course and speed.

"Range . . . mark."

"Four thousand yards." Smithers read the range from the stadimeter scale.

Hubley entered the data into the TDC and within seconds came back with a reply. "Observation checks with the solution in the TDC, Captain."

Tremain smiled. The freighter had not changed course or speed. It meant that *Mackerel* had not been sighted. As he rotated the scope to the left, he caught a glimpse of a smaller ship coming up rapidly on the freighter's starboard quarter. Tremain did not need the identification book to recognize it, for he had seen its type many times before. It was a destroyer escort of the *Matsu* class, plodding the water at nearly twenty-five knots. He could easily make out its ominous five-inch gun turret directly forward of the squatty bridge structure. He could not see it, but he knew that the escort carried a similar gun on its stern.

"*Matsu* escort," he said for the benefit of the men in the conning tower. "It should pass by before we get to our firing position. Down scope."

Tremain slapped up the handles as Smithers lowered the periscope.

As *Mackerel* moved along at three knots to close the range to the freighter's track, Termain weighed his options. He could try to sink the *Matsu* first. Then, with the escort gone, he could destroy the freighter at his leisure. However, a Japanese *Matsu* class destroyer escort was fast and maneuverable. It was fast and maneuverable enough to avoid a Mark 14 torpedo if it saw it coming in time. If he fired at the destroyer escort first, he might get a hit, but most likely the *Matsu* would evade and follow the torpedo wakes right back to *Mackerel*'s position—forcing *Mackerel* to go deep and allowing the freighter to escape unmolested. The attack would be a complete failure and the crew would lose whatever confidence they had left. The choice was suddenly clear to him. This crew *had* to sink a ship. Tremain decided that the freighter would be his one and only target. He would concentrate all efforts on sinking it.

Cazanavette was obviously weighing the same options in his head. He carefully worded a question—to evidently feel out Tremain. "Do you plan on shooting on the generated solution, sir? We might be able to get in one more good observation."

"One is all we'll need, XO. That freighter has not zigged for hours. He's just heading straight for Truk as fast as he can. The TDC solution should be a good one. I'll take one more observation at time of fire."

Tremain turned to Smithers, who had a sound-powered phone hanging around his neck. The young sailor looked nervous, but he was intently listening to Tremain's every word.

"Pass to the forward torpedo room," Tremain said to him. "Open outer doors on tubes one through four and make the tubes ready for firing in all respects. Set depth at eight feet."

As Smithers relayed the orders to the torpedo room, Tremain exchanged glances with Cazanavette. The moment they had been waiting for was fast approaching. They would be firing the specially modified torpedoes. Soon they would know if Konhausen's modifications had fixed the detonators, or if Tremain had just ruined his career for nothing. Tremain gathered from Cazanavette's expression that he inwardly wanted the torpedoes to fail. Then he would be proved right.

Several minutes passed before Smithers received and relayed the report that tubes one through four were ready. Joe Salisbury, manning the sound gear, reported high speed screw noises correlating to the *Matsu*. It was passing across *Mackerel*'s bows, from port to starboard. Salisbury estimated its range at only one thousand yards.

"Generated distance to the freighter's track, fifteen hundred yards, Captain," Hubley reported as the TDC ticker hit fifteen hundred.

Tremain took a deep breath. *Mackerel* was only making three knots of headway, but he still was not sure whether the *Matsu* would be close enough to see the telltale periscope 'feather' on the surface. He noticed that his palms were sweating. The time had come.

"Up scope!" Tremain said. "Final bearing and shoot!"

As the scope glided up Tremain again met it at the floor. He could see the spray drizzle off the lens as he rapidly swung it through one revolution. He quickly saw the fast-moving *Matsu* only a few hundred yards off *Mackerel*'s starboard beam and still heading east. Waves from its frothing wake slapped against the periscope lens. With magnification, Tremain could make out racks of neatly stacked depth charges on the escort's stern. The *Matsu* did not change course and simply drove on. She seemed to be unaware of *Mackerel*'s presence.

Tremain rotated the periscope slightly to the left.

"Damn!" he cursed under his breath as another wave slapped against the lens, obscuring his vision. When the lens finally cleared the freighter appeared before his eyes. It looked to be on the same course and speed. It was simply plowing through the ocean at ten knots, heading for its distant port. Tremain noticed that the freighter also appeared much larger than he had anticipated. He was looking straight on at the ship's starboard beam. It was close enough that it took up most of the periscope's field of view. He could see every detail of her hull, every line and rust stain, even a few crewmen strolling on the deck.

It had to be inside fifteen hundred yards, Tremain thought. He quickly centered the reticle on the single smokestack.

"Bearing, mark!" he called.

"Three four eight," Smithers replied.

"Down scope."

As Smithers lowered the scope, Tremain closed his eyes to wait for Hubley's response. How true the torpedoes ran depended on the quality of the solution in the TDC and the final observation bearing would be the truth teller. If the bearing that Tremain had marked matched the one generated by the TDC then the firing solution was a good one.

Hubley rapidly spun the dials and turned the knobs on the TDC. To Tremain it seemed like it was taking him an eternity to evaluate the observation.

"Bearing matches with generated solution, Captain," Hubley finally reported.

"Fire one!" Tremain said, without hesitation.

Cazanavette depressed the plunger on the bulkhead. A small pressure change, followed by a loud "Whoosh" and a slight lurch of the deck, signified that a shot of high-pressure air had ejected the first torpedo from its tube.

Tremain waited six seconds between each shot.

"Fire two! . . . Fire three! . . . Fire four!"

After similar pressure changes, Smithers relayed the report from the forward torpedo room that all torpedoes had been fired.

Several seconds later, Salisbury reported, "All torpedoes running hot, straight, and normal, Captain."

"Time to impact, fifty-five seconds, Captain," Hubley said.

"Very well. Helm, left full rudder, steady course two nine zero, all ahead full." Tremain then leaned over the ladder railing and called down to the control room, "Dive, take her down to four hundred feet, fast!"

Olander acknowledged the order and *Mackerel* pitched forward as she began her plunge into the deep. Everyone in the conning tower was still silent and perspiring nervously. Some of them had their fingers crossed. Others simply watched their panels. They all eagerly anticipated the results as they waited for the torpedoes to cover the distance to the freighter. Only George Olander's voice could be heard above the low hum of the electric motors as he quietly gave orders to the planesmen in the control room.

Cazanavette made his way over to Tremain.

"You're not going to confirm, sir?" he asked, the question sounding more like an accusation.

Tremain gave him an obligatory answer. "That escort is inside a thousand yards, XO. You can bet we'll get a confirmation of a different sort real soon."

Cazanavette thought for a moment and then seemed satisfied. He went back over to the chart desk and stared at the plotted positions of the enemy ships. Tremain knew what he was thinking. An unconfirmed kill is no kill at all on the record books and it would not be officially recognized back at ComSubPac. But Tremain knew that he had no choice, he had to go deep. The escort was too close for comfort. He glanced at Hubley who was holding a stopwatch and counting each second with his lips.

Ten . . . nine . . . eight . . . seven . . . six . . . five . . . four. . . .

A muffled "Whack," followed by a loud rumble, shook the hull.

Tremain and Cazanavette exchanged glances. The modified detonators had worked. The torpedo had run true.

Tremain could not help but give a small smile. Inwardly, he was breathing a sigh of relief.

Everyone in the conning tower burst out in cheers and the same could be heard coming from the other compartments. The men shook hands and slapped each other on the back as another "Whack!" filled the air . . . then another.

The exultation of the crew intensified with each detonation. The cheers died down for a moment as they waited for the final torpedo to hit, but the seconds passed with only silence.

Hubley looked at his stopwatch. He waited a few seconds more before announcing, "Number four missed."

The single miss did not seem to affect the mood as more cheers erupted. The crew was so elated they appeared to have forgotten that they were at battle stations with a Japanese escort only a few hundred yards away.

Tremain rubbed his temples. Number four had missed but there could be no doubt that one, two, and three had hit the target. His gamble had worked. Now when the court martial relieved him of his command he could at least go to his sentence knowing that some good came of it.

"Quiet down, gentlemen!" Tremain said finally. The celebration amongst the crew had lasted a bit too long for their present situation. "We still have an escort up there!"

"Passing three hundred feet, Captain," Olander called up from the control room.

The hull creaked a little as the boat started to feel the increased sea pressure.

"Captain," Salisbury said, removing one side of his sonar headset, "I'm picking up high speed screws off the starboard quarter, getting louder."

Tremain nodded. He tried to gather a mental picture of what was going on up on the surface. The freighter would be sinking for sure—or at least in its death throes. With three torpedo hits he could not imagine it staying afloat much longer. The *Matsu* would be backtracking, desperately searching for the submarine that had sunk its consort. It would almost certainly see the wakes left on the surface by the exhaust from the torpedo internal combustion engines, then follow them straight back to *Mackerel*'s firing position. That's where the *Matsu* would begin its search. Tremain had to get *Mackerel* as far away as possible from that piece of ocean before the destroyer escort got there.

"Steady on course, two nine zero, Captain," the helmsman reported.

The angle slowly came off the ship, as Olander reported, "At four hundred feet."

Tremain moved over to the chart desk. Cazanavette was plotting *Mackerel*'s dead reckoning position using the sub's course, speed, and simple mathematics.

"We're approximately five hundred yards from our firing position, sir," he said, measuring the distance with a pair of dividers. "It's not much."

Tremain nodded. Then he heard it, as did every other sweating man in the conning tower. The sound came through the hull, faint at first but it grew louder quickly. It was the dreadful "Swish! Swish! Swish!" of the escort's screws churning up the ocean overhead. Those big screws were propelling the *Matsu* at high speed toward *Mackerel*'s position.

"Slow to one third!" Tremain ordered. "Rig for silent running! Rig for depth charge!"

The helmsman rang up one-third speed and the sound of the electric motors quickly faded to a barely audible hum. Throughout the ship the crew quietly shut and dogged the watertight doors, rigging their spaces in anticipation of the worst while listening to the muffled sound of the escort's screws overhead. Everyone stared up as if they could see the *Matsu*'s underside through *Mackerel*'s steel hull and four hundred feet of water.

"The *Matsu* now bears zero eight eight, sir," Salisbury whispered.

The sound of the escort's screws then shifted to a lower pitch and many in the conning tower looked at Tremain as if they expected him to have an explanation for the change.

"She's slowing," Tremain whispered to no one in particular. "She's reached the end of our torpedo wakes, and now she's slowing to see what she can find. What's the bearing now?"

Salisbury turned the hydrophone handles a little. "Zero nine zero, sir."

"How far are we from the firing position now, XO?"

"Eight hundred yards, sir," Cazanavette answered after leaning over the chart momentarily with the dividers.

The *Matsu*'s screws continued to change in pitch and volume for several more minutes. Sometimes they grew louder, other times they faded almost too faint to hear.

She must be going in circles, Tremain thought. He wondered why the Japanese captain had not yet dropped his depth charges. That is what he would have done had the roles been reversed. He did not understand why the *Matsu*'s captain did not unload everything he had on the position marked by the torpedo wakes. It was his best chance of getting them.

Just then Salisbury held up one hand. He turned the hydrophone steering handle slightly and adjusted the sonar headset over his ears. He was listening intently to something.

"Hydraulic noise," Salisbury finally whispered. "She's rigging out her sonar transducers."

Moments later a high-pitched "Ping!" resonated through the water and the hull. It was followed by another, then another as the *Matsu*'s high energy echo ranging sensors scanned the ocean depths, searching for a reflection off *Mackerel*'s metallic hull.

Even though he had heard it many times before, the eerie sound still sent shivers up and down Tremain's spine. The resonating pinging was like a kind of taunting, or psychological warfare. It foreboded doom for any boat that was unlucky enough to fall under the piercing beam of sound energy. It established in every man's mind the fact that they were now the hunted and no longer the hunter.

Tremain surmised his enemy's strategy. The *Matsu*'s captain knew that a submarine on battery power would not be going anywhere in a hurry. He could take his time prodding the ocean for his quarry, conserving his depth charges for the final kill once *Mackerel*'s position was established. Unlike *Mackerel,* the escort had no oxygen or power constraints, and now that her charge was shot full of torpedoes and heading to the bottom of the Pacific, her captain had nothing to do but preserve his honor and prosecute the malevolent submarine.

The active sonar audibly changed while Tremain glanced at the chart over Cazanavette's shoulder. The sound now became what seemeded like two "Pings" in rapid succession. There could be no mistake, the *Matsu*'s probing beam had found them. The sound pulses were bouncing off *Mackerel*'s hull continuously now and the change caused visible tension to appear on the faces of everyone in the room. The double pings continued and then increased in frequency.

"He's found us," Tremain said under his breath, mostly to himself, then immediately wished he had said nothing. He did not need to add to the tension in the room.

The double pings continued to increase in pitch and volume almost incessantly until they were soon audible throughout the entire boat in every space, at every watch station.

"He's sped up, sir!" Salisbury said, having to shout to be heard over the noise. "He's closing us quickly from the starboard quarter. He's too close for a good bearing."

"Right full rudder, all ahead full!" Tremain ordered. The Japanese captain had them. Their only chance to evade was to try to confuse the Japanese captain.

As *Mackerel* slowly picked up speed and began to turn right, the noise only grew louder and the pinging became more intense until it seemed like it was shaking the very hull. The *Matsu* was right on top of them and could not be fooled. Its sonar beam had sought *Mackerel* out and found her. It knew exactly where she was hiding.

"Picking up splashes, sir," Salisbury said.

Tremain turned to Smithers. "Pass the word to all stations, depth charges on the way down, brace for impact."

Smithers relayed the information through his phone set as everyone in the conning tower grabbed the nearest handhold. Tremain's heart was pounding in his chest as he braced himself between the periscopes. He had been through many depth bombings, but the experience seemed to unsettle his nerves more and more each time. He would be lying or mad if he ever said to anyone that it did not affect him. Now, he just tried to concentrate on appearing calm in front of the men around him to take his mind off what was about to happen.

Then, just as fast as they had started, the noise of the screws began to fade, as did the pinging.

"Easy, boys," Tremain said, recognizing the false sense of security. "Those charges have a good four hundred feet to drop. It'll be anytime now."

Suddenly, there was a faint clicking noise outside the hull, then the ocean around the sub exploded.

The powerful depth charges rocked *Mackerel* like a rag doll. Light bulbs burst into a thousand tiny shards. Pieces of cork insulation showered the men everywhere. Hundreds of loose items crashed against the bulkheads and the decks as metal creaked and vibrated to its very foundation. The lights went out leaving the conning tower in complete blackness.

As the rumblings subsided, Tremain heard moans all around him. His head throbbed from the beating he had received from the number two periscope shaft. He could not see the other men with him in the conning tower, but he could hear their heavy breathing.

"Who's hurt?" he said into the darkness.

There was no immediate response, so he reached toward the helmsman's position and clutched what felt like the man's shirt.

"Rudder amidships," he said into the blackness. "Slow to one third."

There was still no response, and Tremain began to wonder if anyone was left alive to carry out his order.

Then someone on the opposite side of the conning tower flicked on a battle lantern and shined it toward the helmsman. Soon the reply came from the direction of the steering wheel.

"Rudder amidships, aye, sir," the helmsman responded weakly. "Answering ahead one third, steering course three five five."

Several more battle lanterns flicked on, and Tremain quickly regained his bearings. He noticed that the air had become much more humid, indicating that the air conditioning plant had shut down during the explosions. He touched his forehead to confirm the welt that was rapidly growing there. Next to him, Hubley picked himself up off the deck and returned to the TDC station. All around him men rubbed their sore wounds where valve stems and other protruding equipment had struck them. Such items were everywhere throughout the ship, sometimes in the most inconspicuous spaces. The crew walked by valve stems and jagged equipment everyday without giving it a second thought, but during a depth charging that equipment could become deadly; many submariners had suffered crushed skulls and impaled shoulders.

In the flickering lantern light, Tremain caught a glimpse of Cazanavette making his way over to him.

"Are you all right, sir?"

Tremain nodded. "Go check the damage, XO."

"Aye, sir." Cazanavette reached for a battle lantern and headed down the control room hatch.

It took him several minutes to climb through the length of the ship, visiting every compartment. When he returned he was out of breath and covered with sweat and grease.

"What's the damage?" Tremain asked.

Cazanavette heaved. "Drain pump was knocked off its foundation, sir, so it's out of commission. Most of the vital bus breakers tripped, that's why we don't have lights. We lost power to just about everything except propulsion. It'll be a few minutes before the electricians can restore it. A couple torpedo harnesses broke in the forward room, leaving one torpedo slightly ajar in its rack. The torpedomen are rigging some chains to hold it temporarily. We've also got minor leaks from valve packing here and there, but nothing serious. The electric motors are fine, the batteries are fine. Mr. Turner is in charge of the damage control efforts with the Cob helping."

Tremain nodded. It could have been much worse, he thought. They had gotten lucky this time.

"Any injuries?" he asked.

"Nothing major, sir. We may have a few broken bones down there, but they're all alive."

"Very well." Tremain moved to the ladder well and called down to the control room, "Dive, how's your depth?"

"We're holding at four hundred feet, sir," Olander replied confidently. The engineer seemed very relaxed under the circumstances. He was leaning against the ladder and casually holding a lantern on the diving control panel so that his planesmen could see their gauges.

Tremain and Cazanavette stepped over loose items on

the deck as they moved over to the conning tower's chart desk.

"I'm sure the *Matsu* isn't finished with us yet and we can't outrun her," Tremain said, looking at the chart. He pointed to the last plotted position of the freighter. "Give me a good course to the freighter's last position, XO."

"Have you got an idea, Captain?" Cazanavette asked as he broke out the parallel ruler.

"No, XO," Tremain said, smiling, "just an old trick. We'll get as close as we can to that sinking freighter. There are bound to be survivors in the water. Then we'll let the *Matsu*'s captain decide whether or not he wants to blow up his own people to get us."

Cazanavette quickly laid down a new course on the plot and Tremain ordered the helmsman to steer for it.

"What count did you get?" Tremain asked Salisbury.

"I counted four depth charges, Captain."

"I agree."

"Well, a *Matsu* carries thirty-six." Cazanavette said, flipping through the identification book. "We've just got thirty-two more to go."

The lights came back on as *Mackerel* crept toward the spot where the freighter had been hit. The screw noises could no longer be heard through the hull, but Salisbury still tracked the lurking *Matsu* on his sound gear. As *Mackerel* neared the last known position of the freighter a monstrous creaking sound filled the water around them. It was a whiny eerie sound that lasted for several minutes then ended with several loud "Pop!"s in rapid succession. The veterans knew that sound well. Once a man heard a ship break up as it headed for the ocean floor, the sound stayed with him for the rest of his life. He never forgot it. There could be no doubting now that the freighter had sunk. As she had plunged to her watery grave her bulkheads had twisted and warped as the pressure increased. Finally the watertight compartments had collapsed and imploded. Anyone who had survived the torpedo explosions and found himself trapped below decks during those final terrifying seconds would have been killed at that moment.

"Scratch one freighter!" someone in the control room said excitedly. It must have been a green member of the crew, because no one else made a comment. The sounds of a ship breaking up were not very comforting to men who were themselves riding on the edge of their ship's depth limits with a looming escort overhead.

Tremain waited in the succeeding silence. The air was getting thicker. Humidity was rising more rapidly due to the temporary power loss and carbon dioxide levels would be rising too.

"Here she comes again," Salisbury whispered. "She's off the port beam, bearing two four five. She's going active again."

Tremain could hear the distant echo ranging through the hull.

"Right full rudder," he said calmly. "Steady on course zero five zero."

Mackerel slowly came around, pointing her stern in the direction of the escort. Tremain wanted to minimize the chance of sonar reflections by presenting the smallest surface area to the *Matsu*'s hydrophones.

"Whoosh! Whoosh! Whoosh!" The screw noise became audible again as the *Matsu* drew closer. Then the powerful sonar pulses shifted frequency and again they began to reflect off *Mackerel*'s hull. The enemy had found them again.

Tremain closed his eyes. The escort captain was good. He had anticipated Tremain's move and had changed his search pattern accordingly. Slowly and methodically, he was narrowing in on the submarine's position.

The screw noise and pinging once again drowned out all other noise in the boat as the escort moved in to attack.

"Come on, damn you," Tremain said with a mad grin on his face. "Give us your best shot."

"Splashes, sir!" Salisbury exclaimed.

"Right full rudder!" Tremain ordered. He would be damned if they were just going to sit there and take the pounding. "All ahead full! Dive, make your depth four five zero feet!"

"Sir, that exceeds test depth!" Olander's voice called up the ladder well in protest.

"Do it, damn it!" Tremain shouted. "And quickly, damn you!"

"Aye, sir!"

The deck lurched slightly as *Mackerel* propelled herself to seven knots and then angled downward to go deeper. Tremain watched the depth gauge as the needle passed the four hundred ten mark and kept descending. The depth charges were on their way down. Tremain was gambling that the *Matsu*'s captain had set them to explode at four hundred feet. *Mackerel* had to get away from that depth, and fast.

Four hundred twenty feet . . . four hundred thirty feet . . .

The hull creaked and popped as the sea pressure pushing in on it increased drastically. Some of the men had their eyes shut tight. Some clasped their hands in prayer. Others stared into space attempting to erase the ominous noises from their minds. Tremain allowed his own mind an instant away from the battle to think of Judy. He wondered if the thought would be his last.

Then the clicking noise sounded outside the hull again as the falling depth charges armed themselves. Half a second later, four distinct explosions shook the hull in all directions. Bodies and equipment flew across the compartment. The lights went out again. More yells and screams came from the blackness as *Mackerel* rocked uncontrollably.

Then, once again, all fell silent.

Tremain heard a few moans and coughs as the battle lanterns once again flicked on. He picked up a lantern near him and shined it on the faces of the men around him. They were dazed but none appeared seriously injured.

Then he sensed that something was wrong. As he got his bearings, he noticed that the deck was still tilted downward. A chill immediately shot through his spine as he realized that *Mackerel* was still diving. Not only was she diving but the deck was angling down more and more with each passing second. The men in the conning tower groped for something to hold onto as the angle approached thirty degrees and books started to launch from their shelves.

Tremain flashed his lantern on the depth gauge by the helmsman who had one foot firmly planted against the bulkhead in front of him to keep him from falling into it.

The gauge read four hundred seventy feet, and it was still descending.

"Dive, take the angle off her!" Tremain shouted as he dangled from periscope shears.

"We're trying, sir!" Olander's voice came up from the control room. There was finally panic in his voice. "Stern planes are jammed on hard dive!"

"All stop! All back emergency!" Tremain ordered. He had to get *Mackerel*'s headway off before she drove herself beyond the point of no return. With the stern planes jammed on dive it would not take long.

Motioning for Cazanavette to take over in the conning tower, Tremain managed to climb down the angled ladder to the control room. There Olander stood behind the two planesmen intently watching their every move. The man controlling the stern planes leaned into his control wheel with his whole weight, desperately trying to level the planes. The bow planesman neglected his own planes to reach over and help him, but the extra weight yielded no results.

"No response, sir," the stern planesman grimaced.

"Shift to emergency hydraulics," Olander said.

The planesman switched a lever on the panel in front of him and tried the wheel once more. The stern planes still did not move.

Tremain checked the gauge on the diving control panel. It read four hundred and ninety feet. The reduced speed was slowing their rate of descent, but they were still going down too quickly. The hull began to shudder and pop under the immense pressure, and several of the men turned pale and began to shake at the terrifying sound.

"We'll have to take local control!" Olander shouted above a gut-wrenching whine, which came from the ship's steel girders.

Tremain nodded. Olander had voiced Tremain's exact thought, although they both knew that the effort would be in vain. Several valves would have to be manipulated back in the aft torpedo room in order to shift control of the planes to the local station. The hull would crack for sure before they could get through even half of the valve line-up.

Then, before any order went out, Tremain heard a report coming from the blackness on the opposite side of the control room. One of the men wearing a sound-powered phone headset was in contact with the aft torpedo room.

"The aft torpedo room reports local stern planes control station is manned and ready, sir," the man announced.

"Order them to place full rise on the stern planes!" Olander shouted after a moment's hesitation. He was obviously somewhat perplexed at the report.

The man on the phone set repeated the order into his mouthpiece and within seconds the stern planes indictor on the diving control panel showed the planes rotating to the level position, and then to full rise. Everyone in the room held his breath as the ship's angle slowly but surely leveled out.

Tremain grinned wildly after the realization set in that they might actually survive this. He assumed that the men in the aft torpedo room had anticipated the need for the local stern planes' controls and had already manned the control station before the order was given. The few precious minutes they had saved by doing so had made the difference between life and death.

"Go to ahead one third, XO," Tremain called up to the conning tower. He needed to maintain some headway on the ship. The water moving over the stern planes was the only thing providing *Mackerel* with the lifting force necessary to keep her from sinking out.

As *Mackerel* established a steady speed of three knots, the depth gauge showed the descent rate slow to almost nothing. The hull still creaked and popped due to the extreme depth, but much less than it had before.

"I'm going to need to pump some water off, Captain," Olander announced. "We're heavy."

Tremain nodded. "Use air. I'd rather have that escort hear one short air burst than the trim pump. No sense in giving him a good steady pump noise to track."

"Aye, sir." Olander gave a few orders and a small hissing noise could be heard as high pressure air from the ship's air banks pushed several thousand pounds of water from the variable ballast tanks.

Mackerel finally stabilized at five hundred and eighteen feet. The hull moaned as it adjusted to the constant pressure, but eventually the unsettling noise ceased. The hull was holding.

Every man's face displayed utter astonishment. None of

them had ever been this deep before, none ever wanted to be this deep again. They each silently thanked the ship-builders at the Electric Boat Company for doing their jobs so well.

Tremain wiped the sweat from his brow and breathed a deep sigh as the lights flickered back to life. He looked up to see a visibly exhausted Tee squeezing his muscular frame through the aft door with Chief Freund in tow.

"Power has been restored, sir," Tee reported. "The servo valve controlling the stern planes was damaged by those last depth charges. We'll have to stay in local control until it's repaired."

"Very well, Mr. Turner. Someone was on the ball back there. If the aft room had waited for our order to begin their valve line-up we would have never made it. Who was in charge back there?"

"Well, sir . . . uh . . . it was . . . " Tee stuttered.

"It was the young ensign, believe it or not, sir," Chief Freund interrupted with a sweaty grin.

"Young Wright?" Tremain smiled and shook his head. "Unbelievable."

"Yes, sir," Freund continued, "Chief Konhausen was up in the forward room when the stern planes got stuck, and Mister Turner and I were in number one engine room. Kil-cran, the leading petty officer who was in charge in the aft room, got himself knocked out by a valve handle during that last barrage. According to the boys in the aft room the ensign just up and took over. He ordered them to man the local control station for the stern planes when the ship started to angle down like she did. Pretty quick thinking for a youngster, Captain."

Tremain had a hard time picturing Wright in charge in the aft torpedo room; the young officer was still bright-eyed and bushy-tailed in his eyes. Still, the ensign had to be doing his homework to know how to take manual control of the stern planes after only being on board for a few weeks. Tremain considered himself to be a hot runner when he himself was an ensign, but he had to admit that what Wright had done was indeed impressive.

Tremain dismissed Tee and Freund and headed back up to the conning tower. Everyone in the conning tower stared at Salisbury on the sound gear. His face plainly displayed the dire knowledge that the escort was still out there.

"Where is she?" Tremain asked.

"She bears zero four five, sir," Salisbury whispered. "Her screw noise is increasing."

Tremain closed his eyes. He did not think *Mackerel* could hold up to another pounding, especially not at this depth. The ship's backbone was ready to break, and it would only take another depth charging like the last one to deliver the lethal blow. There was nothing to do but wait. To come any shallower would be suicide. They could only wait and pray.

The "whooshing" of the escort's screws once again became audible through the hull. Then the pinging started. It grew louder and louder every minute.

"He's right on top of us," Salisbury reported quite unnecessarily.

Tremain gritted his teeth, anticipating the next explosion. He waited to hear the report of depth charge splashes, but it never came. Then, slowly, the screw noise and the echo ranging began to fade. Every man in the conning tower held his breath and glanced at Tremain in disbelief, as if they wanted him to confirm that what they were hearing was true.

As the minutes passed the pings became even more distant until they were no longer audible through the hull.

"He's fading, sir," Salisbury gasped. "I don't believe it. How could he have missed us?"

"We must be under a thermal layer," Tremain said as he

let out a sigh. "These waters are famous for them. His echo ranging can't penetrate it."

Tremain had studied the effects of temperature and salinity layers on sonar operation when he was at PCO School several years back. They were perfect for hiding a submarine, but the trouble was you never really knew where they were in the vast ocean. Tremain had read about new boats being fitted with devices that could indicate when the boat was passing through one. It would have been nice to have one of those devices on the *Mackerel*.

"This little depth excursion turned out to be a good thing," he said. "It got us below the thermal layer. Now let's get the hell out of here, XO."

"An excellent idea, Captain." Cazanavette's face broke into the first genuine grin Tremain had seen on him.

Several minutes passed with every ear listening for the return of the *Matsu*, but it never came. Distant muffled explosions were heard for the next hour as the escort continued to drop charges on phantom sonar returns. Eventually, even the explosions faded too. *Mackerel* had silently slipped away.

It took several more hours for the crew to unwind from the event. They dealt with their post-trauma by fixing valves, replacing light bulbs, stowing equipment, anything to affirm that they were still alive. Many slept, and many more could not sleep. By the time Tremain crawled down from the conning tower and headed to his stateroom, he even saw a few men smiling and telling jokes once again.

As he passed through the door to the stateroom passage, he almost tripped over a sailor frantically running aft with a folded piece of cloth in his hands. It was Seaman Ross, the signalman.

"What do you have there, Ross?" Tremain asked.

Ross appeared embarrassed and then blushed, with a huge toothy grin. "Some of the guys and me were going to do a little sewing before we turned in, sir." He held up *Mackerel*'s battle flag. "We've got something *real* to add to those sampans now, sir."

Tremain smiled at the excited young man and said, "Carry on, Ross."

Chapter 8

"**FIFTEEN** two, fifteen four, a double run of three for twelve, and his nob for thirteen!" O'Connell shouted in jubilation, moving his peg to the end of the cribbage board. Wright rolled his eyes. O'Connell had beaten him for the third time. He noticed Hubley and Tee chuckling at the other end of the wardroom table.

"Better give up, En*swine*," Tee said. "You really are brainless, aren't you? Brainless and dickless."

Wright shot Tee a sardonic smile but said nothing as he gathered up the cards to deal another game. Ever since they had left port, Tee had been tormenting him in one way or another—he seemed to draw some kind of sick pleasure from it. The first week Wright could understand, he was the new officer on board and he rated a little harassment. Wright himself had belonged to a fraternity in college and he recognized the value in a little hazing. He had engaged in hazing himself and had been one of the best at it. But in the fraternity there was always a point when the harassment

stopped and the new guy was accepted. They had been at
sea for over a month now, and Tee still showed no signs of
letting up. Whenever they passed each other in the passage,
Tee would body-check him into the bulkhead. It was such a
common and unpleasant experience that Wright now instinctively checked each corridor for any sign of Tee before
passing through. Whenever Wright had tried to discuss
the matter with him, Tee just dismissed him with "En*swine*,
are you genetically deficient or just brain dead?" or simply
"Shut up, asshole!"

Wright was sure that Margie had put him up to it. She
was getting her revenge on him in her own way, and he had
come to hate her for it. But he was getting to the point
where he could no longer take the harassment. It was bad
enough being cooped up on a submarine for a month. Being cooped up with an unbearable bully was something
else. He had found that the best thing to do to protect his
own sanity was to ignore Tee altogether, though it did little
to thwart Tee's tormenting.

As difficult as it was to deal with Tee on a daily basis,
all was not dismal. In sharp contrast to Tee, the rest of the
officers and crew seemed to have accepted him as a part of
the ship's company. Wright had noticed the change after
the attack on the freighter. That day was still a blur to him.

He could remember going to his battle station in the aft
torpedo room. Tee had told him to go there because he was
new and he would just get in the way anywhere else. The
enlisted men in the aft torpedo room were junior too and
were trying to stay out of the way themselves. Chief Konhausen had been there initially, but he had gone forward
when he learned that Tremain would be making a bow
shot. He had left Petty Officer First Class Kilcran, who was
the most experienced in the room, in charge of the whole
group. Wright was like a fifth wheel and did not have any
particular assignment, so he did his best to blend into the

shadows. He had spent most of the time listening to the speakers in the torpedo room, which intoned the conversations of the tracking party in the conning tower. Wright and the men in the room had heard the whole thing as the captain conducted the attack on the freighter and fired the bow tubes. When the three torpedoes had struck home, Wright had cheered with everyone else. Then the *Matsu* attacked, and Wright's memory of the rest was sketchy. It was his first depth charging, and it had shaken him mentally. He remembered seeing his life flashing before his eyes with each resounding explosion and seeing images of things he had done in his life and other things that he wished he had. He remembered feeling true fear and discovering for the first time in his life that he was indeed mortal, and that he could die in the blink of an eye.

When the *Matsu* came over for the second depth charge attack, the shockwave from the blasts threw Petty Officer Kilcran across the room and into a protruding valve handle. When the pounding ceased and the battle lanterns came on, Kilcran was lying motionless on the deck with a small trickle of blood running through his hair. The other men in the room had resembled lost sheep as they stared at their fallen comrade. Within moments the deck took a sharp angle and left all of them groping for handholds. Wright had immediately suspected that the stern planes were jammed. It had occurred to him only because he had read the casualty procedure just the night before. It was one of the many things he had to read for his qualifications. The procedure had specified some of the symptoms of a stern plane casualty, one being a sudden large angle on the ship. Wright knew what had to be done, and without thinking he had taken charge of the room. He assumed that the control room would soon be ordering them to take control of the stern planes locally, so he went ahead and ordered two men to open up the valves to line up the hydraulics for the local control. Seconds later, the order had come from the control room to take local control of the stern planes. Wright's men were already ready with the controls in their hands, and thus they had been able to level the ship in seconds, saving every man on board from being crushed to death.

Wright was embarrassed for several days after the incident—he was not comfortable receiving so much attention. Whenever he entered a room many of the men would stop whatever they were doing and pretend to hail him. Even the captain had thanked him for his quick thinking. The captain had asked him how he managed to know so much so quickly, and he did not know what to say. He had always been a fast learner, but he had felt more like he was on autopilot during the whole ordeal. He had had his head so deep in the books the last few weeks that submarining was starting to come to him naturally. Unfortunately, the good will extended toward him by the others was not extended by Tee.

"Did I say you could play again, asshole?" Tee snarled as Wright dealt the cards. "Don't you have quals to work on?"

"Leave him alone, Tee," O'Connell said. "He's way ahead on his qualifications, and you know it."

"Yeah, because he gets the crew to blaze off his signatures, they *like* him so much."

Before Wright could respond to the insult to his integrity O'Connell spoke up. "No, they just *don't* like you, Tee. Why don't you give it a rest?"

"Why the hell should I, Rudy?"

"Because maybe I'm sick of you, that's why. Leave him alone."

"Why are you always defending him? You guys must be butt buddies or something." Tee smirked, then glared at Wright. "You know I think you're a piece of shit, Wright. I think you just got lucky the other day. You didn't know jackshit back there in the aft room, and then all of a sudden you saved the day by taking charge. I don't buy it."

"Face it, Tee," O'Connell said. "You're just mad because you didn't get all the glory. I doubt you'd have even known what to do back there."

"There he goes again, Wright," Tee said, his eyes squarely locked on Wright. "He's always standing up for you, you pussy. What have I got to say to get you to stand up for yourself, asshole?"

Wright ignored him and pretended to examine his cards.

"Oh, I know," Tee continued, with a sadistic smile on his face. "How about I tell you how I fucked the shit out of your dead friend's sister the night before we left. How about I tell you how I fucked that whore for all she was worth. And I've got you to thank for it, too."

Wright put his cards down and faced Tee. He didn't care that Tee had had sex with Margie. It was the mention of his "dead friend" that had struck a nerve deep within him.

"Oh yeah," Tee continued, obviously elated to see that he finally had Wright's attention. "After she saw you that night, she was so pissed off that she let me do anything to her. I've got to say I did most of the work, but your dead friend's sister is one great piece of ass, Wright."

Wright stood up and began to move toward Tee, but O'Connell shot an arm out to hold him back. Tee's face lit up with excitement and he brandished his fists, motioning for Wright to come closer.

"Sit down, Ryan!" O'Connell said. "Just forget it!"

Wright leaned forward into O'Connell's arm as he tried to break free in order to get to the object of his anger. O'Connell's arm was all that stood between him and Tee's laughing red face. He wanted to knock that grin right off his face. The big brute could probably knock him aside like a fly, but he desperately wanted to get in just one blow, one blow to make up for all the insults and ridicule he had taken since he had met this galoot.

"Sit down, Ensign!" O'Connell finally shouted, looking Wright straight in the eyes.

Wright saw stern compassion in O'Connell's eyes and it made him think straight once again. He did not want to ruin his naval career over something so insignificant as Tee's jeering comments. After a brief contemplative moment, he sat back down at the table and retrieved his cards, ready to play another hand.

Tee started to say something, but was cut short by O'Connell.

"Shut your damn mouth, Tee," he snapped. "Just sit down and shut up. And leave Wright alone. If I ever hear you saying crap like that again I'll report you to the XO. How the hell can you talk about your girlfriend like that anyway, you sick bastard? I don't know what the hell she sees in you."

"What the fu—" Tee started to speak but was again interrupted by O'Connell.

"And another thing. I've heard that you've been messing with my watchstanders again. Chief told me you had Eckhart down in the control room cleaning during my watch yesterday. If you're going to play Navy Academy, Tee, do it on your own damn watch. My sonar operator is off limits to you. You got that?"

"Your guys always leave the control room looking like shit, Rudy," Tee said and then looked to Hubley for support. "Carl and I aren't going to have *our* guys clean it up, and I'm not going to stand watch with the control room looking like shit. The captain's going to unload on somebody about it someday and it's not going to be me or Carl."

"Keep me out of this, Tee," Hubley said. "Cluttered or not, Rudy's right. You've got no business distracting his watchstanders. You're lucky he doesn't report it to the XO."

Tee slammed his fist on the table, sending the cribbage pegs and board flying into the air. Veins bulged on his forehead and his face turned red with rage. He could see that he was outnumbered here. Even Hubley, his officer of the deck, was not taking his side. He jammed his thick finger in Wright's face.

"You better stay out of my way, asshole," he snarled, then stormed out of the wardroom, leaving the curtain swinging behind him.

As O'Connell picked up the fallen cribbage pieces, he winked at Wright.

"He's easy to spin up," he said.

"Thanks," Wright said. He appreciated O'Connell's interference but he knew that it would only make things worse in the long term. Tee now had another reason to hate him.

O'Connell had stuck up for Wright on more than one occasion since they had left port, and Wright had completely changed his initial opinion about the man. Being O'Connell's junior officer of the deck, Wright had spent nearly the entire voyage with him. O'Connell had shown Wright the ins and outs of standing watch on the bridge, and had helped him immensely with his qualifications. During the past month they had stood watch together in all kinds of weather and sea conditions, during times when Wright learned just how powerful the ocean was. They had stood watch during dark stormy nights when they had to tether themselves to the bridge to keep from getting washed overboard by fifty-foot waves. They stood watch during beautiful tropical days when it was hard to remember there was a war on at all. During the monotonous times they had shared lots of thoughts about life and the world at war. Wright had gotten to know O'Connell quite well in that time. In fact, Wright even considered O'Connell to be a friend. O'Connell appeared tough on the outside, but Wright now knew that he was also a deeply religious man. He had been fighting in submarines since the beginning of the war, and Wright had nothing but respect for him.

"Won't be long now," O'Connell said as he looked over his cards. "We should be heading back in two or three weeks."

"Yeah, we'll be running low on fuel soon," Hubley added.

"We haven't seen much action out here, other than the one freighter," Wright said. "I thought these waters would be much busier, being so close to Truk and all."

"Listen to him, a real veteran now, huh?" O'Connell nudged Hubley. "Yeah, well, that's the way submarine life is. One minute you're praying that the next depth charge won't break your boat in half, the next you're praying for something . . . anything, to come your way. Intense action followed by long periods of boredom. That should be the submariners' motto."

"I'll tell you one thing, though," Hubley said. "The skipper's upset about it."

"About what?"

"About our area assignment. I heard him complaining to the XO the other day that ComSubPac assigned us to a light traffic zone because they don't trust us in the harder areas. He was pretty irate about it. He even told the XO to send off a message to ComSubPac demanding that they give us a new area."

"Yeah?" O'Connell chuckled. "I guess he doesn't want to go back to Pearl with all those torpedoes he had Chief Konhausen modify. How many was it in all?"

"Ten," Hubley said. "And we've only shot four so far. They modified the six in the forward tubes and the four in the aft tubes. The XO wasn't too happy about that either."

"You gotta admit, though," O'Connell said. "The fish worked against the freighter. It sure got the crew motivated, too. I've never seen them this eager for a fight. My lookouts have even been asking to stay on the bridge after their watch and keep looking for contacts."

"Mine too!" Hubley exclaimed. "I've never seen anything like it. Amazing what a little pride can do to a ship."

As Wright listened to Hubley and O'Connell talk about the morale of the crew, something came to mind that he had almost forgotten.

"Pride runs deep," he said quietly, almost to himself.

"What?" O'Connell asked, rolling his eyes. "What the hell're you talking about, Ryan? You sound like you're selling war bonds."

Wright smiled. "No, it's just something one of my instructors at sub school would always say to us at the end of every class. He was some over-the-hill forgotten lieutenant stuck at sub school teaching tactics. He was medically disqualified from sea duty for some reason or another, I can't remember what for. He was the kind of guy you felt sorry for because you could tell that he had dedicated most of his life to the service, and now he was just a wash-up stashed away at a teaching job. The navy had no use for him anywhere else. 'Pride runs deep, gentlemen!' He would always say that as we left class. He was proud all right. You could tell he wanted to go back to sea more than anything. Definitely more than any of us students did. He was always telling us how much he envied us because we were fleet bound."

"Well, I'm envying him right about now," O'Connell said. "Where do I sign up for instructor duty?"

"No kidding," Hubley chuckled.

They continued the cribbage game, and Wright found himself thinking about his old instructor. It took a special sort of man to want submarine duty, he thought, especially after being here and seeing what it was all about. Wright felt like he was beginning to understand what his instructor had meant by *pride*.

TREMAIN leaned on the periscope handles and slowly scanned the ocean's surface while he waited for Joe Salisbury to decode the message. *Mackerel* had come up to the surface just long enough to receive the VLF broadcast then settled back down to periscope depth. Tremain hoped the message contained an answer to his request to ComSubPac. He needed orders. *Mackerel* had not conducted an attack since the freighter sinking two weeks ago, and only two ships had been sighted in that entire time. Both had been fast-transiting destroyers, impossible to catch, and not worthy of *Mackerel*'s valuable torpedoes.

The ship was now patrolling submerged only a few miles south of the Truk Atoll. Through the periscope, Tremain could see the dense foliage of the thin boundary islets surrounding Tol Island poking up over the wave tops.

As he focused on the picturesque island with its clear blue waters, Tremain wondered why Ireland had sent him here. The place was devoid of shipping. Normally, Truk was a high traffic area, but all of the major operations were currently going on in the Solomon Islands, some eighteen hundred miles to the south. Most of the shipping would be there trying to replenish the Japanese bases in a desperate attempt to help them hold out against the American invasion forces that were rapidly accelerating their island-hopping campaign.

Mackerel had only three more weeks to patrol. Then she would have no choice but to leave the area with just enough fuel to get her back home. He knew that if they did not spot a target soon, the crew's morale would drop right back into the gutter. They would blame him for the failure, and so would ComSubPac, regardless of the circumstances.

As he rotated the scope, a small glint in the sky over Truk caught his eye. It was a Japanese plane. While shipping had been scarce, the air activity around the Japanese Pacific bastion had been anything but. Flights and squadrons of Japanese planes flew over during every watch. Some had flown close enough that Tremain had seen the red rising sun on their gray fuselage. He had included a note in the night orders for the watch officers to ensure that the SD air-warning radar was on high alert whenever *Mackerel* was on the surface. The radar was sometimes the only warning they would have that aircraft were nearby.

"Excuse me, sir. The message is ready."

Tremain took his eyes away from the scope to see Joe Salisbury holding out a sheet of paper in front of him. Salisbury took the scope and Tremain read the decoded message to himself. Within moments of reading it his face broke into a smile. Cazanavette appeared and also read the message, with a similar response. The message was exactly what Tremain had been waiting for. He grabbed the 1MC microphone off its hook on the bulkhead.

"All hands, this is the captain. I know this tooling around with our thumbs up our kazoos has had us wondering if ComSubPac has forgotten about us. Well, they haven't. In fact, we have just received new orders. We are to relocate three hundred miles to the west and patrol the area northwest of the Carolines, off Mogami Bank. Shipping activity in that area is expected to be heavy in the next few days. It may interest you to know that this unexpected relocation will burn up a little more fuel than we had planned on, so we will probably be heading home a few days early. Stay sharp! That is all."

A few cheers could be heard from the other compartments. Several faces beamed at the thought of going back to Pearl Harbor early. Tremain knew he had played that card right. He took one more round on the periscope before he and Cazanavette headed down to the control room to plot out the new course that would take them to their new hunting ground, off Mogami Bank.

Chapter 9

MACKEREL leaped in and out of the swells as her four diesel engines propelled her along at fourteen knots. The unpredictable winter weather of the Central Pacific had changed once again. Gray clouds hung low over the seascape, wafted by a cool salt air breeze with the scent of rain. Squalls appeared here and there as smeared patches of dark gray reached down from the clouds to touch the water.

Wright adjusted his jacket and wiped the spray from his binocular lenses after a wave crashed against the base of the conning tower. It was only one of a seemingly endless set of rollers, which crashed across the fore deck spraying the bridge personnel with a salty mist. He glanced over at O'Connell, who was leaning on the bridge coaming peering through his own binoculars. O'Connell seemed unfazed by the uncomfortable weather.

"Poor visibility today," Wright commented.

"I've seen a lot worse," O'Connell said, still looking

through his binoculars. "North Pac, up by the Aleutians, now that's bad visibility for you. Fog is so thick up there sometimes you can't even see the lookouts."

Wright held on to the coaming as another roller lifted *Mackerel*'s bow out of the water and sat it back down with a thunderous crash. Wright was still amazed at how tiny their submarine seemed in seas like these. Once when he was at submarine school, he saw a large cruiser plow through the rough seas off Long Island. The waters before it had yielded to their steel master, parting before the heavy bow. With *Mackerel* it was not so. The seas tossed her mere two thousand tons at will with only the slightest resistance.

Wright looked at his wristwatch. The jostling and rocking had the effect of making a four-hour watch seem much longer. He and O'Connell had been on the bridge most of the afternoon, almost four hours, though it felt like twice that. Hubley and Tee were due to relieve them any time now.

Wright sighed at the thought.

Being relieved by Tee was never a pleasant experience. He always behaved as though he was doing Wright a favor, very condescending and never polite. It was as if he was holding Wright personally responsible for having to get out of the rack and stand watch on the bridge for four hours, disregarding the fact that it was indeed his job to do so. Wright detested being relieved by Tee. But it was a small price to pay for getting out of the weather, after all.

"What's for dinner?" O'Connell asked with a grin, as he always did at this point in the watch.

"I don't know. I'll check." Leaning down to the open hatch, Wright took a long sniff at the warm air rising out of the small opening. "Smells like chili mac, again!"

O'Connell shook his head in disgust. The lookouts up in the periscope shears overheard Wright and reacted in a similar fashion. One of them shouted down, "Man, those cooks have got to learn how to make something else. If they don't,

I'm going to start fishing for our supper while we're on watch."

Wright laughed at the thought and checked his watch once more. It won't be long now, he thought. We'll be out of this intolerable weather and chowing down on chili mac in the wardroom, and even have a game of cribbage or two. He raised the binoculars with a small smile and continued to scan the sea.

BENEATH Wright and O'Connell, inside the conning tower, Tee made his way up the ladder from the control room, conducting his usual pre-watch tour. Hubley was still finishing his dinner in the wardroom, so Tee toured by himself this evening. Glancing around the control room, he caught sight of the petty officer manning the SD radar screen.

"Anderson, what the hell do you think you're doing?" Tee barked, placing his large hands on his hips.

"What do you mean, Mr. Turner?" Anderson knew exactly what Tee meant. He just did not want to give in so easily. He had come to expect Mr. Turner to chew him out at the end of every watch. Every man in O'Connell's watch section had come to expect it. Turner would always accuse them of making a mess out of the spaces. He would carry on about how filthy everything was then refuse to relieve the watch unless everything was cleaned and ready for inspection. Personally, Anderson thought Mr. Turner was slightly insane, not to mention a complete ass.

"Don't give me any of your lip," Tee snapped. "There's a coffee stain on the deck under the chart desk."

"I don't know how it got there, sir."

"I don't care how it got there, either. Just clean it up. I'm not going to take the watch with this conning tower looking like shit."

"I'm manning the radar, sir."

"I don't give a shit. D'you want *my* guys to have to clean up *your* mess, *Petty Officer* Anderson?"

Anderson finally capitulated, as he always did. He hated Mr. Turner, but he had learned not to argue with him. He knew that Turner would just shout until he got his own way. Anderson also did not want to gyp Mr. O'Connell or Mr. Wright out of getting relieved on time. Some officers were not worth the loyalty, but in his mind O'Connell and Wright were. If he did not clean up the mess, Turner would relieve them late for sure. It had happened more than once before.

Grabbing a rag out of a nearby locker, Anderson crawled under the chart desk to clean up the brown stain. It only took him a few minutes to wipe away every last spot. He was away from his panel for mere moments. He was still cursing Turner under his breath when he got back to the radar panel and nonchalantly checked the display.

The wiggly green line of the cathode ray tube display showed a small spike. It had not been there before.

Anderson quickly adjusted the dial to check the range indicated by the spike. He gasped in horror when he read it and a cold chill ran straight from his scalp to his toes.

The spike had to be a contact. It was less than two thousand yards away from the ship, and rapidly closing.

Anderson swallowed hard and choked out a whispered, "Oh my God."

WRIGHT was about to poke his head down the hatch to see what was taking Tee and Hubley so long when he suddenly heard the bridge intercom squawk.

"Bridge, radar!" It was Anderson the radar operator's voice, very agitated. "Aircraft closing! Aircraft closing! Range one mile!"

O'Connell and Wright exchanged brief expressions of horror before O'Connell could grope for the intercom and the diving alarm.

"Crash dive!" O'Connell shouted into the mike. "Crash dive!"

"AAOOOGAAAHH! . . . AAOOOGAAAHH!" The diving alarm sounded and the lookouts sprang from their perches in a mad dash for the hatch. As O'Connell hastened the lookouts through the hatch, Wright desperately searched the sky for the approaching aircraft. The endless gray clouds hung low, making it impossible to see anything above a thousand feet.

The main ballast tank vents opened creating water spouts as the tanks quickly flooded to start *Mackerel*'s rapid descent. The water spouts shot fifty feet into the air, drenching everyone on the bridge. Wright grabbed the coaming to steady himself as the deck began to angle down.

The last lookout was almost down the hatch when Wright heard a noise like hail hitting a tin roof. He looked up in time to see a Japanese bomber, all guns blazing, emerge from the clouds off the port beam. He could see the sporadic stream of tracer rounds extending from the bomber's wings to hit *Mackerel*'s hull just below the waterline. Each shell hit with deck-shattering impacts. As the plane closed the range, Wright heard the staccato typewriter-like rhythm of the Japanese twenty-millimeter guns. He ducked behind the bridge coaming just in time to avoid the high velocity missiles slicing across *Mackerel*'s width, raking the conning tower and the bridge. The sharp impacts seemed to shake his very skin and he felt small bits of ricocheting metal brush past his face and arms. Within seconds, the plane had zoomed over them.

Wright touched his body in several places not quite believing that he had not been hurt. Then he glanced over to where O'Connell had been standing and gasped at the dreadful sight before his eyes. O'Connell's body lay crumpled on the deck, his chest profusely bleeding from two gaping holes. Blood covered the bridge railing behind him and ran along the deck. Blood was everywhere.

Wright stared at O'Connell in shock and disbelief. It was several moments before he suddenly realized that *Mackerel*'s lower decks were already awash and that she was headed down fast. He scurried over to O'Connell and attempted to pull him toward the still open hatch. O'Connell's limp body seemed like it weighed a thousand pounds. The only sign of life was a wheezing noise coming from his punctured lungs.

Shouts from inside the conning tower reached Wright: "For God's sakes, come on! Leave him, sir! Get down and shut the hatch!"

Wright found himself sobbing uncontrollably as he inched O'Connell toward the hatch. They were moving too slowly. He knew they would never make it down the hatch in time. Frothing water began to enter the bridge scuppers, swirling with O'Connell's blood.

Just then, a bloody hand reached up and grasped Wright's arm. "Get . . . below, damn you." O'Connell gurgled. Then he somehow managed a smile. "Ship . . . first . . . Ryan."

Tears streamed down Wright's face as he squeezed O'Connell's hand once more. Then he let go and jumped down the hatch, a torrent of seawater following after him. The water rushed into the conning tower, soaking men and equipment all the way down to the control room. Wright, standing on the ladder in the midst of the downpour, pulled the hatch lanyard with all his might, and, eventually, the hatch fell shut. The outside water pressure helped the hatch to seal. With Wright still clutching the lanyard, Cazanavette brushed up the ladder past him to spin the hatch wheel tight, locking out the sea.

Then, just as suddenly as it had begun, it was all over.
Everyone in the conning tower stood in stark silence as
Mackerel plunged beneath the waves.

"Eighty . . . ninety . . . one hundred feet. . . . " Only
Olander's voice chimed up through the control room hatch.

Drenched and heaving, Wright pressed his forehead
against the cold ladder rungs and released the soaked hatch
lanyard. His mind could not make sense of what had just
happened. One moment, he and O'Connell had been mer-
rily discussing the coming chili and macaroni dinner. The
next, he was leaving his friend to die on the bridge as the
ship submerged beneath him.

Wright heard a noise like a faucet running. To his left
he noticed a small hole, the size of a quarter, in the port
side of the conning tower with a stream of water shooting
through it. Two sailors, one with a wooden plug and the
other with a hammer, quickly plugged the small hole without saying a word.

Then Wright felt a hand on his shoulder. Strangely, it
startled him. He was completely on edge, even shaking. He
looked up into Tremain's eyes. The blue eyes appeared intense. More so than he had ever seen them before. They
were consoling, even understanding, but only for a moment. Then they reverted to their usual cold glaze.

"Right full rudder!" Tremain barked to the helmsman,
not taking his hand from Wright's shoulder.

"Passing one hundred fifty feet, Captain," Olander
called from the control room.

"Very well." Tremain looked at Wright again. "What
kind of a plane was it, Ryan?"

Wright was shocked. Are you mad? he thought. How
can you possibly care about the damn plane? We just lost
Rudy, for God's sake.

"Ryan?" Tremain's voice was compassionate but firm.

Wright's mind cleared enough for him to remember the target identification course at submarine school.

"Twin engine Zeke bomber, sir," he managed to say.

Tremain turned to Cazanavette. "Two bombs, at the most. We'll turn to ninety degrees off our base course and go to two hundred and fifty feet."

Cazanavette nodded.

Minutes later, Salisbury detected two splashes, followed soon after by two shallow explosions. Except for a small shudder, the bombs had little affect on *Mackerel,* cruising down below two hundred feet. The Japanese bomber had missed.

Tensions remained high as Salisbury, with his sonar headset on, heard the bomber fly over twice more, but no more bombs were dropped.

Tremain kept the boat deep for half an hour before returning to periscope depth in a hopeless attempt to find O'Connell. Everyone in the conning tower waited with dismal hopes as Tremain spun the periscope around again and again.

"No sign of Mr. O'Connell," Tremain said somberly.

"He was too badly shot up to be able to swim all this time, Captain," Wright managed to say.

Tremain gave the periscope to Hubley, and turned to face Wright. "What the hell happened, anyway?"

"I don't know, sir."

"Didn't you pick the bastard up on radar?"

"Yes, sir. That's when Rudy ordered the crash dive. It all just happened so fast." Wright tried to piece the images together in his mind.

Tremain turned to the radar station, where Anderson stood forlorn. Anderson was staring impassively at the bulkhead, oblivious to the conversation. Oblivious to the world around him.

"Anderson?" Tremain said.

Anderson did not hear him.

"Anderson!"

"Yes, sir?" Anderson suddenly realized that the captain was speaking to him, though he could barely recognize his own name.

"What range did you first detect the aircraft, Anderson?"

Anderson paused. He did not know what to say. He felt terrible. He felt as though he had personally shot Mr. O'Connell to death. What should he say? What could he say? That he abandoned his post and now a man was dead? That he was ordered to abandon his post?

He glanced at Mr. Turner, standing in the opposite corner. He looked to him for some inkling of guidance, but Turner avoided eye contact with him as if he too felt ashamed—but obviously did not have the courage to step forward and explain everything to the captain. Anderson realized he would get no help from Turner. He was on his own, and he made his choice.

"Sir, I didn't pick up that bomber until he was only two thousand yards away," he said finally. "We've been having all kinds of atmospheric interference all through the last watch, with the weather the way it is and all. I was lucky to even make him out at two thousand yards."

Tremain considered for a moment, then nodded: "The weather will do that to the SD radar. From now on we will have a double lookout in these weather conditions, since our radar cannot be relied upon."

Cazanavette nodded. "Aye, sir."

"We've lost one good man today," Tremain continued. "I know that everyone had a high opinion of Mr. O'Connell. May God bless his soul for his sacrifice. We were very fortunate that we didn't lose the ship. And we have you to thank for that, Anderson."

All eyes in the conning tower turned to look at Anderson,

and Tremain extended his hand with a grim smile. Anderson returned Tremain's handshake slightly confused. "Th . . . Thank? Wh . . . What for, sir?"

"For saving the ship, that's what for." Tremain patted him on the shoulder. "Your keen eye on the radar allowed us enough time to submerge before that son of a bitch could unload his bombs on us. This will, no doubt, call for a commendation when we return to port."

Anderson suddenly felt sick. His heart sank into his stomach. At that moment, he wanted to blurt it all out, to tell the captain everything. But he did not. He could not turn back now. He would receive a commendation for killing Mr. O'Connell, and there was nothing he could do about it.

"We'll hold a memorial service for Mr. O'Connell this evening, XO," Tremain continued. "He will be sorely missed by us all."

The men solemnly filed back to their stations. Expecting the Japanese pilot to radio his base and call for more aircraft, Tremain ordered that *Mackerel* stay submerged until after dark. When night fell on the remote Caroline Islands, the ship once again groped to the surface. Batteries were charged and she returned to her base course, headed for her hunting ground off Mogami Bank.

WRIGHT remained in a stupor the rest of the evening. After picking at his meal in the wardroom, then attending O'Connell's memorial service in the crew's mess, he did not feel much like sleeping. He walked into his stateroom and closed the curtain. George Olander snoozed on the top rack, oblivious to his presence. The middle and bottom racks were empty. The bottom rack was his. The middle rack had been O'Connell's.

Wright stared at the empty rack for a few minutes, then opened O'Connell's locker. Here were all the things that

Rudy O'Connell had used on a daily basis. The things still felt like him, still had his scent. His comb, his razor, his girlie magazines, the letter from his sweetheart back home, all sat in the locker like small pets waiting for their owner to return for them. But he would never return. They were all that remained of him. They were the only indication that Rudy O'Connell had ever shipped aboard USS *Mackerel*.

A small photograph of Rudy's parents and brothers adorned the inside of the locker door. They looked like pleasant people, and all of them were smiling on whatever occasion the picture was taken. It looked like they had all gone on some kind of picnic near a lake, which glimmered in the background.

Somewhere over thousands of miles of land and sea, Wright thought, these same smiling people were sitting down to supper. They would be talking about their day, sharing stories, saying a prayer for their son whose picture probably hung on full display over the mantel. They could not know that that same son and brother for whom they prayed was now gone. They could not know that the memories of Rudy that now filled their minds would have to last them for a lifetime. In several weeks they would receive a telegram, and there would be a woeful day in that happy home. A few weeks after that, they would receive the trinkets and personal effects that Wright now held and touched in his hands. And that would be all. An empty casket would be placed in the ground in the town cemetery, and the weeping Mrs. O'Connell would receive a flag. There would be no body to bury. No closure for them.

Wright thought of his own family. Would they ever see him again? Would they ever truly believe it in their hearts if the war department informed them that he was lost somewhere in the vast Pacific Ocean?

As he shut the locker and crawled into his rack, Wright found himself sobbing uncontrollably. He swore to himself that if he survived the war, he would go and see Rudy's family and tell them how brave and well-liked their son was. He would try whatever he could to provide them with some sense of closure. And perhaps he would find some, too.

Chapter 10

MOGAMI Bank was the northwesternmost part of the Caroline Island group and the closest to the Japanese island stronghold of Saipan in the Marianas chain. Japanese shipping coming from the Imperial homeland normally took an "island hopping" route to ferry badly needed supplies to the hundreds of remote garrisons across the Pacific. Com-SubPac could easily determine this route using a chart and simply connecting the "dots" across thousands of miles of ocean, from Japan to the Bonins to the Marianas to the Carolines and from there to the final destination whether it was in New Guinea, the Solomons, or the Gilberts. This arrangement made the area off Mogami Bank an ideal hunting ground for U.S. submarines since it was the most likely place a Japanese convoy coming from the homeland would enter the Caroline Islands. It was here that *Mackerel* now searched for more prey.

Tremain lounged on his bunk picking the remains of his supper from his teeth as he studied the chart across his lap.

The supper was okay, but not very exciting. The soup had been a bit thin and devoid of vegetables but the meat loaf had been decent. The meals were starting to show signs of the limited provisions on board as was typical after so many weeks at sea.

After the bomber attack it had taken *Mackerel* another whole day to reach the Mogami Bank area. Damage had been light, considering what might have happened. No major equipment had been affected, but several of the bomber's twenty-millimeter shells had punctured the pressure hull and one of the main ballast tanks in eleven places.

The ballast tank was of little consequence. It leaked air slowly, but as long as they conducted periodic high-pressure blows the boat's stability would not be affected. Of greater concern were the holes in the pressure hull: one in the conning tower and the other in the radio room. Tremain was thankful that no one had been injured or killed by either round, but the two small holes would become thorns in his side if he needed to take *Mackerel* deep again. As a temporary fix Tremain had ordered that the holes be shored up with wood planks and wedges, but they still leaked slightly. There could be no guarantee that the makeshift repairs would hold at test depth, or during a depth charging.

The question now remained, Tremain thought: Should he do the safe thing and return to Pearl Harbor? Or should he take his chances and stay on station?

Tremain tossed the chart on his bunk and moved over to his desk, where the letter to Rudy O'Connell's parents lay unfinished. He had wanted to write the thing while O'Connell's image was still fresh in his mind. He knew how quickly a face could fade into the vast recesses of the mind to dwell with all those other lost friends and shipmates. Soon O'Connell's face, like the faces of the men on the *Seatrout,* would live there and come out to haunt him in the sleepless nights.

"Captain?" Cazanavette poked his head though the curtain. "Do you have a minute, sir?"

"Come in and have a seat, XO. What's on your mind?" Tremain normally tried to avoid one-on-one conversations with Cazanavette, but this time he welcomed a break from his dreaded task.

Cazanavette seated himself on the bunk. The torpedo issue had not been discussed between them for several weeks and despite that fact they had managed to keep their relationship professional and cordial throughout the patrol. Tremain had been grateful to Cazanavette for that at least; for not allowing their personal differences to jeopardize the success of the mission. It spoke well for his sense of priorities. After the past weeks Tremain even considered him to be a good executive officer in almost every sense of the word. He had never shown his contempt for Tremain in front of the crew. He supported him when things got rough, and their few heated arguments had taken place in private. Tremain appreciated all of those qualities, but he still had a feeling that Cazanavette was out to get him, watching and waiting for that one time he would slip up, looking for anything that he could add to his report to the admirals back in Pearl.

"Sir, I've overheard some conversations among some of the crew and I thought I should inform you about it." Cazanavette's expression was not confrontational but very serious. He was obviously being sincere. "I think that plane attack and Rudy's death has shaken them up a bit."

"I would expect it to, XO. That's normal."

"Yes, sir, I know, but it's worse than I had expected. They're starting to grumble again. They're talking about hard luck again and even something about there being a curse on this ship. To put it plainly, Captain, the men are skittish. And they're looking for someone to blame. I've even heard them mention your name a few times, comparing you to Captain Russo."

"Oh?"

"The fact that we have not attacked a ship in two weeks hasn't helped any. They had some revived confidence after the freighter, but if they continue like this, that will all be for nothing. I think they're getting to the point where they think that the freighter sinking was just blind luck."

Tremain was struck more by the fact that Cazanavette was sharing these things with him than he was by the news. There was a new tone in Cazanavette's voice.

"Why're you telling me this, XO? I thought you'd want to see me fail." As soon as the words left his mouth, Tremain wished he had not said this. Cazanavette was being professional with him, and he had let a glimpse of his personal emotion show through.

Cazanavette's eyes narrowed. "Sir?"

"Nothing, XO. Forget I said it."

Cazanavette paused. "Sir, I should tell you that I maintain my position on the torpedo exploders. I still think that what you did was wrong. Yes, we did sink the freighter, that's true. But whether the modifications had anything to do with it's another question."

Tremain started to respond, but Cazanavette uncharacteristically cut him short.

"However, Captain, I want you to know that your perception of me is totally wrong. I'm not waiting for you to 'fail', as you say. I'm not that shallow, sir. If you succeed, that means this crew succeeds, and I want that more than anything else." Cazanavette paused. "You might not know it, sir, because this is your first trip with us, but there was something different about this boat and this crew during our last attack. All of the *Mackerel* veterans noticed it. In my personal opinion, I think the difference was you, sir. And if you ask me, sir, it was your leadership that sank that freighter and got us out of there alive, not the torpedo modifications. There was a drastic change in our crew after we sank that ship. You showed them what they could do. And the only reason I'm saying these things is because I care about the officers and crew of this boat, and I don't want them to lose the confidence they have regained in themselves."

Tremain was taken aback. He had been completely wrong about Cazanavette. About his motivations, about his reasoning, about everything. Cazanavette had bared his soul to him and there was no ill-will in it. It was a very rare occasion in the navy for a subordinate officer to compliment another officer on his abilities as a leader. It seldom happened, because fellow officers always viewed each other as competition, and it was usually seen as a sign of weakness.

"I guess that's what I came here to say," Cazanavette continued. "The crew needs your leadership, Captain. And I don't want you to believe it if you hear the crew comparing you to Captain Russo. There's a marked difference between you and Sammy Russo, sir. Russo was not a born submarine skipper—you are. And with you as our captain, I know this boat can do the job. We just need another chance to prove it. I just wanted to make sure you knew how I felt before you made your decision."

"Decision? About what?"

"About whether to go back to Pearl, sir."

Tremain smiled. A sure sign of a good executive officer was that he always knew what his captain was thinking.

"I'm actually considering that very thing at this moment, XO," Tremain said, then added awkwardly, "And, thanks for the kind words. They help sometimes."

Cazanavette nodded and smiled.

His XO was not a careerist after all, Tremain thought. He saw now that they were more alike than he had ever realized. Both of them wanted the *Mackerel* to succeed. Both of them wanted to accomplish the mission. Both of them wanted to restore the crew's confidence in themselves. They wanted the same things. He could not see it before because their methods were so different. Now, finally, on this issue they were in complete agreement.

"All right, XO." Tremain grinned. "I agree. We'll stay on station until the bastards send us another target."

Cazanavette smiled in approval, then left the stateroom without another word. Tremain decided at that moment that he completely trusted Cazanavette to do whatever was in the best interests of the ship and her crew.

Tremain sighed, then poured himself another cup of coffee and settled down to finish the letter to Rudy O'Connell's family.

Chapter 11

"TWO ... three ... four ... five contacts at least, Captain. Some are big ones."

As the men brushed past him to their battle stations, Tremain looked over the SJ radar operator's shoulder to see the green incandescent spikes appear on the display. He had to squint to help his eyes adjust from the red light in the conning tower to the green light of the display. The display showed several radar returns indicating that a Japanese convoy was out there in the darkness, northwest of *Mackerel*'s position.

"Heading southeasterly, sir," the radar operator continued. "I'd say about ten knots."

Tremain and Cazanavette exchanged glances. *Mackerel* had been patrolling Mogami Bank for four days now, and they both knew that fuel constraints would soon force them to head back to Pearl Harbor. No ships had been sighted and they had begun to doubt ComSubPac's decision to send them here. The discovery of this new convoy eliminated all doubts.

"What do you think, XO?"

"It looks like a gold mine, Captain. Judging from those returns I'd say we're looking at three heavies and two mediums. There're bound to be escorts, but conditions are in our favor, it being a moonless night and all. It's so dark out there I doubt they could even see us if we were right alongside them. I just hope they don't have radar."

"Concur." Tremain nodded as he pulled on his bridge coat. "We'll go in on the surface. Take over down here and get me set up to approach the convoy from astern. I want to try to penetrate the formation and do our shooting from the inside. That'll confuse the escorts."

"Aye, sir." Cazanavette began setting up the chart desk to plot the convoy's bearing and range information that would be coming from the radar.

Tremain began climbing the bridge ladder. Halfway up, he paused and called back down to Cazanavette, "Remember, XO, you're my eyes. I can't see a damn thing up there." Then he continued on up the darkened bridge hatch.

When he emerged onto the bridge, Tremain found that the night was even darker than he had expected. He could not see his hand in front of his face. Normally, the red light down inside the conning tower would not be visible at the bridge hatch, but on this night the open hatch glowed dull-red. It was the sole source of light above deck, and thus it shone like a beacon. Tremain quickly covered the hatch with the nearby blackout curtain lest the Japanese see it too.

He allowed several minutes for his eyes to adjust then made his way over to Hubley, who was looking through the TBT on the starboard side. Hubley was looking into black nothingness, attempting to catch a glimpse of something from the far-off Japanese vessels: an open hatch, a flashlight, a cigarette, anything that would give indication of their whereabouts.

Tremain took the conn and drove *Mackerel* entirely on Cazanavette's recommendations. For the next half hour under the SJ radar operator's and Cazanavette's guidance, *Mackerel* sped up to flank speed and slipped around behind the Japanese convoy, the whole time keeping a safe five thousand yards of separation. Cazanavette fine-tuned *Mackerel*'s course until it precisely matched that of the convoy, then he increased *Mackerel*'s speed and she slowly crept up on the convoy from astern. Soon she was so close that Tremain could see the white water from the Japanese wakes breaking over *Mackerel*'s bows.

"What's the picture now, XO?" Tremain spoke into the intercom. "I still can't see the convoy."

"Captain, I've been able to plot the convoy fairly well based on our radar observations," Cazanavette's voice squawked on the speaker. "We're looking at three columns abreast, each column containing three ships. Looks like the heavies are out front, with medium-sized and small ships bringing up the rear. Convoy course has been steady at one three zero, speed has been constant as well at twelve knots. The Japanese don't seem to be zigging, probably because of the visibility conditions. We're lined up five hundred yards aft of the middle column right now, sir."

They think they're safe in this darkness, Tremain thought, so they're trying to make a run for it. They're trying to get into port tonight. They still haven't learned the lesson about the capabilities of American radar.

"Any sign of escorts?" Tremain said.

"Not yet, sir, but if they're patrolling off the convoy's bows we won't be able to detect them. The heavies are hiding that whole area from our radar with their large cross-sections."

"Right, XO. Bring us up between the port and middle

columns. I want to know when we are well inside the heart of the convoy."

Cazanavette came back a few seconds later with some course and speed recommendations and *Mackerel* came to the left and sped up to enter the Japanese formation.

Although Tremain knew their chances were good that the Japanese ships were not equipped with radar, seeing their wakes slapping against his own ship still made him uneasy. There was always a chance that the enemy could get lucky, such as if some alert lookout sighted them in the blackness. Most of the merchant vessels carried guns large enough to sink a ship the size of the *Mackerel*. Tremain took comfort only in the fact that the Japanese lookouts would be directing their searches toward the convoy's beams and not toward the inside of the convoy.

"There, sir," Hubley said suddenly, pointing off the starboard beam.

Tremain looked to see a dark shape, plowing up the sea right next to them. The ship was running parallel to *Mackerel* and was close enough that he could hit it with a small caliber pistol. A few minutes more and he noticed another one on the port side. The ships appeared to be roughly the size of freighters, although it was still hard to tell, even at this close range.

"XO," he keyed the intercom. "We see two ships. One off the starboard beam, the other off the port beam."

After a brief pause, Cazanavette's voice replied, "That checks with the radar, sir. Those are the trailing ships in the middle and port columns. The next ships should be visible right about now."

On cue, Tremain saw two more dark shapes appear off both bows. He suddenly felt more aware of their situation and it made his scalp crawl. He imagined how much more horrifying it would be if somehow it were suddenly bright as day. He nervously chuckled to himself at the thought.

He would be standing on the bridge of a tiny-surfaced American submarine completely surrounded by Japanese ships, some of them less than three hundred yards away.

He quickly shook the thoughts from his mind. He had to keep a clear head.

Tremain keyed the intercom again. "XO, I think we've about pushed our luck as far as it'll go. Open the outer doors on all tubes. Obtain a firing solution on the first two ships in the port column and lock them into the TDC. Let me know when you're ready."

Minutes later came the response, "Outer doors open on all tubes, Captain. We're set up now on the lead ship in the port column. Range, five hundred yards off the port bow."

Tremain paused. Once the shooting started there would be no going back. Their presence would be known and it would be an all-out slugging match between *Mackerel* and the convoy. It would be a fight for survival.

"Fire one . . . fire two," Tremain said into the intercom, before he could think about it too much longer.

The deck shuddered as the torpedoes left their tubes and sped off toward the first target.

"Shift to the second ship in the port column," Tremain ordered. "Fire three . . . fire four."

The vibrations in the deck were followed by Cazanavette's voice. "Tubes one through four have been fired, sir."

"Very well. Set up on the lead ship in the middle column. Stand by tubes five and six."

Tremain had just finished speaking when the night erupted off *Mackerel*'s port bow. Two massive explosions shot flame and debris hundreds of feet into the night sky. The first torpedoes had hit their mark. Tremain and Hubley quickly ducked behind the bridge coaming to avoid the tremendous heat and the shower of debris. Tremain ordered the lookouts down from their perches so that they could do the same.

Then two more explosions came, this time even closer and off the port beam. Torpedoes three and four had hit their target, too. *Mackerel* rocked to starboard as the shockwave hit and then rolled back slowly to an even keel.

Tremain peered over the coaming to see the entire area bathed in the orange light of several thousand gallons of burning oil. The oily slick rapidly became a fiery moat completely surrounding and engulfing the first ship in flame. Moments before, the proud ship had been a tanker for His Imperial Majesty. Now it was nothing but a useless burning hulk. Tremain could easily discern where *Mackerel*'s torpedoes had hit. They had obviously hit her up forward because the ship no longer had a bow. It had been completely blown off, leaving a gaping hole, which rapidly gulped up seawater. Like the sea around it, the remnants of the ship still on the surface were on fire and rapidly settling.

Tremain then turned to check the spot where the second ship had been, but there was nothing there, nothing but burning flotsam. Either the ship had been atomized by *Mackerel*'s third and fourth torpedoes, or else it had sunk within seconds.

The scene was mesmerizing, the heat tremendous. Tremain had to pull his eyes away from the scenes of carnage to keep going. The area was now bathed in the orange light of the fires allowing him to see plainly that the other ships in the convoy were beginning to scatter. They desperately turned to port and starboard in cumbersome maneuvers to avoid their unseen assailant and to prevent colliding with one another. Tremain assumed that none of the enemy ships had seen the *Mackerel* yet, or at least they had not yet fired on her.

In the sporadic light, Tremain noticed the lead ship in

the middle column, a large transport, make a sharp left turn five hundred yards off *Mackerel*'s starboard bow. In conducting the blind evasive maneuver, the transport's captain had inadvertently placed his ship directly in front of *Mackerel*'s bows, lining up his slow-moving vessel for a perfect torpedo shot.

"Set gyro angle at zero on torpedoes five and six," Tremain hurriedly spoke into the intercom.

"Set," Cazanavette answered on the intercom.

"Fire five . . . fire six."

The torpedoes sped from their tubes. Tremain watched as their frothing twin wakes, glimmering in the firelight, traced a direct path to the transport's exposed port beam. Seconds later two ear-shattering blasts lifted the transport's midsection out of the water along with two distinct columns of water that shot high into the night sky. The ship then came back down into the water and bent inward with a sharp splintering crack. It was the sound of the transport's keel breaking in two, and it began to fall apart. The stern and fore sections quickly drifted away from each other. Both sections, including the sea around them, were covered with flailing soldiers and sailors, some gasping for air, some on fire. The transport had been full of troops and most likely destined for the Solomon Islands.

Tremain felt bile in his throat as he forced himself to turn away from the gruesome spectacle. Although he kept compassion for the enemy to a minimum, especially when he thought of his lost crew on the *Seatrout,* he still felt a surge of pain in his heart knowing that these hundreds of men would be left to the mercy of the sea and flame. The other ships in the convoy would not stop to rescue them for fear of being sunk themselves.

"Sir!" Hubley exclaimed, pointing astern.

Tremain turned to see the knifing bow of a freighter

plodding the ocean behind them. The ship was so close he had to angle his neck to look at its super structure. Tremain could not imagine how it had gotten so close, and it was heading directly for *Mackerel*'s stern.

"Hard right rudder!" Tremain shouted into the microphone. "All ahead flank!"

Mackerel's turn felt slower than any Tremain had ever remembered. The feeling was almost certainly brought on by the fact that a four-thousand-ton ship was bearing down on them. The order had come not a moment too soon. *Mackerel* turned just in time to miss the ominous bow of the freighter as it passed by. The submarine then steadied up on course as the cargo-laden vessel drove past her stern.

Several minutes passed before Tremain realized that the freighter had not sighted them. It simply continued to drive on heading northeast at top speed, straight through the burning oil and flotsam of the evaporated freighter. The freighter's sloping deck must have hidden *Mackerel* from the merchant's lookouts when she was close abeam.

Tremain then maneuvered his ship to line up for a stern tube shot on the escaping freighter. He was about to unleash the stern torpedoes when he noticed a dark shape drive into the firelight just beyond the freighter's stern. He had not expected a ship to be there. The newcomer's bow parted the blackened sea before it with ease and must have been traveling at close to twenty-five knots. The squatty hull was unmistakable to Tremain, even in the poor firelight. It was a *Fubuki* Class destroyer, a submarine killer, less than a thousand yards away and heading straight for the *Mackerel*.

"Mother of . . . " Hubley never finished. The *Fubuki*'s foremost five-inch gun erupted in a cloud of smoke and seconds later the shell screamed over their heads and smashed into the waves off *Mackerel*'s starboard bow, throwing up a column of water that doused the bridge.

Tremain wiped the salt mist from his eyes and turned the TBT toward the oncoming destroyer. Diving was not an option. They could not dive fast enough. The destroyer would be on them in minutes. They had only one chance.

"Mark this bearing and standby tubes seven through ten!" Tremain yelled into the microphone. "Set depth at six feet! One degree spread!"

Another shot from the destroyer's foreward gun mount drowned out Cazanavette's response. Tremain and the men on the bridge ducked under the coaming and held on as the ship lurched from the concussion. Again they were doused with spray. The shell had split the air over their heads and then exploded just a few yards in front of the *Mackerel*'s bow.

Tremain fought the urge to stay down behind the protective bridge coaming and swung the TBT around to mark the bearing to the destroyer once more. The bearing had not changed.

That was good, Tremain thought. It was a lot easier to hit a target that wasn't moving from side to side. But the destroyer was driving straight for them and closing fast. What was taking Cazanavette so long?

Just then the XO's agitated voice squawked on the intercom, "Torpedoes ready, Captain!"

"Fire all four!" Tremain shouted.

The deck shook as all four aft tubes ejected their loads. Tremain watched as the four bubbling wakes instantly appeared on the surface and reached out toward the oncoming destroyer. He winced but did not duck, as the *Fubuki* fired again, this time hitting the water just aft of *Mackerel*.

That's it, Tremain thought. The destroyer's gunner had straddled them. The gunner needed only to make a minor range correction and the next shot would hit. The same realization came to Hubley and the lookouts, as they instinctively ducked behind the bridge coaming. Tremain stood tall, dreading the destroyer's next shot, but staring entranced at the charging enemy only five hundred yards away.

Then, right before Tremain's eyes, the destroyer's bow forward of the gun turret blew off in a massive sparkling explosion. One of *Mackerel*'s torpedoes had run true. Tremain ducked away from the shockwave as another blast echoed across the night. Another five-hundred-pound torpedo warhead had done its job. Tremain closed his eyes and rested his head against the coaming, out of breath from the whole ordeal. There were no more explosions, but no more would be necessary.

Loud gurgling and hissing sounds filled the air, causing Tremain to allow himself a peak over the railing at the resulting devastation. Before the torpedoes had hit, the *Fubuki* had worked itself up to a speed of close to thirty knots, and now, with no bow, that same momentum drove the destroyer straight beneath the waves. Like a sea creature, the doomed ship's stern raised high in the air and quickly plunged downward, its exposed screws still turning in vain. Within moments, the destroyer had disappeared, leaving only a fury of frothing eddies and whirlpools to mark its existence.

Hubley and the lookouts gave a jubilant "hoorah!" and passed the word down to the conning tower. Similar cheers came from below.

That's for Rudy O'Connell, Tremain thought.

Tremain quickly ordered *Mackerel* to the south at flank speed, away from the light of the burning tanker. Once at a safe distance he ordered all compartments to check for damage and conferred with Cazanavette to assess the situation.

The remains of the convoy had scattered at top speed in all directions and were quickly heading out of radar range.

No more escort vessels had been sighted, either visually or by radar. Tremain assumed that if there were any, they had left with the single remaining large ship, which had evaded to the east. Tremain decided to pursue one of the slower freighters trying to escape just south of *Mackerel*. With it being the only radar return in that direction, Tremain could be sure that there were no more escorts with it.

Tremain ordered the tubes reloaded and, once again, used Cazanavette on the radar to close within one thousand yards of the freighter.

With a good beam shot set-up, *Mackerel* fired two torpedoes. They waited, but there were no detonations. Tremain quickly recalled that they had not modified those torpedoes, and that they had no more modified weapons ready. The faulty exploder had reared its ugly head again.

Tremain ordered two more fired, hoping for some luck. This time one exploded halfway between the *Mackerel* and the freighter, knocking the bridge personnel down and alerting the freighter to their presence.

Frustrated and cursing, Tremain ordered *Mackerel* to come about and fired all four aft tubes at the fleeing freighter. One torpedo found its mark, slowing the freighter's escape to a crawl. Tremain then refused to fire any more faulty torpedoes and ordered the deck hatch opened to exercise *Mackerel*'s deck gun crew, which promptly sank the stricken ship with two dozen five-inch shells.

When battle stations were finally secured in the early morning hours of the next day, the frustrations felt by Tremain because of the faulty torpedoes did not seem to affect the attitude of the crew. They all appeared to be happy and proud of their little ship. Tremain even overheard a few of them referring to her as the Mighty Mack.

Tremain picked up on the expression and used it the next day when he and Cazanavette penned the patrol report to ComSubPac:

28 March 1943

From: USS Mackerel (SS-244)
To: Commander Submarines Pacific Fleet

Subject: Patrol Summary

The Mighty Mack sank one tanker, one large
transport, three freighters, and one
destroyer. One officer killed in action,
Rudell J. O'Connell, Ltjg USN (102691).
Light damage. Have expended all but two
torpedoes. At fuel limit. Returning to
Pearl Harbor.

Signed

Robert J. Tremain, LtCdr USN
Commanding Officer

PART II

Chapter 12

"**YOU** did a bang up job out there, Jack. I must say, a fine job indeed." Captain Steven Ireland smiled like a politician as he handed Tremain a cup of steaming coffee.

"Thank you, sir," Tremain said, taking the cup and relaxing on the chair in front of Ireland's desk. "But we got pretty lucky. And we did lose a fine officer."

Ireland paused as his face drew grave for a brief moment. "Yes, that." Moments later the solemnity was gone and his face beamed as before, as if he could not afford any more sympathy for the moment.

"I can't tell you how pleased everyone is at your performance, Jack. But then you know how pleased Admiral Nimitz is." Ireland pointed to the Navy Cross clipped on Tremain's left breast pocket. "Congratulations on your second."

Tremain allowed a small smile as he patted the cross emblem affixed with a blue and white ribbon. His khaki shirt was devoid of any other emblems and made the medal look out of place. Medals were not normally worn with the working khaki uniform, but Tremain had no choice. He had received the medal not more than an hour ago, and quite unexpectedly, as he stepped off the *Mackerel* for the first time after arriving at Pearl Harbor. It had been quite a spectacle. There had been a navy band with all the ruffles and flourishes and even a large crowd to cheer the *Mackerel* sailors as they tied their weary boat to the pier. To Tremain's surprise, the commander-in-chief of the Pacific Theater, Admiral Chester Nimitz, presented the medal personally. Admiral Lockwood had been there as well, along with all the other submarine brass, including Ireland.

It's all quite insane, Tremain thought, as he felt the medal between his fingers. You lose a man and practically get your boat blown out of the water by a destroyer, and what do they do? They give you a medal.

They would be taking away the medal just as quick, too, if Cazanavette had not decided to withdraw his report about the torpedo modifications. Tremain remembered that day during the trip back. Cazanavette had come to his stateroom. "I never thought I would say these words, Captain, but I have to put this ship and crew ahead of my own personal integrity," he had said. "I've decided not to inform SubPac. If those exploders don't work, I say let's disable them all." The torpedo failures during the convoy attack had changed the XO's mind. When he had told Tremain, he appeared to be suffering from a deep inner turmoil, and Tremain had tried to assure him that in war a leader must make tough decisions.

Tremain felt for Cazanavette, mainly because he himself had been there before. Cazanavette was on the fringe, young enough to still have faith in the "system" but old enough to see the cracks in it. Cazanavette was gloomy the whole trip back, but he seemed to cheer up a little when Admiral Nimitz pinned a Bronze Star to his chest.

Tremain studied Irelend as he sipped the coffee.

I wonder if old Ireland still has faith in the system, he thought.

"You smell like you've been at sea for seven weeks, Jack." Ireland grimaced jokingly, then saw that Tremain was not in the mood. He quickly returned to the subject Tremain obviously wanted to talk about. "About your lost officer, Jack. . . . "

"Lieutenant Rudy O'Connell, sir."

"Right," Ireland said, as if he had already forgotten the dead man's name. "We've sent along a notification to his people and I'm sure you would like to include something with the shipment of his personal effects."

Tremain drew a sealed envelope out of his pocket.

"Here it is, sir," he said gloomily. It had taken several agonizing nights at sea for him to write the letter, to make it say the right things in the right way.

Ireland took the envelope and stared at it for several seconds. "I always hated writing these things. The worst part of the job."

"But perhaps the most important, sir."

"Yes, of course."

Ireland and Tremain sat in awkward silence for a few moments. Tremain wondered if he should even bring up the subject of his transfer. Then he thought to himself, I've got a Navy Cross on my chest, why the hell not?

"Sir, about my orders."

"Oh, yes. Everything's been arranged, Jack. You've done what we asked you to do here and we're not going to let you down. I've got orders to Submarine Base, New London waiting for you in the yeoman's office. Unfortunately, there are no new boats available right now, but you'll be put in an instructor status at sub school until one is."

Tremain's lower jaw dropped open in disbelief. He did not think it was going to be this easy.

Orders, he thought. He had orders to sub school, that wretched, beautiful little place. And a cushy instructor job. Sure, it wasn't a new boat, but that would come eventually. They were building boats by the dozen back there. And Judy. He would finally be with Judy. They could spend the summer together, picnicking every Saturday on the green lawns by the Thames River. Evenings in New York and Boston. They would have time to catch up on some of those lost years. Judy would be thrilled to hear the news.

Then a thought crossed Tremain's mind. He glanced over at Ireland, who had turned his back to him and was looking out the window at the harbor.

"What about the *Mackerel,* sir?" Tremain asked.

"She's getting a new captain, Dave Stillsen." Ireland still stared out the window but he had obviously been anticipating the question. "You know him?"

"No, sir. Never heard of him before."

"Well, that's no big surprise," Ireland said, turning and walking over to his desk. "He just transferred over from the Atlantic theater."

"Atlantic?"

"Yes, Jack. Does that surprise you? He did his prospective commanding officer tour on *Blackfish* out of Norfolk."

"Norfolk?" Tremain exclaimed. "Sir, pardon my asking, but what the hell does an East Coast sailor know about submarining?"

Ireland chuckled. "Well, Jack, he scored high on all his exams at PCO School."

"PCO School?"

Ireland was acting strangely, Tremain thought. Stranger than usual. What was he up to?

"Anyway," Ireland continued, "it's no concern of yours. You've done your job, and now you deserve a good break with that wife of yours. We've even got you hooked up with a flight back to the States. You'll be leaving next week. Hell, I'm rather envious of you, Jack. It'll be all fancy uniforms and fine meals for you. You're going to be a regular hero back at sub school."

Tremain felt uneasy. Something was not right. Ireland had never acted like this before. The old duffer was being too nice. Something *was* going on, Tremain realized, but he just could not decipher exactly what it was. Yet he would not bet his bottom dollar that the old man was playing straight with him, nice as he appeared to be. The suspicion niggled at the back of his mind that the old manipulator was teeing him up for another real whack in the head.

But before Tremain could think any further along these lines Ireland ushered him toward the door. "If you'll excuse me, Jack. I've got a meeting this afternoon. We'll have lunch before you fly out. Welcome back and congratulations again."

Tremain shook Ireland's hand as he led him out the door. Why was Ireland being so polite? What was going on? Everything was happening too fast. He needed time to think. He was battle-weary but not completely brain-damaged. His instincts kept hinting to him that the old man was up to his usual games again, using schoolboy psychology on him, setting him up for something different from what had just been presented. But before Tremain could say anything, he had his hat in his hand and was standing outside Ireland's closed door, convincing himself with real conviction that the old codger was on the level this time and that Judy would be in his arms within a week.

WRIGHT adjusted his sunglasses as he turned the corner at the enlisted men's barracks and sped down the narrow street. Checking his appearance in the rear view mirror, he screeched the 1939 Ford convertible into the Naval Hospital parking lot, drawing attention from several pedestrians. Wright simply smiled and waved. He felt alive again behind the wheel. The car belonged to Carl and Barbara Hubley. The couple was renting a small beach house on the east side of Oahu for the weekend and did not intend to be seen by anyone, so they had been more than willing to lend the car to Wright.

Wright could not believe that he was back in the land of the living. The sights, smells, and sounds of the beautiful island overloaded his diesel-saturated senses. When *Mackerel* pulled in that morning, Tremain had been gracious enough to let most of the crew check into the Royal Hawaiian Hotel in downtown Honolulu. Wright had rushed over there with Joe Salisbury and George Olander to secure himself a room, leaving Tee stuck on board with the duty.

Strangely, Tee had not complained much about it, and Wright had noticed a distinct difference in Tee in the last few weeks. In fact, Tee had been much better toward Wright, and toward everyone else for that matter, on the journey home. The man was not quite amiable yet, but better, and noticeably so. Wright assumed that either Cazanavette or Tremain had finally put him in his place and had given Tee the dreaded "heart to heart" feared by all junior officers. Whatever the reason, Wright was thankful for it.

Now, Wright had his whole day planned out. He was going to go to the beach with Joe Salisbury and lie on the powdery sand, and drink cold beer, and get sunburned, and watch the beautiful dark-skinned girls walk by. Then he and Joe were going to try to pick up on a few of those dark-skinned girls and hopefully coax them to their rooms at the Royal Hawaiian to take care of some long-awaited yearnings.

That was the plan. But first, Wright had to take care of a small task given him by the XO. Since O'Connell had been in charge of the electrical division, the division was without an officer. As a temporary solution, Cazanavette had ordered Wright to assume the duties until a replacement could be found. As *Mackerel* was tying up to the pier this morning, one of the electricians had suffered a minor shock while hooking up shore power cables and was admitted to the base hospital. As the unofficial electrical officer it was Wright's duty to look after the men in his division, as Cazanavette had pointed out to him just before he had left on liberty. Checking up on hospitalized men fell under the purview of the division officer, even if he was officially on liberty after two months at sea.

Wright planned to make this stop as quick as possible.

"Can I help you, sir?" asked the female attendant at the main desk in the bleak hospital lobby.

"I'm here to see Petty Officer Henry Berganski," Wright answered, looking past her eagerly as if he could catch a glimpse of the sailor somewhere in the hallways beyond.

After filing through a few pages of the register, the attendant said, "He's been admitted to the D wing, sir, third floor. Just take the steps at the end of the hall to the third deck and check in with the head nurse on that floor. Mr. Berganski is in room three twenty-six."

"Three twenty-six, got it," Wright said as he walked briskly down the passage to the stairwell, his waiting liberty the only thing on his mind.

This should only take a few minutes, he thought as he ran up the stairs, skipping every other one. This will be just a quick in-and-out visit. Was Joe already on the beach? Did he already have a girl lined up for tonight? That girl at the desk was kind of cute. I wonder what her plans are tonight. Wright came to the third-floor nurse's station and found no one there. The nurses were obviously busy elsewhere. He glanced at his watch and waited for approximately two seconds before proceeding past the desk and looking for

Berganski's room himself. He found it around the first corner and walked in to find Berganski in hospital pajamas sitting on the edge of one of the four beds in the room. He and his roommates were playing cards around a small table on wheels.

"Hey, Mr. Wright!" he called with a big grin.

"Hi, Berganski. How're you feeling? You winning?"

"Of course, sir. Hey, fellas, this is the guy I was telling you about. This is the young ensign that saved our boat when we got depth charged last time out."

Wright shook hands with the other men. Berganski went on to tell the whole story. From the looks on his roommates' faces, it was the third or fourth time he had told it.

"Sir," one of the men said, smiling. "Can you take this guy back to your boat, please? If I hear that damn story one more time I'm gonna jump out that window over there. We had a nice quiet room before he came."

Wright laughed out loud. He noticed the others start to laugh too, but then they looked past him at the doorway and abruptly hid their cards. Like guilty school children they returned to their beds without another word.

"What the hell are you doing in here?" a woman's voice came from behind him.

Wright turned to see Margie Forester's wrathful face glaring at him from the open doorway. Distracted with thoughts of the beach and liberty, it had never occurred to him that she might be the head nurse on this floor.

"Obviously you didn't get the message last time, Mister Wright," she said. "I don't want to see you around here. I'm not going to let you absolve yourself of guilt by simply apologizing to me."

"Don't flatter yourself," Wright said. He had been at sea for two months putting up with Japanese depth charges and her browbeating fiancé and he was in no mood for her disdainful ridicule. "Did it ever occur to you that I'm not here to see you? I'm here to see Petty Officer Berganski. He's in my division."

Margaret's face softened for a mere millisecond. She noticed that the other men gawked at her, confounded by her outburst at Wright in front of them. In response, she quickly assumed a professional poise.

"All the same," she continued, in a more civil tone, pausing to clear her throat, "it is hospital procedure for all visitors to check in with the head nurse." Glancing at Berganski and then back to Wright, she added, "I'll let it go this time. You can continue with your visit."

Margie turned and left the room, leaving Wright to face the inquisitive expressions of the four men. He decided not to share the story behind Margie's hostility. Ever mindful of his waning liberty time, Wright asked Berganski if he needed anything, then left the men to their resumed card game.

Passing the nurse's station on the way out, Wright had neither intention nor desire to speak to Margie, seated at the desk and apparently absorbed in paperwork. Still, he was surprised when he heard her call his name as he reached the top of the stairs.

"Ryan." Her voice was civil and not hostile, as it had been before leaving the room.

Half wanting to ignore her, he turned to face her, almost despite himself.

"Yes, Margie."

"I heard what happened to Rudy," she said from her chair, her eyes peering at him over the top of the lamp on her desk. "I'm sorry he didn't make it."

"Me, too," he said somberly. He turned to go but she called after him again.

"I also heard what you did," she said. "About how you saved the ship. Berganski's been talking about it all morning."

She looked uncomfortable as she hid most of her face behind the lamp. The words did not seem to flow naturally and Wright got the impression she was forcing herself to say them with each breath.

"I blame you for my brother," she continued softly, "and it's extremely hard for me to say this to you, but I guess I just wanted to say thanks. Thanks for getting Tucker back safely. He means a lot to me."

Wright nodded. His eyes dropped to the floor and after two months of cursing her nightly in his prayers he did not know what to say to her. He thought about telling her that her fiancé was an asshole and the one man he wished had not made it back. He felt like telling her that she was a bitch and that she could go to hell too for all he cared. In his mind, Tee's volatile behavior was mostly her fault, a mere byproduct of her infantile accusation that he was somehow responsible for Troy's death. She had targeted him for abuse and Tee had been more than happy to oblige his fiancée.

Maybe it was Wright's obligation to his dead friend then that held his tongue and kept him from speaking what was on his mind.

He managed a weak smile.

"Anytime," he said, then turned and headed down the stairs to his waiting liberty.

Chapter 13

WRIGHT slouched into a chair at the wardroom table and propped his head onto one hand. He was completely exhausted. He lightly jingled the keys around his neck that he had just received from Tee, who was sitting across from him. As Tee rattled off everything that had happened during the previous day, reading from the duty officer's notebook, Wright checked the clock on the bulkhead. It read 0740. Just a few minutes more and he would assume the position of ship's duty officer. Then he would be responsible for all maintenance, repair, and upkeep activities on the ship for the next twenty-four hours. He was not feeling up to the task.

As Wright came on board that morning he noticed that *Mackerel* was already a beehive of activity. Repair crews from the shipyard and trucks full of spare parts appeared on the pier, seemingly out of nowhere, and began to assault the battle-weary submarine with rivet and welding guns. Wright had had to step over equipment and people and duck past dangling wires and makeshift ventilation ducts as he made his way below to the wardroom. He could hardly keep count of how many men he had seen on board, let alone know what they all were doing. Welders with their oversized faceguards blazed away, grimy mechanics disassembled the diesels into a thousand little pieces, and electricians buried themselves in open panels. The confined spaces forced the workers to brush elbows and stand back-to-back in some spaces, but they worked with a diligence and professionalism that indicated they had done this many times before. It was a complete hodgepodge of sweaty faces and blue uniforms. Wright had heard stories about Pearl Harbor's repair crews, the hard-working men who shared none of the glory but fought the war every day repairing the damage done by the sea and by the Japanese.

As Tee made his way through the list of items, Wright got a good idea of what was being repaired or upgraded today. It was too much information too fast, and he desperately tried to commit it all to memory. He was thankful that Tee had written it all in the duty officer's notebook, a green-colored, oil-stained notebook that now sat amid a scattering of plans and specifications on the table in front of him.

Wright struggled to keep his eyes open as Tee continued. He had a terrible headache.

The alcohol and sun from the day before was taking its toll on his aching body. He and Salisbury had gone to the beach and gotten drunk as they had planned, but they had found no women willing to satisfy their sex drives.

Chief Freund poked his head in the wardroom, ducking under an elephant trunk–like temporary ventilation duct, his hat cocked to one side. "Good morning, gentlemen. Which one of you was the duty officer yesterday?"

"I was," Tee said. "What do you need?"

"You didn't, by chance, see Petty Officer Anderson anywhere about yesterday, did you, sir?" Freund asked. "Did he come by the ship?"

"No. Not that I know of. Did you ask the sentry?"

"Yes, sir. He hasn't seen him either."

Wright was suddenly curious. "What's up, Chief? Is Anderson in trouble?"

"Hope not, sir." Freund shook his head. "None of the boys have seen him since we arrived in port. He missed check-in this morning, so unless I can find him he's now looking at an 'unexcused absence.' That just might get him in trouble."

Wright remembered Anderson. He was the radar operator in his watch-section during the patrol. He was the same man who noticed the Japanese plane in time for the ship to dive, back when Rudy was killed. As far as Wright knew, he always did his job and never caused a commotion. In fact, when *Mackerel* returned to port yesterday, Anderson received a commendation letter for his actions. He did not seem like the kind to go "UA."

"He's not in the brig, is he?" Wright asked.

"First place I checked, sir," Freund said. "He's not there or in any of the local jails either. He's just plumb disappeared. I've got some of the boys going around to the local brothels as a last resort, but it looks like I'm going to need to call the captain."

"I think you should give him another day or two to turn up, Cob," Tee said suddenly, in an unsteady tone.

"Since when did you give a rat's ass about a member of the crew, Mr. Turner?" Freund grinned. "You must be turning over a new leaf or something, sir."

Tee did not smile. He did not respond either. He simply went back to reviewing the notebook.

To Wright, he appeared jittery. He seemed uncharacteristically nervous about something.

"I'll give you a call if I see him today, Cob," Wright said.

"Thanks, Mr. Wright." Freund smiled. "You all have a good day now."

"You, too."

Freund left the wardroom and the two officers continued the turnover process. Wright was shocked at Tee's congeniality as they went through the checklist. He had expected Tee to be back to his usual behavior, especially after a few days in port. Normally, Tee would be condescending and brash. Instead, he read over the work items for the day with seeming sincerity. He said nothing intrusive, nothing confrontational, nothing rude. Maybe he had finally accepted Wright into the wardroom, after all.

"Okay, I relieve you," Wright said, after Tee had finished going through the list. "Have a good time on liberty," he added. He thought he might at least try to make some conversation.

"Huh?" Tee mumbled, not making eye contact with him. "Yeah, Wright, yeah. I'll see you around."

Tucking the notebook under his arm, Tee ducked out the door and was gone.

What's eating him? Wright thought. Something had to be troubling him.

Wright checked the clock. It was 0800. As if on cue, a half dozen supervisors from the shipyard filed into the wardroom bearing a ream of work orders that had to be reviewed and signed. An ear-splitting paint stripper revved up on the hull just outside and steadily emanated a white noise, which Wright and the others had to shout over in order to discuss the planned repairs and maintenance in detail. As the only officer on board, Wright was ultimately responsible for it all. He had to understand every detail of their work because the safety of the workers and the ship rested on his shoulders alone. As an added nuisance, the metal dust in the air infiltrated Wright's nostrils and started him sneezing every few minutes.

Glancing at the clock again, Wright began to think that this day in port was going to be as tough as any he had ever experienced at sea, except for the near fatal depth charging. It was 0801, and he had twenty-three hours and fifty-nine minutes to go on his first day as the ship's duty officer. His head throbbed, his mouth was dry, his tongue fuzzy, and his eyes ached. He should have drunk less and slept more last night. But he hadn't. And so for him it was a case of tough luck and duty calls.

TREMAIN slammed the phone down on the jack and exited the phone booth in the foyer of the Hickam club. Enthusiasm had won out over his misgivings about Ireland. He had taken the old man's words earlier that day in his office at face value. So he had been trying on-and-off for hours to reach Judy.

"Still can't get through, Captain?" Cazanavette asked.

"No. Here I know that I'm going home and I can't even tell Judy about it. It's driving me crazy. Let's go eat."

"All right, sir."

"Look here, Frank. I know we've been at sea for nearly two months, but if you don't stop calling me 'captain' and 'sir' I'm not going to sit down with you. If I wanted that I'd go eat on board with the duty officer. Hell, I'm being relieved in a couple days, anyway. For all intents and purposes, I'm no longer *Mackerel*'s captain. As far as I'm concerned we're just two friends having dinner. Agreed?"

Cazanavette paused before his face broke into a wide grin. "Agreed, *Jack*."

"That's better. Let's go."

The navy officers' club at Pearl Harbor Naval Station was a pleasant setting for any sea-weary man of the gold lace, but it paled in comparison to the delightful little club over at Hickam Field run by the Army Air Corps, at least in Tremain's opinion. The Pearl Harbor club sat in the heart of the busy naval complex and had no view to speak of, which was quite a feat in the Hawaiian Islands. The Hickam club, on the other hand, was tucked away in a quiet corner of an airfield. It was essentially a small building connected to an outdoor pavilion, which stretched over an exquisite green lawn. Only a small sea wall and a few clusters of swaying palms separated the lawn from the rolling ocean. Visitors loved to sit outside under the pavilion and eat or drink enjoying the fresh air and the view. It was the kind of place a person just wanted to pine the night away drinking beer, listening to the waves on the rocks, and feeling the wind.

Tremain had suggested to Cazanavette that they go there for dinner as a sort of "end of patrol" dinner. It seemed like the right thing to do. Tremain had grown to like Cazanavette as a person and as an XO, and he wanted to show him that he appreciated his hard work during the patrol, not to mention his decision to withdraw the report on the torpedo exploders.

They found a table close enough to the bar with a good view of the water and the sunset. They sat and ate and drank and listened to the music for several hours, talking about anything and everything except the war. Tremain learned just how much Frank Cazanavette missed his family back in his home town of Lincoln, Nebraska. His eyes began to water several times when he spoke of his children and how he had missed much of their infancy. It touched an emotional chord in Tremain. Judy had always wanted children, but he had wanted to bring them up in a stable environment. The navy, with its constant deployments, had made that impossible. He had convinced her to wait until his job would no longer require him to go to sea, until he was confined to some desk in Washington. Now, he was not so sure that waiting was the right thing to do. He would have plenty of time to discuss it with Judy when he got back, he thought. Maybe they could get started on kids while he was in New London waiting for his new boat. The thought of it made him warm inside.

"Jack! Frank! How the hell're you two sea dogs?"

Tremain looked up to see a grinning Sammy Russo standing by their table with his hands on his hips. He looked much different from the broken and dejected man who had stepped off the *Mackerel* two months before. His eyes were full of life again. He actually looked younger. Tremain was no psychologist but he would say that Sammy had come close to complete recovery.

"How're you, Sammy?" Tremain said.

"Oh, fine, fine. I just got up to leave and noticed you two sitting over here. Listen, I wanted to congratulate you both on your patrol and your medals. I knew you'd do it, Jack. You're a miracle worker. Old Ireland was right."

"We just got lucky, Sammy. Nothing you couldn't have done," Tremain said humbly, then changed the subject. "So, I hear you're operations officer for Division Seven now."

"That's right." Russo nodded. "Old Ireland's got me grinding away day and night. I hear just about everything that's going on with the boats."

"Did you hear about my relief?" Tremain asked, reluctantly. "Dave Stillsen or something like that. Ireland told me he's an—"

"An East Coast sailor?" Russo interrupted, shaking his head. "Yes, I know. The guy hasn't seen any real submarine combat to speak of, Jack. This is one of those cases where the man's perfect service record and *not* his experience got him the job. Which reminds me . . ." Russo paused and awkwardly glanced at Cazanavette. "I'm sorry, Frank, but I've got something to say to Jack in private. You mind excusing us for a moment? It'll only take a minute."

"Sure. Take your time," Cazanavette said, rising. "I'll go get us some more drinks."

Russo waited for Cazanavette to leave before he sat down in the empty chair. His face drew suddenly grave, alarmingly different from a few second before. The change got Tremain's attention.

"Jack, I probably shouldn't say anything about this, since you're leaving and all," Russo muttered, checking over his shoulder, "but I think we both have a vested interest in this matter. It's something I heard today over at Division about *Mackerel*'s next patrol."

"What's that?"

"Something's brewing over there between the intelligence guys from ComSubPac and Ireland. Ireland had a meeting with them this morning and then another one this afternoon with the chief of staff. After he got out of that meeting, he ordered me to place *Mackerel* on top repair priority."

"Why *Mackerel*? We . . ." Tremain corrected himself: "*They* are not scheduled to leave for another three weeks."

"I asked myself the same question, and it turns out that *Mackerel* is the only uncommitted boat in port right now that has the capability to leave harbor within two weeks, *if* we put her on top repair priority. So, I asked a friend of mine over at the intel unit what's going on." Russo glanced around the table and lowered his voice. "This is all hush-hush, mind you, but he told me that *Mackerel* is being sent on some kind of suicide mission handed down from CinCPac himself. One of those missions where the possibility of success far outweighs the risk or the cost, if you know what I mean."

"What?" Tremain's mouth gaped open in disbelief.

"Yes, it shocked me, too," Russo said. "Especially now that this Stillsen guy is taking over."

That explains Ireland's strange behavior the other day, Tremain thought. "Any idea what the mission is, Sammy?"

"Not a clue." Russo shook his head. "Everybody's tight-lipped about it."

Why on earth would Ireland agree to send *Mackerel* on such a hazardous mission with a green captain on board? Tremain wondered. It just wasn't like him. Tremain was half surprised that he himself was not asked, or ordered, to stay on for another patrol. It just didn't make sense. But then, Ireland was an old friend, one who not only knew him, but also knew Judy, personally. Maybe Russo was right and this really was a suicide mission. Maybe Ireland had intentionally spared him because he didn't want to make Judy a widow.

Cazanavette returned to the table with two beers. "All done?"

"Yes, Frank, thanks," Russo said, standing up. "Stop by before you fly out, won't you, Jack?"

"Sure thing, Sammy. Thanks for the info. We'll be seeing you."

As Russo walked off, Tremain thought about Ireland's behavior the day before. Ireland probably had a hardenough moral dilemma sending him out on that last patrol and now he wanted to replace him before this next mission. Ireland knew that he had not seen Judy in over a year. Now *Mackerel*, the new glory boat of ComSubPac, would be going on a mission from which it would probably never return, and he would be spared, just like with the *Seatrout*.

Tremain glanced across the table at Cazanavette. He was enjoying his beer, oblivious to what Russo had just told him. Cazanavette and the officers and men of *Mackerel* had no idea what they were being chosen for. They had no idea that these next two weeks in port would probably be their last. They would go to sea, thinking it was just another routine patrol, having newfound confidence from their recent success. The new captain, Dave Stillsen, would do as Tremain had done and try to mold the crew to his own ways of running a ship. *Mackerel*'s men would have to adjust, again. Like Tremain, Stillsen would have the same rough times in the first few weeks. Given time, the crew would eventually settle in to his style of leadership.

Unfortunately, on this patrol, they may not have the time, Tremain thought. Cazanavette was a good XO, but he would not be able to cover for the inevitable errors in judgment Stillsen would make. Stillsen, being a green commanding officer with little or no battle experience, would take even longer to meld with the crew. That crucial bond between captain and crew might not fully form until the second or even the third patrol.

Although he had no idea what this new secret mission was, Tremain suddenly felt the overwhelming certainty that *Mackerel* would never return from this one. And all those smiling faces he had grown to love and respect, including Cazanavette's, would perish without a trace in some unknown Japanese waters. Tremain remembered how he had felt when the news of *Seatrout*'s loss reached him. He could still feel it.

"What's wrong, Jack?" Cazanavette asked innocently. "What was all that about, anyway?"

Strangely, all Tremain could think about was Cazanavette's children back in Nebraska.

"Nothing," Tremain said. "Let's just forget it."

Then Tremain lit a cigarette, his first in quite a while, and took a long hard drag.

Chapter 14

"**YOU'RE** going to love this place, Ryan," Salisbury said as they walked along the sidewalk of Kapiolani Boulevard and turned on to McCully Street, their casual pants and loose Hawaiian shirts blending in with the rest of the uniformed and non-uniformed foot traffic. Wright followed Salisbury not knowing where they were going. After getting off duty that morning he had gone straight to the hotel for several hours' sleep, only to be awoken by Salisbury banging on his door in the late afternoon. Wright had reluctantly followed him, and after several visits to various bars near the hotel, Salisbury suddenly got an idea to go someplace different.

Honolulu was alive this evening. The large number of transplanted military personnel that had come to the island since the war started had been a boon to the local economy and a merchant's dream. The street vendors and shop owners were out to make money each night, and tonight was no exception. With storefronts open and thousands of little trinkets on the display tables brought out to the sidewalk, they were eager to relieve any sailor or marine of his meager monthly pay. There were other things for sale too. Prostitutes lined the streets ready to satisfy the urges of the sex-starved men.

Wright and Salisbury came to a two-story building occupying a street corner. The building looked rather drab compared to the others on McCully Street and had no signs or other markings to indicate that it was anything other than a warehouse of some sort.

"What's this place, Joe?" Wright asked, confused.

"It's whatever you want it to be," Salisbury said with an evil grin. "Come on."

Salisbury approached the drab door and knocked twice. A burly Hawaiian opened the door and exchanged a few words with him before letting both men in. Wright was shocked to see that the inside of the club drastically contrasted with its outward appearance. The large dimly lit room was packed with people. The club centered around an island-type bar and two three-foot circular stages, which were surrounded by young American men in civilian clothes and lots of fairly good-looking women in tight-fitting flowery dresses. Music emanated from a record machine in the far corner and a young woman in various states of undress danced on each stage, taunting the howling men with their undulating bodies. The many women in the club were of Hawaiian, Asian, and American descent, though most were locals, and they wore lots of make-up. Overtly flirting with the excited and sweaty men, the women were obviously professionals and Wright did not need Salisbury to tell him that they were ladies of the evening.

"This place is for enlisted only, so keep it under you hat that we're officers, okay?" Salisbury whispered.

They moved to a corner of the room that afforded them a good view of one of the stages, and a middle-aged,

large-breasted waitress rubbed up against them offering
them beers. Salisbury paid her for them, mostly to make
her go away.

"Since we didn't get laid the other night," he shouted to
Wright over the noise, "I thought we'd come here."

Wright nodded and took a drink. Two or three women
had already brushed by him with their hips or breasts and it
was driving his senses wild. He wanted to just grab one and
let all his sexual energy loose on her.

Just then he noticed a commotion near the bar. A small
man, obviously drunk and out of control, was confronting
a rather larger man who was leaning against the bar with
his back to him. The larger man was firmly sandwiched between two groping Hawaiian girls and seemed to be ignoring the drunken man altogether.

"Holy shit," Salisbury said. "Isn't that Anderson?"

Wright caught a glimpse of the drunken man's face between the peering heads in front of him. It was indeed Anderson, the man who had been missing since they had
pulled into port. Wright was stunned by the discovery but
even more taken aback when the man at the bar finally
turned around and faced him. It was Tee.

Tee was dressed in civilian attire and his face was red
like Wright had seen it that night at the officer's club when
he was drunk. Wright watched as Tee said a few words to
Anderson, which Anderson must not have agreed with because he responded with a wild inaccurate punch, which
Tee easily blocked. Tee quickly had Anderson's arms behind his back and passed him off to the club's bouncers,
who had quickly converged on the scene.

Anderson struggled with the big Hawaiians all the way
to the door, shouting obscenities in Tee's direction. Tee
simply shrugged and turned back to the bar, firmly planting
one hand on each of the two girls' round asses.

"What the hell's he doing here?" Wright asked.

"I don't know," Salisbury answered, apparently amused, "but neither one of those girls looks like Margie."

"We better go help Anderson, Joe. As much as I want to do every girl in the place, he'll probably get into more trouble if we let him get too far."

Salisbury begrudgingly agreed to go and they exited the club to find Anderson sitting on the sidewalk leaning against the wall where the bouncers had left him, oblivious to the world around him. Blood trickled from his lip and onto his shirt and it was obvious that the bouncers had given him a few parting shots before they had let him go. He reeked of alcohol, body odor, and urine, and Wright had to plug his nose when they got close to him.

"Is that you, Mr. O'Connell?" Anderson murmured.

Wright paused. To hear the drunken sailor call out his dead friend's name disturbed him.

"No, Anderson," he finally said. "It's Ensign Wright and Lieutenant Salisbury."

"Oh, Mr. Wright." Anderson slurred his speech. "You're a good man, sir."

"Thanks. We're going to take you back to the hotel, now. You know that you've been missing for two days? You even missed your duty day? Cob and everyone's been looking all over for you. You're lucky we found you."

"Where's Mr. O'Connell, sir?"

Wright paused and exchanged glances with Salisbury.

"Mr. O'Connell's dead, Anderson," Wright said. "Remember?"

Anderson's bloodshot eyes shot wide open. He suddenly appeared terrified and groped at Wright's shirt. "He's dead?"

"Right. C'mon, let's get you home."

Anderson's body writhed as he shouted at the top of his lungs. "I killed him! I killed him! I killed him!" He kept shouting the same thing over and over, and each time his voice got softer, until he was eventually whispering it, and then, finally, he was quiet again. He began to cry.

"You didn't kill him, Anderson. That Zeke bomber did," Wright said, trying to console him. He didn't quite know what to make of the man's condition. "You did all you could. The captain gave you a commendation because you saved the ship, remember?"

Wright's words did not appear to help, and the tormented Anderson continued to whisper "I killed him" as the tears streamed down his face. Wright and Salisbury used the moment to heft Anderson to his feet, and then they began to march briskly toward the hotel supporting the drunken man between them.

Ducking into a couple of alleys on the way, they successfully avoided the roving bands of baton-wielding shore patrol, who would have most certainly sent Anderson to the brig had they seen him. Once at the hotel, Salisbury woke Chief Freund from his room, and together the three men hauled Anderson's limp body up to his own room.

Freund thanked the officers for their help in finding the lost sailor and asked them to keep the whole thing between the three of them. They all agreed to keep silent about it, not wanting to see their pathetic shipmate court-martialed. Then Wright and Salisbury called it a night, both too tired to go out again, after lugging Anderson halfway across Honolulu.

As Wright tried to get some sleep that night, he thought of Anderson. He felt sorry for the poor man, who could not forgive himself for something that was not his fault. He also thought about Margie and wondered if she knew how "faithful" Tee really was to her. He was certain that Tee had not seen them and he wondered how Tee would react if he ever informed him that he and Salisbury had been at the club and saw him groping two hookers.

He would probably shit his pants, Wright thought. He

was actually glad that he had this dope on Tee. It made him feel like he had some power over the man. If Tee ever got too unruly again, he would spring this secret on him and watch him squirm.

With a broad smile on his face, Wright faded off to sleep.

Chapter 15

TREMAIN fidgeted in the small waiting area outside Ireland's office. He thumbed through the war news while the enlisted yeoman across the room whacked away incessantly on a typewriter. It seemed that not much had changed in the war since before *Mackerel* left on patrol. On the other side of the world, the war in North Africa still seesawed back and forth, and the Allies still had not driven Rommel's forces out of Tunisia. Offensives and counteroffensives continued on the Eastern Front, yet the Germans had been defeated at Stalingrad. German U-Boat sinkings were on the rise in the Atlantic, but the Allies continued to lose hundreds of thousands of tons of shipping each month. In the Pacific, fighting continued to rage in the Solomon Islands and New Guinea, but Guadalcanal was now securely in Allied hands. A world on fire, summed up in a few headlines.

Tremain tossed down the paper when he heard some loud voices coming from Ireland's office, then the door opened. A navy lieutenant commander walked out laughing with Ireland slapping him on the back. Ireland had obviously just told the man one of his world famous gutter-quality jokes.

"Oh, Jack." Ireland noticed him. "I didn't know you were out here. Great. Now you can meet your replacement. Jack Tremain, this is Dave Stillsen, your ticket back to the States."

Tremain shook Stillsen's hand and smiled pleasantly. The guy seemed like a square. The uniform was immaculate. The hair slicked back. He had a smile that began on one side of his face and ended there too. He appeared to be a little arrogant to Tremain and awfully young.

"Nice to meet you, Jack," Stillsen said in a ridiculously loud command voice. "I've heard a lot about you. It sounds like you had a good patrol last time out. I'm sure you'll be a legend at the sub school when you get there."

Tremain did not like the way he said "the sub school."

"Well, I'm sure you'll be just as successful in *Mackerel* as I was," Tremain said, politely.

"Yes, well, I've got to run, I've only just arrived in Pearl this morning. I'll be seeing you later, Jack." Then to Ireland he said, "Thanks for your time, Captain." Stillsen then grabbed his hat and walked out the door. He was too confident, Tremain thought. Too matter-of-fact. Too much of an imposter. He had a lot to learn.

"What's on your mind, Jack?" Ireland asked.

"Could I see you for a moment, sir?"

"Certainly."

The two went back inside Ireland's office. Ireland poured his usual cup of coffee and sat on his desk while Tremain sat in the chair. He must drink twenty cups a day, Tremain thought. Something was still wrong with Ireland's demeanor. He was too smug about something.

"Sir, I just received word that *Mackerel* has been placed in a priority repair status."

Ireland nodded and sipped his coffee. He said nothing.

"May I ask why, sir?" Tremain finally said.

"You don't need to know, Jack. As far as you're concerned, *Mackerel*'s just leaving early on patrol, that's all."

"*Is* that the reason, sir? Or is there something else?"

"Who have you been talking to, Jack?" Ireland shot back at him.

Ireland was quick, Tremain thought.

"No one, sir. I just think the crew's been through a lot. They have had to do back-to-back patrols, and now I think they should get all the time ashore they can. They're a good crew, sir, and they need some time away from that boat." Tremain was trying to draw it out of Ireland without betraying Russo. So far it was not working.

Ireland set the coffee cup down and crossed his arms.

"Why should you care what happens, now, Jack? You've got your relief. You've got your orders home. Why should the officers and crew of USS *Mackerel* even concern Lieutenant Commander Jack Tremain?"

Tremain raised his eyebrows. He suddenly got the feeling that Ireland was toying with *him*. It was that old sensation of being worked on by a master psychologist. And worked over by one. But to Tremain his old crew still came first, so he went along with this cruddy gamesmanship, even if he had to discount his intelligence and play dumb to do it.

"I'll always care about them, sir. No matter where I am." Tremain paused, then added, "Just like I still care for my lost men on the *Seatrout*."

Tremain saw that his last statement had finally affected Ireland, who looked down at the floor, then rose from his desk and walked over to the window. He tipped the blinds with two fingers and stared out at the waterfront.

"I never had a combat command at sea, Jack," he said with genuine feeling tinged with regret. "I never had the privilege. So I can only imagine what kind of bond can form between a captain and his crew during the heat of battle."

"A strong bond, sir. One that cannot easily be replaced."

Ireland nodded. "I imagine so."

Ireland was guiding him away from the subject, Tremain thought. He could not wait anymore. He had to get the truth from him.

"Sir, is *Mackerel* going somewhere especially dangerous this time?"

Ireland stared straight ahead for a moment, then nodded. He did not take his eyes from the window.

"Somewhere very dangerous, Jack," he said solemnly. "The odds are against their return."

"Sir, you have to keep me on board for this mission, whatever it is," Tremain said quickly. "You know as well as I do that Stillsen is not cut out for this kind of thing. You can't have *that* character trying to prove his command worthiness on a mission like this. It would break up the cohesive unit I've formed them into. And, *worse,* it would happen right before they go into battle. You of all people understand that, sir."

"What about Judy, Jack? Would she understand? Would she ever forgive me for sending you back out one more time?"

Tremain had thought all of this through the night before, tossing and turning, his head spinning with things he would have to say to his lovely and patient and enduring wife. But he felt sure that Judy would understand, eventually. She was that type of person, she had always been.

"She'll understand, sir. I'll write her a long and heartfelt letter. She'll understand that you made the decision for the families of the eighty-five men on the *Mackerel*. Any choice that will increase their chances of survival is the right one. She'll understand that. She always has."

Ireland appeared to consider. He did not say a word for

several minutes as he poured himself another cup of coffee and took several long gulps.

"I think I can get SubPac to buy off on it," he finally said. "You make a compelling argument, Jack."

"Then it's settled, sir."

"All right, Jack." Ireland nodded with a small smile. "Stillsen's already been briefed on the mission, but I'll find some safe place to stash him until you get back." Ireland paused. "And make sure that you come back, you hear me, Jack?"

"Aye aye, sir." Tremain smiled.

"We'll set up a briefing for you and *only* you tomorrow, Jack. This thing is top secret, understand? You won't even be able to tell your XO until you're underway."

"Right, sir." Tremain got up to leave. "Thank you, sir, for understanding."

"Thank you, Jack."

Ireland watched Tremain leave his office. A few moments later he heard the outer door to the division office shut as Tremain left the building.

Soon there was a knock on his door and Sammy Russo entered.

"He's gone, sir," Russo said. "How'd it go?"

"Perfectly, Sammy," Ireland said, winking as he lit up a pipe. "Whatever you told him last night really did the trick."

"I still feel uneasy about this, sir, deceiving a friend and all. What if he doesn't come back from this mission? I'll feel like I had a part in his death."

"I know the feeling, Sammy." Ireland puffed on the pipe. "Every time one of my boats doesn't come home, I know the feeling. The mission always comes first, though. Our goal out here is to win the war, not worry about how many letters we're going to have to write. My goal is to have my submarines do their share. This mission calls for the best we've got and Jack Tremain, *voluntarily* in command of the *Mackerel, is* the best we've got. You can never order a man to go on a mission like this and expect success. You have to get him to want to go. He's going for them now, not because I ordered him to do it."

Slightly sickened by Ireland's orchestral mind games, Russo walked to the window and looked down at his old boat tied to the pier.

"Don't feel bad, Sammy," Ireland said, patting him on the back. "You did your old shipmates a favor. You actually gave them their best chance for survival."

Russo nodded, not taking his eyes from the *Mackerel* below. He had never really liked Ireland. But he had to admit to himself that Ireland did have a point, although a somewhat twisted one.

Chapter 16

THE war room in the ComSubPac headquarters building was small but imposing. It was sparsely decorated with a single conference table and chairs that took up most of the space. It had no windows and only one door. Three feet of insulated concrete shielded each of the room's four walls, to prevent any eavesdropping from the adjacent rooms. Though it was only one level beneath the ground floor, it was virtually inaccessible to anyone except those with the proper security clearance and the all-important "need to know." Even Tremain had to show his identification card twice to get past the marine guards at two separate checkpoints. ComSubPac took the "silent" in silent service very seriously.

Tremain entered the room and noticed an admiral sitting at the head of the long mahogany conference table. Tremain recognized the man immediately as the deputy chief of staff, Rear Admiral Giles. A grim-looking Ireland was there too, along with two other officers wearing the insignia of the intelligence community. They were all sitting quietly along the opposite side of the table when Tremain came in. The admiral sized up Tremain for a tenth of a second, then nodded and pointed to the empty chair to his right.

Since the war began, Tremain had heard many stories about Admiral Giles. It was rumored that he personally engineered and was responsible to Admiral Lockwood for all submarine missions that fell outside of the "traditional" role of a submarine. In other words, he was in charge of the special missions, the missions that men did not come back from. Most submarine captains dreaded the inevitable briefing with the Admiral because it undoubtedly meant that their boat would be an instrument in some impossibly wild plan dreamed up by a person who rode a desk for a living.

"Commander Tremain." Giles spoke curtly, bypassing the unnecessary introductions. He acted as though he had somewhere to go and so wanted to get the meeting over with quickly. "I'm sure you are wondering what all of this is about, so I'll get right to the point. The purpose of this briefing is to familiarize you with the objectives of a new CinCPac operation which will include your submarine."

Include? Tremain thought to himself. Don't you mean sacrifice?

"Tremain, I must tell you first, and of course you know, that everything we discuss here today is classified Top Secret Ultra and is to not be repeated outside this room."

"I understand, sir."

"Good. Now, let's get to it."

Giles motioned to one of the intelligence officers, who quickly flipped on a slide projector atop the table. A poor-quality image of a large ship in drydock appeared on the screen on the wall.

Tremain could not tell what kind of ship it was due to its shroud of scaffoldings and canopies, but judging from its relative size next to the shipyard cranes it looked to be on the order of a capital ship.

"Commander Tremain," the intelligence officer spoke. "This is a photograph of the battleship INS *Kurita*."

"Never heard of it before." Tremain shook his head.

"No, sir, you should not have," the intel officer continued. "This ship has not yet joined the Combined Fleet. She's a new construction ship. This photograph was taken five months ago by one of our operatives in the Kobe naval shipyard. You can see in this photo that the *Kurita*'s hull had just been completed."

"I don't see any turrets," Tremain said.

"They had not been installed at the time of this photo, sir. The next slide is a much better depiction of what *Kurita* should look like today."

The intelligence officer changed slides on the tray and another image appeared of the same ship, this time from a different angle. The ship now looked very much like a battleship. From the photo angle, Tremain could make out two large triple-barreled gun turrets forward of the superstructure with many lesser guns along both beams. Still in drydock, the ship appeared to be enormous, near to, if not larger than, the *Yamato* Class.

"She is the largest Japanese warship ever built," the intel officer said, almost proudly, "displacing seventy-five thousand tons. Her armament includes nine eighteen-inch guns, sixteen five- and six-inch guns and numerous small caliber anti-aircraft batteries. She is powered by eight super-high-pressure steam boilers delivering roughly a hundred and thirty thousand shaft horsepower to four screws, which is expected to give her speeds of up to thirty knots. As you can see, she is armored heavily. Her armor plating is twelve inches thick near the vital spaces. Her normal crew complement is roughly eighteen hundred men."

"Impressive," Tremain said, aware of the admiral's eyes beaming through him. "When was this photo taken?"

"March second, sir," the intel officer said. "A little over a month ago."

"Looks like she's close to coming out of drydock."

"She was launched last week, sir."

Tremain nodded. He almost hesitated to ask his next question.

"What's the mission?" he finally asked.

The intelligence officer paused. He glanced at the admiral and, after receiving a small nod, answered Tremain.

"The *Kurita* is finishing up her dockside trials and will be conducting inner harbor shakedowns next week," he said confidently. "We have obtained reliable information that she will put to sea from Kobe for trials on the twenty-fifth of this month, exactly three weeks from today. Tug schedules for Kobe harbor on that same day confirm this. She will then conduct her initial testing while she transits to Yokosuka."

"Those are *some* informants you've got over there to provide you with information that precise," Tremain said, astonished. "It sounds like they're on the imperial staff."

Tremain had always been skeptical of information received from the intelligence community. He wondered just how reliable this information was. Obviously it's considered reliable enough to risk his boat on some insane mission, he thought.

"They have distinguished themselves as very credible sources, sir," the intelligence officer said defensively. "It may interest you to know, sir, that we have also learned the route *Kurita* will take to get to Yokosuka. We are confident that this will not change. Our operatives have informed us that Combined Fleet headquarters has approved the route and that *Kurita* has already received the official orders through regular message traffic."

The officer changed slides to a large-scale chart of

Southern Japan, focusing on the waterways that run between the islands of Honshu, Shikoku, and Kyushu. A thin red line on the chart weaved through Kii Suido and around the mainland to connect Kobe and Yokosuka.

"This is a projection of what we believe will be *Kurita*'s intended track," the officer said, pointing to the red line. "However, the only thing we are absolutely certain of is that she must pass through Kii Suido at approximately 1800 hours on the twenty-sixth."

Tremain silently gasped. He knew what was coming next.

"Your mission, sir, is to lay in wait for *Kurita* there and sink her when she comes through the strait. She will probably be traveling at her top speed so you will most likely get only one chance."

Tremain could not believe that the young intelligence officer was serious. He half-expected the whole room to break out in laughter any minute now, and tell him this was all just a big practical joke.

How could they expect him to take *Mackerel* within sight of Japan itself and attempt to sink this behemoth, he wondered. Surely, they understood that there were too many variables involved, that things could and would go wrong with every plan. Surely they understood that this mission was essentially impossible?

Tremain waited, but they all sat silent with blank expressions. They all gazed at him as if they had just asked him to run down to the store and buy a loaf of bread.

Had they done this kind of thing so many times that they were completely indifferent? he asked himself. Or was it that they could not conceptually grasp what they had just ordered him to do?

"I have a few questions," he finally said.

"Certainly, sir," the intelligence officer replied.

"Why wait for her there, at the strait? Why not hit her as she comes out of Kobe harbor?"

"Three reasons, sir. One, we don't want the Imperial Navy to be able to refloat her again, as we have done with many of our battleships sunk in Pearl Harbor back in '41. Two, the Japanese have extensive minefields in and around Kii Suido. It would be futile for your boat to attempt to navigate through them, which you would undoubtedly have to do to get to Kobe harbor. And, three, we want you to attack *Kurita* at dusk. This will afford better possibilities for your submarine to escape and will assist us in the primary mission."

"Primary mission?" Tremain asked. He thought he must have missed something.

"Yes, sir," the intel officer answered without emotion. "If the *Kurita* sinks at night, any rescue attempts carried out by the Japanese will be that much more difficult."

Tremain raised his eyebrows.

"Excuse me," he said, "but I don't follow you on that last one. My orders are to sink the *Kurita*, right? What does it matter if her crew is rescued or not?"

The intelligence officer glanced toward the admiral.

"The *Kurita* is not the primary target of this operation, Commander Tremain," Admiral Giles spoke up.

"Then may I ask what is, sir?"

"Put the slide of the *Kurita* back up there, lieutenant," Giles said, and the intelligence officer quickly changed the slide on the tray. "Look at that, Commander. Tell me what you see."

Tremain did not understand what Giles was talking about. The slide was obviously the same photo they had seen before, of the *Kurita* near completion.

"I see a Japanese battleship, sir," Tremain answered skeptically.

"Of course you do," Giles said abruptly. "You're a sub captain and that's all you should see. Tell you where to shoot and you'll do it, right? But when I look at this photo,

Commander, I don't see a battleship. I see resources. I see industry. I see technical knowledge and capabilities. And, *above all,* I see organization. The masterful organization and management it takes to construct not just a ship, but a masterpiece. *Kurita* is a masterpiece, and she scares me. Not because she has eighteen-inch guns, but because she represents Japan's production capability.

"Someone once said that in war amateurs talk strategy and professionals talk logistics. Well, I don't think I have to tell you that this is a war of logistics, an all-out attrition war and nothing more. And like all wars, it will not be won on the battlefield, but rather in the factories and the ship-yards. Whichever nation can out-produce the other will be the sure victor.

"What the lieutenant has failed to get at, and what I'm trying to tell you, is that, while the *Kurita* is what you will be shooting at, it is *not* the target. We have learned that the Kobe Naval Shipyard supervisor and several hundred of his leading managers and specialists will be aboard *Kurita* for her sea trials. They are your *real* targets and the chief objective of this operation. Take them out and the Kobe Naval Shipyard, the best the Japanese have got, will fall flat on its face. Without their experienced managers, morale will drop, production will slump—and that means poorer quality work and fewer ships that our boys will have to fight in the future."

It was now clear to Tremain why Giles wanted to ham-per rescue operations for the *Kurita* survivors. He suddenly thought of those hundreds of flailing bodies he had left in the water after *Mackerel* had sunk that transport off Mogami Bank. Now he was being ordered to kill non-combatants and leave them to the mercy of the sea. The thought made him sick.

"These are civilians, correct, sir?" Tremain asked.

"Yes, civilians indeed. Does that bother you, Tremain?"

Giles asked the question like he was questioning Tremain's manhood.

"I've just never intentionally targeted civilians before, sir. That's all."

"You've been sinking merchant ships for over a year now. Most of their crews are civilian. What makes this any different?"

"Well, the target was always the ship, sir. The intent was not specifically to kill the crews."

Giles sighed, then glared at Ireland. Giles appeared to be fast growing annoyed with Tremain's questions. He was obviously a man who had justified everything in his own mind and had no patience for those who could not see things his way.

"Think of it this way, Jack," Ireland chimed in, "these are not simply civilians. These are the men that produce weapons and warships to be used against Americans. They're a valuable element of Japan's war machine. Targeting them is no different from targeting, say, a factory or an ironworks like we're doing right now with our bombers over Germany."

"If it makes you feel any better, Tremain, this operation has the approval of the Commander in Chief himself," Giles added, "*and* it falls within the guidelines of the international rules of war."

Tremain wondered how much one had to stretch the interpretation of those rules to legalize the killing of civilians. It seemed like more and more wrong was justified with each passing day of warfare, and right was being redefined. War is certainly hell, he thought. It seemed like it got more hellish every day. He could not deny the logic that the war would end sooner if Japan's war production was diminished. And the sooner the war ended, the fewer lives would be lost. And, after all, orders were orders.

Tremain turned to the intelligence officer. "Any information on escorts, Lieutenant?" Tremain asked. Out of the corner of his eye, he saw Giles and Ireland smile in approval. They had won their battle.

"None, sir," the lieutenant answered. "Three to six destroyers, as escorts, and patrol craft would be typical for a capital ship of *Kurita*'s size. We expect heavy air activity over the area, as well."

"A battleship that size and with that much armor will be difficult to sink with one salvo," Tremain commented.

"Yes, sir," the lieutenant said as if he was suddenly excited. "That's why *Mackerel* will be fitted out with special torpedoes that have been modified for this particular mission. Instead of the normal 500-pound TNT warhead, these torpedoes will carry a 750-pound torpex warhead. That should be enough to break the *Kurita*'s keel. Four well-placed hits amidships should do the trick. Unfortunately, these torpedoes have a somewhat reduced range, only two thousand yards, so you will have to be close in to the target."

Tremain nodded. Giles had thought of everything. At least the man could plan well.

"Do you have any more questions, Commander?" the lieutenant asked.

"No, I think that just about does it."

"You will be receiving the particulars along with your sealed orders before you put to sea."

Tremain started to rise.

"Oh, there's one more thing, Tremain," Giles added. "A rather insignificant matter. We'll be sending Commander Stillsen along with you."

"What?" Tremain could not believe what he had just heard.

"He's already been briefed on the mission so I can *not*

risk having him around here. He can't leak information if he's at sea with you."

"Sir, I must tell you that I whole-heartedly protest this decision. This mission will be difficult enough as it is. Having two captains on board will make it near impossible." Tremain could envision it now. He and Stillsen were complete opposites. Every order would be questioned. Every decision he made would prompt a commentary from Stillsen. It would be intolerable, and dangerous.

"There will be only one captain on board, Jack," Ireland said, reassuringly. "That's you. Stillsen will be assigned as a prospective commanding officer under the excuse that he needs more practical sea experience before taking command of his own boat."

"Sir, I still believe that you are jeopardizing the success of the mission by sending him along. Stillsen's presence will create an uncomfortable command climate. I don't need my men to have to deal with that while they're sweating it out under the ocean with the Japanese mainland less than ten miles away."

"Well, Tremain," Giles said, appearing not to have heard a word he said, "he's going, and that's final. Don't worry, you'll get by just fine."

Easy for you to say, Tremain thought. You don't know the first thing about what it's like out there. Nothing about the delicate balance that holds captain and crew together.

Tremain left the SubPac building with Ireland. Once outside, they both lit up cigarettes. Ireland broke the silence with a few more words of encouragement, which did little to help.

"Sorry, Jack," Ireland said. "SubPac bought off on your reasoning for retaining command of the *Mackerel,* but they really screwed us on this Stillsen thing. I fought it. Believe me, I fought it."

Tremain knew Ireland had fought it. And he was at least

a little glad that, outside of the deputy's company, Ireland felt the same way about the situation.

"Well, sir. I asked to keep her for one more mission. I guess I got what I asked for. Nursing Stillsen is a little bit more than I wanted, though."

"Maybe you can throw him overboard, when you get far enough out, Jack." Ireland laughed, patting Tremain on the back.

But Tremain did not feel like laughing.

Chapter 17

WRIGHT stood on the cigarette deck just aft of the bridge in the late afternoon sun. He watched as the crane on the pier slowly lowered a long, dangling torpedo through *Mackerel*'s aft weapons-shipping hatch. Sweaty torpedomen lined each side of the heavy weapon and steadied it as it slid into the angled shaft that led to the aft torpedo room. Down in the torpedo room, more men would be waiting to receive the lethal cargo and position it into its proper rack and stowage space. Chief Konhausen was supervising the whole operation, and Wright thought it would be best if he just watched from a distance and stayed out of the way. After all, he did not know the first thing about loading torpedoes. His only knowledge came from what he had read in the submarine manuals, and he had not had time yet to get to the sections addressing "in port operations."

It had been a hectic duty day so far, much like his last one. *Mackerel*'s repairs were almost finished. The places in the conning tower where the enemy shells had penetrated had been welded and tested. The ballast tank had been sealed as well. The drain pump was now fully functional again, as were the stern planes from their normal hydraulic supply. All that remained now were a few minor jobs that would not keep *Mackerel* from going to sea one way or another. And it was a good thing too, since the submarine's departure date had been moved up once again.

Yesterday they had learned that *Mackerel* would be leaving Pearl Harbor in two days. No one among the officers and crew knew exactly why they were leaving Pearl so early. Wright heard some rumors that they were being sent out on some kind of special mission, and that these torpedoes, which they were now in the process of loading, had been modified in some special way. Whatever the reason, Wright did not care much. To him, it only meant that he would have just one more day of liberty.

He glanced over at the waterfront. In the distance, he could see the top of the naval hospital poking out from beyond the ComSubPac building. Seeing the hospital made him think of Margie, since she was probably there working at this hour and he could see the third floor where she worked. It also made him think of the other night when he and Salisbury had seen Tee with the two prostitutes. He wondered if Margie would ever find out, or if she would just end up marrying Tee only to discover his unfaithfulness at a more painful time.

"Sir?" Wright's daydreaming was suddenly interrupted when Petty Officer Anderson appeared at his side.

Wright snapped out of it and directed his attention to the sailor. Anderson was part of the duty section today, and it was the first time that Wright had seen him since the night he and Salisbury had lugged him to his room at the Royal Hawaiian. Anderson's face had a small scar near his lip where the bouncer had struck him, but he was clean-shaven. His dungaree uniform was clean and pressed, a marked difference from the last time Wright had seen him, though his face was red and his eyes bloodshot and he still looked like he had not slept for days.

"What is it, Anderson?"

"Chief Freund told me what you did for me the other night, sir. I just wanted to thank you, sir," Anderson said distantly.

"That's quite all right, Anderson. We all have rough nights every now and then."

"Yes, sir." Anderson paused, then added, "Sir, could I speak to you in private?"

Several men were working within earshot, applying paint to the conning tower and bridge. Anderson appeared to be on edge and Wright could tell that this was not just a casual request.

"Sure," Wright said. "What about?"

Anderson glanced around. "It's about Mr. O'Connell's death, sir. I'd really rather talk to you about it alone, sir."

"Are you okay, Anderson?"

"I just have to talk to someone, sir."

"All right. I have to stay up here until the weapons load is complete, then I'm going to eat dinner. How about you come by the wardroom after dinner?"

"I have to go on watch after dinner, sir." Anderson sounded agitated. "I really need to talk to you, sir."

"Okay, okay," Wright said. He had never seen Anderson behave in this way before. "Just come by the wardroom after you get off watch and we'll talk all you want. I'll stay up, don't worry."

Anderson fidgeted around, avoiding eye contact with Wright. He obviously was not satisfied with the answer. He looked as if he was going to say something, but then he hesitated as if he was suddenly aware of the men painting nearby. Then without another word he walked away, quickly disappearing down the bridge hatch.

Wright was bewildered by Anderson's actions. He knew something was wrong. O'Connell's death had obviously affected the sailor, but this behavior bordered on an emotional disorder. It sounded to Wright like Anderson needed to talk to a navy chaplain more than a young and naïve ensign like himself.

Wright was befuddled at what to do about it. Chief Konhausen was the only senior enlisted man aboard, and Wright was not sure whether he should betray Anderson's trust by telling the chief. Then Wright suddenly remembered that Cazanavette would be coming down to the ship in the morning to check on the repair progress. He had certainly dealt with these kinds of situations before. He would know what to do. Wright decided that he would discuss Anderson's behavior with the XO first thing in the morning.

He sighed and went back to watching the torpedo load. There was just one more torpedo to go. Every few minutes, he glanced over at the hospital.

AT 2100 hours on Wright's duty day, some of the mechanics planned on testing the ship's drain pump. Wright thought it would be a good idea if he watched the test since it would be the first running test of the new drain pump. One of the mechanics came to the wardroom when they were ready to test and then led Wright down the ladder into the pump room, a small confined space beneath the control room deck plates.

The drain pump itself was the size of a large trash can and was mounted vertically to the deck near the middle of the room. The pump had a suction and an intake pipe connecting it with the ship's intricate drain system. These two pipes passed through an assembly of valves, which branched off into a series of pipes that disappeared into the fore and aft bulkheads and ran to the bilges in every compartment on the ship. Using this network and different valve line-ups, the drain pump could pump water overboard from any compartment on the ship if there was ever any flooding. It was the most reliable and fastest way to get rid of water, and one of the most important systems on the ship. A submarine captain would not think of getting underway without an operable drain system.

One mechanic spoke up, "There's some water in the aft engine room bilge, sir. We're lined up to pump from there. We've got the phones manned in both spaces."

"Very well," Wright said. "Commence pumping to sea."

"Commence pumping to sea, aye, sir," the mechanic acknowledged, then opened two valves and started the pump. It started with a shrill whine, then changed pitch as it took a suction on the pipe leading aft to the engine room bilge. The pump motor was noisy in the small room, but it sounded like it was functioning properly. The mechanic intently watched the pump-discharge pressure gauge for a few minutes before giving Wright a toothy grin and a thumbs up.

Then Wright heard a faint "pop." He had never heard that noise before and he assumed it had come from the pump motor. He immediately signaled for the mechanic to shut it off.

The mechanic flicked the pump motor switch and scratched his head as the pump wound down.

"I don't know what that noise could have been, sir," he said. "I don't smell any smoke. The motor seems to be fine."

"Call back to maneuvering," Wright said. "Maybe a circuit breaker tripped."

The other mechanic, wearing the sound-powered phone set, nodded and made the call. He shook his head as the response came back.

"No, sir. Maneuvering reports that no breakers have tripped."

What on earth could that noise have been? Wright

wondered, now that he was certain it could not have come from the drain pump. It had sounded very faint, almost like it had come from a different compartment, or even outside the ship. It had been a single distinct "pop." It sort of sounded like . . .

Wright grabbed at the mechanic's shoulder. "Who's the topside sentry on watch?"

The mechanic was startled and thought for a moment. "I think it's Anderson, sir."

Wright felt the hair on the back of his neck stand up. He practically knocked the mechanic aside as he bolted up the ladder to the control room. He ran forward through the officer's passage and into the forward torpedo room, praying with every step that his fears were wrong and the noise was not what he thought it was. As he came up the forward hatch and emerged on the darkened deck, he could hear a commotion over on the pier. His heart skipped a beat as he noticed two sailors huddled over a body near the sentry stand at the end of *Mackerel*'s brow.

"Oh, no . . ." Wright muttered, as he hurried across the brow.

The sailors noticed his approach and slowly stood up, their faces somber.

"He's dead, sir," one of them said. "There was nothing we could do for him."

Anderson's body lay face up on the pier between the feet of the two sailors. A pool of dark liquid slowly expanded beneath his head. Blood and pieces of flesh were splattered on the concrete all around the body, along with one spent .45-caliber shell casing. Anderson's trembling right hand still clutched the smoking pistol.

Wright just stood there and stared at the lifeless form of the boy who had come to him for help only a few hours before. The boy he had put off until after dinner.

"We were just up on deck having a smoke, Mr. Wright,"

one of the sailors said nervously. "Nothing seemed unusual. Anderson even waved to us. Next thing we know, Anderson pulls out his gun, puts it in his mouth, and pulls the trigger. It all happened so fast. We . . . we didn't . . . "

The sailor stopped. He could see that Wright was not listening.

Staring hollowly at Anderson's body, Wright could not help but feel a profound sense of guilt. The boy had been crying out to him for help, for someone to talk to. If he had only taken the time to listen, the boy might still be alive.

Chapter 18

6 Apr '43
8:23 PM
Pearl Harbor

Dearest Judy,

Hello, my love. How are you today? I wanted to write to you before I left again, in case I don't get to talk to you on the telephone. We're pulling out in the morning. I know you won't find this a surprise, since I've been doing this kind of thing to you for practically our whole lives together. You have always been so understanding and supportive in the past and I just ask you to bear with me one more time. This is the last time, I promise. I know I've said it in the past, but I'm afraid something bad may happen to my crew if I don't go on this patrol. Please understand.

Steve Ireland has secured me a job at submarine

school when I come back. Can you believe it? Quiet little New London, Connecticut. You and me and nothing but time on our hands. They aren't even sure if I will ever get a boat of my own, now. And at this point, Judes, I have to admit that I don't even care.

Yesterday, a young sailor in my crew committed suicide. It was horrible. I can't tell you what an empty feeling it gave me. I had just given the kid a commendation letter, too.

We had his memorial service this morning. I didn't know what to say. I mean what do you say at something like that?

I miss you so much. All my thoughts are of you and the little things we used to do together. You are my only source of sanity. I close my eyes and I see your lovely face, and it helps me to go on. When this war is over, I'm going to take off this uniform, get some quiet office job somewhere, and spend the rest of my life loving you. Soon, I promise.

By the time this reaches you, I'll probably already be heading home. Pray for us, honey. You are such an angel, and I know He listens to your prayers.

All my love forever,
Jack

Tremain folded the letter and placed it an envelope. He got up and walked across the passage to the wardroom and poured himself a cup of coffee. He rested his weary body against the table as he sipped at the warm fluid.

The officers were all gone, all except Lieutenant Turner who had the duty. He was somewhere else on the ship with the duty section preparing *Mackerel* for tomorrow's departure. Tremain liked the silence in the officers' spaces. It was not often that he could sit in the wardroom by himself and not worry about someone coming in.

He sat down at the table and rubbed his temples.

Mackerel was ready for sea, finally. And it was no small miracle.

He had not been pleased when he heard that their departure date had been moved up several days. But new information about *Kurita*'s sea trials had surfaced, and the SubPac intelligence officers were no longer certain about the date that the battleship would reach Kii Suido. Now, they had given him a week-long window in which the *Kurita* "might" pass through the narrow strait. *Mackerel* would have to leave tomorrow in order to get there in time for the earliest date in the window. Once there, she would sit in Japanese waters and wait for as long as it took.

Admiral Giles had been good enough to lift the requirement that the battleship be sunk at night, something Tremain appreciated, although Giles did not have much of a choice. It made Tremain feel better about the whole operation. Something about targeting shipyard workers still bugged him. The new orders stated that "if the opportunity presented itself," then *Kurita* should be sunk at night, but that the main objective was to sink the battleship "at all hazards." Tremain knew what "at all hazards" meant, and it was a part of the orders he had decided he would refrain from reading to the crew. There was no sense in them knowing that it might be a one-way mission.

He looked at the addressed envelope to Judy on the table.

Would he ever see her again? he wondered. Or would this letter be the last words he would ever communicate to her? He thought about opening the envelope and changing the letter. He could change it to tell her goodbye, but he refrained.

It could do no good, he thought. It would only cause her

to worry, and she knew how he felt if anything were to ever happen to him.

He finished the coffee, placed the envelope in his pocket, then put on his hat. Moments later he was off the ship and searching the base for the nearest mailbox.

"DON'T Sit Under the Apple Tree" played on the officers' club radio and it made Wright smile, something he had not been able to do all day. The horrible memory of the night before was still etched in his brain as he slouched in front of several empty shot glasses on the isolated corner table he had selected. All of the other officers were in town having a small get-together over at the bar in the lobby of the Royal Hawaiian, but he did not feel like being social tonight.

Wright blamed himself, of course, for Anderson's suicide. Anderson had come to him for help and he had turned him away. Wright felt like he had pulled the trigger himself. The events following the suicide were still a confusing blur to him.

The shore patrol had shown up, then the police, then the ambulance. The Cob came within the hour and, soon after, Tremain and Cazanavette had appeared. The ship was a beehive of activity all of the rest of that night, with navy investigators and police taking photographs and asking questions. Five or six different people must have interrogated him. It was not until Cazanavette sat him down alone in the wardroom that things became coherent. Cazanavette asked him a few simple questions, then asked him how he was doing. It was the way in which the XO had asked the question that finally brought Wright back to reality. His tone was understanding, almost fatherly. Cazanavette seemed to know exactly what Wright was going through.

"This is going to eat at you a long time, Ryan," Cazanavette had said. "You're going to play it over in your mind

a thousand times, wondering if you could have done something to save Anderson's life. You're going to need to let
those feelings go, because they'll do nothing but destroy
your confidence in yourself. I've dealt with this kind of
thing before and I can tell you right now that you could not
have stopped Anderson from doing what he did. He felt responsible for Rudy's death, and he was going to kill himself no matter what. Any last minute words from you would
not have made any difference. You're a good officer, and I
don't want to see this bring you down. Let it go. There is
nothing you could have done. Just let it go."

Cazanavette's words had helped, but Wright still felt
responsible.

The memorial service had been nice. It was at the submarine base chapel and the whole crew had shown up in their
whites on their last day of liberty to pay their last respects to
their shipmate. Tremain had said a few things about Anderson. He talked about some of his humorous habits and about
how he had been a good sailor. The crew had been solemn
through the whole occasion, and there were several teary
eyes. Wright had seen Tee crying, too. Tee had the duty today but he had asked Salisbury to take his place for a few
hours so that he could attend the service. The big red-faced
bully had sat in the pew, staring straight ahead, with tears
streaming down his face, his whole body shaking. The image had stuck in Wright's mind.

Wright threw back another shot. It was getting late and
the club was beginning to clear out. He was drunk and he
knew that he would need to leave soon to catch the bus
back to the hotel. He had been wallowing in his sorrows so
much that he failed to notice the woman suddenly standing
beside him.

"Mind if I join you?" the woman said.

Wright looked up and was surprised to see Margie looking down at him. He noticed that she did not smile and he

could not tell if her demeanor was sincere or condescending. She was wearing her uniform and from the disheveled state of her hair it looked like she had just come off shift.

He didn't have the energy to tell her to get lost. Without a word he motioned to the empty chair across from him and signaled the waiter to bring two more rounds.

"This is a surprise finding you here," she said, as she sat down. "I figured you would be with the others at the hotel."

"Why aren't you there?" he muttered. "I think you were invited, too."

She looked away and Wright thought she was choked up, but he was too intoxicated to be sure.

"Yes, well," she said finally. "I thought that I would stop by the *Mackerel* to see Tucker since he has the duty and you guys are leaving tomorrow, but . . . "

Wright saw that there were tears in her eyes as she held her hand to her face to hide it from him.

"But what?" he asked.

"But he doesn't want to see me," she said, wiping away the last bit of moisture from her eyes. "Something's wrong and he doesn't want to see me."

The waiter brought the drinks and Wright was surprised at how fast Margie threw back the whiskey shot and called for another. After a couple of drinks she seemed to relax more as she stared forlornly at the engagement ring on her finger, twisting it several times. They sat in silence through another drink, neither one making eye contact.

"I don't suppose you care about my problems," she said, finally. "Why should you, after the way I've treated you?"

Wright sneaked a few glances at her as she studied the ring. He was beginning to wonder if she was quite as deserving of Tee as he had thought. She probably had no proof that Tee was fooling around on her, but the saying went that "a woman always knew." Her loyalty to him was unexpected and confusing, but appealing all the same. Wright actually felt sorry for her, and for the first time he saw her as his best friend's heart-broken sister and not the snobby bitch.

"I'm sorry about Troy, Margie," he said. "I miss him."

Their eyes met and she smiled warmly at him.

"I know," she said softly, placing her hand on his briefly. "It wasn't your fault."

After another drink the club began to close for the night and they were ushered out by the waiter.

It was a pleasant night with a bright full moon and swaying palm trees in the humid ocean breeze. Wright walked Margaret to the WAVES quarters, a plain two-storied building on the other side of the base. At her doorstep he started to say goodbye, but he could see in her moonlit eyes that she did not want to be alone, and neither did he.

He observed her as she opened the door, the short uniform jacket and knee-length skirt graciously accenting the curves of her body. His sex-starved senses were driven to their full height as they both walked into the darkened dorm room that she shared with another nurse.

"My roommate is on shift this evening," she said as she removed her hat and let her hair fall to her shoulders.

The scent of her perfume made his senses whirl and he impulsively reached for her waist as she turned to face him, bringing her lips to his in a tenth of a second. Half expecting a knee to the groin, he was amazed when he found that her moist lips were most welcoming, her small hand clutching the back of his neck as if to bring him closer. They both had had a lot to drink that night and she met him with no resistance as he unbuttoned her uniform jacket and blouse and let them both fall to the floor. She pressed her heaving breasts to his chest as his hands slid behind her to unzip her skirt. He tugged at it to get it past her curvy hips and then let it fall to the floor as well. She stepped out of it, taking him by the hand to lead him to her room and the perfectly made bed.

With only the light of the moon filtering in through the shutters on the humid night, their sweating and naked bodies embraced with no sounds save for her periodic muffled sighs. Wright held nothing back as he used Margie's body as an instrument to unleash all the stress and frustration he had accumulated over the past months. The pain of losing Troy and Rudy, the hatred for Tee, the guilt for Anderson, the horror of submarine combat, and the confused feelings he had for Margie all culminated in a release of sexual energy that she passionately accepted with complete willingness.

When the dreaded first light of the morning sun appeared in the eastern sky, Wright woke to find a sober Margie sitting on the edge of the bed in a bathrobe, smoking a cigarette.

"You had better go," she said simply, staring at the ring on her hand.

Wright was late and had to get to the ship. As he dressed quickly, he attempted several times to make eye contact with her but she would not meet his gaze. He grabbed his hat and, once outside, he turned to say goodbye but was met only by a closed door.

Nothing made sense anymore, he thought. The abrupt goodbye hurt worse than any of her previous malice ever did. He did not want to leave and thought about banging on the door until she faced him, but the solitary whistle of a destroyer getting underway in the harbor reminded him that *Mackerel* was leaving within the hour, and he still had to get to the hotel to pack his seabag.

PART III

Chapter 19

MACKEREL'S periscope poked above the ocean's surface, and Tremain waited for the lens to clear. The seas were choppy in the North Pacific.

"Dive, come up to sixty feet," Tremain called down the control room hatch.

Slowly the ship came up until the scope lens was no longer molested by the waves and Tremain could get a clear look.

Tremain scanned the azimuth, then called, "No contacts."

"I would not expect any this far out," Stillsen's voice spoke behind him.

Tremain ignored the man and called off a quick weather report, which the nearby quartermaster hurriedly scribbled onto a note pad.

How could Stillsen know what to expect? Tremain thought. Stillsen had never been this close to the empire before. He didn't know what he was talking about, much like most of his conversation over the past two weeks since they had left Pearl. If Stillsen had known anything about the area, he would know that *Mackerel* was now in range of long-range aircraft flying from the Japanese southern home islands. Something Tremain knew about first hand.

"I've seen aircraft where I didn't expect to see any, Commander," Tremain said to Stillsen, turning the scope over to Hubley. "It's always best to be cautious when you decide to stick this scope above the water."

Stillsen acted like he had not heard him. He had not been taking well to Tremain's tutoring.

Tremain had been trying the best he could to bring Stillsen up to speed. He corrected him whenever he said something wrong. He provided guidance when he thought it was necessary. He gave advice where he saw fit, but Stillsen just could not bring himself to accept the subordinate role. It was obvious to everyone on board that he resented not being in command on this patrol. He had already openly criticized several of Tremain's policies in front of the men, enough that even Cazanavette was in an uproar. Stillsen even referred to Tremain by his last name instead of as "Captain," an infraction Tremain would have been well within his bounds to correct, but he held back, hoping that Stillsen would eventually come around. He hoped that the naïve new commander would see the light and realize that he was nothing more than a simple PCO rider that had no useful purpose on the ship.

They had been at sea for over two weeks. They were literally on the Japanese emperor's doorstep, and even now Stillsen could not rise above himself.

"I see no contacts either, Captain," Hubley said.

"Very well. Bring her up to radar depth, Carl. We'll wait until sundown to surface."

Mackerel cruised submerged for the rest of the afternoon, with the radar mast exposed and radiating. When the sun set, *Mackerel* surfaced for the planned high-speed run and battery recharge under the cover of darkness. She would need to get as close as possible to the eastern coast of Shikoku before the next morning.

Tremain had kept silent about the mission for the entire voyage. The crew was still completely in the dark. Rumors were floating around but no one was really sure where they were going. Tremain had planned this intentionally. He did not want the crew to have two weeks to think about their odds for survival. Now that they were close to their objective, it was time to fill them in. He called an officer meeting in the wardroom that evening.

The officers filed in around the table, eager to finally hear the orders they had been curious about for so long. Stillsen was there, too, and he seemed to be slightly annoyed as Tremain went through the entire briefing, just as it had been presented to him at SubPac headquarters. Tremain did, however, choose to leave out the part about the primary target being the shipyard workers. When he finished he asked for questions.

"That's pretty shallow water we'll be attacking in, sir," George Olander started. "Will we be on the surface or submerged?"

"You're right, George, it's damn shallow there. Only eighty feet in some areas. Unfortunately we don't know the *Kurita*'s exact date of departure from Kobe, so we don't know when she'll pass through Kii Suido. It could be during the day, it could be at night. Either way, we'll attack. Luckily, we're in a moonless period, so if we do have the good fortune of attacking at night, we'll have a good chance of making our escape."

"What about land-based radars, sir?" Hubley asked. "Don't the Japanese have them?"

"They most likely do and I'm sure they'll be probing the strait with every one of them. We're going to have to present a low silhouette at all times. Ideally, we will attack on the surface at night. We are counting on our conning tower being low enough that we won't stick out on their radar screens. If we do, with any luck, they'll confuse our return for a fishing boat. We'll slip inside the task force, fill the *Kurita* with torpedoes, then sail away. Once we're twenty miles or so from the strait, the water will be deep enough to submerge safely. Then we'll just dive and cruise away to fight another day. Nothing to it."

Everyone in the room chuckled at the attempted humor. Fighting another day would be the last thing on their minds.

"Sir?" Wright spoke up.

"Go ahead, Ryan."

"What about our torpedoes?"

"The warheads in these torpedoes are much larger than the normal Mark 14s. They should do the job against the *Kurita*'s armor."

"No, sir, that's not what I meant," Wright said. "I meant to ask, are we going to modify the exploders on these fish like we did on the last ones?"

Wright had asked the question innocently enough, but Tremain felt the question stab him like a knife, and he immediately saw Stillsen's expression change out of the corner of his eye. No one had told the ensign to keep his mouth shut about the exploders.

"Modify?" Stillsen intoned. "What are you talking about, Ensign? What the hell is he talking about, Tremain?"

Wright immediately knew that he had erred. The other officers were avoiding eye contact with him. All except Stillsen, whose bird-like eyes were transfixed upon him, waiting for an answer. Wright did not know what to say. No one had told him to keep Stillsen in the dark on the matter.

"I'm waiting, Ensign," Stillsen said, impatiently.

Wright started to speak, but was saved by Tremain.

"Mr. Wright is referring to a modification I ordered my

chief torpedoman to make on several of our Mark 14s during our last patrol."

"What kind of modifications?" Stillsen snapped.

Tremain exchanged glances with Cazanavette. He knew that Stillsen would not let this issue lie. He had found a weakness in Tremain and now he was going to exploit it.

"I ordered the magnetic exploders deactivated, Commander," Tremain said.

"You are not authorized to order any modifications to weapons." Stillsen spat out the words like a tattling schoolboy. "Does ComSubPac know about this?"

"That's irrelevant at this point, Commander," Tremain said. "The fact is, I did it. The fish we're carrying now have also been changed to contact weapons, by my order."

Stillsen gasped.

"There is no sense in pointing fingers and talking about authorizations, now," Tremain continued. "Let's save it for when we're out of Japanese waters. Right now we need to focus on the mission at hand."

"Why wasn't I informed of the modifications?" Stillsen insisted.

"Because there was no need to inform you." Tremain added in a firm voice, "Let's address this issue another time, Commander, in private. I'd like to get on with the mission briefing."

Tremain did not want to argue in front of the other officers. Junior officers should not have to see their captain and future captain in disagreements. It could only damage the command climate. It was exactly the reason Tremain had wanted to leave Stillsen ashore.

"Like hell we'll address this another time. We'll address it now, Tremain," Stillsen said. "You've broken BuOrd regulations. You've modified weapons that have been specifically prepared for this mission. Those torpedoes have been designed to sink the *Kurita* by exploding underneath it. That's the only way they can break the ship's keel. Now how the hell do you intend to do that with contact exploders, Tremain?"

Stillsen's comment had sparked a question in the minds of the ship's officers. Tremain could immediately see the doubt on their faces. They were thinking of what they had learned in sub school. The textbook method of sinking a capital ship was to detonate a torpedo directly beneath it. The gas pocket, created by the explosion, would place a brief but catastrophic tensile stress on the ship's keel, which would snap it like a twig. That was the textbook way to do it, under perfect conditions.

"I don't intend to sink the *Kurita* by breaking her back, Commander," Tremain said. "If we had magnetic exploders that worked properly, then maybe I would. But everyone in this room will tell you that those magnetic exploders are topheavy with problems. I plan to sink her the old-fashioned way, by blowing holes in her side."

"That is not your call to make, Tremain. We have orders. Those orders don't allow us to alter our weapons or our method of attack in any way. Therefore, I insist that you order Chief Konhausen to re-enable the magnetic exploders."

"We're only going to get one chance at this, Dave." Tremain attempted to diffuse the situation. His officers had uncertainty on their faces. "I need reliable torpedoes. I need them to work right the first time. I can't afford to have any prematures or duds. We won't be able to line up for a second shot. Once we've fired that first salvo, every Japanese son of a bitch with an ash can is going to be on top of us."

Stillsen's face grew grave. "I don't think you heard me, Tremain. So I'll say it again. Have Konhausen restore the magnetic exploders."

Tremain locked eyes with Stillsen. He could not believe the man had actually given him an order in front of his own officers. The man had stepped over the line.

"Clear the fucking room!" Tremain shouted.

The officers quickly rose from their seats and filed out of the wardroom in silence.

Tremain drew the curtain shut behind the last man and turned to face Stillsen with an evil scowl. Stillsen started to speak, but was cut off by Tremain's finger in his face.

"Listen to me, Mister Stillsen. You can disagree with my orders, you can disagree with my policies or the way I do things, but that's the last time you'll give me a fucking order in front of my men! Is that clear?"

Stillsen appeared stunned at Tremain's change in demeanor.

"These boys have very few things they can hold on to," Tremain continued. "Hell, they don't even know if they'll be alive tomorrow. The least I can do for them is give them some kind of confidence in their captain and their boat. I'm fucking tired of you trying to break down that confidence. It's evident to me that you have been trying to do that very thing since we left Pearl Harbor!

"Now I know you feel slighted because you're not the captain this time out. You're upset about it so you're going to make life difficult for me. Well, asshole, I've got news for you, you should be thanking your lucky stars that you're not in command. I've seen you make so many green-ass novice mistakes on this patrol, I could write a book about it. You may have finished PCO School but you've still got a lot to fucking learn.

"We are not out here to protect your pride or your snotnosed ego, Mr. Stillsen. We're here to do a job. I know how to get the job done. You don't. Accomplishing the mission goes beyond blind adherence to peacetime rules and regulations that were written by people who didn't know the first thing about actual combat.

"Do you actually think that I would go against regulations

without giving the matter the utmost consideration? I have made my decision, it is my command decision, and I believe it is the best chance we have. That is final! I'm not going to tell Konhausen to change the fish back and jeopardize the mission for your sake, for Captain Ireland's sake, or even for Admiral Giles' sake, for that matter."

Stillsen did not respond. His face was red. Tremain could not tell whether it was out of embarrassment or hate. He suddenly looked much smaller, like the wind had left his sails.

Tremain continued. "Now, I suggest that you take on a much lower profile for the rest of the mission, Mister Stillsen. Watch the crew and the officers and see how good they are at what they do. If you can get past your own arrogance you might actually learn something."

Stillsen still did not speak. He sat with lips pursed and face red. Tremain thought he saw a slight nod. That was enough. Tremain started to leave the room, but stopped short as he remembered one last thing.

"One final thing, Commander. From now on, you don't call me 'Tremain' and you don't call me 'Jack.' From now on you don't call me anything but 'Captain' or 'Sir.' Understood?"

Stillsen stared at him in fuming disbelief for several seconds, before uttering a weak: "Aye aye, sir."

Chapter 20

WRIGHT peered through the periscope at the white-capped waves above. He had been on watch for three hours and the tension in the conning tower got thicker with every nautical mile they eliminated between them and the Japanese coast, although nothing seemed as tense as the briefing in the wardroom the night before. Wright felt like an idiot for bringing up the torpedo modifications and the other officers had jeered him for it after the meeting. Tee was the worst, of course, calling him a dumbass and reverting to some of his previous behavior but with somewhat less vigor. Wright had just smiled with the knowledge that he had shared Margie's bed the night before deployment, not Tee.

He played that night and the morning after over and over in his mind. After leaving Margie, he had rushed to the hotel, packed his seabag, caught a taxi back to the base, and made it to the boat just in time for inspection at quarters. When *Mackerel* shoved off, Wright had been on deck along with Tee and he had noticed Margie standing with some other nurses way down the pier. As *Mackerel* had backed into the channel, Tee shouted orders to the linehandlers on deck, never looking in her direction even once. Since that day Wright wondered if she had been standing there for Tee at all, or if she had been there for him.

As Wright looked through the scope his eye caught a small flicker of light in the blue sky.

"Aircraft spotted, sir," he announced. The sun gleamed off the distant twin-engine bomber's wings as it banked far away to the north.

Tremain came up the ladder from the control room and took the scope from Wright. He swung around a quick scan of the surface, then steadied the lens on the distant aircraft and increased the magnification.

"She's headed west," Tremain said. "Probably headed home after an ASW patrol."

Cazanavette was at the chart desk, plotting the new contact. He measured off the distance with a pair of dividers.

"We should be able to see Shikoku, Captain," he said. "Bearing three four five."

Tremain swung the scope around to the bearing and increased to maximum magnification. Barely visible above the wave crests, he could make out the jagged peaks of a mountain range, lying just over the horizon.

"Right you are, XO. I hold some mountains on that bearing. From here on it gets dicey. Pass the word to the crew. Let them know we're less than fifteen miles from the Japanese homeland. This is the real deal. I don't want any maintenance performed until further notice."

"Aye, aye, Captain."

Equipment failures happened all the time on a submarine at sea. Most of them occurred just after the equipment had received routine maintenance. Tremain did not want any problems that might force him to surface during daylight hours. So much traffic passed through these waters, they would certainly be sighted, and the mission would be a complete failure. The Japanese would never allow the battleship to pass anywhere near waters where they knew a submarine lurked.

"What's the distance to Kii Suido, XO?" Tremain asked.

Cazanavette grabbed the dividers again. "Twenty miles, due north, sir."

"Helm, right standard rudder. Steady course north."

As the helm acknowledged the order, Tremain looked at Cazanavette.

"Well, XO, we won't get there until sundown. The window starts tomorrow. I hope the *Kurita* doesn't decide to come out a day early."

"It wouldn't be the first time our intelligence boys fed us some bogus data, Captain," Cazanavette said with a smile.

Mackerel cruised along at five knots, against the stiff ocean current, slowly closing the distance to Kii Suido. Tremain ordered periodic periscope searches, but also ordered that the scope exposure be kept to an absolute minimum. With Japanese planes flying overhead, it would take only one daydreaming airman to sight the *Mackerel*'s periscope and radio the information back to his base.

At sunset, *Mackerel* came into visual range of Kii Suido. The snow-capped mountains of Honshu were just visible in the last light of the day. Kii Suido was the Japanese name for the entrance to a natural channel that ran between the Japanese mainland, Honshu, and the southern island, Shikoku. The channel itself was hundreds of miles long and ran far back into Japanese territorial waters, allowing access to several key naval ports, including Kobe. The entrance to the channel, Kii Suido, opened southward into the Pacific Ocean and was less than twenty miles across at its narrowest point. Any ship traveling to or from Kobe would have to pass through the narrow Kii Suido to reach the Pacific Ocean. Thus, Kii Suido was the chosen spot for *Mackerel*'s ambush. And even though the twenty-mile strait was still a large area for a submerged submarine to cover, the usable width was further reduced by shoals and reefs, especially for a vessel the size of the *Kurita*.

It did not take a very experienced sailor to look at a chart and determine the few places through which a deep-draft battleship could pass. Earlier, Tremain and Cazanavette had speculated that *Kurita*'s captain would want to have at least a mile buffer between his ship and any shoal water. That left him with a space approximately ten miles wide in the center of the channel. They both agreed to position *Mackerel* at an optimum place between the two points of land, right in the middle of the ten-mile-wide area. And there she would wait for her quarry.

Tremain ordered the entire boat rigged for red light, and left the daunting task of piloting the ship into the strait for Cazanavette, while he ate a quiet dinner in the wardroom. Tremain allowed Stillsen to assist Cazanavette as a gesture of good will, and to bolster the bruised ego of the young lieutenant commander, but he made it clear to both of them that Cazanavette had the conn. Tremain was growing more confident that Stillsen would be a team player and honor his orders.

About the same time Tremain finished his dinner, Cazanavette called the wardroom to let him know that they had arrived at their position.

Tremain made his way back up to the conning tower and took the scope from Cazanavette. The entire seascape was pitch-black save for a few lights here and there, and he knew that most of them were on land. He could make out very little in the blackness. Only Cazanavette's carefully plotted position on the chart gave him an indication of where *Mackerel* was. The chart showed that they were sitting precisely in the middle of the strait.

"Any contacts, XO?"

"Only faint sound contacts, sir," Cazanavette answered, his face illuminated by the red light. "Sounds like fishing boats and distant merchants. That channel could be creating quite a sound duct as well. We could be hearing things that are sixty to seventy miles away."

"Right," Tremain said. "Well, we need to do a battery charge. We have no choice, we'll have to risk surfacing."

"What if there are sampans fishing up there, Captain?" Stillsen asked hesitantly. "What if they see us?"

"Then we'll have to sink them with guns." Tremain managed a smile. "And hope that their relatives won't notice that they're missing until the *Kurita* has already come our way."

Cazanavette nodded and grinned.

"We'll rotate the gun crews frequently to keep them sharp," Tremain added. "Pass the word, if it comes to a gunfight, we'll use the forty-millimeters first, to minimize the noise. Save the five-inch gun as a last resort."

"Aye, sir," Cazanavette answered and turned to the phone talker to wake Hubley, who was the gunnery officer.

"Man stations for battle surface, XO," Tremain ordered.

"Aye, aye, Captain."

MACKEREL broke through the placid dark waves and emerged bow-first from her underwater habitat. She came up surrounded by a bubbly white froth as high-pressure air purged the main ballast tanks. Her stern seemed to hesitate for a moment, then popped up level, as the water receded from her decks and superstructure.

Within seconds Tremain led an entourage of personnel out of the bridge hatch. He immediately put his night binoculars to his eyes to see if there was enough light to use them. Unfortunately, there was not. *Mackerel*'s lookouts would not be able to see any approaching ships until it was too late. Normally a submariner prayed for dark nights, but this was too dark. They would have to rely completely on radar.

As men filed past him with .50-caliber machine guns and twenty-millimeter and forty-millimeter ammunition, Tremain passed the word to man the main deck. Moments later, the deck hatch popped open and several sailors emerged to man the five-inch gun. Within minutes, the ammunition locker was cracked open and five-inch shells were passed to the gun crew.

Tremain looked around to see all of his helmeted sailors standing by their guns, ready for action. It was the first time Tremain had seen *Mackerel* fully rigged for battle surface, and he was proud of how quickly and naturally the crew filed into their stations. *Mackerel*'s array of surface weaponry would be quite impressive to any small boat sailor. On her deck, just aft of the conning tower, she carried a five-inch gun. On the raised deck forward of the bridge, she carried a twenty-millimeter machine gun. On the cigarette deck, she had a Bofors 40-millimeter gun. She also had two portable .50-caliber machine guns mounted on either side of the bridge. It was more than enough fireworks to light up the sky. The sight actually gave Tremain quite a charge. He half-wanted to hunt down a Japanese gunboat and pick a fight.

"Bridge, radar," the bridge box squawked. "I only have a few useful areas on my scope. The two points of land are blocking out almost everything. There appear to be some small returns hugging the shoreline. No other contacts."

"Radar, bridge, aye," Tremain answered. Those small returns are probably fishermen, he thought. "Watch the ranges closely. And aim your beam up the channel periodically. We don't want to get run over by an outbound convoy."

"Bridge, radar. Aye, sir."

Good, Tremain thought. He expected that the Japanese

would have patrol boats in the area, but they did not seem to be around this evening. Still, the thought of being close enough to the Japanese mainland that he could see lights from houses on the shore discomforted him.

"Control, bridge," Tremain spoke into the intercom. "Mr. Olander, you may line up for a normal battery charge."

"Control, bridge. Aye, sir," came Olander's drawl over the box.

Mackerel's huge diesel engines coughed to life and the familiar smell of diesel exhaust filled the nostrils of everyone topside. The noise seemed loud on the quiet waters of the strait, and Tremain had to remind himself that they were still miles away from land. He was comforted by the fact that another ship's crew would not likely be able to discern *Mackerel*'s noise over that of its own engines, but it was only a small comfort.

There were also shore-based radars to consider. Tremain was banking on *Mackerel*'s low profile to keep it from popping up on the Japanese radar screens. He was operating on a lot of gambles, but that was always necessary on a mission like this one.

The strait remained devoid of activity for several hours, as the powerful diesels generated electricity and charged up the depleted batteries. The gentle tidal current, flowing in and out of the channel, slowly pushed *Mackerel* from one side of the channel to the other. Periodically the officer of the deck ordered some speed to position the ship back in the center of the strait.

Tremain remained on the bridge the entire time. The gun crews rotated out, but he remained, unable to force himself to go below.

In the early morning hours, the serenity of the night was broken by the squawk of the speaker box.

"Bridge, radar. Sir, the channel appears to be cluttered with multiple large contacts, around bearing three five zero. Range is now seven miles and closing. It looks like they're coming out."

Tremain's heart skipped a beat. This is it, he thought. The *Kurita* and her escorts were coming out right on schedule.

"Radar, bridge," Tremain spoke into the box. "Any of those returns look big enough to be a battleship?"

"Hard to tell, sir. They're still distant. It's possible."

Cazanavette came up the ladder and joined him on the bridge.

"I looked at the radar scope, Captain. He's right. There are several large contacts in the channel heading for the open sea. They're on a constant bearing heading in our direction."

Tremain checked his watch.

"We still have four hours of darkness left," he said. "Conditions are as ideal as they can get for a surface attack. I just wish we had a little more room to maneuver."

"Yes, sir. I counted at least seven contacts. It's going to get pretty tight when they pass by us. I sure hope they don't have radar."

Tremain nodded. "Go below and start plotting, XO. Let me know when you have a good solution. And have Mr. Olander secure his battery charge."

"Aye, aye, Captain." Cazanavette disappeared down the hatch.

Tremain lifted the binoculars to his eyes and pointed them up the dark channel. He knew he would not be able to see the approaching ships. It was still pitch-black. They were out there, though, and headed this way. Cazanavette would have a better picture watching the radar screen.

A few minutes later, Cazanavette's voice squawked, "Bridge, conning tower. We now have eight discernible radar contacts, constant bearing three five five. Good solution is course one seven five, speed ten knots. Range to the lead ship is four miles and closing. Impossible to tell which return is the *Kurita,* sir. Also, sonar reports high-speed screws on the same bearing. Impossible to tell how many."

Destroyers, Tremain thought. But something wasn't right. Why would the battleship and her escorts be traveling at a mere ten knots? Especially when passing through the narrow strait. All intelligence reports indicated that she was capable of much more.

"XO, bridge." Tremain keyed the box. "Does sonar hear any echo ranging?"

There was a brief pause.

"Bridge, XO. Very little, sir. Sounds more like a fathometer than active sonar pulses."

That made sense, Tremain thought. The Japanese heavy ships would be using their fathometers to avoid running onto any shoals. But why weren't the destroyers pinging away at the water? That was standard procedure for Japanese destroyers escorting heavy warships. Maybe this was not the *Kurita,* after all. Maybe these escorts were protecting a large convoy of slow-moving merchants. That would explain the lack of active sonar. The escorts would be listening, not pinging.

"XO, bridge. What's the range now?"

"Bridge, conning tower. Just under six thousand yards, sir. Still closing at ten knots. We'll be inside their formation in fifteen minutes."

Tremain had to make the decision. Attack or dive. It was now or never.

"Mr. Hubley." Tremain grabbed Hubley's arm in the darkness. "Stow the guns and clear the decks. Get the men below, and hurry."

"Sir?"

"Do it, now! We don't have time to talk about it."

"Aye, aye, sir."

Hubley began barking orders. The gun crews jumped from their positions and started passing the broken-out ammunition back to the storage lockers.

Tremain keyed the call box. "XO, bridge. Prepare to dive the boat."

Cazanavette's voice came back. "Sir, if this is the *Kurita* . . ."

"Understood, XO. Get ready to dive. This is *not* the *Kurita*!"

It took several minutes for the gun crews to rig the weapons for submergence and then get below themselves. Then Hubley ordered the lookouts below and checked the deck for any person who might have been left behind. The range to the oncoming ships closed to three thousand yards as the klaxon rang out two blasts. *Mackerel*'s diesels shut down and water rushed into her main ballast tanks with a loud hiss. Moments later, she disappeared beneath the waves, leaving only a frothy disturbance on the surface to mark her presence.

"Take her down to one-hundred-twenty feet," Tremain ordered. "Rig for silent running."

All of the compartments throughout the ship fell silent as the procession of ships approached overhead. Salisbury manned the sonar headset, and reported as the ships drew closer, "Multiple contacts closing, sir. Multiple low-speed screws."

"Are they warships or merchants?" Tremain asked.

Salisbury raised one hand and closed his eyes as he listened intently.

"Well?" Tremain said, impatiently.

Salisbury opened his eyes and gave a small smile. "Sounds like merchant ships, Captain."

Tremain breathed a sigh of relief as he exchanged glances with Cazanavette.

Within minutes the low churning screw noise was audible through the hull. It grew louder until it reverberated through the whole ship. Salisbury's sensitive ears counted ten different ships, including one escort. It took a good twenty minutes for the entire column to pass overhead. *Mackerel*'s crew stared at the bulkheads, trying not to breathe too heavily, whispering to communicate. It was absurd to think that the Japanese sonar men could hear them if they spoke normally, but whispering felt like the right thing to do.

Stillsen stood in the back of the conning tower, watching Tremain as the screw noises began to fade.

"What if that *was* the *Kurita*?" he asked, then added, "If it was, the mission is a failure."

Tremain did not respond. He wanted Stillsen to know that he was still a visitor, and his comments were not welcome. He glanced at Cazanavette and smiled.

"If it was the *Kurita,* Commander," Cazanavette answered for him, "then she was traveling with a bunch of merchant ships, and an extremely light escort."

"Either way we'll know for sure when they make their turn," Tremain added.

If *Kurita* were in the convoy, it would turn left once they reached the open sea and the screw noises would track off to the east. That was the direction to Yokosuka. If it were simply a convoy of merchants, they would almost certainly head west or continue on a southerly course toward one of the Empire's island garrisons out in the Pacific.

Salisbury listened intently and tracked the convoy, making small adjustments on his hydrophone director. He read off the bearings and Cazanavette plotted them, assuming that the convoy's speed had remained constant at ten knots. Then, about the same time, Cazanavette's plot showed that the convoy had emerged from the channel. Salisbury's bearings started to track off to the west indicating that the convoy had turned right. The *Kurita* could not be among them.

Tremain had been sure of his decision, but he still breathed a small sigh of relief.

After a quick periscope search, Tremain ordered *Mackerel* back to the surface. Again, the guns were manned, and the hunters sat in silence for the rest of the night, watching and waiting for their prey.

Chapter 21

WRIGHT and Salisbury strolled through the forward torpedo room on their pre-watch tour. Since O'Connell's death, Wright had been reassigned to Salisbury's watch as junior officer of the deck. As the two passed from space to space, Salisbury shined his flashlight inside nooks and crannies looking for any sign of problems and directed Wright to do the same. Salisbury was a marked difference from Rudy O'Connell when it came to standing watch. Their shared liberty antics seemed to be a distant memory as the hierarchical positions made their relationship suddenly very professional.

"Always check back there," Salisbury said, shining his flashlight onto a grease-fitting outboard of one of the torpedo racks. "That's a good place for corrosion to occur. Those drain strainers leak all the time."

Wright appeared interested, then went on about his own inspection of the space, trying to find his own rust spot partly because it was his job, but mainly because he knew it would please Salisbury.

Salisbury found the torpedoman of the watch up by the tube breech doors and began speaking to him about the status of the tubes. While Salisbury was talking, Wright moved aft along the starboard torpedo racks, continuing to scan the space with his flashlight. He checked the hidden areas outboard of each torpedo rack, trying not to disturb the off-watch torpedomen sleeping in hammocks all around him.

Wright noticed two sailors lounging near the room's aft bulkhead. He recognized them as Johnson and Dalton. As he drew nearer, he overheard pieces of their conversation.

". . . can't believe they're going to give us to him," Johnson said. "Let him slip up just once and we'll see that his ass is accidentally dropped overboard."

"Yeah," Dalton replied, "I'll be a skimmer again before I take orders from that asshole."

Wright smiled inwardly. He assumed they were talking about Lieutenant Commander Stillsen. The poor man was already jinxed to have a difficult time as *Mackerel*'s captain. Ironically, the *Mackerel* sailors had come to respect Lieutenant Commander Tremain, and they were not so eager to have Stillsen take over when they returned to Pearl.

"Anderson's dead because of him," Dalton said, and the other sailor nodded in agreement.

Wright's ears pricked at what he had just heard. Maybe the men were taking this change of command bitterness a bit too far, since they now seemed to have laid the blame for Anderson's death on Commander Stillsen. Wright could not stand by and listen to such foolishness, especially when it concerned Anderson's death. It was something that he had grown very sensitive about.

The two sailors appeared startled for a moment as Wright approached them from out of the shadows.

"Hello, Mr. Wright," Johnson said with a counterfeit smile. "Anything we can help you with, sir?"

"I couldn't help but overhear you talking about Anderson," he said.

They glared up at the ensign like he was intruding.

Wright continued, "I'm sorry to eavesdrop, but I think you are wrong to blame Commander Stillsen for Anderson's death. If anyone is to blame, it's me. I'm the one who turned him away when he needed someone to talk to."

The sailors looked at each other.

"We're not talking about Stillsen, sir," Dalton spoke up. "We're talking about Mr. Turner. Haven't you heard. . . . "

Dalton, who was somewhat junior to Johnson, stopped abruptly in response to a jab in the ribs from his compatriot.

"Nothing to worry about, Mr. Wright," Johnson said quickly, still smiling. "It'll all take care of itself in due time. Sorry to bother you, sir."

Wright nodded and turned to rejoin Salisbury, but he stopped mid-stride. He was confused. The sailors were obviously trying to hide something. Something concerning Anderson's death, and it had something to do with Tee, although he couldn't guess what. Tee wasn't even on the ship the day Anderson shot himself. How could he have been responsible?

Wright remembered hearing about Hubley's transfer orders. Hubley was to transfer to another command as soon as *Mackerel* got back to Pearl. When that happened, Tee would take over as the new torpedo and gunnery officer. Tee would be in charge of the men of Torpedo Division, the largest division on the ship. Johnson and Dalton were both part of that division, so they would also end up under his command. For some reason, they did not seem to like the idea. They had not been talking about Commander Stillsen at all. The officer they had been talking about dropping over the side was Tee.

Wright suddenly felt a cold chill as he realized that these sailors had not been merely griping to each other, as he had originally assumed. They had not been venting or complaining. They had been plotting an actual threat against an officer's life, and they were dead serious about it.

"Johnson." Wright turned back toward the sailors. "What's going on?"

"Nothing, sir."

"Nothing?" Wright checked that Salisbury was still occupied on the other side of the room before continuing in a forceful whisper. "You just said something about throwing someone overboard. And you also said something about that person being responsible for Anderson's death. That's nothing? What're you hiding?"

"Sir, this doesn't concern you."

Johnson looked irritated at Wright's probing. His arrogance was starting to annoy Wright. Wright had to know. The two sailors knew something about Anderson's death, and he would not let up until they told him the truth.

"Johnson, you tell me right now what you and Dalton were talking about or I swear I will go straight to the XO with what I've heard." Wright immediately saw a response in the sailor's eyes. "We'll see what he thinks of your sneaking and plotting against an officer."

The sailors glanced at each other with panic in their eyes as Wright shrugged dramatically and started to walk away.

"If you must know, Mr. Wright," Johnson said finally, before Wright could take two steps.

Wright turned back to face them.

"Tell me," he said.

Johnson looked hesitant. He contorted his face, then looked around once more to see if anyone conscious was within earshot.

"Sir, this is a big secret," he whispered. "Me and Dalton don't want to tarnish a dead man's name. I don't want to do that. Anderson was a good shipmate. Promise you won't tell the XO, sir?"

Wright needed to know. He had held onto the guilt of Anderson's death for weeks. He needed to know all of the circumstances for himself. "I promise, Johnson."

Johnson nodded. "Thank you, sir."

"Well, what is it?" Wright said impatiently.

"There was no radar interference the day we got attacked by that Japanese plane, sir," Johnson said, checking over his shoulder. "Anderson's radar was working just fine. That bomber got so close to us because Anderson wasn't watching his screen. He left his post to clean up a coffee stain. By the time he got back to the radar, the plane was already on top of us."

Wright was astonished, though a little skeptical. He had been on board long enough to know how quickly rumors spread. He also knew how easily they were embellished and distorted. Sailors were a very superstitious lot and they always needed an explanation for everything under the sun. Random events did not exist. The fact that a random event could cause their deaths or the death of one of their shipmates was not comprehensible. It was even scoffed at. The blame always had to be attached to something or someone. It helped to make sense of senseless things and it gave them something to think about.

"I don't know about that," Wright said. "I was up there, remember. I was the last one off the bridge. Anderson saved our lives by giving us those few seconds of warning. I'll always be grateful to him for that. And you should be, too. And you're right about one thing. You shouldn't tarnish his memory like that."

"He could have given you plenty of warning, sir," Johnson said, sounding annoyed with Wright, "if he'd been at his fucking station doing his fucking job. We could have been well below before that plane got anywhere near us and Mister O'Connell would still be here." He paused and then added, "Anderson would still be here, too, if it wasn't for fucking Mr. Turner!"

"What has Turner got to do with this?" Wright exclaimed.

"It was Turner who ordered Anderson to leave his post, sir, to clean up a fucking coffee stain. A fucking coffee stain, sir!"

Wright's heart skipped a beat. A tingling sensation crept up and down his spine and he suddenly felt cold. He had not believed anything Johnson said until now. Now it was all becoming very clear to him.

"What . . ." Wright muttered.

"You knew about that, didn't you, sir?" Johnson said. "It happened like fucking clockwork at the end of every watch. Turner always had to have his little conning tower looking spotless before he could relieve the watch. Well, this time Turner got bit in the ass. He told Anderson to leave his post to clean up a coffee stain and because of that Mr. O'Connell died. Anderson shot himself because he couldn't live with the guilt. The only reason we haven't ratted on Mr. Turner is because we don't want Anderson's family to lose his medal. That's worth more to us than sending Turner to a general court martial, like he deserves. So we all hate Turner, sir, and we don't want him as our division officer. That so wrong, sir?"

Anderson drunk and almost AWOL, then committing suicide. Turner not acting like himself and crying at Anderson's memorial service. It all fit together now in Wright's mind. He felt both angry and afraid at the same time. Angry at not seeing it before, and afraid of what he now knew about Tee.

"I can see by the look on your face that you believe it, too, sir," Johnson said. "You and Mister O'Connell were friends, right, sir? Well, don't you worry. We'll take care of Mr. Turner when the time comes."

Wright did not respond. His head hurt and he felt a bit dizzy. He left the sailors and made his way back to Salisbury, still conversing by the torpedo tube breeches with the torpedoman of the watch.

"What's wrong with you, Ryan?" Salisbury asked. "You look ill."

Wright rubbed his head, unable to tell him. "Nothing, Joe. Let's just go relieve the watch."

MACKEREL spent all day at periscope depth, holding position between the two points of land with short one-third and two-third bells to counteract the effects of the current flowing in and out of the channel. The conning tower and most of the ship was quiet. The crew had exerted themselves during the night, manning the deck guns, and now most were resting up for the next night. The gentle purr of the electric motors combined with the reduced oxygen levels did well to put the off-watch crew to sleep, and tempted a few of the men on watch to do the same.

So far, the day had been an uneventful one. There had been no sign of the *Kurita*. The officers kept the scope trained up the channel and every hour or so a ship or two would pass through, heading in to port or out to sea. A small squadron of destroyers steamed by at high speed in the late morning, but they passed well clear of *Mackerel* and did not pose a threat. Periodically, a flight of aircraft would appear over the land. Whenever they appeared to be heading in *Mackerel*'s direction, Tremain ordered the ship down to two hundred feet to prevent the submarine's dark shape from catching any attention. After enough time was given for the aircraft to pass, *Mackerel* was back at periscope depth again, searching. It was unlikely that an aircraft would spot the submerged submarine, anyway. A low gray cloud cover had set in and it removed most of the water's translucency.

Waiting was the hard part of submarining, waiting for the enemy and being patient, having faith that they would come. It could be extremely boring, so boring that one could easily forget how close the enemy actually was.

Late in the afternoon, Cazanavette took the conn while Tremain caught up on some sleep in his cabin. Salisbury and Wright were the officers on watch.

"There goes another one," Salisbury said, looking through the scope. "Small freighter, eight thousand yards away. Bearing three zero zero. It's heading up the channel."

Cazanavette came over from the chart desk and took the scope.

"Probably heading to Kobe," he said. "Yep. Here, Ryan, take the scope. Give me a good angle on the bow. I want to see how good you are . . . Hey, Ryan!"

Wright had been deep in thought only a few feet away, but he had not heard a word the XO had said.

"I'm sorry, sir," Wright finally said.

"You need some coffee, Ryan?"

"No, sir."

"All right then," Cazanavette said impatiently. "Take the scope and tell me the angle on that freighter."

Wright took the scope and swung it around until he saw the Japanese freighter. He almost missed it because only its topmasts were visible above the waves. They appeared as two tiny sticks cruising along the northwestern horizon. Shikoku's mountains in the background made the masts even more difficult to discern.

"I can only see the tops of its masts, sir," Wright said. "I can't see any of her hull. I can't tell which way she's headed."

Cazanavette and Salisbury exchanged smiles.

"Well, use what you do know," Cazanavette said in a tu-toring tone. "How many masts do you see?"

"Two."

"Okay, if she were pointing at us or facing away how many would you see?"

"Probably only one, sir."

"Right. So, since you can see two masts, you know that you're looking at one of her beams. Which way is she drawing?"

Wright centered the crosshair on one of the masts and held it steady. He waited and watched as the mast slowly move to the right.

"Right bearing drift, sir."

"Okay, so if she's bearing three zero zero, and she has a right bearing drift, that means she has to be headed which way?"

"Somewhere to the north, sir."

"Okay, so what's the angle on the bow?"

"Starboard one hundred?"

Cazanavette turned up his bottom lip. "Not bad. That's the best you can do with what you know. After you get used to seeing those mast arrangements, and you get used to the different separations on different ships, you'll get better at it."

Salisbury took the scope back. Cazanavette pulled a recognition book out of a locker and handed it to Wright.

"Here," Cazanavette said. "Look up the freighter in here. It's the best way for you to learn."

Wright hated standing watch with Cazanavette around. He liked the man as a person, but he always took it upon himself to teach Wright something. Of course, that was his job as XO, but sometimes Wright was not in the mood for the tutoring sessions, especially today. Not after what he had heard down in the torpedo room. He could not get the thought out of his head. He felt anger brewing deep inside him. As the monotonous watch went by, the anger grew. His anger was directed at one person, Tee. He hated the man for O'Connell's death, for Anderson's death, for not coming forward, and for his treatment of Margie.

Several times during the watch, he thought of going against his word. He thought of telling Cazanavette the whole story. But what good would that do? The whole story really was just a rumor. He knew it was the truth, but he could never prove it to the XO. And besides, how could he expose an internal problem when they were in the midst of such an important mission? It could serve no useful purpose. And Johnson was right; Anderson's name should not be tarnished any further. Wright decided that he would wait, and when the time was right he would confront Tee, and he would seek retribution for all the trouble he had caused.

Chapter 22

TREMAIN rolled over in his rack and stared at his cabin bulkhead bathed in the red glow from the solitary red light bulb in the overhead. He had just come below to relax for a few minutes before going back up to the bridge to spend the rest of the night. *Mackerel* had been on station for four nights now, and still there was no sign of the *Kurita*.

Mackerel had conducted the same routine for the past four days: surfacing at night to probe the channel with the radar, then submerging during the day to search with the periscope and sonar. Large convoys had overrun them on two more occasions, both at night. Both times *Mackerel* barely submerged in time to avoid detection. During the daylight hours, single merchant ships and sporadic aircraft continued to keep them on their toes, but there was no sign of the *Kurita*.

The crew had openly started to doubt the quality of Sub-Pac's intelligence reports. Tremain could not blame them. He had started to doubt the reports himself. Each night had been one nerve-racking experience after another, and it was stretching the crew to the limit of their endurance.

Tremain struggled to keep his eyes open. He knew that he would fall asleep the instant he shut them. So far, this evening had been tense just like all the others.

As evening had fallen on Kii Suido, a dense fog fell too and it now hugged the ocean's surface like a fluffy sheepskin blanket. The fog compounded with the moonless night had made it virtually impossible to see anything, and it was having its effects on the crew. The gun crews were highstrung, fearful that a destroyer could emerge from the fog at any moment. Every sound, every light, every ripple in the calm waters startled them, for they did not have complete faith in *Mackerel*'s radar.

"Captain to the conning tower," the speaker near Tremain's head intoned just as he had shut his eyes.

He rolled out of his rack, not bothering to put his shirt on. Groping through the darkened passage and past several sailors in the control room his hands finally found the cold polished rungs of the ladder, gleaming dimly in the red light. Climbing up into the conning tower, he found Cazanavette and Stillsen huddled near the radar.

"What is it, XO?" he mumbled.

"Intermittent radar contact, sir. Bearing zero zero eight. The radar operator was showing Commander Stillsen how our radar worked, and the commander noticed a small spike, just visible there above the background noise."

"The Commander's got good eyes, sir," the radar man said. "I would have missed it, completely."

Tremain glanced at Stillsen and smiled in appreciation. The young lieutenant commander had been doing much better. He had been taking much more of a learning role since their last conversation, and he was actually becoming an accepted member of the ship's company. Even Tremain did not think Stillsen, taken down a few notches, was that bad an officer.

"What's the range now?" Tremain asked.

"Six thousand yards, sir," the radar operator answered and then abruptly pointed at his screen. "There it is again, sir!"

A small spike appeared above the squiggly electronic line running across the display. When the radar beam came around a second time, the spike was no longer there.

"It could be a sampan, sir, traveling across the strait," Cazanavette offered. "Whatever it is, it's small and it's moving slowly."

Tremain watched the radar screen as the beam swept across the contact's bearing several more times, but the spike did not reappear.

"Could it be interference?"

"Possibly, sir. The fog and the temperature variations outside could be causing it. It could be a phantom return. The right weather conditions will do that."

"Anything on sound?" Tremain glanced at Cazanavette.

"Too much traffic up the channel to discern this contact from the distant ones, sir," Cazanavette said. "The strait is acting like a sound duct, so we're hearing everything for fifty miles down that bearing."

Tremain waited several more minutes but the spike did not reappear. It seemed to have vanished.

"I'm going up to the bridge, XO. Stand by down here and keep watching for it."

"Aye, sir."

Tremain bolted up the ladder and onto the bridge and waited for his eyes to adjust before he moved over to the railing. Hubley was there, staring into the fog. Dawn was fast approaching, and the first shades of sunlight had turned the fog around them into a deep blue haze.

"Have you heard any noises at all up here, Carl?"

"No, sir. It's as quiet as a mouse."

Mackerel was hove to with her bow pointing to the west. Tremain looked into the fog off the starboard beam. Somewhere out there, the phantom contact either existed or it did not exist. Originally, Tremain had wanted to stay on the surface during this day, at least until the fog had cleared. Now he was not so sure. If they were going to be plagued by phantom radar returns it might be better to take her down and listen.

"Wait, sir," Hubley said, raising one hand. "Hear that?"

Tremain bent an ear toward the starboard beam. At first he heard nothing. Then his ear picked up on the foreign noise and he heard it too. It was the low putter of a diesel engine. The noise dissipated in the fog one second, then was clearly audible the next. It sounded close.

"I'd say that's inside two thousand yards, sir," Hubley whispered.

The gun crews had obviously heard the noise as well, since *Mackerel*'s long gun barrels all swung in unison toward the starboard beam.

"Hold your fire!" Tremain whispered and the bridge phone talker passed the order to all of the gun stations.

Cazanavette poked his head up the bridge hatch, wisely avoiding the use of the loud speaker. The other ship was definitely close enough to hear it.

"Captain," he whispered. "We now have him on sonar. Single engine diesel, low revolutions, bearing zero two zero, off the starboard beam."

Tremain squatted down. "We can't dive, XO. He'll hear us for sure. We're going to have to stick it out and hope he doesn't see us."

Cazanavette nodded and disappeared below.

Tremain leaned against the bridge coaming and peered out into the fog. He could see nothing, just a sheet of blue haze. The ship out there could be anything. It could be a trawler, a powered sampan—or worse, it could be a gunboat.

The unseen ship's engine grew louder, then constant. Tremain was sure that it was close enough to hit with a stone's throw.

One of the lookouts gently slapped his hand against the periscope shears to get Tremain's attention and then pointed into the fog aft of the starboard beam.

Tremain saw the shadow of a mast form in the fog. The fog high above the water was thinner than that hugging the surface. Soon after, a large shadow appeared beneath the mast and Tremain immediately recognized the unmistakable short, squatty silhouette of a Japanese patrol boat.

Though only half of *Mackerel's* size, Tremain knew from experience that these little boats carried quite a punch. He could see the long dark shapes protruding from the boat's fore and after decks. He knew that the shapes were twenty- and forty-millimeter guns, and that the vessel probably carried a three-inch gun as well.

The patrol boat was obviously conducting routine guard boat duty. It was probably cruising along in the fog at a low speed to avoid hitting any other shipping that might be in the channel. The fact that the craft was traveling slowly was a good indication that *Mackerel* was still undetected.

Tremain could safely assume that the patrol boat was not equipped with radar, although the Japanese boat would not need it to spoil *Mackerel's* mission. All the patrol boat needed to do was radio his base that an enemy submarine had been spotted in the area and the *Kurita* would not come out for weeks. The mission would be a failure, and, worse, the enemy would send out destroyers to find them.

Tremain glanced at the gunners. Their barrels were trained at the shape in the fog, now less than fifty yards away. They were ready, Tremain thought, if it came to a fight. He guessed that the enemy had not sighted them yet, because the craft's low superstructure sat lower in the fog than *Mackerel*'s bridge.

As the enemy shape became more distinct, it was clear to Tremain that he was looking at the patrol craft's port beam. If the patrol craft stayed on its present course, there was a good chance that it would pass by without seeing *Mackerel*.

All on deck watched intently as the patrol boat cruised quietly along, crossing the submarine's stern. *Mackerel*'s guns trained around, following its every move. The patrol boat did not change course, and everyone breathed a sigh of relief when it finally disappeared into the fog off the port quarter.

"That was too close, sir," Hubley whispered, smiling.

Tremain nodded and rubbed the sweat from his temple. He had been mere seconds away from ordering the gun crews to open fire on the unsuspecting patrol boat.

"I hope the bastards have no more out there, Mr. Hubley," he said.

Hubley started to say something in reply but Tremain quickly motioned for him to stop.

Something was not right, Tremain thought, as he listened. The sound of the patrol boat's diesel engine had been fading before, but now it was growing louder. The patrol boat had turned around.

Tremain looked up in time to see the lookout point into the fog off the port quarter.

"It's coming back, sir. Bow on, this time."

Could the patrol boat have seen them? Tremain thought. It would have fired by now. It must have reached the end of its run and simply turned around to go back up the channel. But it was headed straight for *Mackerel*.

Tremain sucked in a deep breath. He had no choice. The patrol boat would see them within seconds. He had to keep it from sending any radio transmissions.

He reached for the phone talker's arm.

"To all gun crews, when I give the order, target the patrol boat's mast and superstructure."

The nervous sailor relayed Tremain's order into his handset, and *Mackerel*'s guns quickly leveled toward the port quarter.

Tremain waited as the dark shape once again emerged from the fog, heading directly towards *Mackerel*'s port beam. The distance between the vessels closed to sixty yards . . . then fifty yards . . . then forty . . . then thirty. . . .

A solitary voice came out of the fog speaking in Japanese. It sounded amplified, as if the enemy officer was speaking through a megaphone.

Several of *Mackerel*'s sailors looked up at Tremain as if they expected him to respond. The patrol boat was obviously hailing *Mackerel,* and apparently still unaware that the shadowy vessel off its bows was an American submarine. Tremain scowled and each man quickly turned back to his post.

After several hails, the distance between the two vessels closed to mere yards and a searchlight clicked on from the Japanese craft.

Tremain held his breath as the long beam of light cut through the fog and steadied on *Mackerel*'s bridge. Almost instantaneously a Japanese voice shouted an exclamation and the light shut off. Tremain could hear the boat's diesels suddenly cough to life in an apparent attempt to gain speed.

"Commence firing!" he shouted at the top of his lungs.

Mackerel's weapons broke open the quiet night, erupting in a crescendo of rattling automatic weapons. Bright tracer rounds from the 40-millimeter gun walked across the small space of water, creating tall geysers. The gun quickly found its target and settled on the patrol boat's pilothouse, pounding it into pieces with shell after shell. Another searchlight came on but was instantly blown apart by a .50-caliber machine gun burst. Tongues of flame spewed

forth in staccato fashion from every gun on *Mackerel*'s
deck. Water spouts and debris filled the air around the patrol boat as flying shells repeatedly pulverized it.

Mackerel's hull shook as the five-inch gun fired its first
round. The shell missed and splashed into the water well
beyond the patrol craft.

With the enemy's pilothouse and mast virtually destroyed, Tremain prayed silently that the Japanese captain
had not had time to send a message. The patrol boat had
been taken completely by surprise and now he had to sink
her, and fast.

"Tell the five-inch gun to aim for the waterline!" he
shouted to the phone talker over the noise.

Moments later, the five-inch gun erupted again and its
large shell slammed into the patrol boat's bow, sending
metal splinters flying in all directions.

By now, the Japanese boat was close enough that its deck
was completely visible, and *Mackerel*'s guns were chopping
it to pieces, as it came. Tremain could see that the entire vessel was already riddled with holes. It was fast becoming a
wreck, as ammunition began exploding on deck, and anything that was flammable caught fire. The Japanese helmsman had obviously been killed in the first few seconds,
because the boat continued to head straight for *Mackerel*'s
side.

Tremain saw one large-caliber machine gun still opera-
tional on the boat's stern. Two skivvy-clad Japanese sailors
appeared to be the only life left onboard as they struggled
to load an ammunition belt into the gun's chamber. With
their own boat burning around them, they rotated the
gun toward the submarine and prepared to fire.

Tremain grabbed the arm of the sailor manning the
.50-caliber machine gun on the bridge.

"Take out those two gunners!" he shouted.

The sailor swiveled his .50-caliber around and aimed it

at the Japanese sailors. His first burst ricocheted off the deck and kicked up sparks near the sailors' feet. Before he could fire again, the Japanese sailors opened up with their machine gun. The ensuing onslaught of projectiles peppered *Mackerel*'s bridge railing, holing it in several places.

A few feet away from Tremain, the sailor who was loading for the .50-caliber machine gun reeled backward from a round that had hit him in the throat. He fell to the deck clutching his neck and quickly gurgled up blood.

The sailor operating the .50-caliber weapon ignored the fate of his shipmate and leveled his gun at the Japanese sailors once more. This time, his burst hit home. Tremain's stomach turned as he saw one of the Japanese sailor's head explode from a .50-caliber round, his body continuing to fire the machine gun for several grotesque seconds. The other sailor took multiple rounds across his midsection and was mercilessly chopped in two. When the burst finally ended he was nothing more than an indiscernible mess of bloody rags and flesh.

A large explosion from the patrol boat's stern signified that the diesel fuel had ignited. The boat soon lost all headway and began to burn wildly only a few yards from *Mackerel*'s side. It was so close that Tremain began to grow worried that a secondary explosion might damage his own ship or injure some of the men on deck. *Mackerel*'s gun crews continued to pound the Japanese boat without mercy, but the fight was over.

"Cease firing!" Tremain shouted.

It took several seconds for all of the guns to get the word but they soon stopped firing. Spent shell casings covered the decks everywhere. Each gun barrel emitted a pale smoke from its red-hot breech and muzzle. The gunpowder flashes had blackened each of the gun crews' faces and uniforms, and they all stood breathless and wild-eyed after the madness.

The hapless patrol boat showed no signs of life as it bobbed against *Mackerel*'s side. Tremain could see smoking bodies and pieces of bodies littering the deck. The burning and twisted metal that had once been a Japanese boat now resembled a funeral pyre. He smelled the acrid odors of burning fuel oil, burning gunpowder, and burning flesh. Tremain noticed that the men all around him were staring down into the boat, aghast at the grisly spectacle they had created.

The pharmacists' mate emerged from the bridge hatch and immediately went to work on the wounded man, now in the arms of his gunner. But it was too late for the young sailor. The bullet had severed the man's jugular vein and he had already bled to death. His blood covered the deck at Tremain's feet and ran down the bridge scuppers.

Tremain forced himself to turn away. He had to keep a clear head.

"XO, bridge," Tremain said into the call box. "Start up the engines. We need to clear away from that boat before it explodes on us."

"Captain, XO. Aye, sir."

Mackerel's engines started and Tremain piloted away from the burning patrol boat at five knots until it disappeared into the fog and all that could be seen were the flickering fires along her hull. All on deck watched as the roaring fire flared up, then extinguished suddenly as the patrol boat slid beneath the waves. The wind carried a pall of white smoke over to the *Mackerel,* as if to remind her of what she had done.

Tremain ordered the ship prepared for diving. The crew needed a rest, he thought. He did not know whether the Japanese captain had been able to warn his base before his radio was destroyed. Nor did he know if the noise from the gunfight had reached the ears of the fishermen near the coast. Either way, his men were in no shape to stay at their guns.

Everyone on the bridge watched in silence as Petty Officer Grimes' body was placed in a bag and lowered below. They would have to bury him when they left Japanese waters. They could not risk his body washing up on the shores of Honshu and alerting the Japanese to their presence. Until then, his body would be stored in the freezer with the food. It seemed grotesque, but it was the only way. It was the submarine way.

With the guns secure, and all hands below, Tremain ordered the ship submerged. Once safely below the surface, the crew did not celebrate the apparent victory. Partly because of Grimes' death, but also because they realized the gravity of the situation. The evening had been a complete disaster, and now the mission was in jeopardy.

Chapter 23

"**WHAT** if a Japanese fisherman heard the fire fight?" Tee said from across the wardroom table. "What if one of those charred sons of bitches washes up on the shoreline? What if the patrol boat didn't sink?"

"That's enough, Mr. Turner," Cazanavette said forcefully, putting down his turkey sandwich.

The officers sat around the wardroom table, eating breakfast and discussing the previous evening's events. Cold cuts were all that was available since the cooks had been manning the guns most of the night. The officers breakfasted on whatever meats and breads were available.

Tremain had decided not to join them. Partly because he needed some sleep, but mostly because he knew that they needed to vent their frustrations. They would never do it in front of him. It was more appropriate for the XO to hear what they had to say. Tee had been the most vocal so far, pushing the edge of Cazanavette's patience.

"The captain and I have gone over the different possibilities, Mister Turner," Cazanavette said. "The enemy may know we're here, and the *Kurita* may never come out now. But, regardless of those possibilities, we are going to continue the mission. We're going to stay out here until we sink the *Kurita*."

"For how long, XO?" Tee asked belligerently.

Tee had reverted to his old bullying habits, but this time he was directing his venom at Cazanavette. Wright sensed that his tone was more nervous than it was threatening as he eyed him with contempt from across the table.

"We already have one man dead, XO," Tee continued in the face of the fuming Cazanavette. "We're lucky we weren't sunk this morning. This mission is suicide. It was doomed from the start. When is the captain going to—"

"Watch it, *Lieutenant* Turner," Cazanavette cautioned him, but Tee seemed to ignore it.

"The captain is not acting rationally and I think you should do something about it, XO. If you don't I might have to let my father know about this when I see him again. In my opinion Commander Stillsen should take over and get us the hell out of these waters before the Japanese send everything they have after us."

Wright's blood silently boiled higher with every word that came out of Tee's mouth. He hated the man for everything that he was. He was a liar, a cheat, a bully, a murderer in Wright's eyes, and now a coward. As he listened to Tee defy the XO and defame the captain and threaten to use his father's pull, Wright could no longer control himself.

"Shut your mouth, you fucking son of a bitch!" Wright snapped and bolted out of his seat.

Sitting in the chair next to him, Salisbury grabbed Wright's shirt and pulled him to sit back down, but Wright would not budge. Everyone was startled at the quiet ensign's outburst and even Cazavette was speechless.

Tee appeared stunned at first, but then he looked Wright up and down with apparent irreverence.

"What do you know?" Tee said. "It looks like the ensign's testicles finally dropped."

Tee did not see it coming. Neither did Salisbury or he would have stopped it. Wright's fist curved in an arc and struck Tee across the face in a lightning fast blow. Tee's head jerked from the blow and he fell back in his chair until his back met the bulkhead. Wright had made full contact, and Tee's eye was bound to turn black from the punch.

Red-faced and fuming, Tee struggled out of his chair to attack Wright, who was eagerly waiting for him. Before the fight went any further, however, the other officers subdued them both and held them away from each other.

Cazanavette pulled the curtain aside and checked the passage to ensure that none of the ship's crew had been passing by to witness the event. Then he returned to the room with a menacing scowl on his face.

"Wright!" Cazanavette said. "What the hell do you think you're doing? I don't know who you think you are, Mister."

Wright started to speak but Cazanavette interrupted.

"Let me tell you what you are. You're nothing, nothing but a young immature ensign. How can we maintain discipline among the crew when the officers behave in such a reprehensible and despicable manner? You may consider yourself on report for this, Mister Wright. When we get back to Pearl, we'll discuss your future in the navy, if you have any." Cazanavette paused, then glared at Turner. "That goes for you too, Mister Turner. I don't care who the hell your father is, this ship has only one captain, and you're going to shut up and do your fucking job from here on out. Is that clear?"

Wright had never seen Cazanavette so angry. The XO had been up for thirty hours and was in no mood to be trifled with. Wright wanted to expose Tee and tell Cazanavette all that he had learned about the man, but he feared that the XO would only dismiss it in light of his outburst.

"Nobody says anything about this and that's an order," Cazanavette continued in a lower tone. "I want to keep this from the crew for the sake of their morale, and for the sake of this mission." He eyed Wright squarely. "And I want nothing but full compliance and diligence from you. *Understood*?"

"Yes, sir," Wright said.

"All right," Cazanavette said, looking at each one of them in turn. "Let's all get some sleep then."

The officers filed out of the room and into their staterooms. Across from the wardroom, Tremain lay in his darkened stateroom, wide awake. He had heard every word. The scuffle between Wright and Turner had not bothered him. He had seen officers go at it before in stressful situations. It happened.

He was impressed with the way Cazanavette had handled the situation, but he knew that it had not been easy for him. Every submarine executive officer reached a point in his career where he ceased to be just one of the officers and where he became their leader. That was when he was ready for his own boat.

Cazanavette was ready, Tremain thought.

MACKEREL spent the next day submerged to allow the crew to unwind from the morning's action. Periodic periscope searches confirmed that the fog had not dissipated. Instead of a dark blue haze, they now had a light gray haze to contend with. The fog could be a blessing, but it could also be a curse. While it did hide the periscope from any aircraft that might be circling overhead, it also blocked their own view of the channel and of the *Kurita,* if she ever came out. All detections would have to be made by radar or sonar, and the identity of those contacts could not be confirmed with the fog as thick as it was.

At noon, the sonar picked up a trio of screws that were quickly identified as patrol craft. They cruised up and down the channel at various speeds, presumably searching for their missing patrol boat. Tremain prayed that they would not find any wreckage or bodies or any other trace that the boat had met with a violent end. With luck, they would conclude that the boat had run onto some rocks and had disappeared without a trace. Tremain was certain that they would not immediately assume an American submarine had sunk her, because submarines very seldom attacked such small vessels.

"Still hold those patrol boats, sonar?" Tremain asked as he climbed into the conning tower. He had just finished four hours of broken sleep and a coffee lunch. It was now Cazanavette's turn to get some sleep.

"Yes, sir." The sonar man nodded. "All three of them are still nosing around."

Salisbury and Wright were the watch officers. Wright tried to avoid eye contact with Tremain, embarrassed that the XO might have told him about his scuffle with Tee. Tremain gave no indication that he knew about it.

"Still foggy?" Tremain asked.

"Yes, sir, just as bad as before," Salisbury answered from the periscope. "We can't see a thing beyond a few yards."

"Let's come up to radar depth, Mr. Salisbury. I want to get a good picture of what's around us."

"Aye, aye, Captain."

Salisbury shouted a few orders down to the control room and *Mackerel* eased up to forty-five feet, exposing the SJ radar mast.

A sailor came to the conning tower to man the radar panel and immediately began the start-up procedure. He flicked on the power, turned a few dials, and the radar started to warm up. After several minutes he turned the knob that would rotate the dish, but nothing happened. The radar beam remained focused on the same bearing and would not move. He powered down, then conducted the start-up procedure again. Still, the radar would not rotate.

"Problems?" Tremain asked.

"Yes, sir. I can't seem to rotate the radar at all. I am radiating, but only down one bearing."

"Did you check the hydraulic lineup?"

The sailor leaned over and checked the hydraulic supply and return valves and the small pressure gauge beside them. "Yes, sir. Hydraulics is cut in. We have pressure. Something must be fouling it topside."

Tremain instinctively knew what was wrong, but he ordered the ship to the surface to be sure. Once surfaced, he and Salisbury climbed into the shears and inspected the metal shroud around the radar shaft. As Tremain suspected, several rounds from the Japanese machine gun had penetrated the shroud. The metal had been warped and dented just enough so that no tolerance existed between the shroud and the radar shaft. The radar was physically stuck in one position and could not rotate. It was damage they would not be able to repair at sea. *Mackerel* was now essentially without a radar.

Tremain inwardly cursed as he ordered the ship submerged again. Things were not going well. First the fog, then the patrol boat, and now no radar. Without radar to pierce through the fog, they would never be able to find the battleship. Sure, they would be able to hear her as she passed by, but her noise would be combined with the churning screws of her escorts, and virtually indistinguishable. They could never be certain of what they were shooting at. It would be pure blind luck if they sank the *Kurita*—that is, if she ever came out. Everything seemed to be against them. For the first time since they had left Pearl, Tremain thought about calling off the mission.

Tremain noticed Stillsen, leaning over the chart desk. He had been pushing himself hard. Tremain could not remember the last time he had seen the man sleep.

"Why don't you go get some sleep, Dave. You need some, too, you know."

Stillsen looked up at him. His eyes had bags under them and he had not shaved for two days.

"I guess so, Captain," he muttered.

Before Stillsen reached the ladder, Tremain stopped him.

"I didn't get the chance to commend you for detecting that patrol boat last night, Dave. Your sharp eye may have saved the ship. Good work."

Stillsen smiled, the hatchet now obviously buried between them. "Glad I could help, sir."

Stillsen would do all right when he took over the *Mackerel,* Tremain thought. He had learned a lot. The thought gave him brief comfort, when faced with the knowledge that the mission was turning out to be a complete failure. *Mackerel* had nothing to show for her troubles but one dead crewman in the freezer and a five-hundred-ton patrol boat on the bottom of Kii Suido.

Admiral Giles would not be pleased. He would certainly ensure that Tremain's career stalled out and he might even have Ireland relieved of command. Tremain didn't want that to happen to the old bastard, but he could not worry about it now. Part of him wanted the mission to end—to call it quits right now and go back home to Judy.

He had tried not to think of her at all once they left Pearl, fearful that the hope of seeing her soon might cloud his judgment. Now, he could not stop thinking of her. The mission did not seem to make sense any more. Forget the

Kurita, forget the Japanese, forget the war. Seeing her again was all that mattered to him.

In the cold dark silence of the conning tower, Tremain reached a decision. Tomorrow, he would turn the *Mackerel* eastward and head for home.

Chapter 24

MACKEREL'S sonar monitored while the Japanese patrol boats continued to search Kii Suido for the rest of the day and late into the night. The fact that they were out there was reason enough to stay submerged. Tremain saw no point in coming up to the surface. The fog was still around, but *Mackerel* had no radar. It would be too risky.

No other ships came down the channel that night, at least none that they could hear. In fact, the channel was unusually quiet. The lack of activity concerned Tremain. It made him even more certain that the Japanese knew they were here or at least suspected it. He did not expect any more Japanese ships would pass through the area until it had been cleared by anti-submarine forces. He considered that the fog might be the only thing protecting *Mackerel* now. As soon as the fog cleared, and daylight came, bomb-laden aircraft would hover in swarms over Kii Suido, waiting for the moment *Mackerel* showed herself. Once they saw anything, a periscope, a dark shape in the water, or even a surge of bubbles, they would drop their explosives. Soon after, the destroyers would come to finish the job. *Mackerel* would not be able to escape a combined attack from aircraft and destroyers. She would be sunk, her crew would die a lonely death, and the *Kurita* would come out of the Inland Sea only a week late, surviving to eventually wreak havoc on American ships. When all was said and done, ComSubPac would have traded one submarine for one Japanese patrol boat. It was not exactly the way to win a war.

When midmorning came, the channel was quiet again. The patrol boats had faded off into the distant ocean noise. Tremain ordered *Mackerel* up to periscope depth for a look around. He prayed that the fog was still heavy enough to hide them from any enemy planes lurking overhead.

"Stand by to take her down fast. We might need to," Tremain ordered as he flipped down the periscope handles and pressed his face to the eyepiece.

He had to squint at the bright light as the water quickly drizzled off the lens. The fog had started to dissipate and was now a thin sheet of white mist that seemed to intensify the sunlight.

"We're losing our fog cover, XO," he said, not taking his eye from the scope. "I put visibility at one thousand yards. That's quite a change from this morning."

"Bad for us, sir," Cazanavette replied.

Tremain turned the left handle to angle the lens upward. He could not see any blue through the white sheet above. The fog was still thick enough to hide the scope from any aircraft, but not for long.

Tremain slapped up the handles.

"Down scope."

He breathed a long sigh and moved over to the chart desk, where Cazanavette stood.

"What d'you think, sir?" Cazanavette asked.

"I think we've done what we could, XO. Once the fog

clears, enemy aircraft will be all over the place. Night time won't be much better, with no radar and no moon. I've thought it through, and I'm calling off the mission. We're going home."

"Bad luck, sir," Cazanavette said.

Tremain's eyes shot back at Cazanavette. He could not tell how he had meant the comment. The XO's tone left it open to interpretation. Perhaps he did not share Tremain's opinion about their present situation. But it did not matter. He had made his decision. He could not risk their lives and the ship on such feeble odds.

"Plot a course for Midway, XO. Let's get out of here."

The conning tower fell suddenly silent. Everyone in the room had heard the order. They stood at their stations avoiding eye contact with him, almost as if they were ashamed.

"Aye, Captain," Cazanavette finally said.

"We'll pull in there and change out our fish. Maybe Sub-Pac will give us orders for another quick patrol." Tremain said it to try to bolster them with some kind of consolation, but it appeared to do no good.

Cazanavette acknowledged this change of plans weakly, then turned his attention to the chart desk and began laying out the new course for their retreat.

Tremain was stunned at the men's behavior. He had turned them into submarine warriors and damned good ones, but surely they could see that continuing the mission was suicide. Surely they realized that their chances were dismal at best.

Was he wrong about this? he asked himself. Was he making the right decision or was he allowing his hopes of returning to Judy to affect his judgment?

Cazanavette made a few measurements with a parallel ruler and stoically reported. "One three zero is a good course to open Kii Suido, sir."

"Very well, XO. Helm, left fifteen degrees rudder. Steady one three zero. All ahead two thirds."

The helmsman acknowledged and *Mackerel* conducted a slow turn to the left and steadied on the southeasterly course, placing Kii Suido and the Japanese homeland behind her. Her batteries hummed along as she increased speed and steadied at five knots.

As *Mackerel* cruised toward the open sea, Tremain felt strangely out of place on his own ship. The men around him stared blankly at their panels or at the deck. They did not converse. They did not celebrate or joke with each other. There were no smiles at the thought of going home. It seemed that only he had lost faith in the mission.

He had to leave the room. Go to his stateroom, or somewhere, anywhere but there. If he did not, he might decide to change his mind and turn the ship around.

"You have the conn, XO," he said, then jumped down the ladder and proceeded to his cabin, leaving the conning tower in its tomblike silence.

WRIGHT walked aft through the forward engine room. The word had just reached him about returning to port. The news should have excited him, but he still had a one-track mind. He could not get his loathsome feelings for Tee out of his head.

Wright would not come on watch for another three hours, but he could not sleep. He had decided to go to one of the engine rooms to work on his qualifications. He might get kicked out of the service when they returned, but he was going to make damn sure that he went out wearing his gold dolphins. He had worked too hard and spent too many hours with his head in the books not to get them now.

The large diesel rooms were always a good place to get

away from people whenever the ship was submerged. The sleeping diesels required no attention. He found a small nook on the starboard side between two lockers and cracked open the oil-stained technical manual for the ship's 500-kilowatt auxiliary generator. It was a dry read, but it was something he needed to know for his qualification board.

Just then, he noticed the aft watertight door open. Tee emerged and shut the door behind him. He had a clipboard in hand and was obviously carrying out some of his divisional duties. He did not notice Wright at first. Not until he was only a few feet away did he realize that Wright was in the room. He stopped and stared at Wright with the same smirk that had been on his face in the wardroom.

They were the only two in the room. Wright knew that he should ignore him. He should let him go on by and not say a word, but he could not. His hatred of Tee got the best of him. He had to settle this once and for all, he decided, regardless of what it might mean to his career.

Wright put his manual down and stood to face Tee. Standing directly in his path, Wright blocked the passage-way between the two diesels. Tee looked angry but he stopped and did not come any closer.

"What's your problem, dickhead?" he finally said.

"You are, Tee. You're nothing but a damned coward and a liar."

Tee's face grew red and his lip began to quiver. He looked like he wanted to rip Wright's head off, but still he did not advance.

"You're in enough trouble already, asshole," Tee said, slightly regaining his composure. "I'd beat you to a pulp, if the XO would let me."

"Well, you're going to have to," Wright said, barely maintaining his own self-control. "You're not leaving this compartment, until you get through me."

Tee looked long and hard at Wright. Realizing that

Wright's intentions were serious, he sat his clipboard on the starboard diesel bedplate and rolled up his shirtsleeves. Tee outweighed Wright and Wright himself half-wondered what the hell he was getting himself into, challenging the man to a fight, but he was bent on venting the rage inside him. He was determined to settle the score and get revenge for Rudy's death. He quickly unbuttoned and removed his own shirt.

"What the hell's gotten into you lately anyway, Wright?" Tee asked, suddenly in a more appeasing tone. "Don't you know when someone's just screwing around with you?"

Wright did not respond.

Tee paused. "I know I've been an asshole to you, and all. But the bull ensign's supposed to be fucked with. All ensigns have to go through it. It's kind of a navy rule." Tee chuckled, in an obvious attempt to lighten up the situation.

With fists firmly clenched Wright did not laugh or even smile.

"When the next ensign shows up," Tee added, "you can fuck with him like I've fucked with you. That's the way it works."

"I don't care about that," Wright said. "You think I'd risk a fucking court martial for that? Hardly."

"Then what's your fucking problem?"

"You killed Rudy, Tee! You killed Anderson!"

Tee's face turned white. "What the hell're you talking about?"

"Don't act like you don't know, asshole!" Wright yelled. "I saw the way you acted after Rudy was killed. You weren't yourself. You were tense about something. What were you tense about, Tee?"

Tee glanced around the compartment. "Nothing. I was just a little upset at Rudy's death. That's all. We'd been shipmates for a while."

"And it was just a coincidence that you suddenly returned

to your old self again after Anderson shot himself, huh?"

"I don't know what the fuck you're talking about."

"Let me tell you what I'm talking about. You told Anderson to leave his post to clean up some coffee on the day Rudy died, didn't you? Even after Rudy told you not to bother his watchstanders, didn't you?"

"I don't know. Maybe."

"I think you did. I think you did, and I think that plane snuck up on us because Anderson was away from the radar. We didn't dive in time and Rudy got killed. Then you and Anderson were afraid you'd get court-martialed so you kept your mouths shut about the whole thing, blaming it all on atmospheric interference." Wright paused. Tee continued to shake his head and glance around the compartment. He was visibly distraught. "You were able to live with the lie, Tee, but Anderson couldn't. When the captain gave him that commendation letter, he cracked. He couldn't take it anymore. He couldn't live with the guilt and he shot himself."

Tee wiped beads of sweat from his forehead and pretended to smile. "Whew. That's the biggest load of bullshit I've ever heard in my life, Wright."

"You thought no one else knew about your little secret," Wright continued. "But you forgot one thing, sailors talk. They talk to each other. You should have known that there's no such thing as a secret on a boat. Now they're talking about taking matters into their own hands. They're talking about getting revenge on you, Tee."

Tee gave a brief artificial chuckle, but then his eyes fell to the deck and his face grew somber. Wright's words had struck some string inside his warped mind and he suddenly became very quiet.

Wright walked toward him until they were toe to toe. Tee did not move.

"What's it going to be, Tee? Did you do it, or not?"

Tee cleared his throat. His eyes slowly looked up to meet Wright's.

"Yeah, Wright, I guess I did. But it's not like—"

Tee did not finish the sentence before Wright's fist struck him hard in the jaw. Wright could not hear any more of the man's denials. He put every bit of strength and anger he had into his punch. Tee fell backward against the port side diesel engine, clutching his face, his mouth bleeding.

Wright landed two more punches to his temple, then missed with a third, as Tee ducked beneath it. Tee went on the offensive and came up with a strong blow to Wright's midsection. Wright crumpled under the punch and fell to his knees wheezing. Tee had been a boxer at the Academy and knew exactly where to hit a man. Wright was now paying the price. He was bearing the consequences of his actions. He knew that Tee could beat him any day of the week, but at least he had landed a few punches. At least Tee was bleeding. That was some recompense for Rudy's death.

Tee grabbed Wright's hair and pulled his head up, preparing to deliver the knockout blow. Wright opened his eyes to see Tee's large fist, an arm's length away, ready to strike the smashing blow. He shut his eyes, waiting for the punch that would almost certainly shatter his jaw.

But it never came.

Wright opened his eyes again. Tee's fist remained cocked, as he breathed heavily. Wright watched as the pure rage in Tee's red sweaty face slowly transformed to anger, to pain, and then finally to sorrow. He released Wright's hair while practically crying, and then backed off to lean against the port side diesel engine.

Wright clutched his own abdomen as he leaned against the opposite engine. He was sure several of his ribs were broken.

"You're right," Tee finally muttered, sobbing. "I screwed up that day. But it's not like you said, Wright."

Wright looked up at him, skeptically. Tee's expression stunned him. If he had ever seen a trusting look on Tee's face, this was it. Tee's face showed the pain he felt. It was sincere. He was genuinely hurting inside for his actions.

"I did tell Anderson to clean up the coffee," Tee continued. "Rudy got killed because of me. I know that. But you have to believe me, Wright, when I tell you, Anderson and I didn't make any agreement about keeping quiet. He didn't want to tell anybody anymore than I did. We both felt guilty. I know I did. It was eating me up the whole time we were in Pearl. I didn't sleep nights. I drank all the time, and I couldn't even face Margie. I could barely get a meal down. I was too drunk to see how bad it was eating at Anderson. I didn't know he was going to kill himself. If I did, I would have come clean and told the XO about the whole thing.

"I wish Rudy hadn't gotten killed. I liked him. You may not believe me, but I thought of him as a brother sometimes. He and I had seen a lot together. When he got killed, I just panicked. For some reason, all I could think about was how ashamed everyone would be if they found out it was my fault. The admiral would remember me as the failure. My *father* would remember me as the *failure*. My fucking dad, mister fucking navy!"

As Tee hid his face in his hands, Wright thought about how he had seen Tee change from the bully to an emotional wreck in a matter of seconds, just like at Anderson's memorial service. He was certainly unstable and Wright could see that he truly had a moral battle going on inside him. Wright's anger and hatred for him was beginning to transform into pity.

"Sometimes it's not easy to do the right thing." Wright had finally got enough wind to speak. "But we still have to do it. Anderson's dead. He might have had a chance if you had told the XO about everything. He would have been court-martialed, but at least he'd still be alive."

"I know. I hate that," Tee said genuinely. "It eats me up inside to know that. I wish I could change things."

"In a few weeks you're going to take over a division of torpedomen," Wright said. "They've heard the whole story through rumors, and they're not looking forward to working with you. You think they'll ever trust another word you say? You think they'll perform their best under those conditions? How long you going to keep living this lie, Tee? When is that mistake you made going to stop getting people killed?"

Tee nodded slowly and stared at the deck. "I've fucked everything up, Wright. I pray to God that I could take it all back."

"You can fix things, Tee. Tell the XO what happened. Stand up and take the punishment like a good officer. It's the best thing for everyone's sake. It's best for the division. It's best for the ship. It's best for you. Maybe, you'll get some of your self-respect back."

Tee's eyes met Wright's. He nodded. Wright could see the man's inner struggle in his eyes.

"You're right," Tee finally muttered. "That's the right thing to do. And I'm tired of hiding the truth. Let's go see the, XO. I'll explain everything." Tee briefly paused before adding, "I'll explain to him why you hit me the other day, too. He'll probably drop the issue after he hears why."

The hardened man had finally cracked, and Wright saw another side of Tee. He believed that Tee actually did have a conscience. He believed that Tee wanted to do the right thing. And in a small way, Wright felt sorry for him. He suddenly felt very guilty for sleeping with Margie, though he still did not regret it.

Tee held out a hand and helped Wright to his feet.

They had just started to head forward when the fourteen-bell gong rang throughout the ship, followed by the blare of the 1MC.

"All hands! Man battle stations torpedo!"

Chapter 25

THE fourteen-bell gong rang throughout the ship and *Mackerel*'s crew stopped whatever they were doing and fell out of their racks to hurry to their battle stations. Tremain watched as the conning tower quickly filled up with personnel manning phones, chart tables, and other equipment. Hubley brushed past Tremain's arm and started to warm up the torpedo data computer. Salisbury's sonar assistant stood beside him and manned an additional headset. Stillsen came up and assisted Cazanavette on the chart desk. The periscope assistant and another phone talker also squeezed into the tiny space, until Tremain had barely two feet in which to stand between the two periscope barrels. Within minutes the report came that all stations were manned and ready for torpedo action.

Tremain leaned on the periscope shears as he assembled in his head what had happened in the last fifteen minutes. The phone had buzzed in his stateroom just as he had settled down with the logbook to inscribe the entries explaining his decision to return to base. Over the phone, Cazanavette's agitated voice had told him that he needed to come back to the conning tower, and fast. Something had happened. He had raced to the conning tower in less than ten seconds, shoving his way past sailors who had been inquisitively crowded around the ladder.

"Captain," Cazanavette had said excitedly as he met him at the top of the ladder, his hair tousled from removing a sonar headset only moments before. "We have a new sound contact, sir. Several of them."

Tremain had lifted the headset to his own ear and quickly heard what Cazanavette was excited about. Very faint, but very steady, on the same bearing as Kii Suido, he had heard the unmistakable pinging of active sonar. It was not just a single ship pinging, but multiple ships. In fact, the pings were almost continuous, and it had been impossible to tell which ones were pulses and which were returns. Somewhere, not far up the channel, the Japanese had begun to probe the hell out of the water with high energy sound, and it could mean only one thing: a valuable warship was being escorted out of the Inland Sea. Tremain knew that it had to be the *Kurita*.

At four miles from the channel entrance, Tremain had ordered the ship turned around and *Mackerel* had headed back toward the sonar contacts at nine and a half knots. Now, as the men settled in at their battle stations, they exchanged grins. They knew they were going back to get the *Kurita,* and that's where they all wanted to go.

"We're going to eat up the batteries getting into position in time. We won't have much left for an evasion," Cazanavette commented as he and the quartermaster placed a fresh sheet of plotting paper across the chart desk.

"We'll work it out, XO," Tremain said, then smiled with the necessary commander's confidence. Sinking the *Kurita* would be enough, he thought. Anything after that, he would handle as it came. Cazanavette nodded in agreement and picked up the phone to converse with the engineering officer of the watch.

Tremain watched his men as they eagerly prepared for the coming battle. He had certainly turned them into warriors. They had pride and confidence in their ship and in themselves, and they did not want to return to port empty-handed.

Mackerel drained her batteries with every mile of progress, and Salisbury reported that the pinging was getting louder. When the submarine reached a position a mere mile from the channel, he reported many high speed screws across an area spanning five degrees.

Tremain formulated the picture in his head. The *Kurita*'s escorts were coming down the channel at high speed. They were headed straight toward the same spot *Mackerel* had been patrolling only hours before. With their current speed of advance, he estimated that *Mackerel* and the outbound fleet would reach the spot at nearly the same time, but from opposite directions.

Tremain looked over Stillsen's shoulder at the chart. The *Kurita* and her escorts would come down the channel at high speed. When they reached the outlet and the open ocean, they would make a sharp turn to the left and head east, since that was the way to Yokosuka. The battle group would then probably start a zig-zag pattern. Once the *Kurita* began zigging, it would be nearly impossible to line up for a good shot. That's why *Mackerel* had to get to the channel outlet before the *Kurita* did. It was their only chance, the only time the Japanese ship would be traveling in a straight line long enough to get a good torpedo solution on her.

Cazanavette measured off the distance to the channel with a pair of dividers. "We still have a half mile to go, sir. From the sound of those screws, it's going to be close. I recommend increasing to flank."

"Helm, all ahead flank," Tremain said, which brought a smile from Cazanavette before he returned to his plot. Tremain clearly trusted his XO's judgment.

"All ahead flank, aye, sir," the helmsman replied from the forward conning tower wheel and *Mackerel* soon steadied at her maximum submerged speed of eleven knots, her hard-working motors sucking every ounce of electric power the two batteries could give them.

Tremain tried not to think of the straining batteries. After being submerged all morning, they were already quite depleted. Going to flank speed would leave them with very little power for any post-attack maneuvering. He imagined that the electrician on the electric plant control panel back aft was probably already having difficulty maintaining voltage. But there really was no option.

Tremain fought the urge to raise the periscope. The lead destroyers should be inside a mile by now. Depending on the fog conditions he might be able to see them, and maybe even the *Kurita*. But, he did not dare raise the periscope at this speed. At eleven knots, the water resistance would bend it back like a tree caught in a high wind. And if the scope did not break, the escorts would almost certainly sight the white "feather" of spray it would create on the surface.

"I'm getting a lot of pinging now, sir," Salisbury reported. "It's across both bows and moving aft. It sounds like they're about to pass down both sides of us."

The pinging could now be heard through the hull. The lead destroyers were close. They were not listening, but rather using active sonar to probe the depths as they drove on at high speed. The pinging grew louder with each passing second.

From the number of echo-ranging pulses in the water, Tremain estimated there were at least four destroyers above them. He silently prayed that their piercing sonar would not detect *Mackerel*'s steel hull.

"They're passing down both beams, now, sir," Salisbury reported. He had to shout to be heard over the sonar beams.

Tremain again looked at the chart. According to Cazanavette's dead reckoning, *Mackerel* would now be at the outlet of the channel and right in the middle of it, equidistant from the two points of land. With destroyers passing down both beams, he assumed that they had to be inside the enemy formation as well. Now they would also face the danger of being run over by the keel of an enemy ship.

Salisbury's sonar became useless as the sounds of echoranging and screw noises saturated every point on the compass. Nothing was discernible to him and Tremain could only assume that *Mackerel* had remained undetected. He really did not know for certain, but it no longer mattered. They were here and it was time for action.

"All stop!" Tremain shouted.

Cazanavette nodded in approval. They both watched the speed indicator as *Mackerel* slowed. It took her almost a minute to slow to five knots, even with the massive water resistance, and it seemed like a lifetime.

"Up scope!" Tremain finally ordered when the speed log moved below five knots.

The scope came up into Tremain's hands as he met it at the floor, instantly pressing his face to the eyepiece. He waited for the water to rinse off the lens as it poked a few inches above the surface. The water was choppy today, with white caps and rollers, terrible conditions for periscope observations since he would not be able to see past the next wave crest when the scope was in a trough. Tremain cursed as wave after wave slapped against the field of view, obscuring his vision. All eyes in the conning tower were glued to him, waiting for the first report of the enemy.

The lens finally cleared as the scope reached a wave crest. Tremain saw that the fog had partially lifted and had become a broken series of water-hugging clouds. Visibility was good in some directions and poor in others. Tremain panned around quickly, anticipating the next trough.

Off *Mackerel*'s port bow, five hundred yards away, he saw the port side of a four-stack destroyer surging through the seas on a southeasterly course, making at least twenty knots. The destroyer was obviously one of the echo-rangers and Tremain was amazed that it had not yet detected the *Mackerel*. The rough seas and surface agitation must have been hiding them, he thought, as they cruised along at the shallow periscope depth.

Tremain then swung the scope around to the starboard beam. There he saw another four-stack destroyer less than a thousand yards away, with the same course and speed as her sister. That one had not detected *Mackerel* either—or at least it appeared not to have detected her. It simply steamed on, heading away to the southeast.

With the two ships past, *Mackerel* was now inside the formation.

Tremain swung the scope to look up the channel, and was met again by a large roller, which submerged the lens for several seconds. The waves came from the northwest, making it difficult to get a long look on any bearing in that direction. Unfortunately, that was the same direction he expected the *Kurita* to come from. Tremain cursed as another wave doused the lens. Every time the lens started to clear, another roller engulfed it.

"Joe, do you have any good information about what's out in front of us?" Tremain shouted toward Salisbury.

"No, sir. I still have active sonars everywhere. In front of us, on both sides, and now behind us. Lots of screw noise in front of us, too."

Tremain kept his eye to the scope, eagerly waiting for the waves to allow him any small glimpse of what lay ahead. He was looking at bubbles and blue water more than anything else.

Then, finally, the periscope reached the crest of a large roller and briefly afforded him a view beyond. Tremain's heart skipped a beat as the water ran off the lens and the sharp bow of a Japanese destroyer filled his field of view. It was so close that he could not see any of the superstructure, only the pointed bow as it knifed through the water at high speed, tossing the seas to either side. It was headed directly for the periscope.

"Emergency deep, all ahead flank!" Tremain shouted, slapping up the periscope handles. "Destroyer, dead ahead! Rig for depth charge!"

George Olander heard the order down in the control room and immediately flooded the negative tank, bringing on thousands of pounds of water ballast. *Mackerel* hesitated in the surface suction forces, then angled downward and surged beneath the surface with her new weight. The spinning screws assisted in driving her deep quickly.

Those in the conning tower held on to anything they could as the deck heeled forward at a thirty-degree angle. The angle was so steep that Tremain grew concerned that the screws might be spinning out of the water. He watched as the needle on the depth gauge began its slow clockwise rotation, passing through the eighty-foot mark . . . then ninety feet . . . then one hundred feet.

The churning screws of the approaching destroyer became audible through the hull. It was going to be close with *Mackerel*'s stern still shallow enough that it was in danger of being rammed.

The screws grew louder as the depth gauge ticked off each painstaking foot.

When the destroyer finally passed directly overhead, it missed *Mackerel*'s hull by mere feet and the churning eddies spawned by its spinning screws grabbed the submarine's stern and shook it in a corkscrew-like motion. Everyone breathed a small sigh of relief at having avoided the collision, but they soon regained their anxiety as the wait began for the inevitable depth charges.

Tremain was almost certain that the destroyer had detected them. Their scope must have been plainly visible, he thought, and if the Japanese destroyer had not seen it then it could have easily detected the submarine on the sonar as it passed overhead.

He closed his eyes and imagined what must be happening on the surface. The destroyer would signal the other destroyers to converge on the enemy submarine's location. Then they would commence run after run of depth charge attacks, and they would not stop until they saw oil and debris from *Mackerel*'s ruptured hull floating to the surface. After seeing the debris they would drop a few more charges just to be sure.

As *Mackerel* passed two hundred feet, there was no indication of depth charges. Salisbury still had contacts on the surface all around the boat, but he heard no depth charge splashes. The destroyer that had passed overhead just continued on course and faded into the rest of the background noise.

Was it possible that *Mackerel* was *still* undetected? Tremain thought. Maybe the Japanese did not know there was an American submarine in these waters after all. Perhaps the patrol boat encounter of the previous evening had not given them away. The enemy probably didn't expect a submarine to be this close to the Empire's homeland. If they truly were undetected then it had to be a miracle.

Tremain had to decide. If he took the ship deep to avoid a depth charge attack, *Mackerel* would never get back up in time to shoot. By the time they reached periscope depth again, the Japanese task force would have already cleared the channel and made its turn for the open sea. On the other hand, if he came back to periscope depth now, he might raise the scope in time to see five or six destroyers, with depth-charge throwers primed and ready, converging on *Mackerel*'s position. *Mackerel* would not stand a chance. She would be destroyed before she could get below one hundred feet.

Tremain sighed and glanced at Cazanavette, who was leaning over the chart desk with a pencil in his mouth staring at the chart as if it contained the answer. There really was no choice, after all, Tremain thought to himself. They had come here to do a job, or die trying.

"Diving officer!" Tremain shouted down the hatch. "Make your depth six five feet!"

Everyone in the room looked at him in shock as if he were mad. Cazanavette looked up from the chart with his face contorted at first, but then he smiled with his eyes and nodded. He and Tremain both knew what had to be done.

As Olander pumped off all of the water he had previously flooded into the negative tank, *Mackerel* began to glide up. It took several minutes to get the water off, but she ascended more rapidly with every foot of depth due to the increased buoyancy force created by the hull's expansion. As she passed one hundred feet, Tremain ordered all stop once again and waited for the speed log to read five knots.

"Up scope!" he ordered, and the periscope assistant pressed a button. Hydraulic pressure raised the scope out of its well and Tremain again met it at the floor.

The sound contacts still existed on all bearings. Everyone in the conning tower held their breaths and watched as Tremain spun around, checking in all directions. They let out a collective sigh when Tremain announced: "No close contacts. I don't think they've detected us."

Tremain turned the scope back up the channel. Again, a large roller doused it and he found himself looking at the underside of a wave. Several seconds passed before the scope emerged again. As the water ran off the lens, Tremain caught a glimpse of something over the next wave crest.

A dark shadow lay directly in front of the *Mackerel*'s bows. At first, he thought it was another destroyer. He almost gave the order to go deep again, but then the lens finally cleared and Tremain immediately recognized the dark gray camouflaged masts and superstructure of a large Japanese battleship. Tremain could just see her ominous eighteen-inch gun turrets protruding above the visible horizon. The waves hid the rest of her hull from view, but there could be no mistaking, the superstructure was the same as the one he had seen in the shipyard photographs. It was the *Kurita*. She was presenting her starboard bow and was headed on nearly the same southeasterly course as the destroyers.

"*Kurita* two thousand yards off the starboard bow, gentlemen," he announced with a wide grin, not taking his eyes from the periscope. "Let's do this, XO. Stand by for an observation."

Chapter 26

TREMAIN did not have much time to maneuver *Mackerel* into a firing position. The *Kurita* already filled up the entire field of view of the periscope lens. He could see black clouds of smoke billowing from her two stacks, indicating that her monstrous boilers were pouring out steam to turn her engines at high speed. *Kurita*'s freshly painted seventy-five thousand ton hull drove on through the treacherous pass, parting the ocean waves before it, effortlessly tossing them off in shattered pieces. Even the swells did not appear to have any affect on her, unlike her smaller escorts whose structures swayed to and fro in the choppy waters. *Kurita*'s masts and stacks stood vertical and unbending as though she were not underway at all but rather sitting beside the pier. She was a beautiful sight, Tremain thought, the master of her new realm, and a perfect symbol of Japanese engineering, ingenuity, and production capability.

In high power magnification, Tremain could make out small clusters of men standing on the battleship's decks.

A ship of her size would have a crew of over a thousand men, not including the shipyard personnel on board. He wondered if any of the men he was looking at now were shipyard workers. They were too far away to tell. He saw one of the men toss a cigarette butt into the water. Surely, none of them could suspect that an American submarine captain was watching them.

Tremain had to shake himself to get back to the business at hand. The *Kurita* was already drawing quickly to the right. He would have to act fast in order to place the shot. At her present speed she would be past them in only a few minutes.

Lining up the periscope reticle on her forward stack, Tremain depressed the mark button.

"Bearing, mark!" he shouted.

"Zero one nine, sir," the periscope assistant called off.

"Down scope!" Tremain slapped up the handles as the scope slid back down into its well, and he quickly made his way over to Hubley. "Use a range of eighteen hundred yards. Speed, twenty knots."

Hubley turned the dials and knobs of the torpedo data computer in a lightning quick fashion, entering all of the data from the periscope observation.

"She's moving fast," Tremain said to Cazanavette. "She's heading straight down the channel. We'll be hard pressed to get her as she goes by."

"As long as she's in the channel, Captain. We'll at least have a good idea of what course she's on. She won't zig until she's reached the open ocean. Can we get another observation, sir?" Cazanavette asked while scribbling the new information onto his plot.

"There's no time, XO. We've got to turn the tubes to bear now or we'll never get her." Tremain looked over his shoulder at the helmsman. "Hard right rudder. All ahead full."

The helmsman put the rudder over to the right as far as

it would go, and rang up the new bell on the engine order telegraph. The speed would assist the rudder in turning *Mackerel* quickly.

Tremain watched the course indicator dial as the ship's heading swept across north to the right. He needed to position the ship's bows perpendicular to the *Kurita*'s track to minimize the gyro angle settings on his torpedoes and to expose the battleship's full beam to *Mackerel*'s forward tubes. The larger the area that the target displayed, the easier it would be to hit it.

"Course zero seven five is an optimum firing course, sir," Cazanavette reported, from his plot. "That will place us perpendicular to *Kurita*'s projected track."

Tremain nodded. "Very well, XO. Helm, steady on course zero seven five."

"Steady course zero seven five, aye, sir," the helmsman responded.

The course indicator showed that *Mackerel* still had forty degrees to go to get to the ordered course. The slow underwater speed of the submarine made it seem like an eternity to complete the turn. Tremain took in a deep breath. They were only going to get one chance at this.

"Open outer doors on tubes one through six," he ordered. "Make tubes one through six ready for firing in all respects. Set depth on all torpedoes at twelve feet."

The phone talker next to him relayed the orders directly to the forward torpedo room over the phone circuit. Moments later, a small vibration trembled the deck beneath their feet as the large torpedo tube doors were opened hydraulically.

The phone talker received a report over his headset and repeated it to Tremain. "Sir, forward torpedo room reports, outer doors open on tubes one through six. Tubes one through six are ready for firing in all respects. Depth setting on all torpedoes is twelve feet."

Tremain glanced at the course indicator. *Mackerel* was passing course zero six zero to the right. As she edged over to course zero seven five, it took another minute to steady on the course.

"Steady on course zero seven five, sir," the helmsman reported finally.

Tremain glanced at Cazanavette's plot. Cazanavette had plotted a projected track for the *Kurita* using the information obtained from the last periscope observation. According to his plot, she would pass directly in front of them at close range within the next minute. That is, if the *Kurita* had not changed course.

"Final bearing and shoot," Tremain ordered, indicating that he intended to make one last periscope observation before firing. He knew it was risky, but he had to check the quality of the firing solution. He would mark one more bearing to the *Kurita*. If the actual bearing to the target matched the projected bearings coming from Cazanavette's plot and Hubley's torpedo data computer, it would mean that the firing solution was good and he would shoot.

"She's going to be close, skipper," Cazanavette commented unnecessarily.

Tremain nodded. He knew that the battleship would be practically on top of them, but he had to check the solution. They would not get another chance.

"Up scope!"

The periscope came up out of its well and Tremain pressed his face to the lens, immediately spinning around the azimuth. The scope took a few wave slaps, blurring the lens and obscuring his vision.

"Bring us up to fifty-eight feet!" Tremain shouted. He could not afford to miss the *Kurita* because of a choppy sea.

Down in the control room Olander acknowledged the order and *Mackerel* rose up seven feet. Everyone in the room glanced at Tremain momentarily, then kept going about their business. They knew that the shallower depth would expose more of the periscope and give the Japanese lookouts a better opportunity to see it. But there was no turning back now.

The lens now stood well above the waves, allowing Tremain a view unobstructed by the water. He swung the scope around, checking the entire azimuth, making sure that no destroyers were nearby. There really was no way to tell. The patchy fog blocked his view completely in some areas while allowing him to see for several thousand yards in others.

Kurita was indeed there, directly ahead less than a thousand yards away. She was steaming on as before, now presenting her entire starboard beam to *Mackerel*'s bows. With the lens high out of the water, Tremain could easily see every part of her structure and hull, right down to the waterline. She was so close, he had to rotate the periscope through several degrees to see her whole length. Once more, he steadied the lens reticle on her forward stack and pressed the button.

"Bearing, mark! Down scope!"

"Zero six five," the assistant called off as he lowered the periscope.

"Matched!" Hubley reported, indicating that the bearing was close enough to the torpedo data computer's generated bearing to fall within the allowable tolerances to proceed with the shot. Hubley locked the solution into the computer, which electronically transmitted the gyro information to the torpedoes waiting in their tubes.

"Set," Hubley reported.

"Fire one," Tremain said.

Cazanavette reached up and pressed the plunger on the firing panel. The deck shuddered and all ears popped as high-pressure air ejected the first torpedo from its tube.

"Fire two! . . . Fire three! . . . Fire four! . . . Fire five! . . . Fire six!" Tremain intended to place a good spread along the

Kurita's beam. He could see in his mind's eye the six bubbling wakes reaching toward the battleship like long knives.
It would not take long. The torpedo run was less than one
thousand yards.

With only seconds remaining in the run, Tremain raised
the periscope again.

There was the *Kurita,* still steaming ahead, still appar-
ently oblivious to the explosives headed for her underbelly.
While waiting for the torpedoes to hit, it occurred to
Tremain that he had better perform a safety check.

He quickly spun the scope around the azimuth, and almost spun it around too quickly. As he swept past the port
beam, his eye caught something in the fog that had not
been there before. He had almost missed it. A dark shape
appeared in the fog, and then suddenly it grew larger and
darker. Seconds later the shape emerged from the fog and
transformed into the charging bow of a destroyer, heading
straight for the periscope at twenty-five knots. It was so
close that Tremain could see the rust stains around its anchor housing. It could not have been more than three hundred yards away. This time there was no doubting that the
periscope had been sighted. Tremain could even see men
on the bridge wing pointing at it. Then he noticed the destroyer's two forward gun turrets rotate and depress in ele-
vation until they were aimed directly at his lens.

"Emergency deep!" Tremain shouted, slapping up the
periscope handles.

Both the helmsman and Olander were waiting for the order, and the deck lurched forward and down as the *Mackerel*
leaped to flank speed and water flooded into the negative
tank. Yet the initial downward motion stopped suddenly
and Tremain gasped when the depth gauge needle showed
that the submarine was actually rising instead of descending. She had been so shallow that she was now ensnared in
the surface suction forces created by the choppy seas. Every

man in the conning tower held his breath, waiting for the inevitable. There was nothing that could be done.

Two loud blasts split the water outside the conning tower hull and shattered the eardrums of every man. The blasts left them all seeing stars for several minutes afterward. Tremain stumbled between the scopes, getting his bearings, regaining his hearing, and discerning what had happened.

The Japanese destroyer had obviously fired a gun salvo. The shots had been close, too. The only thing that had saved them from being impacted by the lethal projectiles was the few feet of water remaining above the conning tower.

It was hard to determine if the shells had caused any damage, but the two blasts had at least managed to push *Mackerel* down in the water a few feet, finally freeing her from the suction forces. So *Mackerel* now began a very rapid descent into the deep. While she had been caught in the surface suction, Olander had ordered the negative tank completely flooded and he even brought water into the variable ballast tanks. As a result, the submarine was now very heavy and a large down angle soon developed, sending her deeper at an alarming rate.

The men in the conning tower regained their senses in relative darkness due to the concussion of the destroyer's shells, which had shattered all but one of the light bulbs. Tremain noticed Hubley holding his stopwatch near the remaining bulb, counting off the seconds to go for the running torpedoes. With all of the confusion, Hubley had somehow managed to keep track of the torpedo times. With only a few seconds remaining, he began counting out loud.

"Five . . . four . . . three . . . two . . ."

A thunderous rumble drowned out Hubley's voice and *Mackerel*'s deck rocked as the shock wave from the enriched torpex reached them. The crew recognized the sound of a torpedo detonation and cheers emanated from all compartments.

Another detonation followed. Followed by another. Then another. The crew below accompanied each successive detonation with more cheers. They waited several more seconds for the last two torpedoes to hit, but no detonations ever came.

Tremain and Cazanavette exchanged glances. In all, they had four confirmed hits. It was questionable whether four torpedoes would be enough to do the job, but they had done all that they could.

"Sir, I'm picking up some steam noises from *Kurita*'s direction," Salisbury reported. "Maybe we hit one of their boiler rooms."

Tremain forced a smile, but said nothing. It would take more than a ruptured boiler to sink a ship the size of the *Kurita*. The battleship had several boiler rooms. Losing one would only slow her down.

Tremain struggled to banish any more thoughts of the *Kurita* from his mind. He now had more pressing matters. He had to shift his focus to *Mackerel*'s survival and escape. The enemy destroyers would soon be converging on their position.

"High-speed screws are everywhere, sir," Salisbury reported, as if to confirm his deduction. "Active sonar is saturating the water."

Mackerel passed through two hundred feet rapidly. She was still going down fast, and Tremain began to grow concerned that Olander did not have a handle on the depth control.

As she passed two hundred thirty feet, water began to trickle down the periscope barrels. The near miss from the destroyer's shells had damaged the periscope seals, and now the increased sea pressure had blown them inward. The trickles quickly turned into small streams as *Mackerel* went deeper and the pressure increased more.

Cazanavette shined a flashlight up at the periscope seals. "This is only going to get worse, Captain."

Tremain nodded. "Get someone working on it, XO."

Moments later the periscope assistant and another sailor began attempting to seal the scope barrels with rubber gaskets. Tremain watched their efforts with bleak hope that they could do anything to stop the leaks. Leaks from scope gaskets usually needed to be repaired pierside.

"Destroyers are close now, Captain," Salisbury reported. "At least four."

Tremain could hear the sonar beams probing the water. The destroyers would know exactly where to look. The destroyer that spotted them had probably already placed a dye marker on the spot where *Mackerel*'s periscope had been sighted. Now all of the sub killers would converge on that spot.

"Passing three hundred feet sir," Olander called up the hatch.

"Take her to four hundred feet," Tremain called back. "Helm, left full rudder. Steady on course, three five zero."

The destroyers would not expect him to turn up the channel. They would expect him to head for the open sea. Either way, it did not matter, and Tremain knew it. The destroyers could move much faster and would cover every inch of the channel until they found him.

"Depth charges splashes, sir!" Salisbury announced. "They sound close!"

"Continue the dive!" Tremain shouted. "Take her down to five hundred feet!"

Tremain's order would take the submarine well below test depth, but he got no argument from any of those around him. They all knew it was their only chance to avoid the depth charges.

Mackerel continued to dive and had just passed four

hundred fifty feet when the depth charges exploded. Six distinct explosions blasted the water just outside *Mackerel*'s thin metal skin and rocked the hull in every direction. Light bulbs shattered. Pieces of cork insulation rained down everywhere. Men were flung across compartments like rag dolls. The hull shook for several seconds and screams and yells could be heard from other compartments well after the shaking had subsided.

Tremain opened his eyes to darkness and disorientation. He instinctively rubbed his head and felt blood underneath his hair. Somehow he knew that he had been thrown into a hydraulic valve on the port side of the conning tower and his head was spinning from the concussion.

He took a few moments in the darkness to regain his faculties and gather his bearings. He could hear running water close by—it sounded like several different streams. Then he smelled the distinctive fishy aroma of seawater. He noticed that he was sitting on the deck and that the running water was soaking his trousers. The cold sensation helped him to come to, but he still was not sure where he was.

"XO?" he spoke into the darkness.

A battle lantern clicked on. Then another. One shone its beam onto his face. He heard some agitated voices on the other side of the conning tower.

Then he heard Cazanavette shout, "Mister Olander, take the angle off her! We're passing five hundred feet!"

An answer came back. "Olander's knocked out, sir! We're trying to take the angle off!"

"We're going down too fast!" Cazanavette's voice rang out again. "Blow negative! Head for shallower water, Helm, steer course north!"

"Passing five hundred fifty, sir!" another voice said.

Tremain thought he heard the hull creaking. He could feel the vibrations through his numb hands. He tried to speak but he could not.

"Blow bow buoyancy!" Cazanavette's voice instructed. "Blow safety! Blow all main ballast!"

Tremain tried to move, but he still could not see straight. The room was still dark and the few battle lanterns appeared only as a blur to his eyes. He heard the shrill sibilation as high-pressure air expunged water from the ship's tanks.

"Passing six hundred!" someone yelled.

Tremain then heard something that sounded like bullets ricocheting off metal. Somehow he knew that it was the sound of nuts, bolts, and fasteners impacting the bulkheads at high velocity after being shot out of their over-torqued flanges and valves. The hull shuddered continuously, now. Tremain heard someone near him whispering a prayer.

"Passing six hundred thirty!" a voice yelled.

The number jogged something in Tremain's groggy mind. He suddenly remembered. It was burned into his memory. He had seen the number on the chart for the last few weeks. It was the depth of the channel.

His memory was instantaneously confirmed as *Mackerel* slammed into the ocean floor, bow first. Everyone in the conning tower flew forward into a pile near the steering wheel. More shouts and yells came from the other compartments as the deck lurched to one side, then back to the other. *Mackerel*'s anchored bow acted like a pivot in the sand and the angle quickly diminished until her stern slammed into the seabed with another massive crash, sending more shudders throughout the ship.

Moments later the ship settled. All was quiet, save for the creaking of the over-stressed girders, the moaning of the wounded, and the sound of running water.

Tremain smelled something else in the air now. Even in his groggy condition, he recognized what it was.

It was chlorine gas. The batteries were flooding.

* * *

WRIGHT had gone immediately to his battle station in the aft torpedo room when the alarm had sounded. In the same way, Tee had gone to his station in the crew's mess, which became damage control central during combat. They had separated without another word between them.

Wright and the torpedo men around him heard the torpedoes from the forward room hit home. They had just finished celebrating when word came that depth charges were on the way down.

Each man grabbed on to the nearest handhold and began to pray. Wright positioned himself near the depth gauge by the torpedo tubes. He could see that they were already below test depth.

He felt chills as he heard the eerie metallic clicks of the depth-charge-arming sensors outside the hull. Then the sea outside erupted in a series of concussions that rocked the room. In rapid succession, one exploded on the starboard side, then on the port side, then another to starboard, then Wright lost count as he careened across the room and into a sailor near the opposite bulkhead. The hull creaked and whined some more as the shock waves stressed it in both directions.

The room went pitch black as the deck steeped downward and the hull creaked as the sea pressure increased. Wright heard several hissing sounds and knew that the control room was attempting to stop their descent by blowing all of the water they could out of the ballast tanks.

The hull creaked again. Then Wright felt a tremendous jolt. It flung him and some of the men into the forward bulkhead. Then the deck began to level. Wright thought it a good thing at first but then realized what was happening when the stern slammed hard into the ocean floor.

The ship was on the bottom of the channel.

After it was all over, Wright found that beyond a few bruises, he was not injured and grabbed for the nearest battle lantern. All of the light bulbs in the room had been shattered and many of the other men clicked on battle lanterns too. The room was filled with the dank smell of oil and water.

"Who's hurt?" Wright called.

"Rucker's hurt," a voice said. "He's over here."

Wright moved toward the voice to find two men huddled over a prostrate figure on the deck.

"He's hit his head on something sharp," Petty Officer Guthrie said.

Wright could see blood and a messy wound near the man's left ear. The man's body was limp and lifeless and Wright could not see how he could still be alive.

Another man stumbled over to the light, cradling his right thigh with both hands, his dungaree trousers torn open to expose several bright red oozing blisters on his skin. Guthrie immediately instructed the man to sit on the deck and began squeezing the grotesque blisters, causing the man considerable pain. Wright was almost sickened by the sight.

"What happened to him?" Wright asked.

"We must have a hydraulic rupture," Guthrie said as he kept pressing on the man's leg. "The oil has shot up under his skin. Best thing to do is get it all out of his leg."

"We've got leaks over here!" a man yelled.

Wright felt some spray across his face and noticed a valve flange squirting water in all directions. He heard other leaks in the darkness on the other side of the room.

Wright grabbed Guthrie's shoulder. "Leave him, for now. We have to get these leaks under control. Get someone to work on that flange. I'll go check the rest of the room."

Guthrie looked sympathetically at the two injured men, then nodded. "Aye, sir."

Wright crawled around the piping and racks on the room's port side and found three more leaks from pipe welds and valves. Another man noticed that the hatch in the overhead was leaking, too. Eventually, Guthrie and the nine non-injured men broke out wrenches and banding equipment and got to work on the leaks.

Wright manned the sound-powered phone set and established communications with the control room and the crew's mess. As he plugged in the phone set, he noticed the reading on the depth gauge.

It read six hundred forty five feet, well below *Mackerel*'s four-hundred-foot test depth. The fact that the hull was still intact was a miracle, and Wright silently thanked God for the men who built her back in Portsmouth. He was certain that those men never anticipated that she could go this deep.

Wright could hear several reports coming over the phone circuit, as each compartment reported the damage. He waited his turn. He was last in line, since his room was the aftermost room in the ship. As he listened to the reports, he realized just how serious *Mackerel*'s situation was. Each compartment reported leaks or minor flooding, and damaged equipment of some kind. When it was his turn, he reported what he knew.

"Control, aft torpedo room," he identified himself. "Minor leaks from seawater piping. Hydraulic rupture in external hydraulic system. Two men injured."

The report was acknowledged and the circuit was immediately taken up by another damage report. Wright heard something about flooding in the forward battery, then something about chlorine gas, the toxic gas created when salt water underwent electrolysis.

Then the latch on the compartment door spun around and the door opened. Tee stepped inside and glanced around at the damage before approaching Wright. He was making his rounds as the damage control officer. He shone his lantern on Wright's face.

"How're your people doing back here?" he asked,

slightly out of breath, and with no indication that they had been at each other's throats only minutes before.

"All right," Wright replied. "I think we can get these leaks under control. Our injured men need attention."

"Any more damage to report?"

Wright was about to answer when he heard someone shouting over the communications circuit. "Fire! Fire! Fire in the maneuvering room!" the voice yelled.

"Someone's reporting a fire in maneuvering," Wright exclaimed to Tee.

Tee raced for the door. The maneuvering room was the next compartment forward. He opened the door and was met by a billowing cloud of smoke and lapping flames. It was impossible to see beyond the doorframe. Tee leaped back and hurriedly shut the door, before any more smoke could enter the torpedo room.

The men in the room briefly stopped their repairs and exchanged glances. That door was the only way out of the room and now a fire blocked it. Wright, Tee, and the other men in the aft torpedo room were cut off from the rest of the ship now, trapped by a fire in a leaking compartment.

Chapter 27

"**YOU** all right, Captain?" Cazanavette asked.

Tremain walked through the water stream dripping from the periscopes and over to the chart desk where Cazanavette conferred with Stillsen. His head still throbbed, but at least he felt sturdy enough to be on his feet. The cold water felt surprisingly good on his face and it helped to revive him, but he winced as the stream of salt water touched the wound on his head.

Men desperately worked everywhere around him. Some turned wrenches to tighten seeping valves. Others hammered long planks of wooden shoring into place to help support the hull against the massive sea pressure. They all worked by inconsistent and unsteady light from battle lanterns.

As Tremain drew near the desk, Cazanavette extended a hand in an attempt to assist him, but Tremain did not take it. Instead, he managed a polite smile of appreciation and leaned against the bulkhead for support. Cazanavette and

Stillsen both looked like hell, Tremain thought. But then he wondered what he must look like. The room was dank and humid and he could already tell that the oxygen was getting thin. Carbon dioxide levels would be increasing soon.

"Damage report," he muttered. "Bring me up to date, XO."

Cazanavette and Stillsen looked at each other, as if to question whether he was well enough to be on his feet, let alone in command. But one look into his eyes did away with any such thoughts. Tremain was not in the mood for doubting, and finally Cazanavette answered.

"It's bad, Captain."

"Give me everything, XO."

"We're sitting on the bottom of Kii Suido in six hundred and forty feet of water. Don't ask me how, but the hull is still holding, for now anyway. I tried to stop our descent and used up damn near all our reserve air pressure in the attempt. The surface suction forces must have given us a false trim when we were at periscope depth. We were real heavy. Several thousand pounds heavy by my reckoning. I think that's why we went down so fast. That's the only thing it could be. Either that or our ballast tanks have been ruptured, but there's really no way to tell that. We have multiple leaks and minor flooding in almost every compartment."

"I smell chlorine," Tremain added.

Cazanavette nodded. "We have a leak in the forward battery well. We don't know where the leak is. I've ordered the forward battery disconnect switch opened to take it off the bus. In the meantime, we've cleared the whole compartment. I've got two men in breathing apparatus looking for the leak. Besides them, the forward battery compartment's to be used for passage only.

"The forward torpedo room took some bad damage when we hit bottom. The men in there are fighting tooth and nail to stay on top of things. They're up to their knees in water. All the tubes are flooded so the outer doors must be smashed. The inner doors are holding, by the grace of God. If one of those goes, it'll all be over. The worst damage was to the hatch. It unseated from the shock and I don't know if we'll be able to get it completely shut again. Chief Konhausen thinks the hatch ring is bent. They're trying to seal it with block and tackle fastened to the hatch wheel."

"How're we looking aft?"

"Aft could be worse, sir. A panel fire lit off in maneuvering a few minutes ago. They think it's one of the main bus breakers. The compartment filled with smoke before anyone could find out the source, and they had to evacuate it. That room's completely sealed now, so, hopefully, the fire has no oxygen to keep it burning. Of course, now we're cut off from the men in the aft torpedo room, and they have their own leaks to deal with. Turner and Wright are both back there."

Cazanavette stopped as several explosions reverberated throughout the hull. The explosions were well above them, but close enough to send vibrations through the hull.

"And then there's that," Cazanavette said, pointing up. "The destroyers topside are still dropping ash cans about every ten or fifteen minutes. So far, none of them have been very close, which kind of baffles me because they have to know where we are. Anyway, I'm afraid our hull can't take these vibrations much longer. Not at this depth."

Tremain nodded. His throbbing head had magnified the sound of the explosions. "What about the drain pump? Is it working?"

"No, sir. The drain system has been completely mangled. The pump came off its foundation and is lying on its side in the bilge. Much of the drain piping has been ruptured."

"Do we have any of our sensors?"

"As far as we can tell, no, sir. Either the depth charges or the bottom must have ripped off the sound heads. The scopes are still leaking, as you can see."

Tremain was almost afraid to ask the next question. "Casualties?"

"Two dead, sir, Seaman Rucker and Petty Officer Leland. Eight men incapacitated, including George Olander. I think everyone has some kind of scrape or bruise or something." Cazanavette paused. "Oxygen's low too, sir, down to eighteen percent. Carbon dioxide levels are increasing."

Tremain closed his eyes and rubbed his head. His head hurt enormously and he felt very tired. It seemed useless. They were below test depth. Nearly every system had been destroyed or damaged. Oxygen was low. Water was coming into the ship. The next depth charge pattern might split the hull at its seams.

Rucker and Leland were perhaps better off than any of them, he thought. At least death had come quickly for them. He wanted to lie down on the deck and shut his eyes for the last time. His head hurt so much he could hardly stand it. He closed his eyes to briefly shut out the pain and their dismal situation.

When he opened his eyes again Cazanavette and Stillsen were watching him with hopeful expressions. They were waiting for him to say something, to give them the magic orders that would make everything right again and save them all. They suddenly looked afraid to him, and young.

Cazanavette had done well to attack the damage, but he was obviously at the limit of his abilities, and Stillsen did not have the experience to help, though he obviously wanted to. This was the moment in which they needed him, the captain, Jack Tremain. They needed his expertise and his experience. Most of all, they needed his leadership. Someone had to pull the crew's efforts together and give them a chance to live.

But what can I do? Tremain asked himself. Then he thought of Judy. She would be a lonely widow. And a young and beautiful one. She would go for walks on the beach and gaze at the sunset thinking of him. In a few months she would get a letter from Ireland. It would be cold and emotionless, simply stating the standard "greatly appreciate your sacrifice" and some other bullshit. Judy would cry every night for years to come, and there would be nothing to console her but a folded American flag that would do little to recompense her for the years of sacrifice. She would get nothing but a flag and a heartless letter from a twisted old man.

Tremain felt tears forming in his eyes at the thought of her alone and grieving. The woman who had been so understanding all these years, the woman who had waited patiently for the day that he would be hers and hers alone, would be herself all alone. Now she would live out the rest of her years with a broken heart, and he sobbed inwardly because he knew that she deserved much better than that.

"XO," Tremain said as he mustered the energy to stand up straight, the pain still throbbing in his head. He forced himself to keep going. He had to do it for Judy's sake, and for his men's sake. They all needed him right now.

"Are you okay, sir?" Cazanavette asked.

"First, we have to get to the aft battery disconnect," Tremain said, ignoring the question. "It's our only remaining source of power and we can't let that electrical fire eat up any more of our remaining juice. Someone's going to have to enter the maneuvering room and do it."

"Aye, sir," Cazanavette answered skeptically.

"Also, there's no reason for anyone to be in the conning tower, except for the men working on the leaks. So let's clear this room and transfer down to control room."

Tremain did this because the conning tower was perhaps the most dangerous place in a submarine, being a separate section from the rest of the pressure hull. The men in the conning tower quickly secured their stations and filed down the hatch into the control room. Tremain was the last one down, leaving the four men working on the leaks. In his condition he had trouble negotiating the ladder—the rungs seemed yards apart.

Distant depth charges shook the ocean once again. Everyone watched for new leaks to appear, and, when they did, men groped through the outboards and the bilges to repair them. Tremain looked at his watch and began to formulate a plan of attack, trying to ignore the pain in his head.

Remarkably, the pressure hull was still holding.

"**SHHH!** They're telling me something," Wright said, holding his hand to one ear of the headset. The men around him tried to be quieter with their repair work, so he could hear the orders being passed over the sound-powered phone. Most of the leaks in the aft torpedo room had been slowed to a trickle and now they were working on minimizing the trickles. Isolation valves had been shut to seal most of the damaged valves and piping. Some piping that could not be isolated was wrapped in banding material, rubber, sheet metal, and strong pieces of steel plating especially cut for such an occasion.

The men in the aft torpedo room had been working continuously for two hours. They stood ankle deep in a muck of water and hydraulic oil and debris. Two of the battle lanterns had died and the oxygen in the room was getting low. Wright could tell because he was feeling drowsy. He also had a headache, probably because the CO_2 level was reaching the lower limit. He listened to the message from the control room. He could hardly believe what he was hearing. They could not possibly want him to do that.

Tee stumbled over to him. "What did they say?"

"They want us to enter the maneuvering room and open the aft battery disconnect manually," Wright replied, covering the phone with one hand. "They said they tried to get to it twice from the forward side, but the fire re-flashed and beat them back."

"Are they crazy?" Tee shouted. "Holy shit!"

"Maybe. I told them we're at our limit back here. Then the XO came on the line and told me personally to get the disconnect opened. He said to make that our priority. Even above fixing the leaks."

Tee shook his head and rested against the bulkhead. He looked exhausted. Wright and Tee glanced at the working men around them, all breathing heavily. Together, they had been guiding the damage control efforts in the room. Wright could see the black bruise forming on Tee's face where he had punched him earlier. Strangely, Wright found a moment to wonder what kind of thoughts had to be going through Tee's mind. Having just decided to come clean for the sake of his honor only a few hours before, he could not be completely focused now. In the back of his mind, he had to be thinking about it.

"Break out the Momsen lungs," Tee said suddenly. "They can help us to breathe inside maneuvering."

Tee had obviously made the decision to carry out the XO's order. He was the senior man in the room, and it was his call. Two of the men removed the Momsen lungs from a locker. The box-like breathing devices were supposed to be used to escape the submarine when it was disabled and lying on the bottom in shallow water. The Momsen lung gave a person only a few breaths of air for an ascent, and then doubled as a life preserver once the man reached the surface. No one objected to using them. Everyone knew that an escape from a depth of six hundred and forty feet was impossible.

Tee strapped a Momsen lung across his chest and

plugged it in to an air manifold to charge it full of air. He directed two of the sailors to do the same.

"I should be the one going in," Wright protested. "You're the man in charge back here."

Tee smiled as he placed the nostril clamps over his nose. "I know exactly where the disconnect is. I had to open it when we did the battery replacement a few months ago." He paused, then added, "Besides, you're manning the phones. I need you to keep giving the control room clear and accurate reports."

Wright nodded. It was true that Tee knew much better than he where the battery disconnect was, but Wright could see in Tee's face that that was not the real reason he had volunteered himself. Wright wondered if Tee was doing this brave act to somehow vindicate himself for what he had done to O'Connell and Anderson. Wright wondered if Tee would be entering the compartment at all if he had not come clean.

Tee and the two sailors moved to the door and found it to be hot from the fire, so they all quickly donned the driest pairs of gloves they could find. Wright and the rest of the men moved aft to stand by the torpedo tubes and out of the way. Tee peeked through the small sight glass on the door and called back to Wright. "I can see smoke, but no visible flame!"

That was not surprising, Wright thought. The fire had probably burned up all of the oxygen in the room. Wright nodded and passed the word to the control room. He also told them that Tee was preparing to enter the maneuvering room to open the battery disconnect.

Tee made an attempt to undog the hatch, but the latch would not budge. The fire had created a positive pressure in the maneuvering room, jamming the door shut. Wright saw Tee's struggle with the latch and called to him. "We need to pressurize this room to get that door open!"

"No!" Tee shot back. "We'll need every ounce of reserve air pressure to get back to the surface! We'll have to muscle it open!"

Wright knew that Tee understood the consequences of "muscling" open an airtight door to a pressurized room. A real danger existed because there was no telling just how much of a differential pressure existed between the two compartments. It was like activating a bomb of unknown size. Tee directed the two men to help him with the lever and they all found good handholds on the door's latching mechanism. Then, all together, they tried to move it. They grunted and groaned as they put their whole bodies into the hatch lever, but it did not budge. Then Tee asked for a crowbar and once again all three men put their full weight against the crowbar to pry the door's latch free.

Wright thought he saw the lever move slightly. He started to call out for Tee to take it slower, but before he could, the lever moved and the door blasted open with a loud explosion, throwing Tee and his men backward through the air. The explosion was strong enough to knock the men in the back of the room against the bulkhead and it blew Wright's headset off. Like the mouth of an angry dragon, the open door shot forth a long tongue of fire that stretched the length of the compartment and singed the eyebrows of the men by the torpedo tubes, momentarily lighting up the entire room. Wright shielded his face from the intense heat and felt the sleeves of his shirt touched by the flame. It had lasted for no more than a fraction of a second, then it was gone, leaving only a pall of black smoke pouring from the door and quickly filling the aft torpedo room. The men immediately started coughing as they got down on the deck, searching for some breathable air. Wright did the same, and found that he had to get within a foot of the deck to find slightly breathable air.

"How many more Momsen lungs do we have?" he shouted to the men by the locker.

"Plenty, sir," Guthrie answered. "We have enough for half the crew."

"Pass them out. Hurry. Get them charged up."

The men put on the cumbersome breathing lungs and charged them at the nearest air manifold. It gave them some relief from the acrid smoke.

Wright donned a lung as well, but the smoke still stung his eyes as he felt his way across the smoke-shrouded deck. He found Tee, lying face up, in the middle of the room, the oily slush that covered the deck lapping at his blackened cars. The clothing had been burned off the front of his body as had much of the skin on his face, and his eyes stared blankly upward from their blackened pits.

Wright held his ear to Tee's mouth and could hear no breathing. Tee's large frame had taken the brunt of the blast and had shielded the two other men. They lay near him, gasping for air, their Momsen lungs ruptured and useless. Wright quickly called for some more lungs and a few moments later Guthrie appeared with them.

As Guthrie applied the new lungs to the injured men, he motioned toward Tee.

"What about Mr. Turner, sir?"

Wright shook his head. "He's dead."

Wright stared at Tee's still form. Despite all the pain he had caused, despite all his questionable ethics, despite all the harm he had done, his last action had been a heroic one. For the first time in his life, he had put someone else ahead of himself. His father, the admiral, would be proud.

"What now, sir?" Guthrie said in Wright's ear, briefly removing his mouth from the lung inhaler.

Wright looked back towards the door. The fire had subsided now, probably because there was no more oxygen in the room.

"You ever opened the battery disconnect before?" Wright asked between breaths.

"No, sir."

"Well, man the phones, then. And hand me that wrench and those rubber gloves."

Tucking the wrench in his belt, Wright donned the rubber gloves while he recharged his Momsen lung. He would have to open the battery disconnect himself. Although he had never operated it before, he knew exactly where it was from his endless hours of study.

He moved quickly. Blinded by the smoky air, he felt his way through the battered door and into the maneuvering room. The smoke in the maneuvering room was dense, but he quickly felt his way to the electrical panels on the starboard side. Some of the panels were charred, yet others seemed untouched. He groped his way along several feet forward until he found the panel he was looking for. Strangely, he started to think about the time he had first studied the battery system. It was during one of those sleepless nights during his first week on board. Now it seemed like a hundred years ago.

Methodically, Wright unscrewed each bolt on the panel. He knew that his air would be running out soon, so he kept a steady and deliberate pace, removing each bolt one at a time. It seemed like there were so many of them, and he lost count. As he finally removed the last bolt, he felt a suction effect from his Momsen lung. It was out of air.

He quickly reached into the dark panel and found the lever that he knew must be inside it, the lever that would disconnect the aft battery from the ship's electrical distribution system. He clutched the lever with his gloved hand and rotated it slowly through ninety degrees, his fingers starting to lose feeling from the lack of oxygen. With the lever locked in the open position, the aft battery was now physically disconnected from the ship's electrical distribution system. The source of the fire had been removed.

Wright would have breathed a sigh of relief if he had the air to do it. He started to feel light-headed and dizzy as he stumbled back through the door, desperately groping and searching for an air manifold to recharge his lung. In the dark smoke he suddenly lost his orientation and he could not tell whether he was still in the maneuvering room or back in the torpedo room. Without thinking, he threw off the Momsen lung and relentlessly groped around the room. His panicked lungs forced him to take in several breaths of the dense smoke and instantly he fell to the deck and went into convulsions. His lungs tried to cough out the smoke but in their desperate need for air they only brought in more.

Then a hand reached out from the smoke and grabbed him. It was Guthrie. Guthrie put his arm around his shoulder and dragged him the rest of the way out of the room. Moments later, Guthrie had a new Momsen lung on him and plugged it in to the nearest manifold.

Wright was phasing in and out of consciousness, and felt his lungs reject the fresh air. He forced himself to take a deep breath, then he grabbed Guthrie's arm.

"Is it done, sir?" Guthrie said, examining Wright's eyes.

Then Wright lost his senses in phases. He could not breathe, that was his first sensation. The deck suddenly felt very soft, that was his second sensation. Guthrie's face and everything around him suddenly became very dark, that was his third. Suddenly, he felt very cold, and then he felt nothing.

Chapter 28

TREMAIN leaned against the cold steel skin of the port-side diesel in the forward engine room. Struggling to keep his eyes open, he brought his watch into the fading light of a battle lantern. It read 2013 hours. They had been sitting on the bottom since noon. The boat was silent now, as was the sea all around it. He flicked on his flashlight and shone it around the room, its beam stretching off into the thick air. A few trickles remained here and there. Tremain coughed as the smoke and chlorine mixture touched a nerve in his throat. His cough echoed off the metal bulkheads and made him feel like he was the only one on board.

Partially rested, he pressed on, making his way through each compartment, inspecting the repairs. Wooden planks and shoring blocked his path in many places, as did the bodies of sleeping crewmen. The men had been working continuously in the worst of conditions since the *Mackerel* had crashed on the bottom of the sea. They had fought every leaking valve, every leaking pipe, every leaking hatch, until there were none left to fight—at least none worth wasting energy on. All of the large leaks had been patched in some fashion or other, including the periscope seals. The men had pulled together all of their efforts and had exhausted themselves while doing it, and now they slept wherever they could. Tremain even saw a few lying on the deck in some of the flooded compartments, oblivious to the oily muck lapping at their bodies. They were physically drained. Even if they had not been so tired, the lack of oxygen in the ship's atmosphere would have put them to sleep.

Tremain walked through the maneuvering room. The fire damage in the room had been limited to only a few electrical panels. If young Wright had not opened the battery disconnect, they would have never regained access to this vital room, which controlled *Mackerel*'s critical supply of electricity. The aft battery still contained some badly needed energy. Even now, some electricians worked sluggishly on the damaged gear over in the corner, attempting to jumper around the fried circuits with makeshift cables and remove them from the ship's electrical distribution system.

Tremain shone the light down onto the large motors beneath the deck plates. The motors seemed to be in good shape. If the shafts were not bent, they might be able to restore propulsion. But only time would tell. He moved on to the torpedo room. The door bore the blackened marks from the earlier explosion that had killed Lieutenant Turner. The room's atmosphere had cleared a little, now that it had shared its smoke with the other compartments in the ship. Tremain tried to imagine what it must have been like for the men who had been trapped in the room. It must have been a hellish experience. When they had finally gotten through to them, just a few hours before, most had suffered badly from smoke inhalation, young Wright among them. They were all quickly transferred to the forward torpedo room, the cleanest atmosphere left in the boat, but they were all in bad shape. Tremain did not know if the men would make it. But then, he wondered, would any of them make it home?

Cazanavette and Chief Freund came through the door, both out of breath. The XO rested one arm on a torpedo rack before speaking. "The . . . forward battery well has been pumped dry, sir," he breathed, ". . . using a hand pump. We pumped it . . . to the forward torpedo room bilge. And the chlorine levels have stabilized. Still dangerous . . . but stable."

"Good," Tremain breathed, "I've been thinking . . . about our buoyancy situation. . . . We can't be heavy . . . the ballast tanks have to be near dry unless they're ruptured. . . . So we should be close to positive buoyancy. . . . If we can just get some of this water off . . . I think she'll rise."

"And how . . . do we do that, sir?" Freund muttered. "The drain pump's gone."

"We could cross connect the trim and drain systems," Cazanavette said. "But . . . we don't have enough power . . . to operate the trim pump long enough to get it all off."

"I know . . . I know," Tremain said. To utter the words was a labor in itself. "We won't use the pump."

"Then . . . how, Captain?"

"We'll remove the access cover to the negative tank . . . and use buckets to get the water into it . . . then we'll seal it up . . . and use all the rest of our reserve air to blow the water overboard."

Cazanavette grimaced, then nodded. He realized that it was their only chance.

The negative tank was a variable ballast tank that could hold roughly fourteen thousand pounds of water. It was normally flooded to speed up diving. The tank had been blown dry earlier when Cazanavette had tried to stop *Mackerel*'s almost fatal descent, so it should be empty now. Most submariners would have been unnerved at the thought of opening the access hatch to a hard tank while at sea, especially while submerged. It was not normally done, due to the dangers involved. While the access cover was removed, they would have only one protection valve between them and the outside sea pressure. But it was their only chance to get the water off the ship, and Cazanavette and Freund both knew it.

Cazanavette and Freund walked through the ship, rousing the men. They laboriously formed bucket brigades using every bucket on the ship. When there were no more buckets, they grabbed whatever they could find that would hold water. The cooks even broke out some of the empty five-gallon food cans.

The men formed a long line that wound through the passageways connecting the flooded torpedo room bilge with the negative tank access hatch in the pump room. Most of the men were so exhausted that they had to lie on the deck and use only their arms to pass along each bucket to the next man down the line. A full bucket came from the torpedo room, and an empty one returned, to be filled and passed back again. The men worked in three shifts, officers included. One shift worked for fifteen minutes while the others rested for thirty. Fifteen minutes was as long as they could go since they were working on such low oxygen. Periodically, the corpsman would walk by and give any droopy-eyed sailors a breath or two from a Momsen lung to help them revive a little. Momsen lungs had not been distributed to the crew because every ounce of reserve air pressure would be needed to get them back to the surface.

Slowly, bucket by bucket, hour by hour, the water level in the torpedo room bilge lowered, until no more full buckets came down the line. Then the line shifted to the forward engine room, and the water was removed from that bilge in the same fashion. Then the storeroom, and so on, until only a few inches of water remained in all of the spaces.

Tremain watched through blurry eyes as the last bolt sealed the negative tank access hatch shut. His head still throbbed and he did not know how much longer he could stay on his feet. He reached down to the deck and grabbed some water in his hand, then threw it onto his face. Even the cold liquid did not help anymore.

"That's it, Captain," Cazanavette said. "The access hatch is sealed. . . . I've had the men check the bolts for the . . . proper torque."

Tremain nodded and forced out the words. "Very well . . . XO. Man stations. . . . Prepare to surface. Let's hope this works."

The word was passed and the weary crew gradually moved to their posts. Tremain and Cazanavette took up their positions in the control room behind Chief Freund and the two planesmen at the ballast control panel.

Tremain looked at the clock. It read 0134. They had not heard any depth charges for eight hours. Perhaps the Japanese had given up on them. Either way, the *Mackerel* had to surface now or never.

"We may end up in a POW camp, XO," Tremain said.

Cazavnavette did not respond. He did not appear to have the energy.

"Maybe . . . they won't be up there," Stillsen said hopefully.

Tremain looked back at Stillsen and managed a smile.

"All stations report . . . manned and ready for surfacing," a sailor with a phone headset intoned.

"We're ready, Captain," Cazanavette muttered.

Tremain stood up as straight as he could to help give the crew faith. "All right, XO. Use every last bit of air and blow negative to sea."

Cazanavette repeated the order and Chief Freund turned a valve on the ballast control panel. A faint sibilation filled the room as air pushed the water from the negative tank into the sea, then the sound faded away, signifying that the air banks were now empty.

Tremain thought it seemed too fast. It didn't seem like much air had been released. He turned his attention to the depth gauge, as did everyone else in the compartment. Several battle lanterns had their beams squarely focused on it. A hush came over the room as every man's eyes stared at the gauge needle as if they could will it to rise just by concentrating hard enough.

Then, *Mackerel* gave a slight shudder and the needle moved.

Mackerel shuddered again.

Tremain felt a motion in his feet and the deck began to slope as *Mackerel*'s stern slowly lifted out of the sand. The depth needle showed six hundred and thirty five feet and rising. A few men cheered as they watched the needle go, but most just stared with smiles on their faces and prayers on their lips. They had been at death's door and now they might live. If it was to mean years in a Japanese prison camp, even that was better than certain death.

The deck continued to slope downward as *Mackerel*'s stern climbed, so much so that Tremain wondered if the bow would ever break free. It seemed to be firmly anchored.

"I don't know what's keeping the bow from coming up, sir," Freund shouted.

"Try moving the bow planes," Tremain ordered.

The planesman on the bow plane station leaned on the wheel that operated them to no avail.

"They seem to be stuck, sir."

"We're caught up on something and it's fouling the planes," Tremain said, as the deck approached a thirty-degree angle. They all knew the concerns. If the angle got too large, it could allow air to escape from the ballast tanks, and then *Mackerel* would never come up again.

"Helm," Tremain struggled to say. "All back full! XO, tell maneuvering to give us every last bit of battery power we have left!"

The helmsman rang up the ordered speed and Cazana-vette got on the phone to pass the word to the engineering officer of the watch to run the battery to depletion.

Tremain felt the deck lurch slightly as *Mackerel*'s screws spun in the astern direction. A terrifying scratching sound could be heard against the hull outside. It sounded like metal grinding against metal. Then suddenly *Mackerel*'s bow broke free of the ocean floor and the boat lev-eled off. Both bow and stern began rising together, slowly at first, but with an ever increasing rate of ascent.

Six hundred twenty . . . six hundred ten . . . six hundred. . . .

Tremain heard some men sobbing behind him, breaking under the stress. He managed to remember to order the ship to a complete stop and the aft battery placed back on the bus to give the ship some power. As partial power returned to the ship's systems, the replaced light bulbs flicked on, al-lowing the men to move around without battle lanterns. The new and better lighting showed Tremain how bad his ship looked on the inside. Tools, rags, planks of shoring, flash-lights, bolts, pieces of sheet metal, and other miscellaneous items covered almost every inch of deck space.

"Sir," Cazanavette said from near the bow planesman. "We still don't have control over the bow planes. Some-thing must be jammed up there."

Tremain nodded. A hundred explanations went through his weary mind, but he put them all off until later. *Mackerel* was coming up, with or without functioning bow planes, and that was all he cared about at that moment.

As *Mackerel* passed three hundred feet, Tremain or-dered the compartment rigged for red light. With the sonar gone, he had no way of knowing what was above them.

Tremain at least wanted to have the crew's eyes conditioned for the darkness before they reached the surface.

Mackerel passed two hundred feet, then one hundred feet. The air pockets in the ballast tanks expanded as the sea pressure decreased, speeding up the rate of ascent as she got shallower. The depth gauge then stopped abruptly at twenty feet, signifying that *Mackerel* was now on the surface, bobbing like a cork.

Water could be heard running off the conning tower and decks outside. Scrambling up the ladder and into the conning tower, Cazanavette cracked opened the bridge hatch, and fresh air rushed into the ship for the first time in almost twenty-four hours. Through the small opening, good air flowed and quickly filled the entire compartment. Air with oxygen in it and without chlorine. All heads crowded around the hatch for a whiff of the wonderful salt air. The rich air tickled their nostrils and their neglected, oxygen-deprived blood cells ached for more.

Tremain breathed deeply, and the air did his head some good. He wanted to sit down and breathe for a few hours, but he forced himself to follow Cazanavette up the ladder and onto the bridge.

He found Cazanavette in the darkness, both hands on the wet coaming, taking in full lungs of air. Tremain doubted if he had taken the time to look for any sign of the enemy on the sea around them.

Some warped plating around the structure supporting the scopes gave an indication of the barrage *Mackerel* had suffered. He could not tell whether depth charges had caused the damage or the two enemy shells, but both scopes and all of the masts above the lookout perch were gone, ripped away. He glanced over the railing at the main deck and could see obvious damage in certain spots. The deck was missing wooden planking in several spots and the five-inch gun appeared to be mangled.

The night was moonless but clear and the air felt good on his face, although it did little to stop the splitting ache still throbbing in his head. He heard his heart pound in his ears and each beat seemed to make his head hurt more. He fought off the temptation to lie down and finally steadied himself against the bridge coaming next to Cazanavette.

Tremain looked out at the sea around them. The fog had drifted away and the sea was calm, more like a placid lake. He could see no ships in the blackness. The destroyers must have given them up for dead, he thought. Then he noticed a yellow glow on the water far off to the north and he momentarily forgot about his headache. Something was burning out there, several miles away. Though he could not tell for certain, Tremain estimated that the burning object lay in the channel between the two points of land that formed Kii Suido. He had forgotten his binoculars, but noticed that Cazanavette had remembered to bring his and was training them toward the burning object.

"What is it?" Tremain asked.

An exhausted smile formed on Cazanavette's oil-stained face as he handed the binoculars to Tremain, who quickly focused them on the distant object. He saw flames leaping hundreds of feet into the air. It was a dazzling spectacle. Then he noticed the triple gun barrels of a single turret protruding from the violent flames. He quickly made out the rest of the ship. It was the *Kurita*. She was dead in the water and down by the stern. In fact, the water line had reached the aft gun turret and was beginning to extinguish the flames on that quarter. *Mackerel*'s four torpedoes had done far more damage than Tremain had expected.

Through the binoculars he saw three small tugboats moving in and out of the yellow light around the burning ship. They had obviously made an attempt to tow the wounded battleship back to port and had only made it half way up the channel before the *Kurita*'s damage had got the better of her. The fire appeared to be completely out of control. Her stern was so low that the flooding had to be critical as well. Tremain knew that there had to be destroyers out there somewhere, hidden by the darkness.

"Let's try to get out of here, XO," Tremain said. "Get the main engines on the line."

Cazanavette relayed the word down the hatch and the mechanics in the engine rooms set about reviving their precious diesels. Many false starts later, the enginemen managed to get two diesels up and running and soon they were both supplying power to the ship's motors.

Tremain was just about to give an engine order to the helm when Stillsen grabbed his shoulder next to him.

"Sir!" he said, white-faced and staring over the railing at *Mackerel*'s bow. "Don't order any bells! I think I see a mine."

Scanning the dark water off the port bow, Tremain saw the object Stillsen had discovered. It was round, with bulbous protrusions, and it was roughly the size of a fifty-gallon drum. It was indeed a mine, obviously a contact mine, and it was floating just a few yards away, well within its kill radius.

"We're in a bloody minefield!" Cazanavette said in horror. "No wonder those destroyers didn't follow us!"

Tremain thought about backing away from the lethal object, but then noticed a cable extending from it. The cable was difficult to see in the dark night but it coiled several times in the expanse of water that separated the mine from *Mackerel*'s side and it even poked out of the water on *Mackerel*'s starboard side. Tremain could clearly see that it had wedged itself into the small flow space between *Mackerel*'s hull and the portside bow plane.

"Holy shit! We must have picked it up when I turned the

boat north to get into shallower water," Cazanavette said. "Then we must have pried it loose from its anchor when we came up."

Tremain did not care how it had happened. Now all he wanted was to get the cable detached from the *Mackerel*. He did not know how extensively the cable stretched beneath the hull, but it was most certainly tethered to the *Mackerel* at the bow. Thus, any movement of the ship could drag the mine closer.

"I've had a little experience with mines in my former station, sir," Stillsen said. "I was on a minesweeper in the Mediterranean before I came into submarines. I'd like to go down and see what I can do."

Tremain saw no other alternative. "Very well. What d'you need?"

"Just two men and all the line floats you've got should do the trick, sir," Stillsen said confidently. Stillsen found the two volunteers from the torpedo division, and Chief Freund came up with the line floats, which were nothing more than floating balls with holes in them.

Tremain and the bridge crew watched intently as Stillsen gingerly used a crowbar to dislodge the cable from the bow plane, then he measured out the several-hundred-foot-long mine cable and dragged it from beneath the hull, never once taking his eyes from the mine itself to make sure that his actions did not move it closer. Once *Mackerel* was no longer fouled, he placed the floats at regular intervals along the mine cable to mark where it sat in the water, so that *Mackerel* did not run over it again.

Stillsen manned a set of sound-powered phones on the bow and gave directions as Tremain slowly backed *Mackerel* away from the mine and its cable. Several minutes later, *Mackerel* turned her bow toward the open ocean and began to limp away at nine knots.

The burning *Kurita* still glowed on the horizon, and

Tremain saw her stern slip under the water, completely immersing her aft turret. The great battleship was in her death throes. She would certainly sink before morning. Tremain briefly wondered what had become of the ship-yard workers. Had they made it off the battleship in time? Part of him hoped that they had. After all, they were civilians. And strangely, he no longer felt the need for revenge upon his enemies. He no longer felt the need to even the score for his lost men on the *Seatrout*. He no longer felt his personal vendetta. He had lost many friends and shipmates during this war, and he himself had killed many Japanese. How many had he killed tonight? He would never know for sure. The war caused suffering on both sides, and now he just wanted the suffering to stop.

Tremain looked over the rail at Stillsen, who was still on the bow gathering up the phone cord. He had come a long way since they had left Pearl, Tremain thought.

Just then an ear-splitting sound rushed over Tremain's head and a millisecond later the ocean off *Mackerel*'s starboard bow erupted in an explosion that shot a waterspout fifty feet in the air. The sound deafened Tremain and the concussion knocked him and the others on the bridge behind the coaming, but not before he saw Stillsen's body blasted over the side like a rag doll.

Tremain struggled to his feet just as another screeching shell blasted the ocean again only a hundred feet off the starboard bow. Tremain's previous injury responded to the shock waves and he suddenly felt dizzy.

"Destroyer!" Cazanavette yelled, pointing astern. "Destroyer off the port quarter!"

Tremain dragged himself to the coaming and looked aft to see a dark shape less than a mile astern. Through the binoculars he could see that the destroyer was coming at full speed, its ominous shape finely silhouetted against the distant burning battleship.

"Are the aft tubes ready to fire?" Cazanavette shouted into the bridge box.

"No, sir," came the reply, "we have no air pressure to shoot with."

It would not have done much good, Tremain thought. He had noticed through the binoculars that the charging destroyer was doing small periodic course changes to avoid a stern torpedo shot. This destroyer captain knew what he was doing.

Another salvo rang out and slammed into the water near the port bow, showering the bridge with spray. Damage reports came from below the waterline that the hull was leaking in several places. Submerging was out of the question.

"Get the gun crews up here!" Cazanavette screamed into the microphone. He glanced at Tremain in desperation as he took charge on his own initiative, seeing that Tremain was in no condition to even be on the bridge. Tremain's head was spinning and he needed the coaming to stay on his feet.

Mackerel's guns would be mere popguns compared with the destroyer's arsenal, and with her meager nine knots compared to the destroyer's thirty knots, the range was falling away quickly.

"Give me more speed, engine room!" Cazanavette ordered.

Tremain saw that Cazanavette was trying everything he could to save them, but it appeared that the game was finally up. *Mackerel* could not outrun her adversary, and it was only a matter of time before the destroyer's guns scored a direct hit. Another salvo crashed into the water on the port beam, one shell skipping several times before it exploded a hundred yards off the bow.

Tremain wanted to help Cazanavette. He could not abandon him now. There had to be a way, he thought. But it was hard to think when his head was in such pain. Then something suddenly occurred to him. He dragged himself upright and brought his binoculars to bear on the pursuing destroyer, the black smoke now visible from its coughing stacks. He scanned the churning water before the destroyer, glimmering in the distant fires of the *Kurita*. That's when he saw it.

The mine cable, with its small floats, was distinctly visible as several small black dots stretching out several hundred feet across the glistening water's surface, and it lay just to the northeast of the destroyer's position. It would only be visible from *Mackerel*'s perspective and not from the destroyer's, because one could only make it out with the fire light of the burning *Kurita* behind it.

"Hard left rudder, XO!" Tremain shouted.

Cazanavette looked at him perplexed. "Sir, that'll present our beam to them, I don't—"

"Do it, damn you! Steer course north."

Cazanavette shook his head, but he must have trusted Tremain even in his current state, because he relayed the order and the helm responded. No sooner had *Mackerel* turned than a three-shell salvo smashed into the water right where she would have been had she kept going on her original course.

Cazanavette glanced at Tremain, but Tremain had his eyes glued to the binoculars to watch every move of the destroyer. As *Mackerel* steadied on course north, the destroyer continued on its original course, and Tremain started to believe that his far-fetched idea might not work. The destroyer had almost driven past the strung-out cable when it suddenly came hard left and steadied on a northeasterly course in an obvious attempt to continue closing the range to *Mackerel*.

Tremain watched as the destroyer ran over the bobbing cable at flank speed, making maximum turns. Seconds later, the destroyer's stern exploded in a towering column of red flame.

Though he could not see it, Tremain knew what had happened. The destroyer's screws had run over the mine cable and had become fouled. As they had turned for flank speed revolutions, the cable had coiled around the propeller shafts and had "winched" the mine right into the destroyer's stern, where it had exploded on contact.

Tremain also noticed that the destroyer's rudder must have jammed after the explosion because she immediately made a hard turn to the left and continued turning in circles. As her speed came off, the aft deck started to burn intensely. With the binoculars, Tremain could see small shadowy figures against the burning backdrop leap from her deck and into the sea. Moments later, the inevitable happened as the rows of depth charges lined up on her deck exploded in a nightmarish crescendo of heat and flame that could be felt on *Mackerel's* bridge a half mile away.

As the burning mass of fuel oil and metal bathed the sea in a ghoulish red glow, Cazanavette ordered the helm to come back to an easterly course in order to get *Mackerel* as far from the Japanese mainland as possible before the sun came up, and away from any other destroyers that might be lurking.

Tremain nodded his approval and gave a small sigh as he touched the dried blood beneath his hair. He had no sensation in his fingers or in his scalp and he felt lightheaded. He suddenly became too dizzy to stand and he started to fall, but Cazanavette caught him before he hit the deck.

"Take over, XO," he managed to mumble. Then all went black.

Chapter 29

THE room was cold, that was his first sensation. The room was dark, that was his second sensation. The bed was soft, that was his third. He could not breathe, that was his fourth.

Wright woke abruptly with a violent guttural cough. He felt a burning in his throat that did not go away when he swallowed. Within a few minutes, he regained his wind. His head still spun from the drugs they had given him. Then he remembered where he was—or at least he thought he did.

He was lying in a hospital bed. Which hospital, he did not know. There were ten or twelve other occupied beds in the room, and the lights were out. He was the only patient awake.

He vaguely remembered the trip back to Midway. He had stayed in his rack the entire trip, slipping in and out of consciousness and in no condition to do anything but eat and drink. The pharmacists' mate had looked after him the entire time. He had been transferred to the field hospital on

Midway, then after that it got fuzzy. That's when they started giving him the drugs.

He remembered a plane, or was that just a dream? No, he *had* ridden in a plane. They had loaded him onto a plane and flown him to this place. He must be in Pearl.

He looked around. Nothing was familiar. Could this be her hospital?

He wanted to ask someone, but no one else was around, only sleeping patients. They were probably wounded marines from one of the island campaigns. He had no sense of time. How long had he been here? Did she know what had happened? Did she even know that he was on the island?

Her lovely face was still fresh in his mind, as if he had seen it only moments ago. Maybe he had just dreamed it. It had to be night. The blackout curtains were drawn across the windows. Even if she did know he was here, she would be at home by now, asleep, getting some rest for her next shift.

Then he heard a noise. The door at the far end creaked open slowly, allowing the light from the outside hall into the dark room. The silhouette of a woman appeared in the doorway. She was holding a steaming coffee cup in both hands.

Wright's heart jumped in his chest.

Her glimmering hair in the soft light. Her beautifully curved hips. The way her skirt caressed and accented their lovely shape. Her petite delicate shoulders, appearing even smaller when she held the cup with both hands. Her sensuous legs. Her fragrance, unmistakable even from the other side of the room, sweet yet seductive. It had to be her.

"Mar . . ." he tried to speak but quickly broke into another bout of coughs.

She quickly came across the room to his bed.

"Shhh," she said from the darkness. Wright could tell she had a smile on her face, and he wanted to see her face.

She placed a soft hand on his bare chest, and motioned for him to lie back.

He tried to speak, but she stopped him with a gentle finger on his lips.

"You shouldn't talk," she whispered. "Your lungs and throat need time to heal."

He squeezed her hand, then brought it to his lips and kissed it, then he noticed that the ring was no longer there. She withdrew her hand, then leaned over and kissed his lips. After being at sea for so long, he thought her lips felt like the softest things he had ever felt in his life.

"I took my roommate's shift tonight," she said. "I've watched every toss and turn you've made. I just went to get some coffee, but I wish I had been here when you woke up."

She gave him a wink and a smile. "The doctor says you inhaled a lot of smoke. He said you'll probably be assigned to shore duty for a while, if not permanently. I know you probably won't like that, but I'm glad."

He didn't care. He could be happy sitting at a desk for the rest of the war.

"Oh, I almost forgot. A man in one of the rooms upstairs was asking about you. I guess he was on your boat. I went up and talked to him. He seemed very nice. I let him know how you were doing, and he told me to tell you that you had good taste in women."

Wright smiled at her.

"He's a little worse off than you are," she continued. "He's set to be shipped back to the States. I guess the war is over for him."

Wright started to ask who it was, but remembered the burning sensation in his throat.

"He also asked me to give you this."

She pressed something into his hand. It was cold and metallic. Margie took out her small nurse's pen light and shined it on the object.

It was a gold piece of metal shaped into a design. The design showed two oversized dolphins meeting above a surfaced submarine. It was the gold dolphin insignia, the coveted badge worn over the breast pocket of all submarine officers.

Wright immediately recognized this particular set of gold dolphins. It was an old pair. Its dull shine and dingy grooves represented many hard years aboard the boats. He had seen this same set of dolphins many times above the left breast pocket of Captain Tremain.

"So this means you're a qualified submarine officer," she whispered. "Isn't that right, Ryan?"

Historical Note

THOUGH I have made painstaking efforts to provide an accurate historical setting, *Pride Runs Deep* is a work of fiction, and I would be remiss in my duties as a writer if I did not mention some of the historical facts that might be of interest to the reader.

There actually was a submarine USS *Mackerel* (SS-204) on the United States Navy list during World War Two. The real *Mackerel* spent most of the war on the East Coast of the United States serving as a training and experimental submarine for the Prospective Commanding Officers (PCO) School in New London, Connecticut. She also assisted in anti-submarine training for the various Task Groups preparing to take on Hitler's U-boats in the North Atlantic. The *Mackerel* had only one contact with the enemy, during which she exchanged torpedoes ineffectually with a German U-boat while en route to Norfolk, Virginia. While not dramatic, her service was invaluable to the training of future submarine captains and to the development of new submarine and anti-submarine tactics. She was de-commissioned in November of 1945.

There never was a secret Japanese battleship *Kurita*. However, the USS *Archerfish* (SS-311) did sink the secret Japanese aircraft carrier *Shinano* near the same location in November of 1944 while the carrier was on its maiden voyage. The *Shinano* was indeed a "supercarrier" and dis-placed well over seventy thousand tons, the largest warship ever sunk by a submarine. The *Archerfish* was performing lifeguard duty for B-29 strikes against Honshu when she happened upon the *Shinano* and sank her.

I chose early 1943 as the setting for *Pride Runs Deep* be-cause it was a pivotal time for the U.S. Submarine Service. Japanese anti-submarine efforts saw a sharp increase in in-tensity. During 1942, the United States Navy lost a total of only three submarines to enemy action. Throughout that first year of the war, U.S. submarines ranged up and down the waters of Imperial Japan sinking ships at will and fight-ing against a mostly confused enemy. By 1943, the Japan-ese Imperial Fleet had learned how to use the combined forces of aircraft, escort ships, and mines to effectively fight the elusive U.S. submarines. As a result, sixteen U.S. sub-marines were lost to enemy action in 1943, an increase in losses exceeding 500 percent. This marked increase in sub-marine losses had a psychological impact as well as a tacti-cal one. The crews began to calculate the odds of perishing on the next patrol, which were about one in five.

Despite the losses, U.S. submarines sank over five mil-lion tons of Japanese shipping during the war, virtually all of Imperial Japan's merchant capacity. Tens of thousands of brave Japanese naval and merchant sailors died in this dev-astation. In all, the U.S. Submarine Service lost fifty-two submarines and over three thousand five hundred brave men killed in action.

In conclusion, I hope this novel conveys some of the

courage displayed by the combatants and merchantmen on both sides of this epic conflict. Today, Japan and the United States of America are staunch allies, which I think is a credit to both nations. During my time in the submarine service in the 1990s while I was stationed at Pearl Harbor, I found it comfortably ironic that more often than not, a Japanese submarine shared the pier with my submarine. Across the water, I would often see Japanese destroyers moored right alongside our own ships, as if to signify that one-time enemies were now bound firmly together in friendship. And each morning at 0800, the national ensign rose from flagpoles and fantails, thousands of working sailors stopped what they were doing and came to attention, and the "Star-Spangled Banner" would resound throughout the harbor followed immediately by the national anthem of Japan.

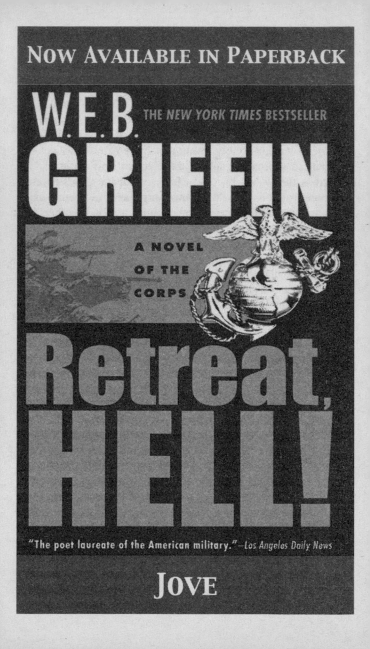

One man has just discovered an
international threat that no one could
have prepared for—or imagined...

Unit Omega
by
Jim Grand

In charge of investigating unusual
scientific phenomena for the UN,
Jim Thompson is the world's authority
on the unexplained.

But when a world-renowned scientist
reports a sighting of the legendary
Loch Ness Monster, the disturbance
turns out to be much bigger—and more
dangerous—than the folklore
ever suggested.

0-425-19321-7

**Available wherever books are sold
or at www.penguin.com**